Praise for th...
New York Times b...
Susan Krinard

"Susan Krinard was born to write romance."
—Amanda Quick

"Darkly intense, intricately plotted, and chilling, this sexy
tale skillfully interweaves several time periods, revealing
key past elements with perfect timing but keeping the reader
firmly in the novel's 'present' social scene."
—*Library Journal* on *Lord of Sin*

"Krinard's imagination knows no bounds as she steps into the
mystical realm of the unicorn and takes readers along for the
ride of their fairy-tale lives."
—*RT BOOK Reviews* on *Lord of Legends*, *4½ stars*

"A master of atmosphere and description."
—*Library Journal*

"A poignant tale of redemption."
—*Booklist* on *To Tame a Wolf*

"With riveting dialogue and passionate characters,
Ms Krinard exemplifies her exceptional knack for creating
an extraordinary story of love, strength, courage and
compassion."
—*RT BOOK Reviews* on *Secrets of the Wolf*

SUSAN KRINARD
Bride of the Wolf

MILLS & BOON®

First published in Great Britain 2012
by Mills & Boon, an imprint of Harlequin (UK) Limited,
Eton House, 18-24 Paradise Road, Richmond, Surrey TW9 1SR

© Susan Krinard 2010

ISBN: 978 0 263 89597 1
ebook ISBN: 978 1 408 97480 3

089-0412

Harlequin (UK) policy is to use papers that are natural, renewable and recyclable products and made from wood grown in sustainable forests. The logging and manufacturing processes conform to the legal environmental regulations of the country of origin.

Printed and bound
by CPI Group (UK) Ltd, Croydon, CR0 4YY

In memory of all the great Western movie directors I love:
Anthony Mann, Delmer Daves, and John Sturges,
and for the great Western actors:
Jimmy Stewart, Henry Fonda, Gregory Peck, Glenn Ford,
Richard Widmark, William Holden, Clint Eastwood, Audie
Murphy, Jack Elam, Eli Wallach,
and Lee Van Cleef.

Prologue

Pecos County, Texas, 1881

JEDEDIAH MCCARRICK WAS DEAD.

Heath rode carefully around the body sprawled at the bottom of the draw, gentling Apache with a quiet word. The horse was right to be scared. Jed hadn't been dead more than a few days, and the scent of decay was overwhelming.

An accident. That was the way it looked, anyhow. Half Jed's skull was bashed in, and his legs stuck out at strange angles. The rocks were sharp around here, and plentiful.

But Jed was a damn good rider. You had to be, in the Pecos, so far from civilization. The old man had been on his way home, just as his letter had said. He would have let go the cowboys he'd hired for the drive once it was finished, and he didn't trust many people. He would have risked riding alone rather than let some stranger get close to his hard-earned money.

That was his mistake.

Heath dismounted and scanned the horizon. Jed's horse was gone, so there was no way to be sure exactly how it had happened. Maybe something had spooked the animal: a rattler, a rabbit, a gust of wind. Heath couldn't smell anything but the stink of rot, no trace of another human who might have been around when Jed died. Any hoofprints or tracks had been blown away. If some drifter or outlaw had helped Jed to his grave and taken his horse, he was long gone.

I should have been with him, Heath thought. But Jed hadn't wanted him along.

The old man hadn't acted like the others when he found out, when Heath was stupid enough to forget all the hard lessons he'd learned. Jed wasn't easily scared. He hadn't yelled or run away or tried to shoot him. He'd pretended it didn't matter, that Heath was still like a son to him.

But Heath had known Jed was lying. He knew what he saw in the old man's eyes. Jed had understood that Heath would never hurt him, but he was still human. The only reason he'd kept so calm and reasonable was that he needed Heath at the ranch to keep Sean in check. He'd been willing to use Heath's secret for his own ends—until Sean was no longer a problem and he could run Heath off like the animal he was.

Heath laughed. It was almost funny that Jed was more worried about his nephew than a man who wasn't even human. The devil knew why Heath had stayed on. He supposed that three years of friendship, of letting himself trust the man who'd saved his life, had held him at Dog Creek. That and his contempt for Sean. He'd owed Jed, and he had meant to pay off the debt. But Heath had been ready to ride out as soon as Jed returned and could deal with Sean himself. That would have been the end of it.

He just hadn't expected this kind of end.

Apache snorted and tossed his head. "Easy, boy," Heath murmured, and knelt beside the body. He touched the bloody depression beneath Jed's thinning hair. The old man had probably died quickly. No sign of knife or gunshot wounds.

Closing his nostrils against the stench, Heath patted Jed's waist and pockets. Nothing. If he'd brought the money back with him, he would have carried it in the saddlebags. Everything he'd received for the sale of fifty percent of Dog Creek's beeves, driven north to Kansas and the rail lines.

Before he'd left, before Heath had made his big mistake, Jed had expected to make a good profit. Enough to buy better stock, make Dog Creek grow into a concern that could compete with Blackwater on its own terms. No more risky investments that brought Dog Creek to the brink of ruin. No more wild ideas. No more foolish dreams.

And no more free money for the worthless peacock of a nephew who thought he could bend Jed around his saddle horn like a twist of rope.

Heath's lips curled away from his teeth. Sean had been Jed's one weakness. It had taken the old man a long time to realize Sean didn't care for anyone but himself. If Jed had lived, he would finally have shown his nephew that he wasn't going to be led around by the nose anymore.

But Jed had waited too long. Once everyone found out the old man was dead and Sean got his hands on Dog Creek, he would sell it to the Blackwells. All Jed's hard years of work gone for nothing.

The wind shifted, momentarily clearing away the stench and the raw feelings Heath couldn't seem to kill. He caught a whiff of a new scent. Old leather and horse sweat, not Apache's. He sucked in a deep breath and followed the smell to the base of the stony hillside that rose up from one side of the draw.

The saddlebags had been thrown far enough back under the rocky overhang that an ordinary man might never have found them. Heath crouched and dragged them into the light. They were full to bursting. He didn't have to open the flaps to know what they contained.

Someone had put the saddlebags here. An outlaw would have taken them just like he would have taken Jed's horse. Had Jed seen someone he didn't know, gotten nervous and decided to hide the bags before he died?

Heath stood up, a knot in his belly. Maybe Jed's death had still been an accident, and the old man had lived just long enough to try to keep the money out of the hands of any stranger who might run across him.

But there'd been another accident some years back, a trail boss who'd gotten his neck broken when Heath—who'd been using his own name then—was there to see it. Only, no one else had. And someone had figured out that he wasn't who he claimed to be, a simple cowhand looking for work wherever he could get it.

Heath had never before been taken by the law despite all his years outside it. There'd been a jail cell and the endless wait for a trial, his fate settled before he ever stood in front of a judge. But they hadn't reckoned on a prisoner who was stronger and faster than any normal man. After he broke out, they'd added another crime to his tally.

Heath tilted his face toward the sky and closed his eyes. If he'd been a normal man, he might have done the right thing and ridden to Heywood for the marshal. No one else in this part of West Texas knew what he could become. The money was still here. There was no reason for anyone to think *he'd* killed Jed. Even if someone remembered that other death hundreds of miles from the Pecos, no one had recognized him in three years, or made any connection between "Holden Renshaw" and Heath Renier.

But if there was a chance, even one in a million, that someone could put those facts together…

Not even a *loup-garou* could hang more than once. Heath had been ready to die plenty of times, even when the wolf inside him kept on fighting to keep him alive. But he could never go back to that cell, those bars, the man-made hell that left him alone in his human body, trapped by memories and feelings he'd outrun for so long. Remembering that the one man he'd let himself trust in nearly ten years had been just like the rest.

Apache nickered, feeling Heath's anxiety. Heath calmed himself down and opened one of the saddlebags. A heavy bag of coins was neatly packed inside. Heath didn't touch it. The other pouch held more coins. And something else. A bundle of small folded sheets, bound together with a bit of frayed ribbon, and a roll of leather tied up with a cord.

Thick paper crackled as Heath unrolled the leather. There were three sheets inside, dense with writing. He smoothed out the first across his knees.

Reading had never been one of his best skills, but he knew what he was holding. As he picked his way down the paper, the knot in his belly squeezed so he could hardly breathe.

The will left almost everything to him. The ranch, the proceeds from the sale—and money Heath hadn't known Jed possessed, locked away in a bank in Kansas City. Money that made Jed a wealthy man.

Maybe Jed had been hiding that money from Sean, or from people he owed. Heath didn't know what had been going on in Jed's mind. He sure as hell hadn't known about any will giving him Dog Creek.

Not that it mattered now. Someone had drawn a dark line all the way across it from corner to corner and blacked out the signature at the bottom of the page.

Hands shaking like a boy in his first gunfight, Heath unrolled the other two sheets. The second was a will leaving everything to Sean, dated two years ago. It, too, was crossed out.

The third will wasn't signed or dated. The name at the top meant nothing to him.

Rachel Lyndon.

He picked up the smaller bundle of papers and lifted it to his nose. It smelled like Jed. And someone he'd never met.

Heath untied the ribbon, and one of the folded sheets fell into the dirt. The letter had been sent from Ohio. The paper was browned, the edges bent as if someone had read it over and over again.

When Heath was finished with it, he put it back with the other letters, rolled up the second and third wills in their leather sheath and set it on the ground. His heart was rattling around in his chest like brush tossed by the wind. He missed his first try at striking a spark; the second time he got it right, and nursed the tiny flame until it was just big enough to burn a sheet of paper. He watched the first will catch and smolder until there was nothing left of it but ash.

The leather sheath rolled sideways in the wind, and Heath picked it up. He was beginning to lose whatever sense he had left. Burning the will didn't solve his problem. Jed hadn't been much good with accounts and paperwork, but Heath couldn't be sure that the ones he had were the only copies. The last unsigned will and what it contained could make it look as if Heath had a motive to kill his boss before Jed finished it. Before Jed went through with the crazy thing he'd planned.

But it didn't make any difference if there were other copies of the will somewhere. Jed's decision made it easier for Heath to be sure of his own. The old man had lied to Heath in more ways than one. Even if Heath hadn't revealed himself, Jed would have ruined everything by bringing a woman to Dog Creek.

Any debt Heath had to the old man had been paid with hard work and loyalty. The woman Jed had planned to marry meant nothing to Heath, and he didn't owe anything to most of the hands, who'd never much liked him anyway. Maurice was too good a cook not to find a place at some other outfit.

He would feel a little bad about leaving Joey, but he had some money he could give the boy before he lit out.

That was his last obligation. Sean could claim the ranch and sell it to the Blackwells, will or no will, and Heath wouldn't try to stop him.

He pushed the sheath and the bundle of letters back inside Jed's saddlebags, carried them over the hill and stripped out of his clothes. The Change was complete in a painless instant. The world came sharply into focus, every scent, every sound crisp as a December morning. He'd know if any human came within ten miles of the place.

Shaking out his fur, Heath picked out a likely spot and set about the task at hand. When the hole was wide and deep enough, he seized the saddlebags in his jaws and dropped them in. He covered the hole, scraping at the dirt with his powerful hind legs. Only when he was finished did he Change again and look over his work.

It was good. The ground was already rough, and a few tossed pebbles made the spot look just like everything else around it. No human would be able to find it.

Heath put on his clothes, secured his gun belt and returned to Apache, who sniffed at him and snorted. Heath mounted and urged the gelding out of the draw. The money could have been useful, but he didn't want anything else from Jed. The old man could lie easy knowing he would keep something of what he'd earned.

A jackrabbit burst from the cover of a dead mesquite and bounded away. A cottontop cried from the brush. Heath felt the wide-open land all around him, beckoning.

One last trip to the house, and he would shake the dust of the Pecos off his boots forever.

"*Adiós*, Jed," he said, touching the brim of his hat.

For the first time in three years, Jedediah McCarrick didn't answer.

"SOMEONE'S COMIN' TO *Dog Creek.*"

Sean could still hear Jed's voice as he guided Ulysses down the steep slope of the draw. "*She'll be makin' things different here,*" the old man had said. "*With her and the money I got from the sale, I'm goin' to make Dog Creek what it ought to be. No more debt, Sean. No more money wasted on your gamblin' and them bad ideas you talked me into.*"

Only it hadn't quite gone as Jed had planned. The coyotes and buzzards had done such a good job that Jed was already unrecognizable. Only his clothes and his gold tooth would identify him now.

Sean kept his distance and began looking for the saddlebags. He searched under every rock and bush, scraped at every rough spot in the dirt, circled the area in every direction until he knew he had to stop if he wanted to get back before the sun rose.

Cursing, Sean gripped the carved ivory handle of his gun and wished he had something to shoot. For the dozenth time he went over the encounter in his mind, searching for a clue, a hint of what Jed had been thinking when he'd hidden his money.

The old man had surprised Sean when he'd sent the letter asking his nephew to meet him at the western border of the ranch. Jed had made sure to arrive on the very day he'd promised. He'd planned it all carefully, just so he could give Sean the news.

Sean closed his eyes and leaned over the saddle horn. The first words had been a shock. He'd always had what he wanted from the old man before. The allowance, the education back East…everything but the life he deserved. The life Jed owed him. The life he could have when he sold Dog Creek to the Blackwells.

Now that was all undone. Sean had shouted at Jed, cursed him, even pleaded at the end. For once Jed hadn't backed down.

"You think you're gettin' the ranch," he'd said. *"You ain't gettin' a penny, not of this money or off the property. As soon as we're married, it's all goin' to her."*

Some woman he'd found in an advertisement for mail-order brides. A female so desperate that she would expose herself in a newspaper, begging for a man to support her. A bitch from some little town in Ohio who had no claim on anything belonging to the McCarricks.

Sean had only meant to scare the old man at first. He'd pulled his gun and asked Jed where he'd put the money.

But Jed hadn't talked. Sean had almost shot him then and there, until he realized just how stupid that would be.

It had to look like an accident, of course. One shot past the horse's ear was all it took. Jed was damn fond of the bronc, but he should have known it had never been fully broken. It tossed Jed so hard that Sean didn't have to lift a finger to finish the job, though he'd had to work a little harder to drive the horse far enough away that he could run it over a convenient cliff.

He'd meant to stay and look for the saddlebags. But he hadn't been thinking clearly. Now he was paying for his lapse.

Jerking sharply on the reins, Sean turned Ulysses for home. The saddlebags might be lost to him, but he wasn't about to give up on the rest. He'd already gone looking for the will Jed had spoken of, searching the house as soon as he could manage it without being seen.

But there had been no will, only a handful of receipts and random papers stashed in a hole in the wall behind the massive kitchen range that Jed had hauled in all the way from San Antonio.

Sean nicked Ulysses's sides with his spurs, and the stallion leaped into a run. The cursed thing had to be somewhere. Maybe Jed had it filed away in some bank for safekeeping. If it was anywhere to be found, Sean would find it.

He rode at a reckless pace back to the house, running Ulysses to complete exhaustion. Most of the other hands, including Renshaw, were still on the range, and Maurice was nowhere in sight. Sean rubbed Ulysses down and returned to the tiny foreman's cabin he'd taken when Holden moved into the house with Jed. He threw a chair across the room, smashed the mirror over the washstand and nearly put his fist through the window. When he could think again, he sat on the edge of the bed and composed his thoughts to an icy calm.

Jed had said the woman would be arriving on the next stage. The stage only came to Javelina twice a month, and Jed had been dead less than a week. Another was due in a matter of days. Rachel Lyndon would arrive expecting to marry a settled rancher who would provide for her needs.

But Jed was gone and she had no lawful claim on Dog Creek. If Sean planned things right, Rachel Lyndon could be encouraged to turn right around and go back to where she came from.

Sean allowed himself a smile and stretched until his bones popped. He would have a little talk with the drifter who'd come by the other day looking for work. Like most men, he was a sheep, easily led and ready to obey a man who knew how to balance bribery and threat.

Whistling a tune he'd heard last week at the Blackwells', Sean went to clean himself up.

Chapter One

THE BABY THRUST its tiny fists in the air and wailed.

"It's yours," Polly said, pushing the bundle toward Heath. "Frankie said so right before she died."

Frankie was dead. It was strange to think the woman he'd visited every month for two years, who'd given him what his body had to have, was gone. For just a minute he almost felt sorry. Whore that she was, she'd done nothing to deserve dying before her time.

But this…

Heath backed away, staring at the red and wrinkled face.

His? It wasn't possible.

But it was. The last time he'd seen Frankie had been about eleven months ago. Heath didn't know a damn thing about babies, but he thought this one was pretty new.

"He's two months old," Polly said impatiently, holding the baby closer to her chest. "Frankie died bringin' him into the world. The least you can do is own up to your part in it."

The letter in Heath's pocket was fit to burn a hole through his vest. It had been waiting for him at the house the day he'd found Jed. He'd gotten only a handful of letters before, all from the old man. Never one like this.

Come right away, the letter said in Frankie's stiff, uneven writing. *You have a son.*

The first thing he'd done was laugh. Frankie was a whore, but she did like her little jokes. Only after he'd read it twice more did he start to think she meant it.

If he'd been in his right mind, he would have ridden north, the way he'd planned, crossing the Pecos at Horsehead and heading into the Llano Estacado before anyone knew he wasn't coming back.

He didn't know if it was the human part of him or the wolf that made him turn south to Heywood, or which part was most scared when he looked at this helpless little mite that had spit on its face and a head almost smaller than Heath's fist.

"It could have been any of the men she saw," he said roughly, heading for the door. "Find someone else."

"Renshaw!" Polly yelled, coming after him. "We can't keep him here!" She shifted the baby in her arms and gestured with one hand at the garish wallpaper and cheap, gaudy furniture that made Polly's room of a piece with the rest of the whorehouse. "We don't have time to look after him, and what kind of life could he have as a whore's son?"

Heath shoved his hat farther down across his forehead. "That ain't my problem."

"He's your kid, Renshaw!"

The hair on the back of Heath's neck bristled. He turned around and closed his eyes, letting the wolf take over.

At first all he could smell over the rank stench of the bordello were traces of the kid's scat, the soap someone had used to wash it away, and a kind of milky musk. Below that was a human scent, but different, like the smell of a colt was different from its dam.

And under that…

Heath tried to tell himself he'd imagined it. It wasn't as if he'd smelled *loup-garou* cubs before. But it was there, undeniable, faint but true. The odds against Frankie lying with another *loup-garou* at just the right time were bigger than Heath could calculate.

Hellfire.

Without warning, Polly pushed the infant into Heath's arms. He nearly dropped it; only his animal reflexes spared it a nasty fall.

"Be careful!" Polly scolded. "Here. Hold him like this."

She adjusted his arms so that they supported the baby's head and tiny body. "There you are, little one," she said in the gentlest voice Heath had ever heard out of her. She tickled the baby's shapeless face with a fingertip. "See? Your daddy's here."

Heath was too numb to say a damn thing. Polly moved to the bed and gathered up a threadbare carpetbag. "This is what you'll need at first. All of us pitched in. Warm blankets, cloths for diapers, a bottle. Enough cow's milk to get you through tonight, and a bottle of formula for afterward. It would be good to find him a wet nurse."

"I don't know any wet nurses," Heath mumbled.

She put her hands on her hips and stared at him with disgust. "You ain't got no tits yourself, do you? If you don't know how to keep him, take him where they'll never know he's a whore's son and find some woman who wants him."

Some woman. Heath caught himself before he could bare his teeth and snarl in Polly's face.

But Polly didn't know what the kid was. What could happen to a 'breed if he ever ended up being raised by people like the humans who'd taken him in, then rejected him as a monster. Or like his real mother, who'd thrown Heath out for being half-human.

Quarter werewolf might never be able to Change at all.

Heath felt the fragility of the wriggling form beneath the blanket and thought of the future he had planned. He couldn't just ride aimlessly into the plains with a baby tied to his saddle.

He would know better what to do when he was away from this place and out on the range where he belonged. Where he'd always belonged.

Polly tossed the carpetbag on the stained rug. "You'd better git. I heard Will Bradley thinks you cheated him at poker last time you was here, and I'm sure you don't want no trouble." She put up her hand to give Heath a shove, then thought better of it. "Mind you do right by him, Renshaw. If we find out any hurt has come to—"

Heath looked hard into her eyes, and she drew back. "Forget you ever saw him—or me."

Her throat bobbed. Someone gave a raucous laugh, and a drunken cowhand, leaning on a skinny whore's shoulder, staggered past the open doorway. Polly rushed out the door and closed it behind her. The baby opened its blue eyes and seemed to look at Heath with a kind of yearning. As if it knew…

With a curse too profane even for the most jaded harlot, Heath transferred the baby into the crook of one arm and picked up the carpetbag. He walked out of the room and left by the back stairs. They creaked under his boots, laughing at him all the way down.

It wasn't easy to figure out how to carry the kid. In the end he rigged up a sling out of one of the well-worn blankets, tying it around his neck so the small, warm bundle was cradled against his chest. Apache snorted in surprise and craned his head around to stare.

"I don't need no lip from you," Heath muttered, reining the gelding away from the bordello. The baby yawned, showing naked pink gums, and Heath's stomach dropped to the soles of his boots. It was so damn *alien*. He could kill it without even meaning to.

That day was just about the longest of Heath's life. He managed thirty miles by dawn, using his night vision to steer Apache along a path over the rough terrain of the desert. Just after dawn the kid started to cry, and it didn't take Heath long to realize that he wasn't saying he was hungry. Heath used one of the other diapers and water from his canteen to clean the baby as best he could, fumbling with fingers made clumsy with uncertainty. Then he found the bottle, filled it from the small flask of milk and stuck the Indian-rubber teat near the baby's lips. It only yelled louder.

Patience was a virtue Heath had learned in long years of running from the law, but it did him no good now. The baby wouldn't take the teat. It was pretty clear that nothing Heath did was going to make it suckle, so he mounted up again and kept on going. The kid was strong. It was *loup-garou*. It would eat when it was hungry.

But he knew there was something wrong when he was forty miles from Javelina and it still wouldn't take the bottle. Its cries got soft, like the whimper of a pup, and it didn't look so pink anymore.

The slow panic Heath had felt only a few times in his life welled up like foul water. There wasn't much of anything between here and Javelina. Dog Creek was ten miles to the north.

There weren't any women there now, unless the Lyndon female had come in on the stage while he was gone. He hadn't figured he would be around to see the spectacle, but instinct told him to run for the only place he'd ever thought of as home.

Instinct had a way of getting him in trouble almost as much as his human heart. The wolf wasn't always right. But he could get the kid proper shelter and a bed at Dog Creek. Even if Jed had already been found, Heath didn't see that he had any choice. He would find himself a wet nurse to look after the boy until he was well again, even if he had to drag some female to the ranch kicking and screaming.

RACHEL LYNDON STOOD at the door of the small general store, watching the dust rise from the street as a heavily laden wagon rolled by. The aged woman crossing the single main street hardly seemed to notice. She brushed absently at the sleeve of her drab dress, her gaze fixed on the faded sign of the tavern next to the store.

She was the only other woman Rachel had seen. It was a rough place, Javelina. A world away from Ohio. A world dominated by the plain, hardy folk of West Texas, a country with far more cattle than people.

Or so Rachel had read. Yet not all the reading in the world could have prepared her for this.

I will have a home, she thought. A home, and a husband who would be steady and respectable and would care nothing about her former life.

But she was still afraid. Afraid of the horses that seemed to be everywhere, snorting and stamping. Afraid of the riders who stared at her as if she were a rare and exotic beast in a cage—she, who was as plain as a sparrow.

She straightened and lifted her chin. Let them stare. They would never see her nervousness. She had as much right to be here as anyone.

Mrs. Jedediah McCarrick. Ellie Lyndon would cease to exist, along with her past. No more loneliness. No more taking any employment she could find, hoping that she might at last outrun the scandal. The end of wondering where her next meal would come from. Of fearing to get close to any man, lest he turn his back on her.

Lest he be like Louis.

She shook off the thought. Here she could be useful. Here she would never be tempted to return to what she had become.

Here she could forget.

A cowhand tipped his hat as he rode by. She nodded, unsmiling. A spotted hound wandered past the door, wagging its tail. She offered a pat. Dogs had always been kind to her. Forgiving.

The sun sank a little lower, driving long shadows before it. She had sent a letter to Jedediah informing him of the anticipated date of her arrival, but the stagecoach had been late. Apparently he had decided not to wait in town all day.

Lamps were lit inside the houses and public buildings, such as they were. The saloon door swung open, and a pair of inebriated men staggered out, singing off-key. Rachel hugged her shawl more tightly around her shoulders.

Everything had gone so well until now—at least compared to the rest of her life. She'd advertised in the *Matrimonial News*, only half daring to hope that some respectable man from a place far away from Sheffield, Ohio, might respond. *I am a single woman, aged twenty-eight, dark haired and with brown eyes, five feet four inches tall and slender, seeking correspondence with an honorable man of some means. Hardworking, excellent housekeeper, experienced in teaching and good with children.*

Jedediah McCarrick had been the fourth to answer. His reply had been the best that could be hoped for: *Dear Miss Lyndon, I am a gentleman of fifty-two years, height five feet ten inches. I own a ranch in Texas and am seeking a wife who will work hard to make Dog Creek a going concern.*

There was nothing the least romantic in it. Why should there be, when there had been nothing the least romantic in her advertisement? Indeed, he met her needs perfectly. He owned property, so she would never be without food or shelter; he would not be a doddering old man at fifty-two, and he wanted exactly what she could provide.

And he had said nothing about wanting children of his own.

The wind, so warm during the day, had grown cooler. So much hope rested on this meeting. Hope she had not dared allow herself for so long.

"Fräulein?"

The owner of the store, a small, wiry German with a sharp, friendly smile, bustled up beside her and introduced himself. "I could not help but notice that you are still waiting, Fräulein Lyndon," he said with what appeared to be genuine concern. "Wouldn't you like to come in? I have coffee, and it is much more comfortable inside."

Rachel summoned a smile, warmed by the offer in spite of her wariness. Perhaps people really were different here.

"That is kind of you, Mr. Sonntag," she said, "but I prefer to remain here."

Mr. Sonntag gave her a long, quizzical look. "You are a relative of Herr McCarrick's, *Fräulein?*"

Her throat tightened. "Yes. I am."

He waited for further revelations. When none were forthcoming, he nodded briskly and vanished into the store.

So no one knew. Surely if anyone in Javelina had guessed her purpose in coming, the owner of one of the town's few businesses would be aware of it.

But she had not really deceived him; she *would* be Jed McCarrick's relative in a matter of days, if not sooner.

Mrs. Jedediah McCarrick.

The thought kept her from panic as another hour passed, and then another. She grew colder. Something must have kept Mr. McCarrick. Perhaps his wagon had broken down or there had been some emergency at the ranch.

The noise from the saloon increased. Rachel picked up her bag. Perhaps it would be best if she went inside rather than make a spectacle of herself, or become an object of derision. She turned to open the door.

The rattle of wheels stopped her. A wagon—a buckboard, they called it—had drawn up in front of the store. The lean, dusty man on the bare plank seat touched the brim of his hat as he settled the horses.

"You Miss Lyndon?" he asked.

Relief nearly choked her reply. "Yes," she said. "Yes, I am."

The man's face clouded. "Well, ma'am, it's like this. Jed ain't coming."

She barely registered the words. "I beg your pardon?"

There was no mistaking the man's discomfort. He squirmed on the seat and cleared his throat.

"Jed sent me," he said, "to tell you that he's changed his mind." He felt inside his coat and produced a leather pouch. "Jed said to give you this, for fare back to Ohio and a little extra for your trouble."

Rachel had never swooned in her life, but the weakness in her legs was such that she feared she might not keep her feet. "There must be some mistake," she whispered.

"I'm sorry, ma'am." The man held out the pouch. Rachel raised her hands as if she could ward off disaster before it could truly become real.

Changed his mind. It was not possible.

"I do not believe it," she said, finding her courage again.

The messenger let his hand fall. "I only know what he told me. If you'd only—"

"I wish to be taken to Dog Creek."

"I don't think that's a good idea, ma'am."

Perhaps it wasn't. Perhaps she would only face further humiliation and the extinction of her last hopes. But she could not go running back to Ohio with her tail between her legs. Not without being absolutely certain.

"If you will not take me," she said, "I shall find another way."

The man's expression of embarrassment underwent a rapid transformation. He scowled and pushed the pouch back under his coat.

"You're making a mistake, ma'am," he said. With a curse and a flick of the reins, he sent his horses off at a fast clip. Rachel began to tremble. She had convinced the messenger of her sincerity, but the effort had taken its toll. She felt breathless and weak.

But the decision had been made. She could not afford to return to Ohio now, even had she wished to. This had become a matter of survival.

Taking a firm grip on her bag, she went into the store. Mr. Sonntag offered to find someone to drive her to Dog Creek in the morning.

"You can stay here, Fräulein Lyndon," he said. "I have several rooms in the back. It is the nearest thing we have to a hotel. No one will trouble you."

Rachel was prepared to refuse. She had no money to repay such unexpected kindness. But in the end she agreed because she could not imagine spending the night on the street like a woman of ill repute.

Are you any better? she asked herself as she settled in the small, plain room Herr Sonntag had assigned to her.

She was. She *must* be. And Jedediah McCarrick would make it possible.

RACHEL WOKE EARLY the next morning. Mr. Sonntag insisted that she share his breakfast of bread and jam, and she was too hungry to refuse. A few hours later a man from the livery stable arrived with a wagon, and Rachel took out a few of her remaining coins, hoping they would be enough.

"It's not necessary," the grizzled driver said. "Sonntag arranged it."

Rachel hurried back into the store to thank the German, but he'd gone out on some business. She resolved that she would pay him back as soon as she was in a position to do so.

The driver, Mr. Sweet, was not inclined to conversation, and Rachel had no desire to reveal herself to a stranger. She concentrated on absorbing the landscape. Beyond the tiny patch of green that marked the spring near which Javelina was situated, this was a stark, unforgiving world, in every way unlike the East. Rachel knew if she allowed herself, she would be very much afraid.

This will be my home. I will learn to love it.

The ride was long and dusty and hot. The road, if such it could be called, was rutted and hard. There was little shade, but the driver seemed to find it whenever there was a need to rest the horses. They passed over dry streambeds and rocky hills, and expanses of brown, hardy grasses.

The landscape changed abruptly as they drew alongside a strip of low green trees and shrubs that marked a rare watercourse. Sweet drove the wagon through the scrub and under a handsome live oak to the bank, where he let the horses drink from the clear, bubbling stream.

"Where are we now?" Rachel asked, breathing in the crisp, welcome scent of water and growing things.

"On the border of Blackwater, the Blackwell ranch," Sweet said. He waved his hand at the opposite bank. "They own all the land to the north of Dog Creek. We're only about five miles from Dog Creek Ranch."

"Then we're nearly there."

"Hardly, ma'am. We got another fifteen miles past the border before we get to the house. There's a good place along the creek about seven miles east of here where we can stay the night."

The prospect of spending the night alone in the wilderness with a stranger did nothing to salve Rachel's worries, but she forgot her concern when she saw a rider approaching from the opposite bank. Even from a distance she could see that he was not like the driver, or the man who had come to tell her that McCarrick had "changed his mind." He rode erect, and his clothing was of a better cut and far cleaner. *A gentleman*, she thought.

The rider guided his horse down the bank and crossed the stream, the water splashing at his horse's knees. "Mr. McCarrick," Sweet said as the stranger stopped before them.

Rachel's heart bounced beneath her ribs. She stared up at the rider's blue eyes, long blond hair and tanned, handsome face. He was much too young and too tall. But his name...

"Good day, ma'am," the rider said, touching the brim of his hat and smiling down at Rachel with bright curiosity. His voice was smooth, a pleasant tenor that bore an accent more evocative of the East than the Texas drawl Rachel had been hearing since her arrival. For just a moment it reminded her of Louis, and she stiffened.

"This here's Miss Rachel Lyndon," Sweet said before Rachel could respond. "She came in on the stage yesterday."

Something flickered across the rider's face, an emotion too quickly gone to grasp. "I'm Sean McCarrick, Miss Lyndon. Jed's nephew. I was just on my way to meet you."

A great wave of relief threatened to wash the starch out of Rachel's spine. She offered her hand. "Good day, Mr. McCarrick. I'm very pleased to make your acquaintance."

He took her hand in his and bent over the saddle to

kiss the air above it. "I'm sorry to have kept you waiting, Miss Lyndon. We'd heard that the stage was delayed and wasn't expected until this evening."

Of course. That explained everything. Everything but the man who had tried to send her away.

"I understand completely, Mr. McCarrick," she said.

"Sean, please."

"Thank you." She hesitated, afraid to push too much. "Is Mr. McCarrick indisposed?"

Sean McCarrick shifted his weight in the saddle. "No, ma'am. He's away from the ranch at the moment and asked me to watch out for you."

Away from the ranch? "I see," she said, suppressing a new spark of panic. "Can you tell me when he'll be returning?"

"He's up north on business that couldn't wait. I expect him anytime now." Sean McCarrick gazed at her with concern. "I'm sorry for the disappointment, but I know Jed will be happy to have Sonntag put you up in town until he comes back."

Rachel's unease blossomed into terror. The man who'd try to buy her off had been correct. Jed didn't want her. He'd sent his gentlemanly nephew to approach her in a subtler fashion, but the result would be the same. She would wait and wait in town until it became clear that Jed was never coming back. Not for her.

Once upon a time, fear and humiliation would have sent her scurrying in retreat. But she'd come too far. Anger bubbled up from some long-quiet source inside her heart.

"I wonder if you might tell me who came to meet me yesterday evening," she said abruptly.

Because she'd learned to watch people's faces, Rachel caught the almost imperceptible flash of dismay in Sean's expression before it transformed into puzzlement. "Someone came to meet you?" he asked.

"Yes. A man who said that Mr. McCarrick had changed his mind and wished me to return to Ohio. He offered me money to leave Javelina."

Sean frowned. "What did this man look like?"

She began to think more clearly. "Lean of frame, of average height, brown hair. He did not give his name."

Sean's frown deepened. "That description fits any one of a dozen men around this part of the Pecos." He drummed his fingers on his saddle horn. "What exactly did he say?"

In brief, concise sentences, Rachel told him. "Who could want to do such a thing?" she asked, watching for any telltale slip in his demeanor.

There was none. He looked out across the desert plain, the muscles beneath his jaw flexing and relaxing. "I can think of only one man who would want you gone," he said. "The foreman at Dog Creek. Holden Renshaw."

"The foreman?"

"He's had a favored place at the ranch he no doubt wouldn't wish to surrender. My uncle has given him far too much trust and control, and as a result…" He hesitated. "To be frank, ma'am, he hates women. I wouldn't be at all surprised if he set a man to watch for your arrival and buy you off."

Rachel could scarcely comprehend what he was saying. It seemed too fantastic to be believed. "Jedediah never mentioned this…this Renshaw."

He shook his head. "Of course I can't be certain he

was behind it," he murmured. "But I do advise you not to mention the incident to him." He gave her an apologetic smile. "I'm sorry this has happened. You can see why it would be better for you to go back to town to wait. Once my uncle is home, he—"

"I beg your pardon, Mr. McCarrick, but that will not be necessary. I assure you that this Mr. Renshaw will not—cannot—deter me in any way."

"But, ma'am—"

"I have every right to be there. You see, Jedediah and I were married in Ohio. I am Mrs. McCarrick."

Chapter Two

HEATH DISMOUNTED, TAKING great care not to jar the baby. The kid had been so quiet those last ten miles that at times he had only known it was still alive by its breathing and slow heartbeat.

He lifted the edges of the blanket away from the baby's face. Sick as it was, it was looking at him the way it always did, as if it could see right into his head.

You'll be all right, he told his son for the hundredth time. *I'll find someone to look after you proper.*

The baby made a soft noise and lifted its hand toward his face. As if it trusted him. As if it knew he wouldn't let it die.

Heath looked around for the ranch hands. Sean wasn't around, as usual. Most of the others were no doubt out on the range, but Maurice and Joey almost always stuck by the house, especially when Heath was away. Joey was a fast rider and could get to the Blackwell place in a few hours.

I should have gone straight there myself. But he hadn't realized how sick the baby was going to get, and the idea of crawling to Artemus Blackwell for help made Heath's hackles rise. Now he didn't have any choice. Blackwell had a wife and daughter, and females knew about babies.

He was about to take the baby into the house when he heard the rattle of a wagon a mile or so up the track that ran west along the creek that gave the ranch its name. He tilted his head to listen. He knew the sound of every vehicle belonging to the ranch, and this wasn't one of them.

The baby gave a thin, whimpering wail. Heath rocked it a little, the way he'd seen Polly doing. The kid went quiet again, and Heath tested the air for scent. The first thing he smelled was Sean on his palomino, Ulysses. The wagon behind him was a buckboard, and there were two people crowded onto the seat, one Heath recognized as Henry Sweet from Javelina. The other…

A woman.

Heath tensed. Strange females didn't just show up at Dog Creek.

Unless Jed had asked them to come.

Cold certainty chilled the air in his lungs. It was *her*. Rachel Lyndon, Jed's mail-order bride. The one Jed had never seen fit to tell him about.

Heath wanted to laugh, but the sound got stuck halfway up his throat. It wasn't as if he hadn't known she was coming, but he'd never thought he would lay eyes on her.

The rattle of the wagon grew louder. Sean and the buckboard came into view, and Heath caught his first glimpse of the woman.

She sat upright on the hard seat, clutching a carpetbag to her chest. Her hair was dark, her body slender, even thin, and her gaze was fixed on the house. There was unease in her scent and tension in the set of her shoulders.

Sean rode straight up to Heath. "Renshaw," he said coolly. "I hope you're prepared for guests."

"Where the hell have you been?" Heath growled.

He didn't really expect an answer, and there wasn't one.

Sean glanced at the blanket, then looked away again without seeing what was inside it and reined Ulysses around to watch the wagon approach.

"She just got in on the stage, nice and ready to take over while Jed's gone," he said. "You'd better clean yourself up. The lady may not decide to keep you on if you don't please her."

Something in Sean's tone told Heath that the son of a bitch was sitting on information that he couldn't wait to let out. He wanted Heath to ask who she was, why some female he'd never seen had any idea of "taking over." He thought Heath didn't know the truth, and he wanted to savor the moment.

But Sean could never keep his mouth shut for long. He smiled, not quite meeting Heath's gaze. "Do you know who she is, Renshaw? Did my uncle tell you before he left for Kansas?"

"I know who she is," Heath said between his teeth. "Rachel Lyndon. Jed's intended."

Sean's smile froze. "You're half-right, Renshaw," he said, recovering his balance. "Her name is Rachel, but it's not Lyndon, and she's not anyone's intended." He grinned and looked full into Heath's face. "It's McCarrick. Rachel McCarrick. She and Jed were married in Ohio.

"She's Jed's wife."

JED'S WIFE.

At first Heath didn't think he'd heard right. He'd read Jed's unsigned will, and the letter from the woman. It had been clear that Jed hadn't married her yet, that he planned to do it soon after she arrived.

Someone was lying. But who?

Heath didn't have the chance to call Sean out. The female was taking Sweet's arm and climbing down from the buckboard, almost stumbling as she stared at the house.

Sean dismounted, tossed Ulysses's reins over the hitching post and went to meet her. Heath gave her a closer look. Her eyes were brown, a few shades lighter than her dark hair. She wasn't pretty, but she wasn't ugly, either. She was somewhere around thirty years, not old, but there was a tightness around her mouth, a kind of tension that told him she wasn't easy in her mind.

So this was the woman who'd written the letter that Jed had carried like something precious. The woman he'd cared enough about to woo and win and bring all the way to Texas.

She looked in his direction. Her shoulders lifted, and she started toward him, her plain brown skirts swishing with each firm step. He could feel her hostility through his skin and in his bones. She didn't even glance at the bundle in his arms.

"Mrs. Rachel McCarrick," Sean said, gliding up beside her. "Holden Renshaw, foreman of Dog Creek."

At first Heath thought the woman was going to back away, but then he realized her hostility covered something else: fear. He could smell it sure as he could smell a skunk at ten paces.

"Ma'am," he said coldly, briefly touching the brim of his hat. "Welcome to Dog Creek."

She studied his face. "*Am* I welcome, Mr. Renshaw?" she asked.

He didn't understand the question, and he didn't much care. She wasn't denying that she was Jed's wife, and that meant *she* was lying. He hated that she was here, hated that she'd invaded this place and claimed it for herself, that a stranger held Jed's loyalty just because she was human.

But she obviously didn't know Jed was dead, and neither did Sean.

"So you're Jed's wife?" he said, making her feel a little of what he was.

She flinched, so slightly that he knew no human would have caught it. "I understand that Mr. Mc—my husband is away," she said.

"He's been in Kansas, selling cattle," he said. "Surprised you didn't know that, Mrs. McCarrick."

Her upper teeth, white and straight, grazed her lower lip. "Of course I knew he had been elsewhere on business, but he was to have returned by the time I arrived."

Maybe she was telling the truth about that part, maybe not. Heath smiled, not trying too hard to make it friendly. "I don't know what you're used to back East, ma'am, but out here, things don't run by clockwork."

"*You* expected me, did you not?"

He knew a challenge when he heard it. Jed had surely planned to meet her when she arrived. Maybe she wondered why his foreman hadn't known to fetch her in Javelina.

"Jed didn't say when you was comin'," he said.

"He told *me*," Sean said.

More lies. "You know when he'll be back, too?" Heath asked with a curl of his lip.

Sean hesitated, and little worry lines appeared between the woman's straight dark brows. Heath came within an inch of feeling sorry for her.

An inch could be a long way if you wanted it to be.

Sean cleared his throat. "Mrs. McCarrick is weary from her long journey," he said. "I'll escort her into the house."

One long stare shut Sean up again. Heath looked down at the baby, so covered up that it looked like a pile of rags. It chose that moment to stir and whimper. Sean jumped. So did the woman. They both stared in disbelief at the lump curled against Heath's chest.

"You know anything about kids, Mrs. McCarrick?" Heath asked roughly.

She blinked at him. "I…I beg your—"

He showed her the baby's pale face. "It's ailin'. Can you make it well?"

Her gaze moved from the baby's face to his, astonishment wiping every other emotion from her features. "Where…whose baby is this?"

"Someone left it, and I found it. Can you fix it?"

Surprised as she was, she landed on her feet just like a cat. "How long has it been since it has eaten?"

"It won't eat at all."

Accusing eyes met his, and she took the baby from his arms, taking care not to touch Heath more than she had to. "What have you been giving it?" she demanded.

His hackles rose again. "Some cow's milk and stuff in a bottle. That's all I had."

"It must have milk. Fresh milk."

Relief burned through his body like strong whiskey. She knew what to do. She could keep the baby alive.

Maybe she could do more than that. She was holding the baby close and humming softly, just like a real mother.

Heath cut the thought before it could get any further. He would be gone with the baby as soon as it could travel. "Go on in," he said. "I'll see to that milk."

She met his gaze with a flash of defiance and

walked toward the house, still cooing. Heath turned on his boot heel and walked toward the barn. Sean stepped into his path.

"What in hell do you think you're doing, Renshaw?" he demanded. "I don't know what kind of game you're playing, but if you think you can order Jed's wife around like a common servant—"

Heath took a single step toward him.

Sean backed away fast, his hands half raised, but his fear wasn't enough to shut him up. "Where did you get that baby?" he demanded.

"It ain't your concern, McCarrick," Heath said slowly and clearly.

"It *is* my concern if it affects Dog Creek."

"You never gave a damn about Dog Creek." Heath leaned into Sean, who took another step backward. "Where did you meet her?"

Sean rolled his eyes like a horse about to spook, then took himself in hand. "In Javelina. Jed told me to watch for her."

"Jed never told you a damn thing."

"He never told you, either." Sean attempted a grin. "If only I'd had a mirror to show you the look on your face when you found out who she was."

Heath bared his teeth. "Take a look at it now."

Hunching his shoulders, Sean laughed nervously. "Wondering what else Jed was hiding from you?"

"I knew he was fixin' to marry."

"But not that he *was* married."

So Sean believed it. Heath saw no reason to set him straight and a couple of good ones not to. Sean would be boiling in his own juices by now, much as he tried to hide it by trying to defend the woman. He'd always expected Dog Creek to be handed to him on a silver platter once Jed was gone. He didn't have to know about the wills, or Jed's death, to realize that his plans for Dog Creek were in trouble, but he was just smart enough not to let on. For now.

"You know what I think?" Heath said, wanting to twist the knife a little deeper. "You didn't know nothin' 'bout the woman until she showed up. Jed knew you'd be riled about it. He didn't trust you."

Sean stood straight and put on an offended look that probably would have fooled most of the folks he liked to impress. "Why should I be anything but pleased that my uncle has found happiness with a woman?"

"You was never interested in anyone's happiness but your own."

"Amusing that you of all people should say that, Renshaw. You've been manipulating my uncle since you first arrived."

Hitching his thumbs in his gun belt, Heath half closed his eyes. "That'll always stick in your craw, won't it? That he chose me over you to run Dog Creek?"

Sean sneered. "He made a serious mistake. There's always been something wrong about you, Renshaw. Eventually I'll find out what it is."

If Sean had been anything more than a weak, puling shadow of a man, full of empty bluster, Heath might have taken his threat seriously. He hadn't forgotten the risk of his being here, but Sean didn't know just how much things had changed, and he sure as hell wouldn't do anything that would push Jed into taking Heath's side over his.

Heath didn't know that Jed had chosen against both of them.

Heath glanced back at the house, where Apache was still waiting patiently. "Look on your own time, McCarrick. Now you're nothin' but a hired hand, and you got work to do. See to my horse."

"I'm not taking any more orders from you, Renshaw," Sean spat. "Mrs. McCarrick's in charge now. Once she realizes what a low-bred barbarian you are, she'll have the sense to turn you out and hire someone more suitable."

"Like you? That why you're bowin' and scrapin' to her?"

"I am a gentleman, Renshaw. I have an excellent reputation in this county. The same can't be said of you. In fact, I would think that the good people of Pecos County would be inclined to believe that you might be a danger to Mrs. McCarrick. A woman alone—"

Heath struck faster than any human eye could follow, clenching his fingers in the fabric of Sean's coat and lifting him off his feet.

"You got a filthy mouth, McCarrick. Too filthy for the likes of Jed's wife." He let Sean drop, and the other man fell to his knees. "You got fifteen minutes to pack up your kit and clear out."

Scrambling to his feet, Sean bunched his fists and crouched as if he was thinking about launching an attack of his own. He had just enough sense to think better of it.

"You can't throw me off the ranch," he said. "I am my uncle's closest kin. You have no right—"

"*This* is my right," Heath said, laying his hand on his gun. "Until Jed comes back, you won't set foot on Dog Creek again."

Sean's hand hovered near his own shiny new gun

with its fancy silver scrolling and ivory grip. "You aren't the only one with—"

"Even if you knew how to use that fancy piece, you wouldn't draw it. Not when you'd be the one left bleedin'."

Sean opened and closed his mouth like a gasping fish. "You won't get away with this, Renshaw. I swear you'll live to regret it."

Heath stepped around Sean as if he were no more than a pile of steaming cow dung and took Apache to the corral himself. Almost since he'd come to Dog Creek, he'd wanted to do what he'd just done. Jed had made that impossible. But there'd been nothing to stop him now, and even if Sean worked up the grit to try acting on his threats, Heath wouldn't be around to deal with them.

Once he'd unsaddled the gelding, brushed him and given him a bag of oats, his thoughts quickly turned back to Mrs. McCarrick.

Rachel. He didn't know what to make of her. He'd known a few females in his life, but she wasn't much like any of them. Not like Polly or Frankie, hardened by a life of catering to the lusts of men. She talked like she had plenty of book learnin', all fancy and proper with her words, looking down her nose at him. But she wasn't soft, like the ladies in San Antonio with their fine airs and frilly dresses.

And she'd taken the baby right away. She'd held it like she cared about its welfare.

Because she didn't know what it really was. And she never would. It didn't really matter if she was lying about being Jed's wife, or what would happen when she found out she never would be. For now, he had a use for Rachel Lyndon. The baby needed her. And as long as that was true, Heath had to try to forget how much he hated her.

SEAN DROVE HIS spurs into Ulysses's heaving sides. His rage had gone beyond shock into a low-burning anger that only strengthened his determination.

"I am Mrs. McCarrick." When the woman had spoken the words, Sean had believed at first that he'd heard her wrong. "Miss Rachel Lyndon," Sweet had said when he'd introduced her. According to the drifter, who had fled as soon as he'd reported his failure to Sean, she had answered to that name in town.

It was a flat-out lie. "As soon as we're married," Jed had said. He wouldn't have phrased it that way if they had already been wed. He'd wanted to make Sean suffer, so he wouldn't have hesitated to announce that the deed was done and his worldly goods would be going to his wife upon his passing.

So Rachel Lyndon was a fraud. Sean could think of several reasons why she might prevaricate, among them her desire to go to Dog Creek in spite of Jed's unexpected absence. She might see it as a way to protect her reputation in a strange place and assert her authority until Jed returned. Clearly she did not believe that he would resent her pretense.

Ulysses stumbled, and Sean sawed on the reins to bring the horse up again. Renshaw might have known that Jed intended to be married, but Sean was certain he hadn't realized that Jed's fiancée was on her way, or he wouldn't have been gone when the stage was due. Renshaw had assumed that Sean hadn't known, either, undoubtedly believing that Sean's meeting with "Mrs. McCarrick" had been the merest chance.

It had been a blessing that Renshaw hadn't believed Sean when he'd made the mistake of saying he'd expected Rachel's arrival. If anyone ever found out what he'd told the drifter to do, or what Jed had said just before he died…

Sean laid his quirt to Ulysses's flank, letting the wind burn his eyes. At least Renshaw didn't know that Jed had intended to disinherit his nephew, or he would surely have rubbed it in Sean's face long since.

But he *had* known Sean would be angry. As barbaric and uncouth as he was, he was not without a certain low animal cunning, and few in the county were inclined to cross him. Sean could still feel Renshaw's hands clutching the lapels of his coat, feel that almost inhuman strength that could put even the most superior of men at a disadvantage.

The bastard would pay for that, of course. And that payment had been a long time coming. Too long. Renshaw had claimed Sean's rightful place as Jed's right hand and confidant. If Jed had done his duty and atoned for his brother's sin of abandonment, it would have been different. But the money and education and petty privileges he had given his brother's cast-off son had never been enough. They hadn't filled the hole Sean had worked so hard to ignore.

If only Jed had loved—

Sean hit Ulysses again, pleased by the stallion's grunt of pain. Those pitiful desires and the weakness that came with them were as dead as Jedediah McCarrick. Sean had set his own path, and it was as clear as daylight.

Renshaw's bizarre rescue of an apparently abandoned infant might play into Sean's hands in ways he couldn't yet predict. Renshaw's open hostility toward the Lyndon woman would certainly work to Sean's benefit. And her apparent belief that Renshaw had tried to bribe her to leave, along with his brutish behavior, made it unlikely that she would ever regard Renshaw with any favor, no matter what she might think about the infant. Sean hadn't lied when he'd told her that Renshaw would hate any woman who set foot on Dog Creek, and not even a brute would be tempted by her dubious charms.

Sean didn't hate her. She was simply an obstacle to be removed. A woman who lied about her marital state must have secrets, and he intended to find them. He could beguile any woman he set his sights on, beautiful or ugly, old or young. Charm her into revealing *her* greatest weakness.

In the meantime, he would assign one of the hands to keep an eye on the woman—and on Renshaw. And he had to find and get rid of the will before he arranged for Jed's body to be found. Jed had used a lawyer in Heywood once or twice to draw up contracts, and such a man might very well have handled the will, as well. Sean would send his most loyal sheep to look for the man. Then he would consider how to approach the lawyer without betraying an untoward interest in Jed's posthumous intentions.

Plenty of ifs, and no guarantees. But Sean had never doubted his destiny. It was as inevitable as the sunrise.

He pulled Ulysses to a sharp stop before the Blackwells' fine two-story house. He would not tell them the entire truth about his eviction from Dog Creek. Amy was very close to dropping from the vine into his waiting hand, and her parents were not far behind. A little finesse and he would simply increase their resentment of the man they believed had persuaded Jed to refuse their generous offer for Dog Creek, thwarting their ambition for undisputed dominance of Pecos County.

They didn't know what ambition was.

Sean dismounted in an almost cheerful mood. As he ran up the steps to the wide, shaded veranda, the door opened and Amy walked out, dressed in a tight pink gown that must have come all the way from Paris.

"Sean!" she said. "I didn't expect you this morning!"

He removed his hat. "Something has happened, Amy. I don't like to trouble you, but—"

"What is it?" She hurried to meet him, gazing anxiously into his face. "Come inside and tell me at once." She took his hand, and as she led him into the hall, Sean knew that he need have no more worries. When he had Dog Creek, he would have this woman. And when he had *her*, he would have this house and all the country from Dog Creek to the Pecos.

And when he was governor, Jed wouldn't be the only one he left lying in the dry West Texas dirt.

Chapter Three

IF IT HADN'T been for the infant, Rachel wasn't sure she could have done anything but stare and bawl like a child.

At first all she had noticed was the primitive look of the place—the ramshackle unpainted buildings, the piles of unrecognizable metal objects heaped around them, the barren earth beyond the single tree by the house and the meager stretch of green that marked the creek. Jedediah's descriptions had always been vague, but she had pictured something very different. The house itself was far smaller than she had expected here in the West, where everything seemed so vast. There was no garden that she could see, no whitewashed fences, no evidence that anyone had ever attempted to make the house a home.

That is why I am here, she'd told herself. But then she'd seen the grim-faced man standing in front of the house, and she knew even before she had been introduced who he must be. When she had first looked into his lean, predatory face, she had known that this was a man capable of doing exactly what Sean McCarrick had suggested. His eyes—as much golden-green as gray etched steel that reflected light like those of an animal—emanated hostility as hot as the stark Texas sun.

Eyes that weighed her with a single glance and found her unworthy. A rival. A threat to his power. He had claimed he didn't know about her imminent arrival, but of course he would have no compunction about lying to her if he had already tried to buy her off.

When he had said "So you're Jed's wife?" in such a sneering voice, she'd been almost certain that he meant to accuse *her* of deception. She had, after all, answered to Rachel Lyndon when the wagon driver had approached her in Javelina. Perhaps he hadn't persisted in his challenge because he feared being exposed himself.

You are no less a liar just because he's a liar, too, she told herself. But she had lied only because she had needed a reason for coming to Dog Creek after she'd learned that Jedediah was away. If her worst, most irrational fears were realized and he no longer wanted her, she would compel him to tell her so to her face. Unless and until that happened, turning back, even staying in Javelina, was not an acceptable option.

And if Jedediah had simply been detained on business, as Sean had said, he would surely understand her reasons for claiming a privilege she did not yet possess.

Rachel opened the door to the house, easing the infant into the crook of her arm as she pushed. She had no reason to disbelieve anything Sean had said; his interest in her seemed strictly and benevolently impersonal, and he had accurately predicted Renshaw's reaction. If not for the baby, she would have deemed Holden Renshaw a thoroughgoing and unredeemable villain.

Yet when he'd held the child out to her and demanded that she help in that rough, deep voice, she'd been struck dumb as a lamppost. What sort of villain would bring a foundling home with him and express such concern about its well-being?

Glancing around the rustic parlor immediately inside the door, she saw that the chairs, like the table they surrounded, were handmade, simple and rough-hewn. She went to the nearest and sat, gently unwrapping the infant as soon as she was settled. Its skin was gray, its face far too thin.

It could not have been more than two months old. She cooed to it, waiting for it to open its eyes. Afraid, though she could see it breathing, that it might die in her arms.

A precious life. Small and fragile in body, just as she felt in her soul.

She lifted the baby so that its downy head rested against her cheek. A curled fist flailed, bumping her mouth. Alive. Wanting to live. Giving her the courage she so sadly lacked.

Whoever you may be, she told it silently, *wherever you have come from, I am here to protect you.*

Blue eyes opened. All babies had blue eyes at first, but this child's were startling, as bright and intent as if they could focus on hers.

"Yes," she murmured. "I see you."

The baby—a boy, she saw, checking under his diaper—gave a gusty little sigh as if he understood. Nursery rhymes crowded into her head, pushing away her fear.

Once, she had sung such songs to the baby within her, certain he could hear her long before he was born. She had felt him move, kicking and punching as if to declare his coming independence.

Little Timothy had lived so short a time. Only long enough for her to sing a few verses of the song she loved most.

> Hush little baby, don't say a word,
> Mama's going to buy you a mockingbird...

The door opened, and Renshaw walked in with a pail in one hand and saddlebags over his shoulder. He set down the pail and moved past her to lay the saddlebags over a chair. In the pail, the milk steamed, fresh and pungent.

Rachel found her composure again and hugged the baby as if it needed protection from the very person who had found him. No one, least of all *this* man, would see her vulnerable.

"We will need something to feed him with," she said briskly.

Without a word, Renshaw rummaged in the saddlebags and produced a bottle and several squares of white cotton fabric.

"Where did you get the bottle?" she asked.

"It was left with the kid," he said. He went to the pail to fill the bottle, but Rachel stopped him with a cry of protest.

"Your hands must be clean," she said.

He glared at her, though his face remained expressionless. He strode into the adjoining kitchen. A moment later she heard the squeak of a pump handle working and a gush of water.

Her heart was beating fast when he walked back into the room, looking like nothing so much as a panther with his lowered head and silent feet. Muscles bunched and flexed under his shirt and trousers, lending power to his grace.

He is handsome, she thought, surprised. It wasn't easy to see at first because of the harsh lines of his features, but she could not deny it.

Handsome, like Louis. And nothing like him. There was a leashed energy in him, a feral quality she couldn't put a name to. It was more than a sense of danger, more than the gun at his hip or a question of dubious intentions. It felt almost as if he could look into her eyes and make her do anything.

Anything at all.

Renshaw startled her by holding his hands in front of her face. "Clean enough for you, Mrs. McCarrick?"

His voice was milder than she had expected, and all at once her certainty of his guilt seemed less secure than it had been only minutes before. She looked up at Renshaw with all the confidence a married woman should display.

"Thank you," she said. "Would you kindly fill the bottle?"

He stared at her a moment longer, then removed the cork, tube and rubber nipple from the bottle, knelt beside the pail and pushed the bottle into the milk. When the bottle was full, he thrust it at her.

"Feed it," he said.

Swallowing fresh resentment, she took the bottle and rested the nipple against the baby's lips. His tiny nostrils flared, and his mouth opened a hairbreadth.

"Mr. Renshaw," she said, fixing her gaze on the baby's face, "I would like to make one thing perfectly clear. I am not an employee at Dog Creek. I am not under your command."

She couldn't see his reaction, but she heard the sudden intake of his breath, as if he was about to speak. She concentrated on the baby again…on the way the rosebud lips opened wider, the miniature fists flailed toward the bottle.

"There now," she said. "That's it." She nudged the bottle into his mouth, and he took it.

Renshaw's worn, dusty boots shuffled on the scratched wooden floor. "Is it goin' to be all right?" he asked.

"It is not an 'it,'" she said. "It is a 'he.'"

"You think I don't know that?"

"One would be hard-pressed to realize it."

Rachel had not lived so sheltered a life that she hadn't heard far worse profanity than he uttered now. "I will thank you not to speak so in front of the baby," she snapped.

"You're tellin' me he can understand?"

Once again she lifted her gaze from the suckling infant, focusing on the dark, strong brows above Renshaw's striking eyes. "What do you intend to do with the child when he's better?" she asked.

For once Renshaw seemed to have nothing to say. If the child was a foundling, presumably abandoned, the chances of his parents coming forward to reclaim him were dubious at best. Wouldn't a man like him be eager to be rid of such a burden, as he had so obviously been relieved to consign the child's care to her?

A man like him. Could she be wrong about him, too quick to base her judgment upon Sean McCarrick's obvious dislike of his uncle's foreman? Had her natural prejudice in favor of Jedediah's nephew, so clearly a gentleman and so comfortingly respectful, colored her perception of this man?

Rachel bit her lip and watched him from the corner of her eye. "There is no need for you to remain," she said. "The baby will rest after he is done feeding. You may return to your work."

His brief laugh was more of a bark than an indication of amusement. "Oh, so I have your permission, Mrs. McCarrick?"

She averted her face quickly. "You have set me a task, Mr. Renshaw, for which you are ill suited, as I am unsuited for yours."

"There ain't much food in the house. We ain't fitted out for a lady."

One might almost have taken it for an apology. "I will make do," she said.

"I'll send Maurice to find out what you need. What he don't have in the cookhouse, he can get in Javelina." He cleared his throat. "Do you need anythin' else for the baby?"

"Yes. As many clean cloths as you can get. And—" She almost blushed. "It is better if the baby has mother's milk. A wet nurse, a woman who has just had a child herself…"

"Is that all?"

His mockery had returned, tempered by something else she couldn't quite name. "I will see that you know if there is anything else," she said.

He lingered for a few heartbeats more, then opened the door and went outside. Rachel didn't breathe again until she had counted all the way to ten.

"There now," she said to the baby. "He's gone. You don't have to be afraid."

The infant burbled, bringing up little milky bubbles. She set the bottle on the table, picked up one of the rags

Renshaw had taken from the saddlebags, laid it across her shoulder and gently positioned the infant over the cloth.

He did exactly what he ought to do, and promptly fell into a deep, contented sleep. Rachel almost imagined she could see the color coming back into his skin, the roundness of health returning to his thin body.

She sang to him for a while, afraid to disturb him, and then looked for a place to lay him down. There was no cradle, of course. She ventured cautiously into the short hall and looked into the two rooms that led off from it.

One, the smaller, was clearly the province of a man, though it was tidy enough. The bed, covered with an Indian blanket, was neatly made. The walls were bare save for a faded photograph of a pretty, dark-haired woman in a white dress. The air smelled faintly of horse, perspiration, leather…and *him*. He might be un-polished and blunt, rude and uncivilized, but these were not the quarters of an ignorant boor.

Who was the lady whose picture was placed across from his bed where he could see her every night before he went to sleep? A relative? An actress he admired? A former lover?

She backed away hastily and turned to the other room. It was as plain as the rest of the house, but somehow softer, with a quilted coverlet in muted tones and an empty vase on the table beside the bed. The house might not be "fitted out for a lady," but some attempt had been made here, and the bedstead was wide enough to accommodate two sleepers side by side.

Jedediah got that bed for me. No one had ever cared so much for her happiness. Unwanted tears seeped into her eyes. When he returned, everything would be just as it should.

The bed was soft enough for a baby. She laid one of the spare cloths on top of the quilt and set the child down. He didn't wake as she removed his diaper and carefully pinned on another. He would need a bath soon, but recuperative sleep, now that his stomach was full, was far more essential.

It felt strange, even wrong at first, to lie on the bed as if it belonged to her. She reminded herself that it was for the baby and settled him into the crook of her arm with a sigh she almost dared think of as contented. She tried to stay awake, certain that Holden Renshaw would soon come striding into the house with more questions and demands.

But her own body insisted on claiming its due, and she drifted into that half-world where anything was possible.

I will wait, Jedediah. I will not be afraid. I will make you happy.

And no one, not even Holden Renshaw, would stop her.

IT WAS DONE. Heath had committed himself, and there was no going back. Much as he hated the situation, much as he wanted to get as far away from humans as he could, he was bound by the baby. And the baby was bound to the woman until it was healthy again.

Not "it," Heath reminded himself as he strode toward the bunkhouse. *Him.* Damn the woman. *Wash your hands. Fill the bottle. Get back to work.* She talked like a schoolmarm and gave orders like a cavalry sergeant.

Sure, the fear he'd smelled on her never completely went away. Most humans could feel that he wasn't one of them without knowing why. He could make just about anyone afraid by staring them down or showing his teeth, and Sean had probably said plenty bad about him. Heath hadn't exactly tried to prove the bastard wrong.

But Rachel had stood up to him, even though she must have had other things than him to be scared of. Whatever her reasons, she'd come a long way to a strange place to marry a man she could hardly know and found him gone. She must feel mighty alone.

Like everyone was alone in the end. Heath had no sympathy for her. She'd come here of her own free will. She hadn't said much about herself in the letter he'd read; maybe those details were in the rest of the correspondence Heath hadn't looked at. The words she'd written in her fine hand hadn't been at all poetical, the kind Heath reckoned you'd send to a lover, just talk about when she planned to arrive and how she was looking forward to making Jed a good wife, whatever that was.

But there was something too quiet and humble in those words. Not like the woman he'd just left. It was as if they covered up secrets. Secrets she didn't want even Jed to know.

Heath took off his hat and scrubbed at the sweat on his forehead. Rachel Lyndon was a puzzle, and he had no use for puzzles. She obviously had reasons for lying about being Mrs. McCarrick. He didn't much care what they were, or why Jed had chosen her. He would let her keep that secret so she wouldn't have to worry about her "reputation" living on a ranch full of men.

Hell, he wondered if she'd even figured out *how* her reputation could be ruined. If she'd ever taken a man into her body, he would eat something far worse than his hat.

Heath stopped in the middle of the yard. Mrs. Mc-Carrick's body was of no interest to him. Even if she hadn't been Jed's intended, he wouldn't have given her a second glance. Too thin. Too unyielding. She wore the ugliest clothes he'd ever seen on a woman, and she wasn't a wild hog's idea of pretty. Even the most jaded whores knew how to tart themselves up. Frankie had been like that. She could almost make a man feel as if he was more than just another coin in her pocket.

But she'd still been a liar and a fake. Like all women.

Heath slammed his hat back on his head and kept on going. He had other things to worry about right now. Getting the things the woman needed. Finding a wet nurse. Where in hell was he supposed to locate a female who had a suckling infant and wanted to come out to the ranch to take on another?

"Holden!"

Joey skidded to a halt in a cloud of dust, grinning from ear to ear. "I'm so glad you're back!"

Heath kept walking, wishing the kid wouldn't make him care that he'd be leaving without saying goodbye. "Where you been?" he muttered.

"Out with Charlie, brandin' strays." He skipped alongside Heath, his yellow hair flopping into his eyes. "You know I ain't no shirker, Holden. I always do my share."

"I know you do."

"Is it true what I heard? About the lady?"

Heath sighed and stopped outside the bunkhouse door. "What'd you hear?"

"She came in from Javelina with Henry Sweet. She ain't pretty, and she talks diff'rent. She says she's—"

"Who told you all this?"

Joey ducked his head. "I was listenin'. You ain't mad, are you, Holden?"

Mad at himself, not at Joey. The kid was too good at eavesdropping, and it bothered Heath that he hadn't heard or smelled Joey nearby. He'd been too distracted by Rachel's arrival, and that kind of distraction was a dangerous thing.

"Sean was spittin' mad at you," Joey said, grinning slyly. There was no love lost between him and Jed's nephew, who'd always treated him like dirt. "Thought you'd never make him leave." His grin went flat. "Is it really true that the lady is Jed's wife?"

Heath grabbed Joey by his sleeve and pulled him back toward the stable. "Help me saddle Bess."

The boy wouldn't be put off. "Jed never said nothin' 'bout gettin' hitched! You didn't know, did you?"

Bess stamped and cocked her ears as Heath walked into the stable. "Guess he wanted it to be a surprise."

Joey brought the saddle. "When do you think he's coming home?"

Lying to the kid felt wrong, but Heath had been ready to lie a lot worse. "Haven't heard from him in a while. He's probably investin' some of that money he got for the herd, maybe even buyin' up new stock."

"Oh." Joey followed Heath as he led Bess outside. "You don't like her, do you?"

"Why shouldn't I?"

"You don't like no females. I could tell you was mad as a hornet."

Heath swung up into the saddle. "She's Jed's wife,

and you got other things to worry about. I need you to talk to Maurice about askin' the lady what she needs to be comfortable and make sure she gets it. I have somethin' else to do."

Joey gave Heath that look of pure trust that always made his chest tighten. "Things ain't goin' to be the way they used to anymore, are they?" the boy asked.

"Guess we'll have to wait and see."

His words finally silenced Joey, though the boy was clearly not satisfied. Heath felt the kid's stare raking across his back as he rode out.

It wasn't going to be easy on Joey when he found out Jed was gone, and Heath wouldn't be around to make it any easier. But maybe he would be able to do something he wouldn't have been able to if he'd left for good the day he found Jed's body.

Sonntag knew just about everything that went on in the county. He'd be able to tell Heath if anyone could use a boy to do small jobs around a ranch for food and shelter. And he'd know if some local woman had a new baby, though it could be complicated getting such a female to come to Dog Creek to act as a wet nurse.

He would make her come, if he had to. The kid was more important than any woman's preferences, even if she was the queen of England herself.

JOEY WATCHED HOLDEN ride off, twisting a frayed piece of rope in his hands.

Holden was upset. Joey had known him for three of his sixteen years, ever since Holden had come to Dog Creek as a hand, and Joey could read his friend's feelings like a book.

It wasn't hard to figure out why Holden was riled. Jed hadn't told him about getting married, and that must have hurt, the same way it hurt Joey. Holden was used to knowing everything that went on at Dog Creek.

And Joey couldn't remember a single time when Holden had ever said something nice about a female. If he even knew any.

Wiping his hand across his nose, Joey stared at the house. He hadn't risked staying around while Holden had been tussling with Sean, but something mighty interesting must have happened. If the lady coming to Dog Creek meant Sean was leaving for good, he was glad she'd shown up. Jed might be a little mad at first, but not for long. He loved Holden lots better than that no-good polecat Sean.

But what would Jed say when he found out about the baby? Where had it come from, and why had Holden taken it in?

Joey shook his head. That was a real puzzle. He'd never seen a baby, leastwise not up close. And he badly wanted to meet the lady. He would have to have a look-see for himself. Maurice could wait just a little longer to hear all the details.

Pushing his hat down on his head the way Heath liked to do, Joey crossed the yard. He paused in front of the door, tucked in his shirt and knocked.

No one answered. Joey opened the door, poked his head inside and heard singing. A woman singing a lullaby.

A hard lump settled in Joey's throat. It was a song he knew from when he was a little kid, before…

You're not a little kid no more. A song couldn't hurt him, and neither could a lady, Jed's wife or not.

He strode down the hall, hesitated just shy of the open bedroom door and knocked softly on the door frame.

The lady sat up, and Joey caught a quick glimpse of the bundle lying beside her, pinched the brim of his hat and stood up as straight as he knew how.

"Howdy, ma'am," he said in his deepest voice. "Name's Joey Ackerman. I work with Mr. Renshaw. He asked me to check in on you."

Clear brown eyes met his. "How do you do, Mr. Ackerman," she said very seriously. "I am pleased to make your acquaintance."

Joey tucked his hands behind his back. "You're Jed's wife."

Her eyes seemed to get darker somehow, like a storm cloud brewing on the horizon. "Yes. I am Mrs. McCarrick." She was quiet for a while, and Joey had a chance to study her. She wasn't exactly pretty, and she was thin, like she hadn't had quite enough to eat. Joey knew what that felt like. The way she was sitting, like she was going to pop right up any moment, reminded Joey of a filly he'd seen once, looking calm but just about shaking with the need to run as fast as her feet would carry her.

He shifted his gaze to the bunch of blankets. "You, uh, need anything, Mrs. McCarrick?"

"I have all I need for the time being, Mr. Ackerman. Would you like to see the baby?"

Joey didn't need another invitation. He moved to the side of the bed and peered into the screwed-up little face. Its eyes were closed, and its lashes were very long and very delicate.

"It looks right young," he murmured. "Did Holden really bring him?"

Mrs. McCarrick stroked the baby's silky hair. Joey watched the caress with a sort of hunger he hadn't felt in a long time.

"So it would seem, Mr. Ackerman," Mrs. McCarrick said.

"Joey, ma'am. No one calls me Mr. Ackerman."

"Of course. Tell me, Joey. Have you known Mr. Renshaw long?"

Joey swelled up with pride. "Since he came to Dog Creek, 'bout three years ago."

"I can see that you think well of him."

"Sure. I been here since I was eleven, and he's the best foreman we ever had. No one can work cattle or ride and break horses like he does. It's like he has some magic power over 'em." He shuffled his feet. "You shouldn't judge him by how he acts sometimes, ma'am. He ain't as mean as he looks."

She tilted her head, considering his words as if they were important. "And Jedediah?" she said. "Are he and Holden good friends?"

It was a mighty strange question to ask, he thought, 'specially since she was Jed's wife and should know things like that. "Jed never trusted nobody like he trusts Holden." He rubbed at the fringe of hair above his upper lip. "You didn't know much about Dog Creek before you came, did you, ma'am?"

"Only from Mr. McCarrick's description. He and I married in Ohio."

"Guess this is quite a change for you, ma'am."

She shifted around, tight as rawhide drying in the sun. "Have you been to Ohio, Joey?"

"Me? No, ma'am. I like it here just fine." He searched her eyes. "Hope you like it here, too, Mrs. McCarrick."

"My name is Rachel, Joey."

Rachel. It was about the prettiest name Joey had ever heard. "You must be tuckered, ma'am. Rachel," he said. "I'm goin' to talk to Maurice, but I'll be around case you need anything. Just whistle."

She smiled, and Joey thought that smile changed her face completely. "I'll do that, Joey. Thank you."

His feet hardly touched the floorboards as he left the house. Now that he'd seen her, he didn't understand why Holden didn't like her. She was a right proper lady, and he could see she liked the baby, even if she'd never seen it before today.

Maybe she'd like *him*, too.

Joey nearly ran to the bunkhouse. Holden was wrong about Rachel. She was going to make Dog Creek a better place.

As soon as Jed was home, everything was going to be just fine.

Chapter Four

"Merci, *Maurice.*"

The big Frenchman beamed, his round face reddened from the sun and his eyes twinkling with effusive good humor. Rachel had liked the cook, who turned out to also be the blacksmith and launderer, from the moment he'd entered the house with offerings from his own stores in the ranch cookhouse. Like Joey, he seemed delighted to meet her and eager to see her well settled.

"It is nothing, *madame,*" he said. "I am honored to assist the wife of Monsieur McCarrick."

She returned his smile. "I hope I will be able to lighten your load at Dog Creek," she said. "I can certainly assume the washing duties."

"*Mais non*, *madame.* It is not necessary."

"I came here expecting to work hard, and that is what I intend to do. I may, however, require your advice as to what my husband prefers to eat."

"Ah, the talent of cooking is wasted here, *madame,*" he said with an exaggerated shrug. "Beef, beans and biscuits. Biscuits, beans and beef."

She laughed. "Then it shall not be so difficult, *n'est-ce pas?*"

With a great sigh, Maurice shook his head, bowed and left the house.

Rachel's heart was almost light as she laid the loaf of bread on the table and took up the knife Maurice had brought. Between him and Joey—and perhaps Jedediah's nephew, whom she wanted very much to trust—she was beginning to feel she might have friends at Dog Creek.

Joey had been perfectly charming. He was every bit the boy trying to be a man, earnest and serious. But he hadn't been able to conceal his fascination with the baby. Or his natural friendliness and willingness to help.

In that respect he was very little like the man he so obviously admired.

Rachel's smile faded as she cut a slice of smoked salt pork. It felt strange to be alone in this house now that the sun had set. The first night noises had brought her to an uneasy alert: coyotes howling, ominous scratchings from behind the walls, the keening of the wind. She was just frightened enough to be angry. Angry that Renshaw hadn't come back to visit the baby. That his brief show of solicitude before he had left had been worth so little.

But of course he had no concern for *her* at all.

Checking the lantern to make sure it was still burning well, she listened for the baby in the bedroom. He was still asleep, oblivious to the loneliness that lay so unexpectedly heavy on her own shoulders. She had thought she was accustomed to such loneliness; she'd had so few people to rely upon during her years of struggle. It was ridiculous that she should feel bereft when she was soon to have companionship and a true purpose.

The bitter thought she could never quite conquer rose to mock her hope. *What would they think if they knew my shame? If they guessed how thoroughly I have deceived them?*

Even Jedediah knew nothing of it. How much more would Holden Renshaw despise her if he was aware of her deepest secret?

Why was his opinion of any concern to her at all?

He will never know. No one here will ever know.

Someone rapped on the door. Her heart fluttered treacherously. Had Holden Renshaw finally returned?

But it was not the foreman. Sean McCarrick tipped his hat and smiled in that same very charming way when they'd first met.

"Mrs. McCarrick," he said. "I hope I'm not disturbing you."

"Not at all." She stepped back to let him enter. "Would you be seated?"

He glanced at the table and her plate. "I see that Renshaw actually considered the possibility that you might be hungry."

"I am sorry I haven't much to offer you, Mr. McCarrick."

He took one of the chairs and removed his hat. "I don't expect anything, ma'am. I just wanted to be sure that you and the baby are safe and well."

"He is sleeping, thank you."

"He's all right, then? I admit I was surprised when I saw Renshaw with him. He's the last man I'd expect to care about an abandoned child, let alone bring one home with him."

Though she had entertained the very same thought, Rachel found herself bristling at Sean's comment. "Yet he did so," she said tartly.

He regarded her with obvious curiosity. "Has he won your good opinion, Mrs. McCarrick? Offered some defense of his attempt to send you away, perhaps?"

"I did not ask him about it."

"I completely understand." He smoothed his fine woolen trousers. "It wouldn't be wise to confront him, under the circumstances. You'll have ample opportunity when Jed returns."

Rachel could not feel at ease, though there was no reason why she should not. They sat quietly for a few moments. Finally Sean cleared his throat.

"I've come for another reason, Mrs. McCarrick," he said. "I've left Dog Creek."

"Left?" she echoed. "But why?"

"I see you are not aware of what transpired after Renshaw gave you the child. It must seem strange to you, ma'am, but it has become impossible to continue here in my uncle's absence. As I believe I mentioned before, Renshaw abuses the authority my uncle left him, and he treats…well, I have come to find his behavior intolerable."

That was no surprise, considering the way the two men had glared at one another that morning. Harsh words had hardly been necessary to establish their mutual dislike.

"I'm sorry to hear it, Mr. McCarrick," she said.

"Sean, please." He smiled warmly. "Your concern is gratifying." He glanced over his shoulder toward the door. "I have no desire to create trouble for you, which is why I have come to speak with you while Renshaw is absent. He has resented me ever since he came here three years ago. It has always been his intention to turn my uncle against me and steal Dog Creek." He sighed. "Jedediah is a good, honest man—too trusting, I'm afraid. As difficult as it is to believe, Renshaw has been very skilled in making himself Jedediah's confidant. He schemed to convince Jed that I was unworthy to act as foreman."

Renshaw hardly seemed capable of such subtlety, but Rachel had not seen him with Jedediah. "It's a terrible thing to be shut out by your own people," she said, her voice thick with memory.

"It is, ma'am. A hard thing indeed." He leaned forward, searching her eyes. "You speak as though you know how it feels."

Had she been just a little less uncertain, she might have confided in him. It would be such a relief. But she knew it would have been the height of folly to admit even part of the truth.

"My parents died when I was very young," she said.

"My deepest sympathies, Mrs. McCarrick."

"Rachel," she said, trying to smile. "It was a very long time ago."

"I was also an orphan," he said. "When my father died, Jedediah took me in and raised me as his own son." He laid his hand over hers. "We have something in common, Rachel. I think we'll be good friends."

His words were too bold, and she drew her hand away. "I hope you will feel more welcome here when Jedediah returns."

He leaned back again. "I hope you'll speak to my uncle on my behalf. I have no doubt he'll listen to you." He hesitated. "I also hope you'll take my advice, Rachel, and remain alert to any attempts Renshaw may make to undermine your position here. He will no doubt attempt to frighten you away."

"I am Jedediah's wife," Rachel said. "Even if he were to dare attempt it, I assure you that I will not allow him to intimidate me."

"I believe you. I don't believe he will resort to physical means, but he is by nature a violent man. Be wary." He rose abruptly. "I've taken too much of your time. If you should need an advocate, I won't be far away. I'm staying with the Blackwells and hope to have employment with them very soon. Send a hand with a message to Blackwater anytime."

It seemed a gallant offer, though Rachel could not quite shake the feeling that Sean expected greater intimacy than she was prepared to give. She rose to see him to the door. "Thank you for coming, Sean," she said. "You have made me feel very welcome."

"The least I can do for kin." He tipped his hat. "I hope to see you again soon, Rachel."

As soon as he had gone, she went back to the bedroom. The baby was just beginning to stir. He opened his blue eyes and smiled.

She knelt beside the bed. "What am I to think, little one?" she asked him, tracing his cheek with a fingertip. "I ought to trust Jedediah's nephew. He is the closest thing I have to kin here, and he has been kind."

So few people had ever been truly kind to her. Yet she couldn't feel entirely easy with Sean or the things he had said, and upon reflection she began to understand why. He had admitted to a certain weakness of character in his unwillingness to stand up to Jedediah's foreman in his uncle's absence. He had suggested that Renshaw had attempted to bribe her in Javelina, yet he had not confronted the foreman with his suspicions. He had clearly suggested that she might find it difficult at Dog Creek while Jedediah was gone—that Holden Renshaw could be a threat to her, even capable of violence—yet he was leaving nevertheless. His offer to be her advocate seemed little more than empty words.

And there were other questions. Was she to believe that Jedediah possessed such poor judgment that he would listen to unjustified criticism of his own nephew by his foreman? Was Holden Renshaw so consumed by jealousy and greed that he would scheme to undermine Sean at every turn? Had he given the baby into her care while simultaneously intending to drive her away? How could he hope to make her leave when he had accepted her as Jedediah's wife? She could make no sense of it.

He ain't as mean as he looks, Joey had said. The boy seemed to look up to Holden Renshaw as an older brother, perhaps even a father. His account, brief as it was, could not be more thoroughly opposed to Sean's.

But that only meant she must be even more wary. She knew that if she reported Sean's visit to Holden Renshaw, or confronted him openly with what Sean had told her, she would get no closer to the truth. Guilty or not, Renshaw would simply deny Sean's accusations and doubtless fling a few of his own.

That Renshaw could be dangerous she did not doubt; she had determined as much from the very beginning. She did not like him in the least. But those considerations could not possibly illustrate the full truth of his character. Had she not recognized even before Sean's visit that her first impressions might be wrong?

Eyes like brooding thunderstorms, gliding muscle and a panther's grace...

Kicking vigorously against the blankets, the baby gurgled. Rachel shivered and kissed his silky forehead, relieved to turn her thoughts to something less perilous. It was already clear that the child would recover from whatever had ailed him. He would live, and thrive, and grow.

"We shall do very well together, you and I," she said.

For as long as she was permitted to keep him. She would have given a great deal to do so, though her feelings seemed dangerously impulsive. If his parents were never found…if Jed were willing to accept him…

It was too soon to hope. She would go on as she always had, minute by minute, hour by hour, taking each day as it came.

She lay down beside the baby and listened for Holden Renshaw long into the night.

THE UNSEASONABLY hot morning sun had robbed Javelina of life. Anyone with sense was indoors at the saloon next to the general store, in the livery stable or in the few houses that lined the single dusty road through town.

Heath stopped in front of the saloon, helped Lucia Gonzales to dismount from her mule and secured the animal's lead to the hitching post. It had been a long and dirty ride from the Gonzales place at the far western border of the ranch, but Heath had found what he needed.

He'd expected the pay he'd offered would be enough to convince Lucia to leave the tiny farm her husband and sons struggled to keep alive. There had been an argument between the *señora* and her man, but it hadn't lasted very long. Lucia was to live at Dog Creek with her own baby for as long as she was needed, and Luis and their three nearly grown sons would just have to get along without her.

As much as Heath hated to admit it, Lucia was as

close to a truly decent woman as he'd ever met. She had made him welcome, insisting he stay overnight in their tiny *casa* so that she and Heath could start fresh in the morning. And she hadn't complained once during the ride. She was so quiet he barely knew she was there at all.

Just the opposite of Rachel Lyndon.

Hell. He needed a drink. "We'll go in for a spell," he said, giving Bess a command to stay put. "The saloon has a dining room that caters to the stage trade. They'll have somethin' for you there."

Lucia smiled at him. "*Gracias, señor.*"

He didn't like being thanked any more than he liked being beholden. He gestured for her to precede him, and they walked through the side door that led into the dining room with its two small tables. It was empty except for two of the three women who lived in Javelina. Neither one of them offered a greeting as Heath showed Lucia to the other table.

"You wait here," Heath told Lucia. He walked into the saloon and leaned on the bar, catching the bartender's eye.

"One lemonade," he said. "And a whiskey. Straight."

Riley gave him a startled, curious look and went after the drinks. The handful of men at the bar and tables—drifters and unemployed cowhands, mostly—looked up at Heath and went straight back to their drinks. Heath ignored them and picked up the whiskey Riley brought him. The stuff almost always made him feel a little sick; the smell and taste were too strong for his *loup-garou* senses. He drank it anyway.

The bartender plunked the lemonade on the bar and set him up for another drink. "Heard Jed's still not back from Kansas," he said, wiping a glass with a stained towel.

Heath downed the second drink without answering.

"Heard about Jed's missus," Riley said.

Heath ordered a third whiskey and nursed it, turning the glass around in his hands.

"They say you found a baby, too," Riley persisted.

"That's right."

It was obvious that Riley wanted to hear a lot more, but he didn't ask. Heath finished his drink, threw down his money and returned to the dining room with the lemonade. He gave it to Lucia and walked over to the store.

Sonntag greeted him with his merchant's smile, hovering expectantly. "You found the lady?" he asked.

Heath nodded briefly. Sonntag was one of the few folk in the county who never seemed wary of him. He picked up a roll of cheap cotton and a few other things he thought Mrs. McCarrick might need before Maurice came to town with the wagon. Sonntag called his attention to a fancy painted cradle he claimed he'd just gotten in from San Antonio.

"The best money can buy," the storekeeper said in his thick German accent. "Where did you find the baby, Herr Renshaw?"

Heath straightened from his inspection and gave Sonntag a steady look. "Be best if people kept more to themselves and worried less about other people's business."

Sonntag stood his ground. "You have done a good thing, Mr. Renshaw."

Heath nudged the cradle with the toe of his boot. "Ain't got much call for somethin' like this in Javelina."

The storekeeper's eyes gleamed. "For you, Herr

Renshaw, and for the new bride, I would offer an excellent bargain." He pushed up his spectacles. "How is Mrs. McCarrick?"

"Fine," Heath said through gritted teeth. He strode to the counter and removed a few coins from his money pouch. "You get any more of that jam in?"

"One jar." Sonntag cocked his head. "No cradle today, Herr Renshaw?"

"I'll think about it." Except he wouldn't be thinking about it at all, because he wouldn't be making any more personal stops in Javelina if he could help it. Sonntag hadn't had any ideas about helping Joey find work somewhere else, and Heath didn't figure anything new would crop up in the next few days. He went out for his saddlebags, dropped them on the counter and left Sonntag to pack his purchases while he looked over the patch of wall the town used for announcements and the rare advertisement.

When he saw the poster, it was like looking in a cracked mirror. The face in the drawing was almost completely covered with a full black beard, mustache and long, unkempt hair. The eyes were the same, but the artist had the nose wrong. The scar across the wanted man's neck was knotted and ugly. Heath Renier, accused of murder, rustling and armed robbery, had last been seen near Dallas four years ago.

"Quite a villain," Sonntag said, coming up behind him. "I would not wish to meet *him* in a dark place."

Heath let out his breath very slowly. "When did this come in?"

"From San Antonio, with my new goods yesterday. It is a great deal of money, *nicht wahr? Ach*, what I could do with such money!" Sonntag shrugged. "But men like that are not easily found. His appearance may be nothing like this picture after so many years."

Heath returned to the counter and grabbed the saddlebags. "Maurice will be along for more later."

"Very well, Herr Renshaw." Heath could feel Sonntag's stare as he left the store, weighing him, wondering. He touched the neckerchief around his throat.

If Sonntag or anyone else had recognized Holden Renshaw as Heath Renier, he would have been arrested by now. But it was a bad sign that they were putting out posters this far south and west. It meant the law was still on his trail and getting closer.

The kid had to get well soon, though Heath would be safe a while longer if he was careful. Coming into Javelina all normal-like, after everything that had happened, probably even worked in his favor.

Just as he put Lucia up on the mule, he heard hoofbeats behind him, coming fast.

He turned around. Amy Blackwell's bay mare pulled up hard, raising dust hip high.

"Holden Renshaw," she said, her pretty face twisted with anger. "I hope they hang you for what you've done."

Heath's heart slammed a dozen times before he got it under control. He touched the brim of his hat.

"Afternoon, Miss Blackwell," he said. "Reckon they have some hangin' rope at Sonntag's. You mind tellin' me what I've done first?"

"You know perfectly well," she said, tossing back the blond hair she always wore loose around her shoulders. "Sean came to us as soon as you ran him off."

The tension went out of Heath's body. He'd never doubted that that was where Sean would have headed first. He'd been in good with the Blackwells for some time, playing up his education at some fancy school back East and the highfalutin manners Jed had paid so much for. Sean had hankered after Amy, too.

Looked like he was getting her.

"Sean tell you why?" he asked. "Or did he just howl like a burnt coyote?"

Her gloved hands tightened on the reins as she shifted on her sidesaddle. "Must there be a reason when a gentleman is run off his own ranch by a jealous cowhand?"

Heath let her see the edges of his teeth. "It ain't his ranch yet, Miss Blackwell. If he promised to sell you Dog Creek, he's layin' you a false scent."

Amy edged her mount a few steps back and flung up her head like a rebellious filly. "You may be interested to know that we intend to employ Mr. McCarrick at Blackwater. He is not without friends."

"You want Sean for a friend, Miss Blackwell, that's your lookout. But he'll use you, just like he uses anyone he thinks he can string along."

Amy swung her arm up, and for a split second it looked as if she might try to hit him with her quirt. She didn't. She just stared at him, hate and confusion in her eyes.

"When Sean's uncle returns, he will hear about this," she snapped.

"It's Sean who should be scared of that, ma'am."

With a sharp, angry cry, Amy jerked her mare around and kicked it into a run.

"The *señorita* is very angry," Lucia said solemnly.

"Yeah."

"When will Señor McCarrick return?"

"Soon." Heath took the mule's lead. "Let's get on home."

It was near evening when Heath and Lucia reached Dog Creek. He smelled something wrong as soon as they got near the house.

Joey was waiting for him in the yard, his wiry body vibrating with tension. "Holden!"

Heath dismounted and helped Lucia dismount. "What is it?"

"The hands! They all up 'n left…'ceptin' me 'n Maurice. They rode in from the range a few hours ago. Didn't say a word, just lit out again right away."

Heath pulled off his hat and raked his hand through his hair. "Where the hell'd they go?"

"Don't know. But—" He bit his lip. "Maurice says Sean was here talkin' to El and Gus last night."

Sean. Heath hadn't seen this coming, and he should have. The son of a bitch would have made the most of Heath being gone. He had a way of making people follow him. People like Amy, too blind or stupid to see through his lies.

The force of his own anger pulled him up short. Why was he so mad? It wasn't as if he had to worry about problems like this much longer.

"This here's Señora Gonzales," he said to Joey. "You show her into the house."

"But, Holden, we ain't done brandin'! What are we gonna do?"

"We would have let most of the hands go in a couple of weeks, anyway. Now git."

Joey didn't like it, but he did as he was told. He touched his hat to Lucia and led her to the house. When he returned, Heath set him to unsaddling the mule.

"How'd it go with Lucia?" he asked.

"Mrs. McCarrick was sure happy to see her. They

showed each other their babies like they was prize bulls."

Heath was in no mood for laughing. He saw to Bess, shouldered the saddlebags and headed for the house, aware that he stank of sweat and horse and needed a bath.

And he needed a run. A good, hard run to clear his mind and remind himself that he was almost free.

He entered the house without knocking. The whole place smelled of warm human bodies, strong coffee and something good cooking in the kitchen. Rachel was sitting at the table, the baby in her arms. Lucia sat beside them with her own kid, and Heath could see that he'd interrupted their talk. The dim light made Rachel seem different somehow. Not sharp and skinny, with a tongue like a knife, but gentle, like Lucia. It gave him a strange, unsettled feeling in his chest.

Especially because she didn't look scared now, or suspicious, or angry. She almost looked happy, as if she'd just been given some pretty ribbon or one of those shiny copper pots he'd seen at Sonntag's.

She almost looked glad to see *him*.

"I have been speaking with Lucia," she said with a smile that gave a sparkle to her eyes. "I am grateful that she is willing to help us."

Grateful. He hated that word; it bothered him worse than her smile. He didn't want to hear in Rachel's voice or see it in her eyes, or care if she was glad to see him or not. None of it was real.

He'd planned to do whatever she told him, treat her right so she would stay as long as he needed her. But now that he saw her again, all "grateful" as she was, the old bitterness was rearing up, stronger than reason or sense. Rachel Lyndon troubled him too much, and a day and night away hadn't eased that feeling. Every time he was around her, it only got worse.

Lucia didn't make him feel that way. She was quiet. She hadn't tried to argue or order him around. And she would never betray him, because she would never know any more about him than she knew now.

If Lucia took over the baby's care, Heath might never have to speak to Rachel again.

"You mind leavin' us alone, *señora?*" he said to Lucia.

She gathered up her baby, nodded to Rachel and went into the hall.

"That wasn't necessary," Rachel said, some of the light going out of her eyes.

"How's the kid?" he asked.

"Much better than when you brought him. He will be better still when he has…" She hesitated, getting a little red in the face. "When he has the nourishment he needs."

Heath didn't let his relief lead him off track. "Now that Lucia's here," he said, "you won't have to look after the kid no more."

She blinked and clutched the baby a little tighter. "I beg your pardon?"

"You heard what I said."

"Perhaps you misunderstood my request for a nurse. Mrs. Gonzales has a family of her own. I would not impose upon her any more than necessary. And I certainly have no plans to surrender the baby's care to anyone else."

Confusion wasn't a feeling Heath suffered often, but this woman had him balancing on a broken fence rail with prickly pear thick on either side. She couldn't really care as much as she pretended. She was acting on some female instinct, the way any animal did, the same way the wolf in him knew how to be a wolf without ever being taught.

Animals could turn on their own get, and so could human females. They could throw their young away if they got too troublesome, turn from love to hate in an instant. And Rachel Lyndon wasn't even the kid's real mother.

Rachel looked up then, and Heath saw that her eyes were wet. She was afraid again, but not in the same way as before.

She was afraid he would take the baby away.

You're crazy. But somehow he knew he was right. She *wanted* to keep the baby, even though she didn't know the first thing about what he was.

Because she didn't know what he was.

Easing down into a chair, Heath looked at his callused hands. *Loups-garous* healed fast, and a Change could erase most all the damage that could be done to a man by wind and weather, knife and gun. But if you pushed your body hard enough, even a hundred Changes couldn't erase all the marks left by a lifetime of hard living.

He almost reached up to touch his neck again, that one wound so bad it had almost killed him. The scar he'd never lose. He remembered that wanted poster in the general store. How did he think he could ever take care of the baby, even when it was old and strong enough to do without the things only a female could provide? What kind of life could *he* make for a child?

Better than the life *he'd* had. The kid would never know what it was like to…

He shook off the memories and looked at his son.

The boy seemed to be holding Rachel as hard as she was holding him, his little fists clenched in the shawl around her shoulders and his head snuggled under her chin. He turned in her arms just enough so he could look back at Heath.

There wasn't any way the kid could understand what Heath had said, but his little round eyes spoke just the same.

I need her.

Hellfire.

"I ain't interferin' between you and Lucia," he said, looking away from both of them. "You do what you think is right."

A little at a time, Rachel's shoulders relaxed. She rested her cheek against the baby's, looking just like a picture of the Madonna Heath had seen once in a church. Benevolent, distant, untouchable.

"You must be very tired, Mr. Renshaw," she said, her voice a lot easier than his thoughts. "Lucia will rest in my room. If you will hold the baby, I'll make biscuits and coffee."

A Madonna who wanted to cook for him. And wanted him to hold the baby.

"I don't expect nothin' like that from you, Mrs. McCarrick," he said gruffly. "We got Maurice."

"I'm sure he is an excellent cook."

"Good enough for us, I reckon. Maybe not what a *lady* is accustomed to."

The word *lady* came out sharper and angrier than he'd meant. He only had to see the new stiffness in her body to know she was back to old Rachel again.

"You cannot possibly have any idea what I am accustomed to," she snapped.

"The way you talk says plenty," he snapped back.

"Because I have an education? How is that proof of prosperity, Mr. Renshaw? In fact, I have known what it is to—"

She clamped her lips together and blushed. He saw pain in the hollows under her eyes and in her pinched lips. Pain he had noticed before but didn't want to see.

Who in hell was she? And what exactly had she "known"?

"Mr. Renshaw," she said suddenly, the way someone does when they want to change the subject in a hurry. "There is another issue we must discuss. Where do you propose to sleep tonight?"

The question caught him by surprise. She must have noticed the other bedroom and realized it was his. It made sense that she would want him out of the house right away.

But there was that sense of something hidden that Heath had felt before; it was in her voice and in her eyes, crouching behind her propriety, clawing its way closer to the surface and shredding what was left of the Madonna's mask. An unexpected wildness in the brown eyes that glanced at him and quickly away.

He flared his nostrils to take in her scent, so subtle under the stronger smells—laundered cotton, the lingering fragrance of soap, a hint of perspiration. And another he knew as well as he did every bend and twist of Dog Creek.

The truth caught his body before his mind. His cock hardened, straining against his britches, and his breath came short.

Rachel was *aware* of him. Not just as Jed's foreman, someone she didn't like or trust, but as a man. Male to her female. Her scent gave her away sure as the smell of bluebonnets announced the coming of spring. She was thinking about things no married woman should. Things he had decided a prim-and-proper lady like her would probably never think about at all.

And he was thinking the same, even though she wasn't pretty, couldn't be trusted and thought he was beneath her.

When she ought to be beneath *him*, her legs wrapped around his waist…

Heath cursed under his breath. Didn't matter who or what she was. He couldn't stop his body from reacting. He'd never been inclined to fight what it needed, even when he wanted nothing as much as to stay far away from anything with tits.

Once, years ago, he'd make the mistake of touching a woman like her. *Her* kind always denied that kind of wanting because it went against what they wanted to believe. Females like Frankie expected nothing but money from a man. They were as honest as any woman could be; they knew what they were and didn't try to pretend any different. He could leave their beds and never have to look at them again.

If he ever got into Rachel's bed…

Heath didn't want to think about that. He didn't want to feel anything for Rachel Lyndon. Not even mindless animal lust.

He grinned at her. "That an invitation, *Mrs.* McCarrick?" he asked.

Chapter Five

SEEING HER FLINCH didn't help nearly as much as Heath thought it would. She went so pale that he thought she was going to swoon, and he almost got up to catch her.

She didn't swoon. The color rushed back into her face, and her eyes went so cold that they could have covered the range in ice.

"I see I have been mistaken in assuming that you were worthy of my husband's trust," she said.

If a man had said that to Heath, he would be looking at a broken jaw. But Heath had never come close to hitting a woman. Not even the ones who'd tried to kill him.

"I'll be movin' out of the house tonight," he said, getting up.

She set to rocking the baby, pretending Heath didn't exist. That rankled more than any spiteful thing she could have said.

"Did Joey tell you about the hands?" he asked, just to make her look at him again.

The poisoned air between them cleared away, and it was all businesslike the way it should have been from the first. "He mentioned something about their leaving," Rachel said without taking her eyes from the kid. "It will be difficult to run the ranch without them, will it not?"

"It ain't your worry, Mrs. McCarrick."

She met his gaze with that familiar spark of defiance. "It is if it affects the baby."

"It won't. I already know where I can—"

What in hell was wrong with him? He was explaining himself to her like some sniveling clerk telling his boss the missing money wasn't his fault. The kid was making him go soft as a banker's hands.

And it wasn't as if *he* had to worry about running the ranch much longer.

"The baby's your lookout," he said. "Dog Creek is mine." He got up. "Thanks for the coffee."

"You didn't have any."

"Thanks for the offer, then." He turned to go and stopped again. "Somethin' else. You came to Dog Creek with Sean McCarrick. Where'd you meet him?"

She hesitated. "On the way from town. He said that Jed had sent him."

"He's a liar. Jed never told him nothin' about you." The stubborn set of her jaw only made him angrier. "Maybe he told you some stories. Maybe you don't believe anythin' I say. But he's the one who got all the hands to leave. He can't be trusted as far as you can spit."

"I don't spit, Mr. Renshaw." But her tart reply masked an uneasiness Heath could smell a mile away. "Why would Mr. McCarrick do such a thing?"

"'Cause he'd do anythin' to see the ranch fail rather than see me keep it goin' till Jed—" He broke off, unable to give voice to the lie.

"You hate him," she said.

"Not half as much as he hates me."

"He left Dog Creek because of you."

"Who told you that? Joey?"

"I…" She bit her lip. "Yes."

"I should have run the son of a bitch off a long time ago."

"What did Sean ever do to you?"

"It ain't just what he's done. It's what he *is*."

"And what are *you*, Mr. McCarrick?" Her glance fell to his Colt. "I was told that the West could be a violent place. Is that why you carry that gun?" She swallowed. "Would you use it on someone you hated?"

"What in hell did Sean tell you?"

She pulled back like a turtle into its shell. "Nothing," she said quietly. "I'm sorry for asking."

He doubted that very much. Her opinion of him was fixed, no matter what her body wanted. And he didn't care what she thought of him. He didn't.

But the Colt, as much a part of him as the hand that wielded it, hung heavy with her scorn. He'd used it more than once on someone he'd hated, someone who wanted to kill him. But not since he'd come to Dog Creek. It was a piece of his old life, one he hadn't quite been able to let go, but he'd never planned to use it on a man again.

You ain't doin' it for her, he told himself as he unbuckled the belt, dropped it on the table and went to leave.

"Wait. Please."

He waited, though he didn't want to be around her one more minute. "Ma'am?"

"I understand that we have neighbors. The Blackwells."

He wondered why she'd brought that up now, and who had told her about the Blackwells. "Yeah," he said. "We share a border with Blackwater along Dog Creek. They have the biggest spread in the county."

"I see. There are ladies at Blackwater?"

"Amy and Mrs. Blackwell. Fine ladies the both of them." He frowned. "Why?"

"Would it be expected of me to visit them?"

What Jed knew about visiting manners could fit on the tip of a lizard's tail, but he did know he didn't want Rachel involved with the Blackwells. "You just got here," he said. "The Blackwater house is near twenty miles away. No one's expectin' you to run around the county just yet."

She nodded so fast that he knew that was what she'd hoped to hear. "Thank you, Mr. Renshaw." All stiff and formal again. And that was a very good thing. Heath pinched the brim of his hat and walked out, an itch between his shoulder blades, anger in his gut and the ache still in his loins. *She'd* put those feelings there, and they were going to stick as long as he stayed at Dog Creek. And if she couldn't get her own lust under control, she would be suffering the same way.

That didn't make him feel much better. He didn't want her distracted. Little as he wanted to admit it, Rachel was right about one thing: no one else could take care of the kid as well as she could. Even if she believed Sean's lies, whatever they'd been, that wouldn't affect her feelings for the baby. The feelings she believed were real.

His pace slowed as he got near the cabin that Sean had vacated and he would soon be occupying again. He'd been thinking a lot about what he had to do to make the baby well so the two of them could get away. He'd thought about Joey's future. He'd even tried to warn Rachel about Sean.

But even then he hadn't let himself think about *why*

he had to warn her, or what she would do once Jed was declared dead. Sure, he'd driven Sean off the ranch, but that had been more for himself than for her, and Sean would only stay gone until Heath wasn't around to make sure he did.

What was the point in warning her, anyway? She didn't believe what he'd told her, and her opinion of Sean, whatever it was, wouldn't affect Heath when he was hundreds of miles away or change anything Sean decided to do.

There was a ball of lead inside Heath's chest worse than anything he'd felt since he'd left the house. When he'd buried the saddlebags and the wills, he'd stopped caring what happened to Dog Creek. Jed's intended hadn't been real to him then, and he'd never even dreamed of the baby's existence.

The kid would be taken care of, no matter what Heath had to do to make sure of it. But there wouldn't be anyone to stand beside Rachel. Sean was a coward and a weakling, all hat and no cattle, but he was smart in his own way, and he did have friends in the county. He didn't know that the greatest obstacle to his ambitions—Jedediah—was already out of his way, but that wouldn't keep him from scheming about how to make sure Jed's wife never got what he thought was his by right. Even once the truth was out and the new will, if Jed had left other copies, made Sean's claim harder to push through.

And if Sean ever suspected Rachel was lying about having married Jed…

She'll leave, Heath thought. *She might think she wants Dog Creek for her home now, but that'll change. She can't fight on Sean's level.*

Heath reached the door to the cabin and stopped. He owed Rachel something for taking care of the kid, but the rest wasn't his problem. She wouldn't want his help anyway; she might feel sorry about losing the baby, but she wouldn't mourn when *he* was gone.

Still, it wouldn't hurt much to give her the means to tide herself over once she left Dog Creek. That would have to be enough.

Stepping back from the door, Heath went straight for the stable. He had one more job to do before the day's work was done.

WHAT WAS WRONG with her?

Rachel sat up on the bed and dropped her head into her hands, fruitlessly. The baby lay undisturbed beside her, oblivious of her feelings. That was the only blessing.

Oh, how she had tried to prepare herself for Holden Renshaw's return. She had been so certain that she could face the foreman again with composure and objectivity, with all the polite and distant neutrality that was absolutely necessary under these precarious circumstances.

She had failed. She had been so grateful when Lucia had arrived; Renshaw had been gone so long because he had been fulfilling her request for a wet nurse, and that could only count in his favor.

But then he'd told her that she didn't have to care for the baby any longer, and it had seemed that her worst fears were being realized. She was just a tool to him, a tool to be tossed aside when she was no longer of use. Just as Sean had said, Renshaw was scheming to drive her away.

For a little while, anger had bolstered her resolve.

She'd felt safer behind that shield, protected from his glittering, uncanny eyes. Then he'd turned the tables on her again. *You do what you think is right.*

Trusting her. Forcing her to once again question Sean's suggestion that Renshaw had been behind the attempted bribe in Javelina. Compelling her to let down her guard again, until she had almost gone so far as to tell him…

Rachel lifted her head and stared blindly at the bare wall. She'd almost made an admission that would show Renshaw just how desperate she had been to leave her old life behind. And then, afraid that he would think too much about what she'd almost said, she had blurted out the question that had been in her mind ever since she had looked into his room.

Where do you propose to sleep tonight?

His gaze had met hers, and she'd felt as if he were stripping off her clothing, dress and corset and petti-coats and undergarments, to reveal her quivering nak-edness. For one awful moment she had imagined what it might be like to give herself to such a man, feel his long limbs and hard muscles moving against her body.

She closed her eyes. No matter how resolutely she tried to shut the memories out of her mind, no matter the terrible consequences that had come from her one and only indiscretion, she could still feel it. Feel the ecstasy of Louis lying over her, inside her, arousing such painful joy that she had become a wanton, lost to all reason.

That wanton should no longer exist. She should have died on the day her aunt had cast her, penniless, into the street. When the life sheltered within her, the fragile flame sparked by what she had thought was love, flickered out.

But that shameful other self had outlived the infant Rachel had wanted so badly. Oh, she had managed to believe herself cured during the hard years that followed, through Jedediah's epistolary courtship and her journey from Ohio. She had told herself that what she must do with Jedediah would be only a way of making him happy, a task no different than sweeping the floor or washing his shirts.

That was all it ought to be, all she should want. But then she had met Holden Renshaw, with his animal intensity and beauty and hint of savagery.

If she had been vigilant, she would never have allowed the wanton to notice Renshaw's whipcord body or the way his hat brim didn't quite hide the sensual depths in his eyes. She would not have minded his being so near, his strong hands resting on the table within a few inches of hers, because she would not have been aware of him as a man at all.

But she had not been vigilant enough. The wanton had wormed her way back into Rachel's body, little by little, so that Rachel hadn't even known it was happening. When Renshaw had insinuated that she was inviting her into his bed, she had known it was no less than she deserved. He had sensed what she was, even if he didn't know the circumstances of her fall.

She scrubbed at her face as if she could wipe away her shame. Had the foreman been testing her fidelity to Jedediah, or had the desire she'd seen in his face been real? Either possibility was damning.

Rachel rose from the bed and walked slowly back into the parlor. Holden's gun still lay untouched on the table. He hadn't said he wouldn't kill a man he hated, but she had sensed that he'd done something extraordinary when he'd taken off the weapon and left it with her. It was as if he'd cut off a part of himself.

Hesitantly, she reached out, and her fingers grazed the evil-looking thing. Who was telling the truth? She could no longer make herself believe that Holden had sent the driver to warn her away from the ranch. He would confront her directly, not hire someone else to do it. So who *was* behind the bribe? The only obvious alternative was Sean McCarrick himself.

Feeling more than a little unsteady, Rachel sat down again and rested her forehead against her palms. If Sean had hired someone to bribe her, then nothing he said could be believed. He certainly did not wish her well. And if he had known she was coming, he could not be as ignorant as Holden believed. He must have known she and Jedediah were not married, yet he was clearly unwilling to refute her claim and arouse suspicion against himself. For the same reason, it seemed unlikely that he would tell anyone else.

But why was he *her* enemy? Yes, Holden had said he would do anything to see the ranch fail, but how could driving her away further that goal when Jedediah was soon to return? Could Sean be jealous of Jedediah's attention? He must have known she would tell Jed what had happened, but he clearly believed she would continue to take his word for Renshaw's guilt. He had even asked her to take his part against Holden.

There were far too many mysteries at Dog Creek. Rachel knew she ought to share her thoughts about Sean with Renshaw, but she was not yet prepared to trust him completely, nor could she trust her own judgment where he was concerned.

Who *was* Holden Renshaw? If she didn't make sense of the enigma she knew lay beneath his rough exterior, she would have no defenses against him at all.

And she would need every available defense before Jedediah returned. Against Holden, against Sean… and—most of all—against herself.

THERE WAS EVEN less left of Jed's body than the last time Heath had seen him. The worst of the stench was gone, but the ground and air all around his bones were thick with the musk of scavengers.

It wasn't possible to keep Jed in one piece, so Heath moved the body in three pieces, laying it back down under the overhang. He crouched there for a little while, staring into the empty eye sockets and wondering whether he should just make sure once and for all that no one ever knew the bones belonged to Jedediah McCarrick. All he would have to do was take away the belt with its unusual buckle and Jed's gold tooth.

But ruining what was left of Jed seemed wrong, and in the end it wouldn't change anything. Whether or not Jed was found, he would eventually be declared dead in the eyes of the law, and what was going to happen would happen anyway.

Heath rolled a few stones over the old man, covered him with a good layer of brush and dirt, and returned to the place where he'd buried the saddlebags. The ground hadn't been disturbed; he dug up the saddlebags, refilled the hole and buckled the bags to Apache's saddle. He didn't let himself relax again until he was back at the foreman's cabin.

The gnawing guilt that Heath had begun to feel much too often made his hands clumsy when he reached into one of the bags. He weighed a handful of coins in his palm. Plenty here to give to Rachel, and more for Joey. Jed would have wanted them safe.

Heath reached inside again, feeling deeper until he touched the bundle of letters and the sheath holding the wills. If he'd wanted to know more about Rachel Lyndon—if her hopes and dreams and fears really mattered to him—he could have read the rest of those letters.

But he didn't want to know. She could keep her damn secrets to herself.

He kept the handful of coins, buckled the saddlebags and pushed them under his bed. He would have looked for a better hiding place if he had to keep it here more than a few days, but none of the few people left at the ranch was going to go snooping around his cabin. The money would be safe until he figured out a way to give it to Rachel without raising too many questions.

He didn't sleep much that night; the cabin held in the heat, and he'd let himself get used to the bed in the house. At dawn he rode out to help Joey hunt for strays. When he came in off the range, Charlie Wood was waiting for him.

The man looked more than a little sheepish; he'd lit out with the rest of the hands, and Heath was none too pleased to see him back.

"Reckon I didn't like the idea of workin' at Blackwater," the man said, scratching at his raggedy three-day beard. "I been here a long time. Don't seem right to leave."

Charlie's words only confirmed what Heath had suspected. "All the men went to Blackwater?"

"Yessir."

"Ain't you gettin' better pay there?"

"That don't matter to me, Mr. Renshaw. I don't much trust Sean. He's got sneakin' ways about him, 'n he's a liar. He told the Blackwells that he chose to leave Dog Creek, not that you threw him out."

"Too bad you didn't think of stayin' earlier. Maybe we don't need you no more."

Charlie removed his hat and turned it around in his hands. "I know I made a mistake, Mr. Renshaw. I really want to come back."

Heath grunted. If he didn't take Charlie back, Joey would try to do all the rest of the early-summer work himself. He was just that way.

"You can stay, Charlie," he said. "Long as you prove your worth."

"Thanks, Mr. Renshaw." Charlie saluted and ambled toward the corral, leading his piebald gelding. Heath frowned. Charlie had been with Jed a long time, but he'd never struck Heath as the kind who would give up good pay for loyalty.

Shrugging off his speculation, Heath looked after his mount, then fetched the account books from his room in the house—glad that Rachel was in Jed's room—and went over the figures in the foreman's cabin. Dog Creek was still solvent, but without Jed's money, Sean wouldn't have nearly as much as he wanted once the ranch was sold. As soon as Heath was finished, he headed for the cookhouse to talk to Maurice, who had come back with a wagonload of supplies from Javelina.

He knew he was only putting off going back into the house to clear out his things. Rachel wouldn't always be hidden away in Jed's room. He'd have to talk to her again sooner or later, if only to see how the kid was doing.

Rachel must have heard him thinking about her, because she came out of the house a moment later, wearing a different but still plain dress and carrying a worn-looking parasol. Her gaze went straight to the horizon, as if she was expecting Jed any minute. The shadow of her parasol made her eyes hard to read.

What did she see when she looked out over the Pecos? She couldn't love this country, not the way Jed did. How could she, coming from the green, settled land of the East? This territory was good for hunters and cattle, not for women. Not even the Blackwell females, who were rich and had the leisure to stay inside and keep their pretty hands clean.

According to Joey and Maurice, Rachel had only been out of the house a few times while Heath was gone fetching Lucia, once to walk along the bank of the creek, once to study the ground near the house, and once to talk to Maurice about the supplies she needed. Maurice had told him that she'd asked only for things a woman required for cooking and cleaning and such, nothing for herself. No pretty dresses or perfume or lace or the kinds of fripperies "real" ladies were supposed to want.

She'd also insisted on taking on some of the washing. Heath had seen the shirts hung out on a line she'd stretched between the house and the old pecan tree. She'd been touching things men had worn close to their skin. Things *he* had worn.

Heath shoved those thoughts far back inside his mind the way he'd shoved Rachel's letters into the saddlebags, and turned to walk away. But she had seen him. Her body went stiff as a fence post.

Damn if he would let her run him off now. He went to join her.

"How's the kid, Mrs. McCarrick?" he asked.

"The *child* is still improving, Mr. Renshaw," she said. "As you would know if you had come to see him."

She was right. He needed to know just when the boy was healthy enough to travel, but he wasn't going to admit it.

"I just saw him yesterday," he said. "Or was it me you wanted to see?"

Damn him for a fool, taunting her with what he wanted to forget. But Rachel didn't take his bait.

"I know you are a very busy man," she said in her most formal voice.

Heath cleared his throat. "Maurice told me that you took in some of the washing."

"Does that surprise you, Mr. Renshaw?"

"I thought you wanted to take care of the baby."

Her chin jerked up. "I keep him with me when Lucia is not feeding him. Many women are capable of doing more than one thing at a time." She folded her arms across her chest, and Heath couldn't help but notice that she was fuller in the bosom than he'd realized. "I am not accustomed to being idle, nor did I come to Texas to drink tea and lounge about in the parlor."

Trying to figure her out was worse than useless. Heath knew she'd already been cooking. She'd offered to cook for *him*. She intended to be just the kind of wife Jed would have needed, baking pies and cleaning and washing and doing everything else women were supposed to do.

But Jed wasn't here. Heath would have expected her to wait until her husband came back before taking on so much.

With a speed that left her no defense, he seized her hands and turned them palm up. The fingers were long and slender, but her fingertips were marked with calluses that could only have been earned with steady labor.

She snatched her hand away. Her breasts rose and fell rapidly, and she looked about ready to hit him.

"I'll ask you to keep your hands to yourself," she snapped.

He almost laughed, but it wasn't from humor. "You done hard work before," he said.

The cool, prim lady was gone now, replaced by that wild thing he'd glimpsed yesterday in the parlor. "Have you seen enough?" she demanded.

He didn't want to speak the real answer to that question. "Dog Creek has gone a long time without the services of a lady," he said.

"Then you had best begin getting used to it."

She looked so ornery that Heath was dangerously inclined to admire her spunk. "You should be inside with the kid," he said.

"He is sleeping, and Lucia is watching him." She glanced toward the barn, and her voice got a lot quieter. "There must be cows that need milking."

He tipped his hat back on his head. "You want to milk the cow?"

"Do you doubt that I am capable of it, Mr. Renshaw?"

"That's usually Joey's job."

"If I'm not mistaken, you need all your remaining hands on the range with the cattle. Isn't that so?" She waved her hand to the north, where the desert grassland stretched out beyond the creek. "Shouldn't you be out there yourself?"

It sounded too much like another order, and Heath

let himself be provoked. "You plan on bein' the one runnin' things once Jed comes back, Mrs. McCarrick?" he asked. "You figure you can bully him the way you did the men you knew back East? You should know it ain't quite the same out here, ma'am. Or do you need more proof of that?"

She dropped her parasol and her body curled inward all at the same time, as if he'd called her a whore to her face. He reached out and caught her arm. It was so tight that he was afraid it would snap if he pressed too hard.

"You'd best get back into the shade, ma'am," he said, trying to keep the anger out of his voice. Anger not at her, but at himself. He'd sunk pretty low by using Jed against her when Jed was never coming back.

He picked up the parasol, keeping his grip, despite her resistance, all the way back to the shade, and sat her down in the old rocking chair Jed used to favor on summer nights, when he would smoke his pipe and talk to Heath about his dreams.

Rachel recovered quickly. Whatever had made her so upset didn't stop her from standing again and pushing her face up to within an inch of his.

"This cannot go on, Mr. Renshaw," she said. "You may not like me, and I may feel the same about you, but we must both live here until Mr. McCarrick returns. I will no longer engage in these ridiculous battles with you. I will treat you with the respect due your position, and you will do me the same courtesy."

Heath didn't have any choice but to look straight into her eyes. They weren't just plain brown like he'd thought, but all kinds of tawny colors, like the pelt of a panther when the sun hit it just right. His gaze dropped to her mouth. Her lips weren't as thin as he'd remembered, either. In fact, they were the prettiest thing about her face, besides her eyes.

She took a sudden step back. Her little pink tongue darted out to touch her lips, and Heath's cock started up again.

"Do we have an agreement, Mr. Renshaw?" she asked, her hands held rigidly at her sides, as if she was afraid *she* might touch *him*. "Do we have a truce until Jedediah returns?"

Heath was damn grateful that she didn't have a wolf's hearing, or she would know just how fast his heart was beating. "If that's the case," he said, "you'd better start callin' me Holden."

"I prefer—"

"You want the truce or not?"

"Yes. I take it that is your condition?"

"Yes. And I'll call you Rachel."

"Very well," she said shortly. She stepped back again until her skirt brushed the rocking chair. "Now that that is settled, we must have a serious discussion about the infant."

"Why?" Heath asked, tensing up himself. "You said he was doing good."

"Doing *well*," she said, and then blushed. "The baby is growing stronger every day, Mr. Ren— Holden. But we must consider…" She swallowed. "If he has family, they must be located."

"Family?" His stare must have scared her a little in spite of her bold talk, because she sat down and clenched the arms of the chair so hard that her knuckles went white. "I found him all by himself. There wasn't no one else around."

"*Where* did you find him?"

"An empty dugout between here and Heywood."

"What is a dugout?"

"A shelter dug out of the side of a hill."

"What kind of family leaves a kid alone in a place like that?"

Heath turned and paced to the end of the porch. "You were mad when I said you didn't have to take care of him no more. You changed your mind?"

"No! It's just that I…" The chair squeaked as she shifted position, and her voice went very quiet. "Just because someone abandoned him doesn't mean that there aren't other kinfolk who would want him."

He has kinfolk, Heath wanted to shout. He clamped his teeth together instead and thought about what he was going to say.

"I wouldn't know how to find them," he said at last, facing her again. "The kid had no name on him, nothin' to say where he belonged. Folks in Javelina know about him now. If anyone wanted him, they'd have said when I was in town. I could ride to some other towns, ask around. But I won't find out anything."

Her body seemed to go boneless. "It does seem an impossible task," she murmured.

"I don't much care for folk who throw their kids away like rotten meat," Heath growled.

She looked up, and he wished he hadn't said it. Her eyes had gone soft just the way they had when she'd been "grateful" for Lucia. "Anyone of decency would abhor such a thing," she said.

Was she *approving* of him?

"You think I'm decent, Rachel?" he asked, smiling in a way that usually sent enemies cowering and everyone else to thinking better of crossing him.

"I don't know."

Honest. Straightforward. You would never think she could lie about anything.

"That's mighty nice of you," he said, "considerin' just yesterday you thought I was a killer."

"I…" She kept her chin up, even though he could smell that she was ready to run. "The gun is still where you left it. You are welcome to take it back."

The anger was passing through him now, breaking up like storm clouds as they tore apart on the wind. "You keep it. In case I get tempted to use it on somebody I don't like."

She backed toward the door. "If that is what you wish," she said.

Heath shoved his hands in his pockets and watched her hurry into the house. Her hips swayed, though he was pretty sure she didn't intend to show off her womanly charms to him.

Did she really meet Jed in Ohio, even if they didn't get married? Did she share his bed?

Or had she known other men, lain beneath them panting and bucking and crying out as she…

It didn't matter how many men she'd had. He still wanted her. Worse, he was starting to respect her, and that was a lot more dangerous. Every minute they were together…

Get out, he told himself. *Take the boy now.*

And have him get sick again? Maybe die, because his pa was scared of a woman?

Heath drove the toe of his boot into the ground. The only thing to do was keep up that truce Rachel wanted and try to pretend he wasn't every bit the puling coward Sean was.

Chapter Six

"DON'T WORRY," Amy said in a soothing voice, leaning on Sean's arm. "That man will be gone soon, and then everything will be all right."

Sean smiled because it was necessary, not because he had any inclination for it. He'd taken pains to get Amy in his pocket, and now he had her—not that there'd ever been any real doubt—especially once Colonel Blackwell's previous foreman had suffered an unexpectedly serious "accident" on the range three days ago and Sean had offered himself as a replacement. Artemus Blackwell would be watching him carefully, so he would have to start putting in a full day's work from now on. But if that was what it would take…

He stared out over the carefully tended garden to the neat ranch buildings and the plains beyond, seeing nothing but the blackness of his own rage. His men had returned from Heywood yesterday afternoon. El and Gus had located Jed's lawyer, the only one in town, and had broken into his office. They'd found exactly what Sean had been looking for—and not at all what he'd wanted.

Three wills. One made out to Sean, leaving the ranch and Jed's bank account to his nephew. One giving everything to Renshaw. And the last and most recent naming one Rachel Lyndon the recipient upon the completion of her marriage to Jedediah McCarrick.

Gripping the porch rail, Sean closed his eyes. Even after all Jed's threats to disinherit him, even after he'd unsuccessfully tried to buy Rachel off in Javelina, he'd never quite believed it. Against all sense, he'd convinced himself that Jed was only trying to scare him.

Now he couldn't deny it any longer. Jed had betrayed him. It was small consolation that the third and unsigned will confirmed that Rachel Lyndon had never married Jed. The first two wills had been rescinded in expectation of Jed's signature, rendering them moot. If not for Rachel, Renshaw would have had everything.

"You're upset," Amy said, clutching his arm. "I warned Renshaw myself, Sean. He knows he can't stand against my family, and we are on your side. Once your uncle returns, we will make sure Renshaw pays for what he's done."

Sean swallowed a laugh. Once Jed's death was discovered, the wills would be made public, and everyone would know what Jed had intended. Renshaw would take the greatest pleasure in Sean's humiliation.

Unless Sean found a way to turn the wills and their contents to his advantage. He had considered forming a temporary alliance with Rachel against Renshaw, at the same time letting him learn anything he could use against her if and when that became necessary. But her wariness and lack of enthusiasm when he'd spoken of Renshaw's evils had convinced him that the foreman had already poisoned the waters against him. She would never be any more cooperative than when she had refused to return to Ohio.

Rachel's current position depended upon her maintaining her deception. And while she might be persuaded to leave the county under threat of exposure, Sean couldn't be sure he could get her out of the way before Jed's death was revealed and his own situation exposed to the public.

The wills themselves—assuming he could come up with an acceptable way to explain his knowledge of them—would be the best proof of her deception, but the risks of using them to force her hand were manifest. Even the one to Rachel alone could raise far more questions than it answered. And even without any wills or proof of Rachel's fraud, Sean could still assert that Jed had not made his intentions clear and dispute any claims "Mrs. McCarrick" might make on Jed's property. A sympathetic judge would certainly take his part over that of a woman no one knew. The Blackwells were already on Sean's side, and a few well-placed bribes would ensure his success.

But that wouldn't be enough. Unless she were shown to be a liar, Rachel would still receive benefits she hadn't earned. And the very fact that Jed had loved and trusted Heath so much that he'd almost given the scum everything he owned…

"Sean?"

He ignored Amy, his brain afire with speculation. What if Renshaw *had* known about Jed's wills and his decision to disinherit his nephew? He would have been laughing at Sean all this time, fully aware that he could eject his rival and make it stick, even after Jed returned. He might even know that Rachel Lyndon wasn't really Jed's wife, playing along only because he understood how much her presence would rile his enemy.

But all Renshaw's assumptions would be based on

the expectation that neither Sean nor Rachel knew about Jed's plans. And he must surely be angry that he, too, had been disinherited because of Jed's fiancée.

Sean released his breath. No, Jed would never have revealed that second will to Renshaw. The date indicated that Jed had had it drawn up only a few months before the one leaving everything to Rachel, perhaps in a fit of anger at Sean. And it seemed unlikely, given his high-handed behavior, that Renshaw knew anything about the will leaving everything to Jed's bride-to-be.

A pity. Renshaw was ruthless and without scruples of any kind. If he had believed himself disinherited, he would have had motive to kill Jed himself.

Renshaw could have killed Jed.

"Sean?" Amy said again, worry in her voice.

Patting her hand, Sean looked deeply into her very common hazel eyes. "I'm sorry, darling. I've been a little preoccupied."

"Tell me," she said, pressing his arm again. "I can help."

He sighed and shook his head. "I'm concerned about my uncle. I would have expected him to return by now."

Her lips pursed in a ladylike frown. "You haven't heard from him yet?"

"Not a word."

"Mrs. McCarrick must be worried, left alone with that man."

Naturally Sean had informed Amy about Rachel's arrival soon after he had arrived at Blackwater, leading her and her parents to believe he had known of her coming and supporting his judgment that it had been better to leave Dog Creek rather than put Jed's wife into the middle of a bitter conflict. Amy had offered to visit

Mrs. McCarrick to make sure she was all right, but Sean had discouraged her. Renshaw, he had told her, would only regard her as an enemy, and the foreman was unlikely to trouble Jed's wife unduly for fear of angering his employer.

"Well," Amy said when Sean didn't respond, "I'm sure Mr. McCarrick will be home soon, and he'll see right away how badly you've been treated. He is a nice man."

Naive words indeed from the daughter of a fine old Southern family who'd created their own small empire with money, luck and ruthlessness. Ironic when Artemus Blackwell so resented Jed for refusing to sell Dog Creek. Any resemblance between Jed and Artemus ended with their interest in cattle. The Blackwells were aristocrats; Jed was of humble origins, unlettered and unpolished.

And Amy thought he was "nice."

He tucked her arm through the crook of his elbow. "We'd best go in to breakfast. Your parents will be waiting."

"Oh! I've lost track of the time. Mother and Father do like promptness." She smiled at him seductively. "Let's go for a ride after breakfast. I've hardly seen you the past few days."

For all her ladylike ways, it took only a little scratching to find the dross under Amy's well-bred veneer. She was a wildcat at heart, but he would tame her. *She* would never stand in his way.

"You know I have work to do, darling," he said. "Your father will hardly think well of me if I shirk it."

She pouted but didn't press the issue. They went inside to the dining room, where Sean respectfully greeted Colonel and Mrs. Blackwell. The butler they'd brought with them from Georgia seated the family, and he and the maid began to serve the elaborate breakfast in the European fashion.

This will all *be mine*, Sean thought as he smiled into Mrs. Blackwell's colorless face and sipped his coffee. Money. Servants. A house finer than anything west of San Antonio. Power. All the things he'd wanted since Uriah McCarrick had dumped his only son at his brother's ranch like a pile of manure.

One step at a time, he reminded himself as he dabbed at his mouth with his napkin. Jed was gone, and eventually, when he was ready, Sean would make sure his body was found. But only when he knew just how to use it.

Sean excused himself from the table with a bow for the ladies, changed his clothes and saddled Ulysses. Charlie Wood found him as he was ready to ride out.

"Mrs. McCarrick's settlin' in comfortable," Charlie said once they'd found privacy in the foreman's cabin, a bottle of whiskey on the table between them. "Don't look as if there's much chance of her quittin' the place anytime soon."

It was no less than Sean had expected. "Renshaw?" he asked.

"Well," Charlie said, scratching his ear, "they don't like each other none, that's plain. He ain't tryin' to win her favor. But she's startin' to make herself useful around the place, and I think he respects that."

Sean clenched his fist on his knee. "Has he replaced the hands?"

"No, sir. Him and Joey and me take care of everything that needs doin' on the range."

"You haven't learned anything more about the child?"

"I asked Lucia Gonzales and Maurice and the boy, but they didn't know nothin', either. Mrs. McCarrick dotes on it."

"And Renshaw is still interested in it?"

"Yup. Mighty strange, if you ask me."

Sean downed his whiskey, pulled out a handkerchief and wiped at his upper lip. The baby was a minor complication. Maybe even a useful one, if both Rachel and Renshaw really did care about it—fantastic as it was to think the man capable of any such emotions.

Caring was always hazardous. It made a man dangerously vulnerable. Sean had learned that lesson well.

In a worse mood than when he'd started, Sean sent Charlie back to Dog Creek with instructions to report again in two days. Then he mounted Ulysses and, kicking him into a gallop, rode out of the yard and set out for Willow Bend along Dog Creek, six miles southeast from the house, where he was to inspect a bunch of cattle Artemus Blackwell planned to sell in Crockett County.

Two hours later he arrived to find that a number of DC cattle, cows with calves and a handful of mavericks, had crossed the creek and mingled with the Blackwater beeves.

Sean pulled up at the hill overlooking the creek. Holden and Joey couldn't watch every stretch of the creek or keep an eye on every unbranded calf, even in the diminished herd. He kicked Ulysses down the slope and joined the hands who'd been waiting for him.

"We was just waitin' on your word to cut them out, Mr. McCarrick," Gus said, shifting nervously in his saddle. "You want us to drive them Dog Creek beeves back over the creek?"

"Now, why should you do that? We will take the mavericks. El, you will drive the Dog Creek beeves north away from the creek. Let Renshaw come and find them."

The hands exchanged quick glances. "Yessir," El said, and started in one direction, while Gus circled in the other, crooning to keep the animals calm. They cut out the DC beeves, and El drove them away from the creek. Sean briefly inspected the Blackwater cattle and instructed Gus to bring them in the next morning.

Sean was about to head back to the ranch house when he heard hoofbeats across the creek. Ulysses jerked his head up and snorted. Sean reined him around.

The rider was coming fast, bent low over his roan's neck like a monkey. Sean recognized the straw-colored hair stuffed under the oversize hat and the frayed blue bandanna as the boy brought his mount to a skidding halt on the opposite bank.

"Damn thief!" Joey Ackerman yelled, his hand hovering over his rifle scabbard. "Those are our beeves!"

Sean leaned back in his saddle. "You'd best watch what you say, boy. Wild accusations are likely to make you plenty of enemies."

"I'm right proud to call you my enemy, McCarrick," Joey said, glaring at Sean as if he had the nerve to back up his words.

Yawning widely, Sean let his hand rest on his thigh near his holster. "You overestimate your own significance. Run on back to the nursery before I lose my patience."

"You ain't goin' anywhere with our beeves!"

"They happen to be mavericks, boy. You're a little too late."

Joey's prominent ears turned red, and he reached for

the rifle. "I seen you stealin' more than mavericks. Holden's comin' after me. He'll teach you to regret your thievin' ways."

Sean felt his hands growing moist inside his gloves. Holden was on his way, was he? He glanced with feigned indifference at Joey's hand on the rifle butt, sighed and turned Ulysses around. Gus and El were watching, frozen and useless, from the top of the rise.

"You stop right where you are!" Joey shouted. "You damn yellow belly!"

For an instant Sean considered shooting the boy. He could certainly make sure that Gus and El backed up his story of self-defense, and no one in Pecos County, least of all Renshaw, knew how skilled he had become or how eager he was to try his Remington revolver on something other than coyotes and rabbits.

But Joey was small fry. Sean had only begun to consider a way of ruining Holden Renshaw by more deliberate means, but it involved considerable risk to himself and rested on the most fragile tissue of possibilities. The temptation to finish it now was great. If Renshaw really was on his way…if he could be goaded into a rash attack…

Ignoring Joey's curses, Sean rode on up the hill. "Do you have your whip, Gus?" he asked.

"Yes, Mr. McCarrick, but…what're you fixin' to do?"

"Give me the whip."

Gus unwound the bullwhip from around his saddle horn. He handed it to Sean without another word.

"You wait here," Sean said. "And whistle if another rider comes this way."

He didn't wait for Gus's answer but rode back down

the hill, removing his gloves. Joey was aiming his rifle right at Sean's chest, but his hands were shaking. He'd never shot at a man before, and he clearly wasn't eager to begin now.

"Put that down, boy," Sean said softly. "You don't really want to start any trouble."

"You…you back off, McCarrick," Joey stammered.

"Just put the rifle away and we'll talk."

"I don't got nothin' to—"

Joey yelped as Sean uncoiled the whip and snapped it at the boy's horse, startling the roan into a sudden hop. Joey lost his balance for a critical moment and was bumped out of the saddle. The rifle spun away and landed out of his reach.

Sean dismounted and walked casually toward Joey as the boy clambered to his knees. "We'll have that talk now," he said.

Though he wasn't pleased to admit it, Sean could almost admire the way Joey took his punishment. He bore it stoically for the first few lashes, covering his face with his arms to make himself as small as possible. But by the eighth blow, he'd begin to whimper like the pup he was.

"Mr. McCarrick!"

Gus pulled up beside him and jumped off his mount, sweating so profusely that his bandanna was soaked through. "You could kill him!"

"Wouldn't that be a pity."

The man made a grab for his arm. "The kid's taken enough. Let him go."

"I'll stop when I'm ready. Or would you prefer that I tell the sheriff who broke into that lawyer's office in Heywood?"

Gus backed off, rubbing his hand over his mouth and

twitching like a bug on a pin. Joey had uncurled enough to look, tears streaming over his cheeks and hatred burning in his eyes.

"When…when Holden gets here—" he croaked.

Sean raised the whip again just as something dark and low raced toward him, and he caught a flash of white teeth before they clamped down on his right arm.

He screamed in pain and instinctively tried to loosen the animal's hold. Gus scrambled away, his face pinched in fear. The wolf's jaws ground through cloth and flesh until its teeth found bone. Sean felt his bladder loosen as the wolf began to pull him down.

"Shoot it!" he cried.

If Gus answered, Sean didn't hear it. He was fighting for his life, and the wolf was winning. Its eyes were glaring red slits, its rangy body so powerful that no one man could hope to overcome it. It pinned Sean underneath its heavily furred chest and snarled in his face. Dizzy with pain, Sean thought he could hear its voice promising him a slow, painful death.

Somewhere a gun went off. The bullet should have hit the wolf in the middle of its skull, but the animal was no longer in the bullet's path. It stood several yards away, grinning at Sean through a muzzle stained with his blood.

"Kill it!" Sean yelled. Another bullet whizzed past him, and another. The wolf danced out of the way with a few neat steps. Sean would have sworn it was laughing. He fumbled for his gun with his left hand, but by the time he got it out, the wolf had disappeared.

"Mr. McCarrick!"

He heard Gus's voice through a haze of pain. "Go after it," he said. "Hunt it down!"

"I can't leave you like this," Gus said. "I've got to bind up your arm, and—"

Sean lashed out blindly, catching Gus across the face. "I want that vermin's hide, do you hear? I want it skinned alive."

El knelt beside Gus. "He's half-crazy, Gus," he whispered. "We got to get him back to the house right quick, else he'll bleed to death."

A long shadow blocked the sun from Sean's face. "Now, wouldn't that be a cryin' shame."

Sean raised his head, struggling to focus on the man standing over him. Renshaw, grinning just like the wolf, all teeth and bloodlust. Joey leaned against him, shivering but smiling just as triumphantly.

"You done a very stupid thing, Sean," Renshaw said in a low, easy voice. "You hurt one of my boys."

Sean pushed himself to one elbow, cradling his mangled arm against his chest. "Gus," he said, "help me up."

"I think you'd best stay put," Gus said, the words coming out as if someone were holding him by the throat.

"That's right good advice," Renshaw said. He glanced down at Sean's wet trousers. "Best send your boys to bring you some clean britches before the Blackwells see what a coward you are."

The humiliation almost gave Sean the strength to rise, but he couldn't get any farther than his knees. His gun had fallen to the dirt beside him. He felt for it carefully, pretending to catch his balance.

Renshaw's boot connected with his wrist, knocking his arm from under him. "Now, that ain't polite," he said as Sean lay drowning under another wave of agony.

"Joey, you have anythin' to say to this fly-blown skunk?"

Joey spat with perfect aim at Sean's feet and leaned more heavily against Renshaw. The foreman shifted his hold around the boy's shoulders.

"We got to get you home," he said gently. His eyes fixed on Sean again, tearing at Sean's flesh as viciously as the wolf's teeth had done. "I can't give you the whuppin' you deserve right now, but this ain't the last you'll be hearin' from me. I ain't no little boy." He turned his back on Sean, every motion shouting his contempt, and helped Joey into his saddle. He jumped up behind the boy, took the roan's reins and urged the horse alongside his own waiting mount while Joey slumped against his chest.

"Help me up!" Sean snarled. Gus and El lifted him to his feet. He pulled off his bandanna with one hand and tried to bind it around his arm, compelled to accept Gus's help to tie it off. He was already weak from pain and loss of blood, but if he were of a mind to be grateful, he would have been forced to admit that he was lucky to be alive. A slightly different angle of attack and the wolf could have torn out his throat.

The torment was excruciating as the hands half carried Sean to his horse and maneuvered him into the saddle. He refused to allow the animal to be led; he'd already shown far too much weakness in front of the men.

He looked over his shoulder. Renshaw and the boy had gone only a short distance, moving slowly to accommodate Joey's lacerated back. Sean turned Ulysses around to watch them. They were still within rifle range for a man with the necessary skill.

"Shoot him," he ordered Gus.

Gus and El stared at him as if he'd lost his mind.

"I don't want you to kill him. I just want to give him a little taste of what he can expect if he ever tries to make good on his threats."

"But…but, Mr. McCarrick, he'll come after me."

"I'll protect you."

"But he's—"

"You'll be safe from him at Blackwater, but you won't be safe from me."

Like most men, Gus was ill equipped to conceal his true feelings. He was scared to death—more scared, at the moment, of Sean than Renshaw. He pulled his rifle from its scabbard and lifted it to his shoulder.

He was good. Sean saw Renshaw jerk and slap his hand against his shoulder. Sean wheeled Ulysses in a tight circle and rode down the other side of the hill, Gus and El on his heels. He only slowed when he was sure that Renshaw hadn't come after them.

His assumption had been accurate; the foreman was soft when it came to the boy. He would want revenge, but he wasn't going to seek it at Joey's expense.

Sean reined Ulysses to face the hands, swallowing a cry of agony. They refused to meet his gaze.

"You didn't see what happened here today," he said in his softest voice.

El blinked and licked his lips. "I wouldn't say nothin', Mr. McCarrick."

Sean looked at Gus. He was hesitating just a little too long.

"Do you have some difficulty with my request?" Sean asked.

The hand kept his eyes fixed on the ground. "Won't Renshaw tell?"

That was a question Sean had already asked himself and answered with hardly any thought at all. Renshaw wouldn't have the nerve to approach the law or the Blackwells. He wouldn't tell anyone in Javelina. There was no predicting what he would say to Rachel, but Sean didn't think Renshaw would involve a woman. His pride would prevent it. He would keep the whole incident to himself until he could take justice into his own hands.

"He won't talk," Sean said. "He knows my word is worth fifty times as much as his and the boy's."

"You *are* goin' to protect me?"

"Oh, yes. And you will always be on my side, Gus, because if you don't do as I tell you without question or complaint, I'll inform everyone that *you* tried to kill Renshaw."

"I…I understand, Mr. McCarrick." Gus's Adam's apple bobbed under his bandanna. "What about the wolf?"

"I will inform the Blackwells of the attack and advise them to gather a hunting party, which I will lead myself."

Neither of the hands had anything more to say. Sean ordered El to stay with the Blackwater cattle and told Gus to ride with him back to the house.

Half-delirious though he was, Sean struggled to keep his mind on the consequences of what he had done. He'd begun by thinking he would provoke Renshaw into an open attack, but he couldn't have predicted that he himself would be incapacitated and unable to defend himself.

He had miscalculated this time, but so had Renshaw. Yes, Sean had to admit that Renshaw was physically stronger than he was; he had never let himself be provoked into an open battle for that very reason. Renshaw would try to get Sean alone, challenge him to a bare-knuckle fight and beat him to within an inch of his life, believing that Sean would never confess to suffering such a humiliating defeat.

But he continued to underestimate Sean, believing the primitive laws by which he lived were the only ones that mattered. When the foreman came to fulfill his promise of retribution, Sean would be prepared. The fight would be on Sean's terms.

And if that didn't settle things, there was still the possibility of framing Renshaw for Jed's death. Either way, he would destroy Renshaw completely. Just as he would the wolf. They were two of a kind, the man and the beast, vermin to be eliminated without hesitation.

Chapter Seven

RACHEL HEARD SOMEONE yelling outside. She put the baby down on the bed, made certain he was secure and ran to the door.

The voice belonged to Maurice. He had run out into the yard, his blacksmith's leather apron flapping, to meet the rider who had just come in. As Rachel burst through the door, Maurice reached up and caught the boy Holden was easing down from the horse's back.

Joey. Rachel left the door open and ran to meet them as quickly as her skirts would allow. She slowed only a little as she approached Holden's horse, finding her courage and taking part of Joey's weight in her arms. The shreds of his shirt, crimson with blood, hung around his thin shoulders.

"He has been whipped, Madame McCarrick," Maurice said. "He is badly hurt."

It was not the time to ask how it had happened. "Get him inside," she told Maurice, glancing up at Holden.

"Can you help him?" Holden asked in a hoarse voice.

He was slumped over Apache's neck, his mouth set and grim with anger and worry. His eyes were almost yellow in the harsh afternoon light.

"I'll do what I can," she said. "We'll need—" She

broke off in shock. Holden's shirt and vest were soaked in blood from his collar to his waist, and down the length of his right arm.

"You're injured!"

"It looks worse than it is." He eased out of the saddle with far less than his usual grace. "What do you need?"

She clung to her composure by a thread. "As many clean cloths or rags as you can find. Use clean shirts, if you must. Hot water, of course. And I'll need Lucia. She has gone out to the creek."

"I'll find her. Get inside and help the boy."

"But your injury…" She looked into his eyes and understood that there was no point in further argument. She ran back into the house, where Maurice had eased Joey onto the bed in the second bedroom, which Lucia now occupied. The boy was stretched out on his stomach, and the look of his back brought the gorge into Rachel's throat.

"If you will, Maurice, please help Mr. Renshaw find supplies. I'll do what I can here."

The Frenchman nodded and hurried out of the room. Rachel knelt beside Joey, whose dirty face was streaked with the tears he was trying so hard to hide.

"It will be all right," she said, stroking his hair. "Lie quietly now."

He shut his eyes and tried to nod. She strode into the kitchen, took a cast-iron pot out of the cupboard and filled it with water. Once she had the water set to heat, she unfolded several dishcloths and wet them under the pump. She wrung out the excess water and hurried back into the bedroom.

It was difficult to know where to begin. She knelt on the foot of the bed and bent her head close to Joey's.

"I will be as gentle as I can," she said, "but this will hurt."

"Yes'm," he whispered.

The strips of his shirt were already glued to his flayed skin. Rachel wanted to weep. She laid the wet cloth against his left shoulder. Joey flinched, and she could hear him fighting sobs.

"I'm sorry, Joey," she said.

"It's...all right, ma'am," he croaked. "Can you sing?"

She tugged gently at one of the strips, freeing it from his back a fraction of an inch at a time. "A little," she said. "Would you like me to?"

"My ma used to sing to me," he said, "when I was a baby."

In so many ways, he still was. She wet another portion of his ragged shirt and began to sing.

When the blackbird in the Spring,
'Neath the willow tree,
Sat and rock'd, I heard him sing,
Singing Aura Lea.
Aura Lea, Aura Lea,
Maid with golden hair;
Sunshine came along with thee,
And swallows in the air.

She was about to begin the chorus when Holden walked into the room, followed by Lucia with her baby. The Mexican woman exclaimed and rushed to the bed.

"Madre de Dios! Pobrecito!"

Rachel paused in her work, meeting Holden's eyes over Lucia's dark head. His gaze was as steady and unrelenting as ever, but there were deeper lines bracketing his mouth. Lines of pain.

"Lucia," she said, "will you see to the baby?"

"Sí, sí!" Lucia hurried out.

Holden crouched beside the bed, setting down a bulging flour bag.

"How you doin', boy?" he asked in the gentlest voice Rachel had ever heard from him.

"I'm okay," Joey said. He moved as if he was trying to get up, and Rachel uttered a word she hadn't spoken in years.

"Don't move, Joey! Please, Holden, keep him still."

Gray-green eyes flashed to hers. "Keep on singin'."

If it hadn't been for the severity of Joey's condition and Holden's obvious pain, she would have blushed and stammered like a schoolgirl. But she sang, steadily pulling the saturated cotton from Joey's wounds. When Maurice popped his head in, Rachel asked him to fetch the hot water. Its warmth eased a little of Joey's discomfort, and once his shirt was off, she was able to clean the lacerations. She took great care to remove any threads or bits of cloth that might have entered the wounds during the whipping.

"Did you find cloths for bandages?" she asked Holden when she was finished.

He opened the flour sack and held it out to her. As their fingers touched, Rachel forgot the verse she had been singing. His hands had been coated with blood when she'd seen him in the yard, but he had carefully washed them.

"What will you do now?" he asked.

"Bind him up as best I can and let him rest. Time is the great healer."

"Holden?" Joey murmured.

Renshaw leaned closer. "I'm here, boy."

"Why did that wolf help me?"

"I guess he just knew Sean was no good."

"I ain't never…seen a wolf like that before," Joey said, his voice growing fainter. "I don't want no one to shoot it. I…"

He trailed off.

Rachel paused in her work and glanced anxiously at Holden. "How is he?" she asked.

"He's out cold."

"He's probably fainted from the pain. That would be a mercy."

Holden's lip curled up, exposing his even white teeth. He looked like nothing so much as a hungry wolf ready to savage its prey. Rachel was almost afraid to speak again.

"I'm almost finished with Joey," she said. "I'll need to examine your shoulder."

He stared at the bare wall, now bereft of the painting that had hung there. "I don't need no healin'."

"Please. Let me see your injury."

"It ain't necessary."

Rachel got off the bed and approached him as she would that very wolf he so resembled. "I am afraid I will have to disagree, Mr. Renshaw." She swallowed. "Would you remove your waistcoat and shirt, please?"

If he chose to ignore her, she knew very well that she couldn't do anything about it. His will was more than equal to her own, and his strength many times hers. But he eased out of his waistcoat, making not a sound, and with a swift, awkward movement pulled the shirt over his head.

Rachel caught her breath. His entire right shoulder was painted with blood, and there was a small hole in the hard muscle at the top of his arm. She pressed her hands to her mouth.

"You've been shot," she said faintly.

"I told you, it's nothin'."

Indeed, the wound wasn't bleeding now, in spite of the wealth of gore. If she hadn't known better, she would have said that it was closing even as she watched.

That, of course, was impossible. "Is there still a bullet…inside?" she asked.

He wouldn't look at her, wouldn't so much as acknowledge her question. She touched the margins of the wound with her fingertips. His arm tensed.

"There *is* something inside," she said. "It will…have to come out."

His lip curled again, this time in mockery. "You know how to remove a bullet, ma'am?"

"No. But I have—"

"I can fix it myself."

"You propose to stand in front of a mirror and poke a knife into your flesh?"

"I've done it before."

"Not this time." She got to her feet. "Please stay here with Joey, in case he regains consciousness."

Lifting the pail, she returned to the kitchen, dumped the water and thoroughly rinsed the bucket, then filled it with what remained of the hot water and set it aside while she took the thinnest kitchen knife from the wall. She opened the stove door and placed the knife blade just inside, letting the metal sit until it was red-hot.

She leaned heavily over the sink, feeling almost faint. She had tended wounds before, as she'd implied to Holden. But this one should be in the hands of a doctor.

Holden would never consent, of course, even if there

were a resident doctor in Javelina. She must do what she could on her own.

The water steamed as she carried it and the knife, its handle wrapped in a cloth, into the bedroom. Holden was still crouched beside the bed, watching Joey's face. His own held an expression of worry that revealed more emotion than he would ever have consented to show *her*.

She set the pail down with such force that water sloshed over the side. She reached for the support of the bed as she lowered herself to her knees.

"Have you any liquor?" she asked.

"Don't keep any here."

"I cannot emphasize too strongly how much this is likely to hurt."

He finally met her gaze, and she thought she must be going mad. There was humor in his eyes, humor at his own expense.

"I've felt worse," he said.

Perhaps he had. Perhaps he'd been shot more than once, but she saw no evidence of it on his body. The body she had never seen so fully exposed, the broad chest and shoulders, the beautifully sculpted muscles designed to create a thing of beauty and sleek power…

Hesitantly, she reached for the red-stained bandanna around his neck. He caught her hand and held it in a grip that could have crushed her fingers if he'd truly meant to hurt her.

"Leave it," he said.

"It's filthy. It must come off, or there might be—"

"Leave it."

They stared at each other. Gradually Holden's grip softened, and she became frighteningly aware of the feel of his callused palm on hers, the slow movement of his thumb stroking the back of her hand.

She snatched her hand free, and he let her go. Calming herself with a few deep breaths, she dipped a clean cloth in the water and began to bathe his chest and shoulder. She could feel his gaze on her as she stroked over the planes and valleys of his hard physique. She brushed his small nipple, and he sucked air through his teeth.

For a moment she couldn't move. She looked down to avoid his eyes, focusing on the ridged stomach and the waistband of his trousers.

A mistake. A terrible mistake. He was clearly aroused, his…masculine parts straining against their confinement. She remembered Louis, naked in the hotel room where they'd so often met, erect with lust for her. She remembered the gush of wetness between her legs, the same wetness she felt now.

God help her. She had not imagined her desire for him, or imagined his for her.

Long fingers curled around her wrist. Holden pulled her arm up and placed her hand on his chest. His heart was beating as forcefully as hers.

"You'd better finish," he said in his roughest voice.

Somehow she managed to do so, kneeling behind him to clean the entrance of the wound. She picked up the cooled knife, and her hand began to shake.

"It's all right," he said. "You can't hurt me."

"If I make a mistake—"

"You won't."

The confidence in his voice almost reassured her. She positioned the knife over the hole in his shoulder, lowered it, grazed the ragged flesh with the tip.

"Do it," he ordered.

He didn't move, didn't even gasp as she pushed the knife inside. Almost immediately it struck something hard, not far below the surface. She moved the knife against the bullet, and Holden gave a low grunt.

"Should I stop?" she whispered.

"Go on."

Working by instinct, she wedged the blade under the bullet and lifted it. A gush of blood spilled from the wound, and then the bullet was out. It fell onto her skirt, and she stared at it, unable to move.

"You done it," Holden said.

She had. But there was still infection to worry about, fever…

"Don't worry," he said softly. "I heal quick."

Slowly she bent over his back, resting her forehead against his untouched left shoulder. His breath shuddered in and out. His warmth penetrated into her skin, his scent of sagebrush and sweat and man overwhelming her senses.

You are a whore, Rachel Lyndon.

She straightened, her body feeling as fragile as bone china, and washed the wound. The bleeding had stopped. The hole already seemed smaller than it had just minutes ago. She felt inside the flour bag and found several strips of cotton long enough to bind around his back and shoulder. Holden remained still, unnaturally so, as if the whole process had been no more painful than a pinprick.

"I'm finished," she said, scooting back on her knees so that she could no longer be tempted to touch him. "Are you all right?"

He looked over his shoulder, his stark profile untroubled by any sign of emotion. "Much obliged," he said.

She tucked her feet underneath her skirts and rose. "You must be sure to keep your wound clean, and change the bandages regularly. And you must rest."

He watched her as she returned to the bed. She could feel him following her every movement with concentration so intense that she could hardly keep her countenance.

Doing her best to ignore him, she checked to make sure that Joey's back hadn't begun to bleed again. He stirred and groaned. Holden bent close to his head again and whispered a few words, which quieted the boy.

"Joey will have to remain in bed for several days," she said. "He must continue to lie on his stomach."

"He won't like to stay down," Holden said, gingerly touching his own bound shoulder. "But after what he's been through, he'll do it just to make sure he don't have to suffer through any more of this 'healin'.'"

She stiffened. "I'm sorry if you found my ministrations inadequate."

"Your *ministrations* were just fine."

Rachel couldn't mistake his emphasis. Her body purred like a contented cat.

God help me.

Seeking desperately for a neutral topic of conversation, she remembered that she still knew nothing about the circumstances of his and Joey's injuries.

"What happened, Mr. Renshaw?" she asked.

"You said you'd call me Holden."

She folded her hands in her lap to stop their shaking. "Who did this?"

"Best you not know."

"Not know?" She slid from the bed and faced him, unable to control the anger in her voice. "It is as much my business as yours, if I am to be patching up your injuries."

Holden gave her another of his penetrating looks. "It won't happen again."

"That's not good enough. I insist—"

All at once he was on his feet, tall and forbidding, his brows drawn down over darkened eyes. "Out-laws," he said.

Rachel's mouth went dry. Outlaws? Here? "Who are they? Where did they come from? Have you sent someone for the…police or sheriff or whoever handles these matters here?"

"They won't be back," Holden said.

His words were so grim, so final. What had he done? He had not taken the gun he had given her, but perhaps he had access to other weapons. Surely he could not have fended off criminals without a weapon of some sort.

She fought to keep from staring at his lean, powerful body, so suited to the kind of violence such a battle would require. Her gaze moved from his beautifully defined pectorals to his ridged stomach and the arrow of dark hair leading to the waistband of his trousers.

"Th-these outlaws," she stammered. "Did you—"

"No one's dead yet," he said, reading her expression. "But if they do come back, if they come anywhere near the house—"

"Surely the baby is safe here!"

"I ain't talkin' 'bout just the baby."

Had she imagined the warmth in his voice? "Are they common here, outlaws?"

"So long as you're at Dog Creek, you won't come to no harm. But maybe you'd feel safer livin' in town."

"I have no intention of running away. Not because of outlaws, and certainly not because of anyone else."

It was impossible to read his expression. He seemed about to speak again when Maurice appeared at the door.

"I have more cloth, *madame,*" he said to Rachel. "Are they all right?"

"Joey will heal," Holden said. "I'll be back on the range in a few hours."

"You will not," Rachel said.

Holden folded his arms across his chest.

Maurice looked back and forth between them, his eyes bright with curiosity.

"You got no say in it, Mrs. McCarrick," Holden said. "There's only me and Charlie and Joey now, and Joey'll be off his feet for a few days."

"Why don't you hire more hands?" she asked, exasperated. "Or if that is not possible, I can certainly do some of the things Joey did, at least near the house."

Once again Holden's eyes were on her, weighing, measuring.

"You said you wanted to milk the cow."

A little thrill of fear delayed her answer. "Yes."

"Reckon we might use your help."

The turnabout didn't surprise her as it might have done only hours before. Had her treatment of Joey improved his opinion of her? Or had their unwonted intimacy, her hands on his body…

Holden's nostrils flared. He made a slight, almost imperceptible gesture with one hand, and Maurice retreated, his surprisingly light tread quickly receding down the hall.

"You stay with Joey," Holden said. "I'll let you know when we need you."

She moved away, hoping to put a safer distance between them. "I am delighted that you think I am suited for such work after all," she said.

He met her gaze with a look that brought the wanton to her knees. "Yes, ma'am," he said. "I don't doubt you'll be *very* good."

Before she could recover her senses, he walked out of the room. Afraid to jar Joey and wake him if she sat on the bed, she felt her way to the chair against the opposite wall and fell into it.

I will not give in. He will not win.

And neither would the wanton Ellie Lyndon.

Rachel rose and went to the small window, where she gazed at the bleak western horizon.

Oh, come soon, Jedediah. Come soon.

LUCIA WAS ROCKING the baby in her arms when Heath entered the room. Her own child lay on the bed, kicking and babbling.

"Señor Renshaw," Lucia said, her round face creased with worry. "Is all well?"

Heath bit back a retort the woman didn't deserve and gave a short nod. "Joey's all right," he said.

Her dark gaze took in his half-dressed and bandaged condition. "You, too, are all right?"

"A scratch," he said.

"*Bueno.*"

He couldn't say the same. He'd lied to Rachel about what had happened, just as he was lying to Lucia now. But he'd decided, halfway between the creek and the house, that he couldn't tell her the truth, and he'd convinced Joey to keep the secret. If Rachel knew what Sean had done…

Hell, it would give him plenty of satisfaction to make her see what Sean really was. But Rachel was as unpredictable as Texas weather. He didn't know how she would react, whether she would think he was lying or charge off to confront Sean at the Blackwells'. Even if she didn't, she would probably figure that Heath wasn't going to let Sean get away with it.

Why did it matter what she thought? How many times had he asked himself that question?

"Did you come to see the *niño?*" Lucia asked.

He looked down at the curled pink fists poking out from the top of the blanket and the snub of a nose that wrinkled as he came nearer. "How is he?"

"He is very strong. And happy. He never cries."

And he no longer looked even a little gray. Heath had seen the improvements a few days ago, but he'd made himself wait to make sure there would be no question about the kid's health. It was a good thing he had, or he wouldn't have been able to save Joey or take care of Sean.

"Do you wish to hold him?" Lucia asked.

He backed away. "I'm in no fit state," he said. "Can you keep him for a while?"

"It is no trouble. But the child misses Señora McCarrick when she is away. I see it in his eyes." She cradled the baby close again and crooned to him in Spanish. Heath crept out and headed straight for his cabin. As soon as he was inside, he pulled the bandages from his shoulder, wadded them into a ball and tossed them on the table.

The wound was nearly healed. He'd told Rachel the truth when he'd said he could fix it himself. It would have closed fast on its own, ejecting the bullet naturally even if he stayed in human shape, but a single Change would have taken care of it in less than a minute.

But he couldn't have left Joey. And when he'd seen how gentle Rachel was with the boy, he'd wanted her hands on him, her slender fingers brushing over his chest, soothing and making him hurt all at the same time. He'd forgotten the danger when she'd leaned her head against his shoulder, when he'd felt her breasts pressed against his back.

He spun around and hit the table with his fist. It didn't make any sense, but it didn't do a damn bit of good to deny it. He didn't just want her. He didn't just respect her grit or her skill. He was starting to *like* her.

She'd treated Joey as though he was more than just a scrawny, unlettered orphan. She'd stroked his hair and sung to him with the same kindness she'd always shown the baby. And she'd cared about Heath's pain just the same as she'd cared about Joey's.

But liking her was unnatural. He didn't *like* women. And it only made things worse, so bad that he'd reminded her to call him Holden and told her she would be safe at Dog Creek. He'd had enough sense to suggest she leave the ranch, but he hadn't argued when she'd refused.

Then there was the hunger between them that wasn't even close to going way. It wasn't just her scent, or how she got so wet when he was close to her. Not even the deliberate way she tried not to notice his hardened cock. It went deeper than he could understand.

He should have despised her for betraying Jed, even in her heart. But he couldn't. Rachel Lyndon might know what she wanted, but she would never act on it. She would keep fighting her desire even while her body shouted an invitation for him to take her. And he would keep making it harder for her with stupid jokes meant to provoke and punish her for his own weakness.

Heath pushed his hands through his hair and sat on the edge of his bunk. *Find yourself a whore.* There was one in Javelina who would be happy to take his money. Rachel never had to know how far he'd fallen.

He got up again, filled a pail from the outside pump, and took a clean pair of britches and a shirt to the shed the hands used as a bathhouse. He stripped down to the skin and poured the water over himself, letting the shock of the cold wash away his lust.

It wasn't enough, but the only other way he knew to work it off wasn't safe right now. He'd taken a big enough risk in attacking Sean in wolf shape in broad daylight, however much he'd enjoyed it.

Just the way he would enjoy making Sean pay.

Heath rode back out to the western reach of Dog Creek, where he found the beeves Sean had tried to drive off back on the right side of the creek. He drove them east a little ways, then kept on going, smelling out any strays or mavericks he and Joey might have missed, and marking their locations for branding.

By the time he was back at the house, it was nearing sunset. He saw to his mount, made sure that Apache was resting well after the day's exertion, and checked up on a mare that was expected to foal any day now. Going to see Joey would be about the worst thing he could do. *She* was with him.

He was ready for a good run. Once twilight had faded from deep purple to black, lit by the nearly full moon, he walked out onto the range, shed his clothes and Changed.

Chapter Eight

NOTHING COMPARED TO running as a wolf. Heath had ridden plenty of good horses at top speed across prairie and open range, both in his years as an outlaw, and as hand and foreman at Dog Creek. But not even the fastest ride could compare to sweeping over the ground on your own four paws, the wind in your fur, leaving the rest of the world in your dust.

Memories coiled in Heath's still-human mind like rattlers waiting to strike. The first time he'd discovered he could Change, he'd had no other *loups-garous* to show him the way and ease him through the transformation. He'd stumbled along in a shape he hadn't learned how to control, assaulted by sounds and smells and sensations he didn't have a name for.

He'd known since he was old enough to understand anything that he didn't belong to the Mortons. He hadn't known his real name then. They'd taken him in when he was little more than a baby. They'd given him food and shelter. But he was never their son, not in their eyes or his.

He'd thought for a while that Ma Morton had loved him, even though Pa Morton had worked him like a slave from the time he was big enough to help around the farm. When he'd proven stronger than most boys his age, he'd been given enough work to kill a horse, and Ma hadn't been able to stop her husband. Regular beatings reminded him just what he was worth.

When he turned twelve, he'd realized that he was different from the Mortons in ways even he hadn't guessed. He'd thought a lot of times about running away, finding someone else like him, but he didn't leave the farm until Pa Morton saw him Change and tried to kill him.

It hadn't gone Morton's way, that fight, even though Ma had turned against him, too, screaming about monsters and freaks. Heath healed his own wounds with a single Change. At fourteen he was on his own. Being a wolf meant he could survive, even when he didn't have money to buy food and clothes and shelter. But he couldn't always stay a wolf in a human world.

So he'd learned to steal. Little things, at first, things no one would miss. He was faster and stronger than regular folk. He could smell twice as good, and hear the same way. By the time he began his search for his own kin, he had a pair of good mounts, several changes of clothes and enough money in his pocket to let him keep looking.

It had taken him four years to learn his real name and track down others like himself. Only, they didn't want him. He was half human, and the Reniers didn't tolerate 'breeds or *loups-garous* who lay with humans. His ma had sent him far from her home and given him to the Mortons, people who wouldn't ask any questions about where he'd come from. She'd thrown away her own child to stay in good with the ones who despised what she'd done and the child she'd borne.

The Reniers had kept Heath out of their territory. He

hadn't been able to see his real ma, tell her just what he thought of her. But he'd known his real name. And he'd used it when he turned back to his thieving ways.

Heath stretched his muscles and raced low to the ground, laying his ears flat against his head. Neither humans nor *loups-garous* wanted him, so he'd tried not to want *them*. But he could never figure out if he was more wolf or more human. He kept on looking for people he could trust. Men who would stand by him against the law, even if they found out what he was. Women who could prove that not all their sex were like Ma Morton and the *loup-garou* female who'd tossed him aside.

Every one of them had betrayed him.

A flash of white bounced out of Heath's path. He could have taken the cottontail with a single snap of his jaws. He let it go and ran to the southern border of Dog Creek, then kept on going toward the Rio Grande, over the harsh and waterless desert no man claimed.

This was where Jed had found him with a couple of beeves he'd rustled from Dog Creek. Jed hadn't tried to shoot him the way any other man would have. He'd noticed Heath's skill with the animals and offered him a job. It had been stupid of the old man, dangerously reckless, but Heath had decided then and there to change his life. Someone trusted him for no reason, and he was going to pay him back in kind.

Because of Jed, he'd given up his outlaw ways. He'd taken up honest work, proven himself, been raised to foreman. He'd recognized Sean for a sneaking, greedy liar and warned Jed against him. He'd trusted Jed more than he'd let himself trust anyone in years.

But he'd never let Jed know what he was. Until he'd made one terrible mistake.

The earth was so hard that Heath's paws began to scrape raw even as his claws tore furrows in the iron ground. He opened his mouth to suck in air, tongue lolling, eyes narrowed to slits. If Sean had been around just then, he wouldn't have been as lucky as he'd been that morning.

False dawn was breaking when Heath headed home. He hadn't outrun his crazy thoughts or the feelings he didn't want. Lust and hunger still rode his tail like a tick that wouldn't let go.

When he was back to the place where he'd hidden his clothes, he Changed again. There was no trace of the wound on his shoulder. He would have to hide it for a while so no one would question how it could be gone so fast. He got dressed, pulling on britches and boots, shirt and vest.

The neckerchief always came last. Rachel was right; it needed washing. But he wouldn't give it up. He'd worn it since the last time he'd been betrayed by a "friend," his throat slit wide open nearly all the way to the bone. He'd been left for dead, his life's blood leaking out of his body.

Heath didn't believe in miracles or divine providence, but he'd managed to Change. When he'd Changed back, the scar was there, healed over, ugly as sin.

He touched the scar, feeling the hard ridge of puckered skin. It was the one and only wound the Change hadn't undone. He'd stop trying to figure out why. It could identify him, no matter what else he might do to make himself look different, so he'd tied the bandanna around his neck and never took it off except when he was completely alone.

Pushing his hat onto his head, Heath went to the house. Joey was lying on his belly, sleeping, and Rachel was slumped against the bed, her head pillowed on her arms. Heath wanted to go into the room, kneel beside her and stroke her dark hair.

Turning quickly, he went back outside, saddled Bess and headed for Javelina, arriving by early afternoon. A woman was looking at bolts of cloth when he entered the store. She left quickly.

Sonntag frowned. "Sometimes you are not so good for business, Herr Renshaw," he said.

Briefly Heath wondered if word had gotten out about the fight with Sean, but he figured Sean would make sure it didn't. "I won't be here long," he said. "You still got that cradle?"

The storekeeper's expression brightened. "Do you wish to see it again?"

"I want to buy it."

With a smile of satisfaction, Sonntag fetched it and set it on the counter. "It is direct from Germany," he said. "The finest workmanship, the best—"

"Yeah." Heath slapped down the bills. "Wrap it up for me."

"*Sehr gut.*" As the shopkeeper went to work, he began to chatter. "Have you heard, Herr Renshaw? We have had an unusual visitor in Javelina."

Heath glanced at the wall where he'd seen the wanted poster. It was still there. "What kind of visitor?" he asked.

"A bounty hunter. He came to inquire if anyone had seen the man on the poster."

Long practice kept Heath from showing any reaction. "Did he have any luck?"

"*Nein.*" Sonntag finished with the package and tied

it up with a piece of string. "He left after only a day, but he said he would be back."

Heath nodded shortly, grabbed the cradle and left the store. When he'd first seen the poster, he'd known he would have to keep his guard up and his eyes open, and that hadn't changed.

Maybe no one had recognized him, but a bounty hunter meant someone figured he was in the area. He needed to finish what he had to do fast.

Or he could leave Sean alone, give Rachel the money, get the baby and leave today.

He stopped in the middle of the street, forcing a mounted cowboy to swerve around him with a muttered curse. He couldn't do it. He'd seen something in Sean yesterday that he hadn't expected. Sean hadn't just made threats this time. He'd attacked Joey, knowing the likely consequences, and tried to bait Heath. He'd gone plumb crazy.

Even if Heath gave up on the revenge he'd planned for Joey's sake, if he got Joey to take the money and leave as soon as he was fit so Sean could never hurt him again, Heath knew by now that he couldn't convince Rachel to pack up and leave, at least not before *he* left. Not when he'd tried so hard to make her stay. She thought she was keeping the baby and Jed was coming back.

You could tell her you know her secret. But even that might not be enough. And Heath's gut was telling him that Sean wouldn't stop at trying to intimidate her so she would leave. He wouldn't dare hurt her the way he'd hurt Joey, but he could make her life hell before she gave up pretending and realized she didn't belong in the Pecos.

Heath's growl was so loud that the cowboy twisted

around in the saddle to stare at him. It wasn't any good. He would have to do more than just give Sean a good thrashing. And no one, including Rachel, could ever know he'd done it.

"Herr Renshaw!"

Sonntag's voice brought Heath out of his dark thoughts. The shopkeeper ran up to him, waving an envelope. "I almost forgot." he said. "There is a letter for Mrs. McCarrick."

Feeling an unease he couldn't explain, he took the envelope from Sonntag's hand.

It was from Ohio. He didn't know the name on the back of the envelope. Kinfolk? Rachel had never mentioned having family, or any friends she'd left behind. Who was writing to her from Ohio?

Hell. If she did have connections back East, at least she would have somewhere to go. Why didn't that make him feel any better?

"Thanks," he told Sonntag, who was hovering curiously. He mounted and rode out before the shopkeeper could ask any questions. His fingers itched to open the envelope, but he left it alone and clucked to Bess, who swiveled her ears and broke into an easy canter. When he got back to Dog Creek around sunset, Maurice came to meet him, puffing and dripping sweat.

Immediately Heath thought of Joey. He dismounted and grabbed the Frenchman by the shoulders.

"What's wrong, Maurice?"

"The mare, she is foaling."

Heath let out his breath. "She's all right?" he asked.

"*Non.* The baby is not coming out right, *n'est-ce pas?*"

Heath swore. The mare was Jed's best, a half Thoroughbred he'd bought in Dallas. Jed had bounced around like a colt himself when he'd found out the mare was in foal.

"Where's Charlie?" Heath asked, heading for the stable.

"I have not seen him since I spoke to him yesterday."

Having Charlie was better than having no hands at all, but not by much. "Ask Mrs. McCarrick to heat up some water," Heath said. "You'll have to see to Bess."

"Madame McCarrick is with the mare. She was so good with the boy, I thought she might help the mare, as well."

Alarm brought Heath to a halt. What in hell had Maurice been thinking? A troubled foaling was no place for a woman. No place for Rachel.

Heath strode into the stable. Lanterns had been lit and hung on hooks on the walls, though Heath didn't need their light. He could smell the mare's distress.

Rachel was standing at the wall of the loose box where the mare had been quartered, her hands clasped behind her back. It was clear that she hadn't been dressed to leave the house; her skirts fell close to her legs, as if she wasn't wearing petticoats, and Heath could see that she'd left off the corset females used to shape their figures. Her hair was loose around her shoulders, a fall of night that didn't look anything like the severe style she usually wore. She was concentrating so hard on the mare that she didn't see Heath until he was at her side.

"How's Joey?" Heath asked.

She jumped a little, her eyes wide and dark in the lamplight. "He is still resting. The baby is with Lucia. She's staying in my room with me while Joey recovers."

Rachel looked like she wanted to ask him where

he'd been, but she closed her mouth instead and looked back at the mare. Lily was lying on her side, grunting and straining to push out the foal that wanted to be born.

"She seems to be in pain," Rachel said. "I didn't know what to do for her."

Heath shut out Rachel's smell, and tried to ignore her tumbled curls and the unbound curve of her breasts. "Not much you can do," he said. "I'll try to help her, but I need to find out what's wrong first. You go on back to the house. This won't be pretty."

"I've witnessed births before."

He wondered if she was lying. Her face was white with strain, but her jaw was firm and her lips were set. "Have you ever put your arm inside a horse?" he asked.

Her eyelids fluttered. "I'm afraid I…don't know much about horses."

Admitting a weakness wasn't like her. Heath felt as if he were walking that narrow fence again, only the cactuses on either side had grown so many spines that he couldn't see the tough green flesh beneath.

"Then you can't be any use here," he said gruffly. He walked into the loose box, hung his hat over a post and knelt beside Lily. She tried to lift her head and groaned.

"Settle down, now," Heath said, running his hand over her neck, barrel and croup. He could feel the foal moving inside, struggling just as she was. "You ain't alone now."

For a while all he did was soothe her, getting her muscles to relax. He almost forgot that Rachel had ignored his advice and was still there. Maurice came in with two pails of steaming water and set them down a few feet away. He mopped his face with a handkerchief and glanced at Rachel.

"Are there any rags left in the house, *madame?*" he asked.

"I believe there are. I'll go get them."

Heath could hear the relief in her voice. She left the stable, and some of the tightness went out of his muscles.

"Keep her inside, Maurice," Heath said. "Say anything you have to, but I don't want her here."

"That is easier said than done, *monsieur,*" Maurice said. "*Madame* is most formidable."

Maurice didn't know the half of it. "She's still a woman," Heath snapped. "Last I looked, you was still a man."

Maurice drew himself up as if he wanted to talk back, but he lit off without a word. Heath scrubbed his arms up to the elbows and turned all his attention to Lily. He was just feeling inside her when Rachel returned.

"Is she any better?" she asked, setting down the flour sack of rags.

Heath would have damned Maurice for a coward except for one thing. He was going to need help after all. Maurice had been right. The foal wasn't in the right position, and Lily could still decide to fight him. He couldn't turn the foal and calm her at the same time.

"You still want to help?" he asked without looking at her.

"What…would you like me to do?"

She was scared, but Heath didn't have time to coddle her. "Come in here and sit near Lily's head. Talk to her, quiet-like. Keep her calm."

For half a minute Rachel didn't move, only stood staring into the loose box. Either she would run, or she would find her courage.

But he didn't think she would run. She wasn't going to admit defeat, least of all to him.

Finally she took a step inside. Her shoes rustled the straw as she traced a wide circle around Lily, coming to a stop near the mare's head. She took a breath.

"Will she—"

Heath looked up. "Will she what?"

"Never mind." Rachel smoothed her skirts around her knees and knelt beside Lily. Her hands were shaking. Heath wanted to grab them and hold them still, stroke her wrists, soothe her as he'd tried to soothe the mare.

"She won't bite you," he snapped. "Lay your hands on her. She ain't no different than Joey."

Rachel laughed. He realized then that he'd never heard her laugh before. Even though it was a small and nervous sound, there was also a kind of warmth in it.

"I wonder if Joey would agree," she murmured.

"He wouldn't mind."

She hesitated, her hand in the air, and then slowly laid it on Lily's neck. The mare quivered at the stranger's touch and then settled again.

"She likes you," Heath said.

"Does she?"

"Horses know when people like them."

"But I've heard that they—" She broke off and tucked her legs to the side. "I'm afraid my knowledge of horses is very limited."

It was the second time she'd said as much. "No horses in Ohio?" he joked.

She looked at him sharply. "Of course there are horses in Ohio. It's just that I—"

"You didn't have much to do with 'em."

"No." She stroked the mare's cheek with her fingertips. "I have never been employed in any work that involved dealing with horses."

He wanted to ask her what kind of work she *had* done, but this sure as hell wasn't the time. "You'll have to learn quick," he said.

Lily's barrel rippled, and she groaned again. Rachel leaned close to the mare's head and whispered in the flattened ear.

"The foal's leg is bent back so he can't move freely through the canal," Heath said. "I have to straighten it out. You just keep talkin' to her. Tell her it's all right."

"All right." Rachel kept her face near Lily's while Heath positioned himself by the mare's hindquarters.

After that, Heath didn't have much time to think about anything but the horse. He worked his hand and arm inside, felt for the foal's fetlock, and pulled its knee up so that he could straighten out the leg. When he got the foal in the right position, Lily moaned with relief. Next time she pushed, her water broke, and soon the foal began to slide out, one hoof after another followed by the muzzle. Heath wiped the white sac away from its nose, and then the baby came the rest of the way out, wet and glistening. Heath situated the foal to help it breathe and began rubbing it down with the rags.

Rachel pressed her hands over her mouth. Her eyes were wet with tears.

"He's all right now," Heath said. "Healthy and strong. Long legs, like his ma."

As if she'd understood, Lily gave a great, gusty sigh of satisfaction. Rachel brushed the mare's forelock just the way she'd stroked Joey's hair.

"You're a brave girl," she whispered. "You should be proud."

Heath stopped for a minute, his throat suddenly as tight as a hangman's noose. He didn't feel any lust for Rachel now, but the liking and respect he'd begun to have for her, the desire to protect her, were only getting stronger. She had a quality he hadn't seen in many people before: compassion. Not only for babies and half-grown kids, but for animals, as well.

Would she feel that way about a wolf? Or a man who could turn into one?

Never. Never again.

Lily moved suddenly, and Rachel shied away. The mare rolled to her knees and then clambered to her feet. She went straight to her baby and began to lick him. Legs like knobby sticks wobbled as the colt learned how to stand on his own.

"Won't he fall?" Rachel asked, keeping her distance.

"They're all born like this. Ready to run."

"Won't he need to…eat very soon?"

As if he agreed, the colt started nosing for Lily's teats. Rachel's face took on the color of a Texas sunset. "I must seem a terrible coward."

There she went again, acting as if she cared what he thought. "You ain't no coward," he said roughly.

Her eyes were all confused now, half soft and half wary. "When I said I didn't know much about horses…when I was very young, I was almost trampled by a team pulling a carriage."

Somehow Heath managed to swallow his curse before it came out of his mouth. "How?" he asked.

"I was…living in Cincinnati and didn't look when I was crossing the street. It was very foolish of me."

"Why weren't your folks lookin' after you?"

"They weren't nearby at the time." She laced her fingers together in her lap. "I never had occasion to be close to horses after that."

So she'd had good reason to be afraid, especially if she hadn't found the chance to stand up to her fears.

"You didn't have to tell me that," he said, careful not to look at her again.

"I know."

They were both quiet for a while, watching the mare and the foal in a kind of easy companionship Heath hadn't known since Jed had died. His nose had started to clear of the odors of blood and birthing and horse sweat; he could smell Rachel again, the woman-scent, clean soapiness mingled with the musk of her skin. She wasn't aroused, not yet, but he was starting to be.

He cleared his throat. "I'll stay with them a spell," he said. "You rest."

"I am not tired."

Make her go. Yell at her, mock her, show her who's boss.

But he couldn't. Not after what she'd done, how brave she'd been. He tried to pretend he was easy with her, as easy as he would be with a cross-eyed eighty-year-old spinster.

"Where're your folks now?" he asked.

Her answer was long in coming, and when she finally spoke, her voice crept as quiet as a pocket mouse.

"They died when I was five years old."

If Heath had been smart, he would have stopped there, without asking another question or listening to anything else she said.

"How'd it happen?" he asked.

"A fire," she said, her emotions tucked away where he couldn't see. "It was an accident. The house burned down, and I was the only one…" She scooped up a handful of straw and let it sift through her fingers. "It was a long time ago."

But you didn't forget. Not something like that. "You had other folks to take care of you," he said.

She dropped the rest of the straw and brushed the chaff from her hands. "Where did you come from, Holden? Have you always lived in Texas?"

She had turned the tables on him, easy as falling off an ornery bronc in a rainstorm. He considered not answering. Maybe she would leave if he didn't.

"I been here long enough," he said.

"And your family?"

He'd never told anyone about the Mortons, or the Reniers and the mother who'd thrown him away. "Haven't seen 'em in years," he said.

"I'm sorry."

His short laugh was as nasty as he could make it. "Don't be."

Any other woman would have had the sense to get up and walk out. Rachel just kept sitting there, her breathing slow and steady.

"Joey is an orphan, isn't he?" she asked.

"He is. But don't go askin' him about it."

"I didn't intend to." Those eyes were on him, hitting him harder than a longhorn bent on murder. "He thinks the world of you."

Heath shrugged.

"You'd give your life for him."

Maybe he could get her to leave if he made her disgusted with him again. "I wouldn't give my life for nobody," he said.

"You were hurt when you stood up to the men who hurt Joey," she said. "You could have been killed."

"If I'd thought that, I wouldn't have helped him."

If she'd gotten up and turned her back on him then, he would have been glad. But she only shook her head.

"I think there are many things you would die for."

She was wrong, but he didn't know how he could convince her of it without telling her about his years outside the law. Why was it so damn hard to decide whether he wanted her to keep despising him or start liking him? Why was he letting a woman keep setting him off balance when he should have learned better long before he ever met her?

"I confess that I wasn't sure whether or not you had killed those outlaws," she said when he didn't answer. "Now I'm certain you didn't."

"You don't know a damn thing about me. Maybe your first instincts was right."

"I'm quite certain they were wrong." She looked away, maybe realizing she was letting him see too much. "What did Joey mean when he said a wolf had saved him?"

Heath was surprised she'd remembered what Joey had said, but he was glad she was ready to talk about something else. He was safe telling her at least part of the truth.

"A wolf attacked one of the outlaws when he was whipping Joey," he said.

"Attacked him?" She cast him a worried glance. "Is that common here? Are there many wolves in this area?"

"Less than there used to be." Humans hadn't yet

driven them out of West Texas the way they had in other parts, but mostly they stayed away from Dog Creek because Heath warned them off. "It ain't usually in their nature to come after people."

"Then why did this one attack the outlaws?"

"Most animals can smell something rotten. Maybe the son of a bitch was just too big a temptation."

She shivered. "Then it wasn't really trying to help Joey?"

"Maybe, maybe not." He thought of her cowering from him and felt himself starting to bristle. "You ain't scared, are you?"

"I like dogs.…"

"Wolves ain't dogs. But if you don't bother them, they won't bother you."

Rachel nodded, but he could see by the way her fingers worked in her skirts that she wasn't convinced. She glanced around the stable, watched Lily and her colt for a minute, and then settled her gaze on Heath again.

"I should look at your shoulder," she said suddenly. "It must be painful after what you did for the mare."

The last thing he needed was for her to touch him again. It was crazy she didn't know better herself. Maybe if he showed her he didn't need her help anymore, she would leave him alone. Maybe she would even get a little spooked wondering how he could have healed so quick.

He removed his vest, tossed it aside and unbuttoned the top of his shirt, pulling the collar wide open.

Rachel gasped. He let her look her fill and then buttoned the shirt again.

"It's gone," Rachel whispered.

"I told you I heal fast."

"But that's not poss—"

He grabbed his vest and jumped to his feet. "Joey needs your tendin', not me. I'm goin' to get some grub. You sleep."

He didn't get far out the door. Rachel came after him, her little feet moving fast and sure.

"Who are you, Holden?" she asked. "What are you running from?"

Only a *loup-garou* could move as fast as he did then. He spun around, and she stumbled back, raising her hands and turning her face aside.

"What're *you* runnin' from, Rachel?" he asked hoarsely. "When you answer my question, I'll answer yours."

He turned and kept on walking.

Chapter Nine

THE LETTERS LAY on Heath's table, the bundle from the saddlebags and the one he'd just brought from Javelina.

Leave them be, he told himself. All this time he'd managed to keep from looking at the bunch from Rachel, except for the one he'd read when he'd found the saddlebags. He'd told himself he didn't care enough to read them. He didn't want to know more about who she was or where she came from, or why she'd wanted to marry Jed. He'd been safer staying ignorant.

But the last couple of days had changed things. She wasn't just a puzzle anymore. She was starting to wear away at his strength and certainty, making him question and doubt when he had to be most sure of himself and what he had to do.

For all the good she'd done, she couldn't possibly be what she seemed: kind and brave and worthy of trust. He'd seen her weaknesses, like her stubbornness and sharp temper. But there had to be more, and worse. Somewhere in those secrets he knew she was keeping, in the wildness he sometimes saw in her eyes. Why she lusted after Heath when she was marrying another man. Why it was so important to her to make a home with a man she might never have met in a place as hard as the Pecos.

She's an orphan. She didn't have no one to take care

of her. Was that why she clung to the baby so hard? Had she grown up like Heath, more a slave than a daughter?

Heath rested his chin on his fists and stared at the letters without seeing them. He was going to make sure Sean couldn't bother her anymore, but he was still taking the kid. There had never been any question about that. She wouldn't even suspect it was coming.

If it hadn't been for what had happened in the house and the stable, the way they'd talked and the soft things she'd said to him, maybe Rachel would have known better than to believe anything he said. Maybe she wouldn't feel betrayed, knowing that he had lied to her all along. Lied to her about more than she could ever guess.

But *she* was lying, too. And if he knew why, he wouldn't have to care that she'd started to trust him. He wouldn't have to feel anything but relief when he rode out.

He picked up the bundle, untied the string and spread the letters on the table. They had been put in order by date. He looked for the oldest one and started reading.

It was the first letter Rachel had written to Jed after he'd answered her advertisement in the marriage catalog. Heath could hear her voice speaking the words, telling Jed about herself in formal sentences written in a fine, delicate hand. She'd written about a few things she'd never told Heath, like the jobs she'd had—shopgirl and housekeeper and teacher—and her education at the orphanage, where she'd lived from the age of five, and later at a teachers' school. She talked about what she wanted in a marriage: a good, steady husband, a home of her own, a chance to work and make a new life.

But there were things she *hadn't* told Jed. About her fear of horses. How fiercely she could stand her ground, even when she was afraid. How good a mother she was. She didn't mention kids at all.

Heath set down the first letter and began the second. This one wasn't as formal. There was a kind of excitement in the words, as if she'd begun to realize her dreams just might come true. She was letting her heart show a little, letting Jed see more of what was inside her. The vulnerability she tried so hard to hide from Heath. The warmth and generosity.

That wasn't what Heath wanted to find. He threw the letter down and started the next. But none of the others said much more about her past. They were full of hope, plans she'd shared with Jed, talking about their first meeting and what would follow. If she felt any doubts, she didn't show it. She sounded happy.

Heath crushed the last letter in his fist. She'd been *happy* before she came to Dog Creek, expecting so much, wanting what she was never going to have.

Slowly Heath retied the little bundle of letters. Nothing. Nothing to condemn Rachel, nothing to make it easier on him. She hadn't complained to Jed about suffering, but Heath had a pretty good idea what her life had been like with no kinfolk on her side, taking any job she could so she could eat and have somewhere to sleep. Ready to take any chance at finally having a place of her own.

Knowing what she'd been through only made things worse. But Heath could rest easy about one thing: she'd never talked about having children, or even wanting them. She might be a little upset when she lost the baby, but she would get over it. With the money Heath left her, she could still make a new life somewhere. And if she really wanted to stay in Texas, there wasn't any reason why she couldn't find another man to marry her, out here where women were hard to come by.

Another man.

The wolf inside Heath stirred, growling, ready to attack. He sat very still until he could think with his head instead of his animal appetites.

He reached for the letter Rachel had received from Ohio. He knew from what she'd written to Jed that she didn't have any real kinfolk or friends, not any who'd been willing to help her. But someone had cared enough about her to write.

There wasn't much left of the wax seal after the letter's long journey from the East. Heath broke it open and took the scented paper out, wrinkling his nose against the stench of perfume.

He read it three times to make sure he understood. He felt as if all his blood had hardened and cracked like mud baking in the sun.

Rachel did have somewhere to go. She had a future waiting for her, even if she never married.

But the letter said something else. *No one should be compelled to pay for a single mistake for the rest of their lives.*

One mistake. A mistake that had cost Rachel the easy life she could have had. Only, Heath still didn't know what that mistake had been.

He tucked the paper back inside the envelope and took the bundle of letters back to the saddlebags thrown across his bunk. He took out both bags of money and turned them upside down, spilling the coins across the blanket.

Rachel wouldn't need Jed's money anymore. She wouldn't need anything from Heath at all.

"Holden?"

Turning fast, Heath saw Joey standing the doorway. He cursed himself for letting the kid slip under his awareness again, but there wasn't any undoing it now. The boy was staring at the money, all wide-eyed and wondering.

Heath stepped in front of the bunk. "What the hell are you doing up?" he demanded. "Git on back to bed."

Leaning one hand against the door frame, Joey stood up tall, grimaced and quickly smoothed his expression. "I'm all right," he said.

"Sure you are. You're pale as a lizard's belly. How'd you get away from Mrs. McCarrick?"

Joey took a step toward Heath and staggered. Heath caught him.

"She doesn't know," Joey gasped. "I snuck out."

Heath half carried the boy to the rickety wooden chair and made him sit. "Soon as you're able to walk, I'm takin' you back to the house."

The boy's jaw set. "First you tell me where all that money came from."

It was clear Heath would have to tell Joey something. The boy seemed amiable to most folk, but he could be pretty damn stubborn when he was riled.

He also looked up to Heath, just the way Rachel had said. Heath had never craved that kind of worship. And it didn't mean that Joey wouldn't turn out just like Jed if he knew even part of the truth.

Trust wasn't possible anymore. Heath didn't want Joey to suffer any more than he had to. The boy would be hurt when Heath disappeared, even more when he found out Jed wasn't coming back. But Heath couldn't stand to see the look in his eyes when he realized just how much Heath had deceived him.

"Jed left it," Heath said slowly. "He thought there was a chance he could be delayed comin' back from Kansas, so he left this money so Mrs. McCarrick could keep things goin'."

Joey chewed that over for a minute. "You knew he was gonna be comin' home late?" he asked.

"Jed thought there might be a chance."

"Then why didn't he tell you to watch out for Mrs. McCarrick?"

"I don't know. I don't always know what's goin' on in Jed's mind. Maybe he didn't expect her to show up when she did."

"Sean lied when he said he knew she was comin'."

"'Course he did."

Puffing up his chest, Joey shook his forelock out of his eyes. "When're you goin' after Sean, Holden? What're you gonna do to him?"

"He ain't comin' near you again. That's all you need to know."

"But I want to help!" Joey started to get up, grew even paler and plunked back down again. "I can distract him or somethin'. Just tell me what you want me to do."

"I want you to go inside and rest."

"But, Holden, I'm tough! I'm good with my rifle, and—" His face was going red. "I want to kill him."

"I know you do," Heath said grimly. "But you won't."

"We could get him somewhere so no one would ever know. You don't have to do it. I'll shoot him myself!"

Heath got up and stood over Joey, arms crossed to show he was serious. "There ain't goin' to be no shootin' of any kind. You're no killer, and you'd be more a danger to yourself than Sean."

Joey went stock-still, as if someone had punched

him in the face. "You think I'm a baby because I didn't fight Sean."

"Don't be a fool, boy. You're goin' back to bed." Heath picked Joey up before the kid could protest, carried him into the house and laid him facedown on his bed. Joey stayed where he was, refusing to look up when Heath left the room.

Without meaning or wanting to, Heath went across the hall to Rachel's room and stopped before the closed door. He could hear the call of a coyote somewhere on the range, the nicker of a horse in the stable, the scuffling of a mouse on the other side of the wall.

And he could hear Rachel's breathing, soft and deep. She moved around on the bed, cloth brushing cloth. The baby was stirring, as well; Heath could smell milk and that particular scent that had gradually become so much like his own that he wondered how he could ever have doubted the boy was his.

Laying his palm against the door, Heath opened it very slowly. Rachel was on her back, her face turned up, her hands gently cupped as if to gather the moonlight. The sheets were bunched around her feet, leaving only the thin nightdress between her skin and the warm night air. Heath walked into the room, his boots as silent as a wolf's paws, and watched the rise and fall of her breasts, the brown of her nipples and the shadow between her thighs. Her lips were parted, her face softened in sleep. She was almost beautiful.

She wasn't Mrs. McCarrick. She was Rachel Lyndon. She didn't belong to any man yet. He could wake her right now, kiss her, make her open up to him the way he knew she wanted him to. All he had to do was reach out and touch her.

A low gurgle stopped him. The baby was looking up at him from the crate that served as his bed as if he knew exactly what was in Heath's mind. As if the boy were chiding him for even thinking about taking advantage of his mother.

She ain't his mother. She never could be.

Heath turned around and walked out. He returned to the cabin, stuffed the wills and letters back into the saddlebags, buried them under the money bags and shoved the bags back beneath the bunk. He undressed so quickly that he tore his shirt and popped a button from his britches. His cock was on fire, and his head was fit to bursting with the savagery of his thoughts. He Changed and ran again until the sun was skirting the horizon.

What are you running from? Rachel had asked him.

She would never know the answer to that question. But now that he knew she'd made a mistake big enough to keep on paying for, maybe he could finally get the answer to his.

LOUIS CAME TO Rachel as he had so many times before in her dreams, smiling, methodically removing his clothing with the fastidiousness he revealed in nearly everything he did. Even his lovemaking had an air of precision about it. But he was good. Very, very good.

Tonight he was even more tender, even more attentive to giving her pleasure. She was panting and wild with need by the time he had finished, eager to feel him inside her, easing the loneliness that had been so much a part of her life before Aunt Beatrice had materialized like a stern, haughty angel to lift her from poverty and despair.

When it was over, Louis rolled onto his side and played with a lock of her hair, twisting it around his finger.

"Not much longer, dearest," he said, lifting the lock to his lips. "Your aunt is ill. She'll surely pass on soon, and we'll be rich."

Rachel tried to ignore his casual indifference to Aunt Beatrice's health. She wasn't a kind woman, but she had saved Rachel's life.

"My aunt has recovered before," she said coldly.

"Fate cannot be so unkind to us." Louis rose up on his elbow and kissed her forehead. "You will never want for anything again, Rachel. I will make you happy."

But I will have the money, she thought. She banished such treacherous speculation and smiled. "Be patient a little longer," she said.

The lamps flickered. Rachel felt herself rising up from the bed, floating so high that she could look down upon Louis as if he were a mere figurine, a statue of a complacent Greek god certain of winning his chosen mortal's devotion.

I love him, Rachel thought. But her body was growing heavy, her heart transforming to a lump of rock and ash, her stomach expanding and filling with a weight that bore her steadily downward.

She came to rest on the bed again, but Louis was no longer beside her. He stood in the shadows, his features, picked out in writhing shadow, contorted in disgust.

"Look what you've done!" he spat. "You've destroyed everything. You've ruined all our chances with your lust."

Rachel pressed her hands to her swollen belly. "No, Louis. We made this baby with love."

"Love! What does love matter to me? Did you think

I'd marry an ill-favored whore like you for anything but money?" He gave an ugly laugh. "I'd advise you to get rid of the child before you find yourself out on the streets again."

With a cry of fury, Rachel struggled to rise. Louis laughed again and turned to go.

He never got to the door. It crashed open, and a man walked in...a man tall and broad-shouldered, his face hidden in the shadow of his wide-brimmed hat. The stranger touched his belt, and Rachel caught a flash of metal.

"This man botherin' you, ma'am?" the stranger asked in Holden's voice.

The hot breath of violence blew like a gale through the room. Rachel tried to raise her hands, tried to speak, but before she could find the words the stranger was gone and a huge, black animal crouched in his place. The wolf looked once at her with hungry yellow-green eyes and then leaped right for Louis's throat.

Most animals can smell something rotten. Maybe the son of a bitch was just too big a temptation. Holden's words pounded in Rachel's ears as she helplessly watched the beast reduce Louis's neck to a gory lacework of torn flesh and dripping blood. He staggered like a bad actor on a makeshift stage and fell, his last breath bubbling from the hole in his throat. Rachel closed her eyes, and when she opened them again the stranger with Holden's voice had returned.

He stood over Louis, exhaling menace and malevolence like bitter sleet. His face remained in shadow. His eyes glittered green and cold.

"You don't have to worry no more, ma'am," he said. He began to remove his waistcoat, and she could not misunderstand what he intended. Part of her wanted to lie back on the bed, let this man take her without protest.

But the other part could still see Louis lying broken on the floor. Rachel backed away, reaching for a garment that was no longer there. A mirror rose out of a darkened corner, and she caught a glimpse of herself, a woman she didn't recognize, voluptuous and beautiful.

"No," she whispered, banishing the wanton. But the stranger wasn't listening. He had removed his shirt, and now he began to work on the buttons of his trousers. She could not look away.

"No," she whispered. "I can't."

He laughed and tilted up his hat to reveal Holden's hard, cruel face. "Sure you can. You're a whore, ain't you?"

And without another word he drew his gun from the holster at his hip and aimed it right at Rachel's heart.

Choking with horror, she sat up, throwing the sheets aside. Afternoon sunlight streamed through the bedroom window. She touched her chest and then her stomach, feeling for the life inside her.

But her womb was empty. As empty as it had been the night she had lost her child.

She scrubbed at her face and looked into the crate that lay on the floor beside the bed. The baby slept undisturbed among his blankets, his tiny body completely relaxed in the way of the very young. Rachel knew by the light coming through the window that she'd slept through the night and well over half the day; Lucia must have tended him without making a sound.

Now she was left with nothing to do but remember the dream and wonder what had put such terrible images into her mind.

Yes, she had asked about the gun and at first imagined him one of those gunmen she had read about in some penny dreadful. They had spoken of wolves. But Holden knew nothing of her shame, however he might taunt and tease and try to provoke her.

Or desire her.

She shivered and reached for her shawl. The Holden in the dream had been cruel and murderous. The real man was capable of small cruelties and mockery and cutting remarks, and he was certainly capable of defending himself and Joey.

But she had seen him gentle, too…oh, so gentle. His affection for Joey had been undeniable, little as he would care to admit it. He'd let down his guard with the boy. She hadn't expected him to do so again, not in her presence.

In the stable, he had done much more than that. He had allowed her into his world, permitted her to help, to watch him work with his hands and heart. A heart big enough to care for a creature that should have been no more than a useful tool to a man like him.

A man like him. A man she seemed no closer to understanding now than when they had first met. A man whose gunshot wound had inexplicably healed overnight. A man she so desperately wanted to touch far more intimately than when she had bound his shoulder.

A man who, against all sense and reason, wanted a woman like her.

She stood before the washstand mirror and began to unbraid her hair. What had possessed her to confide in *him?* Why had she admitted her weaknesses, the very kind he must hold most in contempt? Why had she given him anything that might let him guess, even a little, how desperate she was…or how deeply she had felt about his loyalty to a boy not his kin?

What are you running from, Rachel?

She shook out her hair, feeling the soft strands whisper around her neck. No one but she had touched it in a half-dozen years. She slipped her nightgown off over her head.

The mirror didn't reflect everything. Even when she stood well back, she could only see her upper body. But it was not the figure and form she had seen in the dream, all lush curves and stunning beauty. She cataloged her many faults, from the too-firm arms made strong with labor to the hollow under her ribs. Her face was equally unprepossessing. She had always known that it wasn't pretty, even if the other children at the orphanage hadn't told her again and again. Her brows were too thick and straight, her nose a little crooked, her mouth painfully ordinary.

Only her eyes sometimes seemed a little more attractive, unusually dark and fringed with thick lashes.

She passed her hand over them, blocking them from her sight, and poured water from the jug into the basin. Slowly she bathed herself, moistening the sponge and brushing it over her skin. A real bath was a nearly unbearable temptation. But she would be compelled to venture into the shed next to the bunkhouse in order to avail herself of it, and that frightened her nearly as much as the horses.

Not because someone might accost her, but because such a sensual pleasure might crumble her already fragile resolve and let her believe she could be desired for nothing more than herself. Let her forget the terrible consequences of playing with fire…

As if he had felt her despair, the baby began to cry. Rachel quickly finished her ablutions, hooked her corset, pulled on her drawers and petticoats and knelt beside him. He quieted almost as soon as she gathered him into her arms. She stroked his thick, black hair and smiled into his eyes.

He had changed so much in the eight short days she had been with him. He had not only completely recovered from his initial illness, he'd become astonishingly robust, challenging both her and Lucia to keep him content.

She hadn't forgotten how Holden had suggested she give up the baby to Lucia, and she still didn't understand why he had done so. Why had he been so angry when she had made the dutiful suggestion that they attempt to find the boy's parents? Why did it seem that he—

An astonishing idea formed in her mind. She turned it this way and that, shook her head, and laughed. How could Holden Renshaw possibly have a son?

But was it really so impossible? A man like him must have had many women, and it took so little effort to make a child. He would surely feel no compunction about lying to *her* about such a thing.

But what had happened to the mother?

Unable to bear the speculation, Rachel rocked the baby until he'd fallen asleep again. Lucia arrived a short while later. Rachel put on the oldest of her three dresses and visited Joey in the second bedroom. He was much better, and so restless that she wondered if she would have to summon Holden to keep the boy in bed.

In the end, simply warning Joey of her intention to call on Holden was sufficient to convince him to lie still a little while longer. On the way out of the house, she met Maurice, who was holding a large, lumpy package under his arm.

"Monsieur Renshaw wished you to have this, *madame,*" he said with a little bow. He set the package down on the table and stepped back, obviously waiting for her to open it.

Her mouth suddenly dry, Rachel fetched a knife from the kitchen and sliced through the twine that bound the package. The paper fell away to reveal an infant-size cradle, painted with delicate pink and blue flowers.

She gave a little cry of pleasure and stroked her finger over the polished wood. The cradle rocked gently.

"Mr. Renshaw brought this?" she asked, her elation giving way to uncertainty.

"Oui, madame. He purchased it in Javelina."

He did it for the child, Rachel thought. "Please thank him for me, Maurice."

The Frenchman regarded her with a suspiciously satisfied look on his round face. "He will wish to hear this from you."

"Is he near the house?"

"He is just preparing to ride out."

"So late?"

"He has business away from the ranch." With a brief salute, Maurice lumbered out the door.

Rachel lifted the cradle in her arms. She never could have afforded such a treasure, even if she hadn't lost Timothy.

Sniffing away foolish tears, she took the cradle into the bedroom and filled it with blankets. The baby took to it right away, grinning broadly and laughing in apparent glee. It was all of a piece with his unusual strength, and increase in size and awareness of his surroundings.

Lucia was already preparing to feed him, so Rachel resolved to find Holden before she lost her nerve. He wasn't in the yard, so she stopped by the stable. Lily appeared not to have suffered any lasting effects from her harrowing experience the night before. The colt was much steadier on his legs, and, like all babies, he was voraciously hungry.

She lingered there longer than she had intended, reminding herself that there was no shame in sincere thanks for a kindness, even one intended for another. She readjusted her bonnet and strode toward the door, determined to pretend that last night's confessions—and today's dream—had never occurred.

Charlie Wood was walking into the stable just as she was leaving and told her that Holden was in the corral behind the building. She found Holden busy with the girth strap of his big brown horse. She hesitated a few yards away, staring into the shadows that obscured his face beneath the wide-brimmed hat. The dream returned in all its passion and fury. She could see the ripple of muscle as he removed his shirt, his hand reaching for the gun….

She was an instant away from turning back for the house when he straightened and saw her. A series of emotions flickered over his face: pleasure, uncertainty, annoyance, anger, though surely she had imagined those first two. Within a few seconds his expression had become a perfect blank.

He wants to forget about last night, too.

"You woke up late," he said gruffly.

"Yes. I don't know what happened. I'm sorry."

Holden shrugged. "Reckon you had the right to sleep in."

It was a kind of approval, however grudging, and she

didn't know how to answer. "Is he the colt's father?" she asked, indicating his horse.

Her question clearly startled him. He laughed, husky and low, with barely a hint of mockery.

"Hardly," he said. "Apache's a gelding."

Rachel felt her face grow hot from more than the relentless sun. "He's a very fine horse."

Holden slapped the animal's glossy rump. "That he is."

Rachel waited for him to speak again. He didn't. She clasped her hands at her waist and swallowed.

"I wished to thank you for the cradle," she said.

Apache's bridle jingled as Holden adjusted a strap. "He needed it, didn't he?"

So much for a graceful acceptance. How could she have expected otherwise? "We can't continue to call him 'he,'" she said. "If we are to keep him, he must have a name."

He rested his hands on the scarred saddle and gazed out at the horizon. For a moment she was terrified that he had changed his mind and was prepared to look for the parents after all.

"Reckon you're right," he said without looking at her. "You have a suggestion?"

How was it that he could keep surprising her every time she believed she had begun to understand him?

"Don't you have ideas of your own?"

"Why should I?"

If he were the boy's father, surely he would show a little more interest in such an important matter. "You found him," she said with a hint of challenge. "It seems only fair that you should have a say in naming him."

Holden shrugged. "You've made yourself his mother, haven't you?"

There was no mistaking the angry note in his voice, and she could make no sense of his response. "I am the only mother he has, and since he has no father—"

Apache jerked his head up, shying from some imagined danger, and Rachel stopped. Holden spent the next minute quieting him. "Don't you want your own kids?" he asked softly.

Invisible claws raked down her spine. "That has nothing to do with this child," she said. "I feel certain that Jedediah will be glad to have such a sturdy boy as his son. Wouldn't you?"

Beyond her suggestions that they might look for the child's real parents, she and Holden had never openly discussed the baby's future. Holden had been adamant about keeping the baby at Dog Creek, but under what circumstances was never clear.

Whatever the truth of the baby's origins, Holden was clearly not prepared to give her the satisfaction of a straightforward answer. "What if Jed turns the boy off?" he asked.

"I would take him away with me," she said in a rush.

He frowned and pushed his hat up. "You'd leave Jed for the kid?"

She was weary of his relentless inquisition and too hurt to speak sensibly. "Perhaps the child means little to *you*, Mr. Renshaw, but I would do anything for him. I can never have children of my own."

Holden's face darkened with some strong emotion. "You're barren?"

The word was cruel, but she couldn't deny its accuracy, or her utter stupidity in letting the admission escape her lips. She had told no one of the doctor's prediction after her miscarriage, not even Jedediah. There were so many children in need of adoption, children just like the girl *she* had been. She had convinced herself that he would understand.

But in fact she had had no way of knowing *what* he would think. She had clung to hope because the alternative was unbearable.

"You lied to Jed," Holden said, as if he were commenting on the weather.

"We…we never discussed children at all. I would have explained before he and I were—"

She had almost said "married." Almost admitted that she had deceived Holden and everyone at the ranch because she'd been afraid of losing her place here in Jedediah's absence.

Surely Holden couldn't have guessed what she had been about to say, but what she *had* admitted was bad enough. His lids were half-closed, his nostrils flared, his mouth drawn in an unbending line.

"I would ask," she said steadily, "that you do me the courtesy of allowing me to explain…to speak to Jedediah on this matter before you tell him. I believe he will want the baby. Unless you have some better plan for him that you have not shared with me?"

Rubbing his hand across his mouth, Heath became very interested in a buckle on his saddle. "Ain't my business to tell Jed about it."

Her frustration reached the boiling point. Where did the truth lie? In Holden's former protectiveness or his present indifference? Did he still consider her some kind of enemy, or had their time together in the stable marked a change she wasn't even sure she wanted?

What did *he* want of *her?*

"I have never seen you hesitate to tell anyone anything," she snapped.

He turned back to her, leaned against his horse and folded his arms across his chest. "Oh, I hesitate," he said. "If I didn't, I might ask you some questions you don't want asked."

The feeling drained from her legs. "Please do not allow any inconvenient scruples to interfere with your curiosity."

His eyes were every bit as hard and cold as they had been in the nightmare as he asked, "Did you ever love Jedediah McCarrick?"

Chapter Ten

CONCEALING THE DETAILS of her past and her motives had become almost second nature to Rachel over the years. She had expected a much more dangerous question. Even so, she could find no answer until several raw, painful moments had passed.

She wanted to tell Holden it was none of his business, just as he had told her such matters as the running of the ranch and the presence of outlaws were none of hers. She found herself stammering instead, speaking aloud what she had never decided in her own heart.

"Of…of course I love him," she said. "I would never have come here if I did not!"

His expression didn't change. "You'd be sorry if he hadn't married you?"

Her arms had gone numb. "He is a kind, good man. I want to make him happy."

"You sure don't act like it."

The ground steadfastly refused to swallow her. "If you…if you think because I didn't tell him about my inability to…to bear children—"

"I was thinkin' more about what *you* want, Rachel." His gaze raked over her, up and down and sideways. "What you expected when you came here."

Until their conversation in the stable, Rachel had never believed him very interested in her reasons for marrying Jed or coming to Texas. But he had guessed she was running from something, as she had guessed the same of him. Had all his earlier questions been tests of her devotion to her husband, tests that she had failed by admitting her barrenness and suggesting she would leave Jed for the baby? Was Holden truly loyal to Jedediah after all? Did he feel obligated to discover every one of her motives now that she had made yet another stupid confession?

"The West is a land of opportunity," she said, as if she were a schoolteacher reading from a primer. "I saw this opportunity and sought companionship in order to build a new life. When I met Jed—"

"In Ohio, where you was married."

"Yes. I knew at once that Jed would be…that we could be happy."

"And were you happy, Rachel, when he took you into his bed?"

He was speaking almost too softly for her to hear, and there was no one about, but Rachel felt as if the entire world must be listening. Sensation almost like pain filled the numb places in her body.

"I am not surprised," she said, shaking, "that you have no conception of the kind of companionship a good marriage entails."

"I know about male and female," he said, casually crossing his booted feet. "Was there someone before Jed, Rachel?"

She could hardly believe what he was saying. "You…you have—"

"Reckon you have some experience of the kind a

man would appreciate. You must have satisfied Jed well enough. But was the old man enough for you? Maybe you didn't want to tell him about not havin' kids because you hoped you'd never have to share his bed again?"

Air suddenly seemed in very short supply, not nearly enough to feed the rage she ought to feel. "I would never…I would never deny my husband his due."

"And it don't matter if he satisfies your needs, since you ain't got no call askin' to be pleased? You think it's better not to hanker after somethin' part of you is afraid of, 'specially if Jed don't much care?"

The fight went out of Rachel all at once. "Why?" she asked, her voice breaking. "Why do you take such pleasure in tormenting me? You know nothing of what Jed and I share. Why is it so impossible for you to believe that he…that he and I…"

He straightened and closed the space between them to three feet. Two. "It's hard for me to believe," he said, "because you want someone else."

She closed her eyes. Denials would win her nothing. He knew.

"It is part of being human," she said. "Just as it is to know whether wanting something is right or wrong."

"And is it so wrong, Rachel?" He had come so close that she could feel his breath stirring the loose tendrils of hair that had escaped from beneath her bonnet.

Wrong. Oh, yes, so very, very wrong. But she wanted him to cup her face in his big hand, touch her lips with his, meet his tongue with hers in a feral dance of desire.

Apache snorted as she stumbled backward. Holden reached for her, and she fended him off, arms flailing.

"Don't touch me!" she snapped.

He leaned back and stretched, popping bones. "Never planned to, Mrs. McCarrick."

He didn't try to pursue her as she ran back to the house. Once she was inside, she pressed her hands to her mouth and struggled to fill her empty lungs.

"Señora McCarrick?"

She turned to face Lucia's gentle concern with a frantic smile. The baby was in the Mexican woman's arms, and Rachel rushed to take him. She held the baby close and bounced him, humming an aimless tune.

"You have quarreled with Señor Renshaw?" Lucia asked.

Rachel kept her voice low for the baby's sake, but she knew Lucia would not be deceived. "Men…men can be very difficult, can they not?"

Lucia nodded solemnly. "*Sí, es verdad*. Is there anything I can do?"

"No, thank you. How is Joey?"

"He has gone out again, though I told him you would not wish it."

Of course he had, since Rachel had not been there to stop him. "You should lie down and rest, Lucia," she said.

Lucia gazed at her for a few moments longer and then left. Rachel carried the baby to the table and sank into a chair.

IT WAS ALL out now. The wolf could not be put back in the trap. She could never again hope to make Holden believe that she was indifferent to him, if she had ever really possessed that hope at all. He might indeed have been testing her fidelity and commitment to Jedediah, proving to himself that she was unworthy, but there had been so much more beneath his words. He might never seriously consider approaching his boss's wife, but his body had betrayed him. He might think he was in control, but he was deceiving himself as much as *she* had been.

She had not loved Jed. She had never met him, in Ohio or elsewhere; she had not had the chance. But she had hoped to learn to love him. Now she could hardly imagine a life of contentment with him and the baby. *If* he accepted the boy. If he accepted *her*.

The baby gave a soft little cry, and she tried to sing as the tears rolled over her cheeks. If she had anywhere to go, money of her own, she would never be parted from this baby.

But she had neither of those things.

"You deserve so much," she murmured to the child, "and I have so little. But I can give you one gift." She brushed her check against his, and he grabbed at a stray lock of her hair. "Would you mind if I gave you my father's name? He was a good man, even though I hardly knew him."

The baby grinned and pulled on her hair with that focused strength that always astonished her. She gave a watery laugh.

"Very well. I shall call you Gordon. Gordie. And if Mr. Renshaw doesn't like it, he can go hang."

"You're sure about this?" Sean asked.

Charlie nodded. "Somethin's different between 'em, Mr. McCarrick. They still argue and fuss, but it ain't the same. They stare at each other all the time. They're like panthers bitin' and scratchin' just afore they're fixin' to—" He grinned, showing his yellow teeth, letting insinuation finish the sentence for him.

Sean leaned back in his chair and glanced toward the door of his cabin. This was a development he had not expected. It had been scarcely more than two days since the incident at Dog Creek. Just as he had anticipated, no one at Blackwater seemed to suspect what had happened. The Blackwells were certainly ignorant of it, and had listened with horror to his account of the wolf attack. The hands had kept quiet…and so, it appeared, had Renshaw.

But this new twist…

"Last time, you told me they didn't like each other," he said, pinning Charlie with a hard stare. "Why should I believe that your observations are accurate now?"

"I can only say what I've seen, Mr. McCarrick."

"And how do you account for this change?"

"If you don't mind me sayin', Mr. McCarrick, when Renshaw came back after what happened at the Creek…"

"Go on," Sean said impatiently.

"Well, Mrs. McCarrick, she fixed the boy right up, and Renshaw, too. Woman took the bullet out of his shoulder. Mebbe that had somethin' to do with it."

Sean steepled his fingers under his chin. He could well imagine the intimacy that could occur during the treatment of a gunshot wound. Renshaw was certainly an animal in that regard, as in every other, and he wouldn't hesitate to betray Jed if he thought he could get away with it. But he had every reason to resent Rachel, and given her distinct lack of alluring physical charms and her frigid demeanor…

You fool. If Renshaw was party to some alteration in their relationship, it would not be based upon Miss Lyndon's physical attractions or his uncontrollable lust.

Animal cunning. The foreman must have discovered some advantage in softening his attitude and behavior toward her.

But why? What had changed? Rachel must have come to believe that Renshaw was not behind the bribery attempt in Javelina, or surely *she* would never soften toward *him.* Had she confronted him about the incident, in spite of Sean's warnings? Had she considered who else might have wanted her gone?

He shook off the thought and returned to the intriguing subject at hand. "Have you seen any indication that this attraction between them has gone beyond looks and conversation?" he asked Charlie.

"Don't reckon they've admitted what's goin' on yet. And Mrs. McCarrick...I don't think she's ready to put horns on Mr. McCarrick."

Sean grimaced. She might be a fraud and a thief, but she would have to maintain the fiction of being Jed's pure and loyal wife, even if she were the kind who would whore herself out to any man who wanted her. Still, the very fact that she couldn't have been wanted by many men in her life would make her twice as vulnerable when an overbearing, brutishly handsome man like Renshaw pursued her.

"Did Renshaw tell her the circumstances behind his and the boy's injuries?" Sean asked.

"He told the other hands something about outlaws. Reckon he said the same to her."

One lingering concern dispensed with, though Sean was hardly surprised. Renshaw had behaved exactly as he'd predicted.

In every way but one.

"What about the baby?"

"Mrs. McCarrick's still mighty attached to it, and I'd say Renshaw is, too."

Sean's fist tightened, and his bandaged arm—stitched up by Colonel Blackwell himself—protested his slight movement, and he had to bite his lip against the pain. "I seem to have underestimated you, Charlie," he rasped. "I wouldn't have taken you for a romantic."

"Huh." Charlie took rolling papers and a small pouch of tobacco out of his pocket, and began rolling a cigarette. "Didn't say nothin' about no romance."

Of course he hadn't. And unless the woman and Renshaw were blatant about their attraction, it would be difficult for Sean to take advantage of it.

That there was an advantage to be taken he had not the slightest doubt. But until he understood Renshaw's motivations, he would have to continue to be cautious.

Sean watched Charlie puff on his cigarette and thought of his own, much finer ones, left back at the house when he'd finished luncheon with the Blackwells. He couldn't roll one for himself without inviting a great deal of pain, and he wasn't prepared to ask Charlie to make one for him.

In the two days since his injury, he'd had little choice but to spend most of his time close to the house. He'd been out on the range today, collecting the beeves that had been left at large after the humiliating incident by the creek, but he'd been careful to make sure he was never alone.

Renshaw hadn't come after him, but Sean did not for a moment suspect that the foreman had given up on his notion of punishment, whatever form that might take. Charlie had said that Renshaw's injury hadn't seemed to trouble him after the first day, but even the foreman must have enough to keep him busy with the boy off his feet and only Charlie and the fat Frenchman to work the ranch.

No, Renshaw hadn't come. But the lobo had. The big black brute had showed up on the other side of the creek just after the beeves had been gathered…bold as brass, pacing up and down the bank in broad daylight, as if daring Sean to come after him. Sean had been very careful to show no emotion around the hands, and he had not accepted the beast's invitation.

But it wasn't over. Tonight he would be going back to the spot with men who could be trusted to back him up and see to it he got the killing shot.

Sean grinned. That pleasure would go a long way toward easing the pain of his wounds. As for Renshaw's possible dalliance with Mrs. McCarrick…

A man of character took what was handed to him and made the most of it. As he was about to do now.

"You've done well, Charlie," he said. He withdrew his money bag and laid several coins on the table beside his chair. "Continue as you have been. Report any further changes to me."

"Yessir." Charlie got up, pocketed the money and headed for the door.

"Charlie."

The older man stopped. "Somethin' else, Mr. McCarrick?"

"I believe that Gus is in the bunkhouse. Send him to me."

"Yessir."

Once Charlie was gone, Sean gave in to the pain and slumped in his chair. For a few moments he was unaware of anything but the fire in his arm and the rage it evoked. He forced his thoughts into focus again, knowing he needed to be clearheaded when Gus arrived.

Gus edged his way into the cabin, his hat in his hands. He'd been nervous as a cat ever since he'd shot Renshaw, and Sean had let him stay near the house to show that he had the hand's best interests at heart.

Now he was going to remind Gus once again that the obligation went both ways.

"I have a little job for you and El," Sean said. "You'll be riding for Heywood. Tonight. You should reach it by sundown tomorrow."

"H-Heywood?" Gus stammered.

"You should be familiar with the place, Gus. You broke into the lawyer's office there. Now you're going to burn it down."

SEAN MCCARRICK HAD been lucky again.

Heath kept Apache to a walk, in no hurry to return to the house. When he'd left, he'd been hoping against reason to find Sean somewhere along the creek, Change, then give Sean a good taste of his own medicine. The odds were against him; Sean was more likely to be sticking close to the house, nursing his wounds and hoping Heath wouldn't make good on his promise.

The odds had been better than Heath had expected, though it hadn't done him much good. Even though he'd found Sean with Gus and another hand along the same stretch where the whipping had happened, the coward had kept the creek and a safe distance between them. He'd been smart enough not to make a fatal mistake.

A bird sang in the mesquite bosquet beside the creek. Apache twitched his ears and bobbed his head, letting

Heath know that he wanted a drink. Heath steered the gelding down to the water, dismounted and sat on the bank while Apache plunged his nose in the water.

Mistakes. Heath took off his hat, slammed it on the ground and turned his face into the evening breeze. Why did he keep making them? It had all gone wrong from the moment Rachel had come out to thank him for the damn cradle.

'Course, he hadn't actually had a plan other than to keep asking questions until Rachel said something that revealed what mistake she was "paying for." But when she had started in about the boy's name, he'd been thrown naked into a thick patch of dog cholla. He'd gotten mad for no reason—or maybe because she'd been the one to remind him his *son* needed a name—and made her defend herself just for caring about the kid. Then he'd started baiting her again, telling himself he was testing her, knowing all the time that he was really trying to hurt her.

That hadn't worked out quite the way he'd meant it to. She'd been so quick to say she would choose the boy over Jed, giving the lie to her claim that she loved the man she'd supposedly met and married in Ohio. Heath had been torn between being mad on Jed's behalf, admiring her and worrying over her attachment to the boy.

Then she'd confessed to being barren and lying to Jed about it, and talked about Jed accepting the boy. Heath hadn't even known what he was doing when he'd started asking her about the kind of love she had for Jed. If they'd lain together. If he'd satisfied her.

Maybe he'd wanted to make her admit it. Make her admit to that wild thing inside her. Admit she wanted *him*. Not with glances or touches she justified as healing, but with her words. Her lips. Her whole body.

Heath laughed hoarsely. She'd passed the test, hadn't she? She was staying true to Jed after all, and he still didn't know if she and the old man had ever met.

Stripping out of his clothes on the way, Heath walked into the creek and got himself wet, scrubbing at his skin with handfuls of grass from the bank. A kingfisher skimmed the water a few yards away, and a catfish swam close enough for him to catch it. He let it go, ducked his head under the surface until he felt short on air, then rose and shook the water out of his hair.

Plenty of mistakes, all right. One after another for the past ten days. If it had been his aim to drive Rachel further away, he reckoned he'd achieved it. She probably thought he would rip off her clothes and throw her down on the nearest bed next time he saw her. Could be if she had the means she would leave the ranch right now, with the baby.

Pushing his hair out of his face, Heath climbed from the creek and let the air dry his skin as Apache grazed. He couldn't let her go yet, of course. He couldn't touch her, couldn't hate her, couldn't put her out of his mind no matter how many lies she told.

And he couldn't tell himself anymore that she would get over losing the boy.

Apache nuzzled Heath's shoulder, and Heath took the big gelding's head between his hands.

"It's easy for you, ain't it?" he said. "Livin' day by day. No future, no past."

It should be easy for the wolf, too. And it would have been, if Heath had ever figured out what he really was. The wolf in his pure form didn't struggle over every little feeling. He didn't harden his heart one minute and let his resolve crumble the next.

But Heath had never been purely one thing or the other. He'd used whatever part of himself helped him survive. Once he'd had to fight to stay alive, and that had kept him sharp. He'd gone soft since he'd given up the old ways. If he hadn't let himself get soft, he wouldn't be imagining what it would be like to grab Rachel and the boy and ride off with the both of them, leaving the old Heath *and* the new one behind forever.

Imagination, like trust, was a kind of poison that would destroy you little by little until you didn't know you were already dead. Some things couldn't be changed, and thinking they could was just another kind of dying.

Apache nodded, butting Heath under the chin. Heath gave him a final pat, put on his clothes and mounted, letting the gelding follow the narrow track back to the house. It was just dark when he took Apache into the stable, rubbed him down and gave him his dinner. Without stopping at the house, he left his clothes in the stable, Changed and set out west for the place where Dog Creek flowed into the Pecos River.

Unlike the creek, the Pecos was wild and treacherous, fordable only at a few crossings within this hundred-mile stretch. Heath stood on the high bank for a while, watching the brown, salty water surge and bubble.

The river was a killer. It had taken the lives of horses, cattle and men ever since the first settlers had come to this raw country. It couldn't be slowed or tamed or bargained with. And like Apache and the wolf, it lived forever in the present.

That was the way Heath told himself *he* had to keep living, too. No future, no past. Just doing what he had to do one more time and forgetting anything that could stop him. Just the way that now, for a little while, he would let himself forget he was human.

JOEY FINISHED TIGHTENING the cinch around Acorn's barrel and made sure his rifle was secure in its scabbard. The three-quarter moon was bright, so he would have to be careful; if any of the Blackwater hands were out tonight, they would see him as clearly as he would see them.

Don't be a fool, boy. Holden's words still stung as much now as they had that morning. They'd eaten away at Joey all the time he'd lain flat on his stomach, shaming him over and over. *You're no killer, and you'd be more a danger to yourself than Sean.*

Grinding his teeth so loud that they squeaked, Joey swung up into the saddle. He'd thought a lot about what he should do, lying on that bed. Maybe Holden was right. Maybe he wasn't a killer...not good enough, anyway, to do the job proper. He'd have to get mighty close to Sean, and even if he got away, it wasn't him likely to be blamed, but Holden.

He didn't want that to happen. Holden had said he would punish Sean, but it didn't look to Joey like he was in any hurry. Well, Joey wasn't going to let anyone keep thinking *he* was a coward. His back still hurt like the devil, but he couldn't stay at Dog Creek one more day knowing Holden still considered him a boy, a child, too stupid and weak to take his own revenge.

By the time he returned, he would have proven that he was smart, brave and clever enough to stand by Holden's side no matter what. He would never let himself be scared and helpless again.

Acorn snorted as Joey swung up into the saddle and headed west. He would start by the creek right where Sean had hurt him. He didn't want to go there. That was why he had to. And it was likely that at least some of the Blackwater beeves were still there.

The one thing Joey wasn't afraid of was the wolf. It was his friend, a spirit-animal like the Indians talked about. He just hoped it never went anywhere near Sean McCarrick until Holden was through with him.

It took him nearly three hours to get to Willow Bend, keeping Acorn at a slow and steady pace. He saw right away that there were plenty of cattle on the other side of the creek, bunched up on the bank and under the live oak trees. Humming softly, Joey crossed the creek, rode around the herd and peered closely at a few lean flanks.

Sure enough, they were Blackwater cattle. It didn't look as though there were any mavericks or unbranded calves left, but that didn't trouble him. He'd set out knowing he would be breaking the same law Sean found it so easy to ignore.

Grinning, Joey patted Acorn's neck. The gelding knew just what to do. Together they drove a dozen Blackwell beeves across onto DC land, ignoring the animals' indignant moans and grunts of protest. Once he had the cattle well away from the creek, Joey planned to build a fire just big enough to heat the running brand tied to his saddle. It wouldn't be a perfect job, but when he was finished no one would be sure if they were Blackwater or DC beeves.

The night was still except for the distant yips of coyotes and the peeping of crickets. Joey was a good mile away from the creek when he heard a horse come up behind. Someone cocked a gun.

"Stop where you are."

Joey knew that voice. His stomach rolled over with fear and hate. He raised his hands.

"Get off your horse," Sean said.

Joey knew there was about a one-in-a-hundred chance that he could have gotten away, but he was so frozen that he could barely fall out of the saddle.

"Turn around. Slowly."

Joey turned. Sean was staring down from the back of his palomino stallion, backed up by two hands whose weapons were drawn and ready.

"You can't stay away, can you, boy?" Sean asked, leaning easily over his saddle horn. "It seems I owe that brute of a lobo some thanks for bringing me to the creek at so fortuitous a time."

Joey's mouth was too dry to spit. He jerked up his chin. "I don't know what you're talkin' about."

"If the beast hadn't been seen in this vicinity earlier this evening, I wouldn't be here. A pity it turned out to be such an unreliable ally." He stretched, wincing as his injured arm shifted where it hung in a sling against his chest, and for just a moment Joey forgot to be afraid.

"You didn't get it, did you?" he sneered.

The look on Sean's face wasn't pretty. "It eluded us—this time. But fortunately we have you."

Joey knew then that he didn't have a chance. It was obvious that Sean and his men had been trailing him since he left the creek. They had him dead to rights, and there was nothing he could say to defend himself, even if anyone would listen.

"Something tells me that Renshaw won't be coming to your rescue this time," Sean said. "And I don't imagine that you could survive another whipping. Then again, that isn't the usual fate of rustlers, is it, boys?"

One of the hands, a Blackwater man named Cash, shook his head. "No, sir," he said. "It's hangin'."

Sean smiled, his eyes half lidded like a bobcat in the sun. "That seems fair. Don't you agree, Joey? We'd be within our rights to string you up from the nearest tree, and no one would complain."

Joey could feel his bladder begin to loosen. He should stand up to Sean, even if he paid with his life. Stand up and show the bastard what it was to face an honorable man.

But Sean had turned him into a thing that didn't deserve to be called a man. He didn't want to die. He was young. He loved the big sky and the wide plain and the oaks by the creek. He loved Holden. He loved being alive.

And if he was hanged and Holden found out, Holden wouldn't just beat Sean up the way Joey had expected he would after the whipping. There would be blood and more blood, all of it on Joey's hands if he let himself be killed.

"I'm sorry, Mr. McCarrick," he whispered.

"What was that?" Sean twisted in the saddle. "Did you hear what he said, boys? He's sorry."

"Ain't that nice," Cash said.

Audie, the other hand, looked away and didn't answer.

"What'll you do to prove it, Joey?" Sean asked with his devil's smile.

"I'll give you everythin' I've saved up from my pay," Joey said in a rush. "I'll never come near Blackwater again."

"Very impressive," Sean said. "But I don't think I can trust you, Joey. You want revenge, and you won't give up until you have it." He sighed. "No, I think we'll have to hang you. Cash?"

Cash produced a rope, already fitted out with a noose. He held it up and dangled it over his horse's withers.

"Audie, get the boy's mount. He'll walk back to the creek."

It was the longest mile of Joey's life. Sean talked companionably with Cash as if Joey didn't exist. When they got to the creek, Cash made a show of finding just the right tree, a tall oak with a strong, outthrust branch.

Joey fell to his knees. Cash forced him up and chivied him toward the tree. Sean tossed the rope over the branch. Cash took another length of rope and started tying Joey's hands behind him. Audie brought Acorn up to stand under the tree.

"Help him up, Audie," Sean ordered.

Joey fell again. "Please, Mr. McCarrick," he blubbered. "I said I had money. But I didn't tell you how much. There's hundreds. I'll give it all to you."

"Hundreds?"

Joey bobbed his head, catching a mouthful of dirt. "I swear it. I just have to go back to the ranch to get it, and—"

"Where did you get that kind of money?"

Panic sucked Joey's thoughts dry as Dead Man's Draw in early winter. "I…I found it."

Rough hands lifted him to his feet. "Where?" Sean demanded, pushing his face close to Joey's.

"In…in a hole," he lied desperately. "In some saddlebags. Someone buried it."

"And just where was this hole, Joey?"

"I don't remember."

"He's lyin'" Cash said. "Let's just hang him, and—"

"Shut up." Sean smiled, as evil a look as Joey had ever seen. "Maybe I'll take you up on your offer, boy. You go get the money, and I'll send a message telling you when and where to bring it."

It was too late to back out now. Joey felt ready to puke, knowing how he'd betrayed Holden by telling about the money Jed had meant for Rachel and running the ranch. And now he'd have to steal it.

"Don't think of going back on your word, Joey," Sean said, slapping his quirt against his leg so that Joey remembered every blow of the whuppin' Sean had given him. "If you do, I'll send the law to bring you in. No one will doubt my testimony as to your crimes."

Joey didn't doubt him for one second. "I...I understand, Mr. McCarrick."

"Good boy." Sean chucked Joey under the chin as if they were friends. "Go home and wait for my message."

Cash untied Joey and let him get back up on his horse. Joey could hardly hold the reins. Audie swatted Acorn's rump so hard that the gelding broke right into a gallop.

Joey didn't try to slow the horse. He couldn't feel his legs. He couldn't feel any part of himself except his heart, and it was hurting more than he thought anything could hurt.

Tonight he'd wanted to prove to Holden that he was a man and not a kid, smart and not a fool. He'd done worse than fail. Sean had made him just as bad as *he* was.

The worst thing he could do now was return to Dog Creek and wait around for Sean to tell him when to bring the money. Only one thing was going to stop Sean now, and that was Holden.

He'd promised Joey that he would punish Sean, and though Joey didn't know exactly what he planned to do, it was bound to be soon.Then Sean wouldn't dare make good on his threat to hang Joey for rustling.

Then maybe I can come back.

Joey turned west and kept on riding.

Chapter Eleven

RACHEL WALKED SLOWLY around the gelding Maurice had saddled for her, pressing her damp palms to her skirts. The Frenchman had assured her that Jericho was gentle enough for a beginner, and she prayed his judgment in such matters was sound. She had hoped to ask Joey's opinion this morning, but he, like Holden, was still absent.

Worrying about Joey would serve no purpose until Holden had returned and could look for him. And she certainly didn't want to think about *Holden*. She smiled at Maurice to conceal her unease and turned her attention to the gelding. He eyed her mildly and blew air through his lips.

"Do not worry, *madame,*" Maurice said, looking almost as nervous as she felt. "He is *un cheval admirable.*"

"Yes." Rachel wet her lips and looked at the mounting block. It did not seem sufficient to help her climb up on the animal's massive back, but she was determined to try. At least she would not be compelled to leap into the saddle as Holden seemed so adept at doing.

dea had come upon her in the sleepless hours awn. She had thought it might be easier to go r work after Holden had left, but the opposite had proved true. She had scrubbed dirty clothes and sewn and mended until her fingers were raw and her back ached, but not even complete exhaustion had been sufficient to give her a good night's rest. When she'd slept at all, she had suffered from dreams of Louis and Holden, violence and betrayal.

It was after one of those nightmares that she'd thought of learning to ride. She was beginning to feel just how isolated one could be in Texas. She would be all but useless on a ranch without an ease around horses and an ability to handle them. Once she could ride on her own, she could leave the immediate area of the house, go to town, even visit the neighbors, without relying upon Holden or one of the other men to take her.

If Jed were here, she wouldn't have to rely on Renshaw for anything.

The more she could reduce her dependence on him, the better. At the moment, she feared his return every bit as much as she feared this docile animal. Conquering one fear might make it easier to conquer another.

Now she stood in the yard, a few stray chickens scratching and pecking around her feet, hoping Jericho couldn't sense her fear the way some animals were supposed to do. Fixing her mind's eye on her goal, she approached the mounting block. Maurice murmured to the horse and stroked his cheek. Jericho bobbed his head as if to offer encouragement. She lifted her skirts—the widest and least constricting she owned— and climbed onto the block. The plain Western saddle seemed as far away as Ohio.

Maurice had shown her how to mount. She grabbed the saddle horn, gripping it so tightly that her fingers stung, and put her left foot in the stirrup. Jericho didn't move. Rachel pulled her skirts above her knees, revealing her unadorned cotton drawers, and swung her right leg up and over. For a moment she balanced precariously between the saddle and empty air, and then she leaned just a little and plopped onto the hard leather. The air burst out of her lungs in a rush of relief.

"Very good, *madame*," Maurice said with a grin. "*Très bien*."

She closed her eyes and let awareness move slowly through her body. It felt very strange to be up so high on the back of such a creature, strange and yet not as terrifying as she had imagined. Jericho was very warm and very solid. He shifted his weight a little, and she found that her balance adjusted without any thought on her part.

She hooked her right foot into the other stirrup, grateful that she'd brought one pair of very worn but practical boots with sturdy heels. She wished she'd had equally sturdy undergarments; she was afraid that after a while the saddle would begin to chafe.

But she didn't intend to do too much today. Just enough so that when she saw Holden again, he would see she was not utterly dependent upon him. He would understand that she had no need to put up with his outrageous behavior. And that she would be a good wife for Jedediah, in every way.

"You are all right, *madame?*" Maurice asked, shading his eyes against the rising sun.

"Very well, thank you. Would you be so kind as to lead him a few steps, Maurice?"

The Frenchman obligingly pulled on the lead rope, and Jericho began to move. Rachel rocked backward and held on to the saddle horn for dear life. But as Maurice led her in a wide circle, step by slow step, she began to glimpse—oh, so distantly—what it must be like to be one with such an animal, riding fast across the desert.

She laughed at such an image of herself and concentrated on matching her body's movements to the horse's gait. Jericho and Maurice were wonderfully patient. A dozen circles increased her confidence beyond anything she would have believed possible, and she found herself looking across the yard, past the stables and corrals and outbuildings to the vastness that had intimidated her for far too long.

"Maurice," she said, "I would like to ride a little farther out."

Following her gaze, Maurice scratched the thinning brown hair under his cap. "Are you sure, *madame?*"

"Quite sure. If anything should happen, I will not hold you accountable. It is entirely my decision."

He gave her a dubious frown, shrugged and pulled Jericho forward. Rachel let the gentle rocking lull her into a kind of contentment she had almost forgotten was possible. Before she knew it, nothing blocked the view of the creek, desert and distant mountain beyond. Soon it would be time to turn back, leave old Jericho to his rest, and return to Gordie.

She was just about to say as much to Maurice when Jericho pricked his ears, flared his nostrils and stamped one large, iron-shod hoof. Maurice tried to quiet him, but it was clear the horse had seen or heard something Rachel and the Frenchman could not. Rachel dug her feet into the stirrups, feeling a shiver race through Jericho's muscles.

The wolf seemed to rise up out of the very earth, its black coat grayed with dust. In the instant it took for

Rachel to recognize it for what it was, her only thought was that it was the most beautiful thing she had ever seen.

Maurice cried out in his own language. Jericho snorted, ears back, and crow-hopped. Rachel lost her seat, her right foot slipping from the stirrup and her body tilting sideways. She grabbed frantically at the saddle horn, but her fingers could find no purchase. Her next try caught Jericho's mane, and with a desperate burst of strength she pulled herself back into the saddle.

As swiftly as it had appeared, the wolf was gone. Maurice murmured soft, singsong words to Jericho, who settled almost as if nothing had happened.

"Madame?" Maurice said, gazing anxiously up at her. "*Êtes-vous bien?*"

"Yes. Only a little startled. May we go back?"

Quickly Maurice turned Jericho toward the house. Rachel leaned forward and wrapped her arms as far as she could around Jericho's neck. As they passed the inner corral, a man came running from the direction of the foreman's cabin.

Holden—hatless, bootless and naked except for his neckerchief and half-buttoned trousers—came to a sudden stop a few yards shy of Jericho and continued at a walk, his brows a solid dark line over his eyes. He went directly to Jericho's left side and held up his arms.

Suddenly boneless, Rachel let herself slide into his embrace. He swept her up, spoke brusquely to Maurice and carried her into the house.

Lucia, sitting at the kitchen table with Gordie in her arms and her own Pepito in the cradle on the chair beside her, rose quickly as Holden entered. Gordie stirred and wriggled, trying to turn his little body toward the door. Holden continued into the hall, nudged Rachel's bedroom door open with his foot, kicked it shut behind him and laid her on the mattress. He sat on the edge and leaned over her, his arms braced to either side of her shoulders.

"What in hell do you think you were doing?" he demanded.

Rachel was not quite dazed enough to ignore the accusation in his voice. She lifted one hand to push him away, preparing an equally scathing reply. The moment her palm touched his chest, she forgot what she had been about to say.

Holden sucked in his breath. She could feel his heart under his ribs, beating almost as fast as hers. His skin was slightly damp, muscle and flesh hard as stone under her fingers. The fierce anger in Holden's eyes changed to another kind of passion, and she had perhaps a moment of warning before he caught her lips with his own.

Rational thought had no part in her response, or in anything she did then. She raised her arms and pulled him down, opened her mouth to his, let his probing tongue silence her gasp of pleasure. She ran her hands over the bunched muscles of his back and shoulders, glorying in every powerful line and plane. She closed her eyes and let his sheer masculinity sweep her along a path she had shunned for so many long, lonely years.

She moaned in protest as Holden drew back, mourning the loss of what he denied her. But he didn't apologize. Nor did he rise and walk away. He continued to lean over her, his eyes searching hers.

"Rachel," he said softly. "You could have been killed."

His words had the effect her ever-weakening discipline could not. The jolt of realization took the strength out of her arms, and she lowered them close to her sides. Her skirts were in disarray, pushed up almost to her knees, but she was in no position to straighten them. Holden still had her trapped, pinned to the bed, but she could not have moved if she tried.

What in heaven's name have I done?

Holden seemed not to notice the tears of shame stinging her eyes. "You should have waited for me to come back," he said. "I would have showed you what you needed to know." His finger drifted close to her face and stroked across her forehead, pushing a damp tendril of hair back among the others.

"I…I didn't need your help," she whispered.

"Sure you didn't."

He wasn't taunting now. His voice had a sound that in any other man she might have called tenderness.

"Maurice…" She firmed her voice. "Maurice said Jericho was Jedediah's gentlest horse."

In one fluid motion Holden rose from the bed and went to stand at its foot, every hint of uncharacteristic tenderness erased from his expression. The name of his employer hung between them as if it were written on the air in scarlet letters.

"I don't know what got into Jericho," Holden said, his jaw so tight that Rachel was amazed he could speak at all. "He ain't usually spooked so easy, not even by—"

He broke off, and Rachel knew she had found a subject she could grasp as a shield against her humiliation and the raging assault on her senses.

"Did you see the wolf?" she asked.

"I saw it."

His answer was curt, and Rachel could almost feel

him withdrawing into himself, so far that no words of regret or apology, even if she could speak them, could possibly reach him. But she knew he wasn't only regretting that he had broken faith with his employer, just as she had done with the man she was to marry. If he felt contempt, it was not only for her.

He had also been afraid for her, as if she was something precious. Someone to cherish, and not only for Gordie's sake. He was furious at his own weakness. He didn't want to want her any more than she wanted to desire *him*.

Oh, yes. She was quite safe now. As long as she didn't so much as glance at his superbly displayed physique, the symmetry of his broad shoulders, his eyes, his lips. She rose onto her elbows and tried to decide how she might get up without doing anything that might be deemed provocative.

"Was it the same wolf that attacked the outlaws?" she asked stubbornly.

Holden went to the window and simply stood there, his hands at his sides, his trousers riding low around his hips. "Looked like it."

"Why did it come here?"

He turned his head so that his profile was limned in golden light. "He shouldn't have been there. He shouldn't have been so close to the ranch after dawn."

"You won't…you won't shoot him if he comes back?"

His laughter cracked like brittle glass. "You don't want me to?"

Rachel scooted across the bed and swung her legs over the side, smoothing her skirt as she stood. "He was beautiful," she said.

Every muscle in his back seemed to clench at once. "Most people wouldn't agree with you."

"I know I should have been afraid, but I wasn't. He didn't try to hurt anyone." She walked backward until her shoulders rested against the door. "I think he meant to help Joey."

"Don't make the mistake of believin' a lobo thinks like a man."

"Perhaps more men should think like lobos."

He looked straight at her, his remarkable eyes suffused with so much pain that she could hardly keep from gasping. "Don't get too fond of that lobo, Rachel. Sometimes wolves take calves and sheep. That's their nature, 'specially when folks drive off their natural prey. He's likely to get himself kilt sooner or later."

"Please. Don't speak that way." She heard the rising emotion in her voice and calmed herself with great effort. "Will you give your word that you won't hurt him?"

"Not if it matters to you so much."

"It does." She swallowed. "I want to…thank you for your assistance."

"It won't happen again."

He wasn't talking about the wolf now. He was giving her the same warning he was giving himself: don't get into any more trouble. Because it wasn't just words now, innuendo and blunt questions about her carnal needs and desires. One more misstep…

There wouldn't be one. She could still draw back from the brink, and so could he. Holden Renshaw, for all his roughness, had a conscience. She had her past. And what was left of her honor.

"If you're goin' to ride," he said, his voice as easy

and cynical as always, "you'll have to learn to do it right and proper. I'll take you out tomorrow."

"You needn't," she said. "Maurice is willing—"

"*I* need to see you in the saddle and able to handle Jericho before I'll be satisfied," he said, looking at the door instead of at her. "I'll put you on Banner this time. You afraid to try again?"

"No, I…am not."

"Good." He started toward the door, and she moved hastily out of his way. He went past her without a single glance.

"Holden."

A tremor went through him, making him seem for a moment as skittish as Jericho had been in the presence of the wolf.

"There is something you should know about the baby."

He swung around to face her, his expression suddenly open and raw with emotion. "What about him? Somethin' wrong?"

"Nothing at all. It is simply that I have taken the liberty of giving him a name."

His expression closed again. "You named him?"

She bristled. "You seemed uninterested, and no child should be without a name."

Two steps took him to the door and out of the room. Rachel followed him into the parlor, where Lucia was still holding Gordie. She rose as Holden stopped before her.

"Señor Renshaw?"

Holden peered into Gordie's face. The baby looked back at him with serene interest. Rachel came up behind Holden, careful not to get too close, and smiled at Gordie. He smiled back.

"What's his name?" Holden asked, his voice little more than a whisper.

"Gordon, after my father."

Holden's lips moved, silently repeating the name. He lifted his hand toward Gordie and let it fall again. "Ain't too bad," he said gruffly.

With those three words he did more than grant his approval. He gave her a gift that she sensed he gave rarely, if ever: his trust. And oh, how terrible a gift it was.

"I call him Gordie," she said.

"Gordie." Holden raised his hand again, brushed the blanket near Gordie's face with his fingers, moved them just enough to touch the soft, pink skin. Gordie cooed, batted at Holden's hand with his own and took firm hold of Holden's finger.

Standing frozen, as if he feared a single movement might injure the boy, Holden cleared his throat. "He's strong," he said.

"Very strong," Rachel said. "And very precocious, which you would know if you spent more time—" She broke off, cursing herself for being so ready to quarrel again. Heightened emotions of any kind were perilous.

She searched Holden's face for some telltale sign of anger. Not so much as the twitch of an eyelid gave him away. He slipped his finger from Gordie's grasp.

"Looks like he's well now," he said. "Reckon you can take him out of the house if you want."

Her pride in Gordie made her risk a smile. "Indeed. I do take him into the yard when I work near the house, but he should do well with longer outings very soon, provided it is not too warm."

"He's a Texas boy," Holden said. "He'll get used to

the sun." He glanced at the floor, seemed to remember his shoeless state and edged toward the door. "I got to look for Joey."

"You knew he was gone?"

"Didn't see him in the spare room. I'll find him." He looked straight at her for the first time since they'd left the bedroom. "You stay away from the horses until I come for you tomorrow."

His bare feet made no sound as he left the house. Lucia offered Gordie to Rachel, and she reached out to accept him into her arms.

Tomorrow she would be very close to Holden. What could he be thinking? How was she to be near him and pretend that nothing had happened?

What in God's name was she to do now?

"*Señora*, you are shaking," Lucia said.

Rachel was afraid to look up. How much had Lucia heard, or guessed? What would such a good woman, a selfless wife and mother of four, think of her employer now?

"It is nothing," Rachel assured her. She hesitated. "You must miss your family very much."

Lucia smiled with the warmth of deep affection. "They are spoiled, *mis muchachos*," she said, "but they understand what I do is necessary."

"And so very deeply appreciated," Rachel said, pressing the other woman's arm. "I hope they realize what a treasure they have in you."

"When do men ever realize such things?" Lucia met Rachel's gaze, the warmth mingled with compassion and sympathy. "Sometimes it is separation that brings such understanding." Still smiling, she lifted Pepito from the cradle and carried him into the hall. Rachel felt the weight of silence and isolation fall over her like a shroud.

Love could be a miracle. Lucia was living proof of the great good it could do when it was given and received in equal measure. But it could also be a curse.

"Why does love cause so much pain, Gordie?" she murmured. "Why were we given hearts at all?"

He raised his chubby arm and waved his fist until it connected with her chin. She kissed his dimpled knuckles. He had answered her question in his own wise little way. She would accept all the pain in the world as long as she had the heart to love this child. Even if that was the only kind of love she would ever know.

THE EARLY-MORNING light hurt Sean's aching eyes. Ulysses was sluggish after the work of retrieving the cattle Joey had stolen, but Sean was in no mood to indulge him. He was eager to get back to the house and a hot bath, where he could think in peace. If it hadn't been for the very satisfactory conclusion to his encounter with Joey, he would have been in a thoroughly bad temper.

But he wasn't. Seeing Joey so terrified of him had been gratifying in itself. That—and the knowledge that he now had complete control over the boy—would almost have been enough to make up for his failure to find the wolf. When one included the money…

The money. Found, Joey had said, buried in a hole. Its very existence might, of course, be a lie, but Sean didn't think so. The boy knew he would die if he'd lied, just as he knew he would be punished if he spoke of this second encounter to Renshaw or anyone at Dog Creek.

That left the question of who had buried the money, and why.

Kicking Ulysses into a canter, Sean worked to put his thoughts in order. He had known very well that Joey could not have forgotten where he'd found such a treasure, and in hindsight, he knew he ought to have pressed the point. But he had developed his own theory, and it was far more intriguing than any lie Joey might have told him.

Joey had found Jed's saddlebags.

If he had, he must have found them between the day Jed had died and Sean's return to the scene of the old man's death. Which meant Joey must have seen Jed's body. But he hadn't told anyone about it, or all of Texas would know by now.

Unless he had told only one man: Holden Renshaw. And if Renshaw did know that Jed was dead, he had carried on a very effective masquerade for the past two and a half weeks. In which case he hadn't wanted anyone else to know that his boss was gone for good—including Jedediah's "wife."

Sean smiled acidly. That, of course, would alter a great many things, answer some questions and raise others. Perhaps Joey hadn't found the money and the body at all. Perhaps Renshaw had. If, even in the absence of any knowledge of the multiple wills, Renshaw knew or guessed that Jed had planned to disinherit Sean, he was unlikely to think that the inheritance would come to him instead. Renshaw would naturally assume that Jed's final heir would be his wife.

And that would explain the attraction Charlie had observed between Renshaw and Rachel Lyndon. Renshaw would have every reason to curry her favor, even seduce her, to ensure that he would remain in control of Dog Creek when the "bereaved widow" found herself stranded in Texas with no knowledge of how to run such an outfit.

But Renshaw's understanding was still fatally flawed. His contempt for Sean would temper his ability to recognize Sean's intelligence and strength of purpose in fighting for what should be his. And the wills…

In a matter of days, the lawyer's office in Heywood would be lost to an "accidental" conflagration, leaving no evidence of the break-in that had occurred immediately before. As far as the world was concerned, Jedediah McCarrick's will would have been lost along with the office.

One will, however, would be on its way to Sean. The one he could use to destroy Holden and raise himself above any future suspicion with regard to Jed's death. The tissue of possibilities Sean had constructed was still fragile; until he questioned Joey again, much more thoroughly, he could not be sure that his theory would hold.

Oh, but if it did…

The vision of perfect revenge distracted Sean so much that he hardly noticed when Ulysses snorted and came to a stop a quarter mile north of the creek. With a sudden sense of danger, Sean jerked the horse in a tight circle. A mounted figure was riding toward him out of the west at an easy lope, and after a few moments' observation Sean was certain it wasn't one of the hands or a member of the Blackwell family.

Instinctively he reached for his gun with his right hand, remembering that he had moved the holster only when the searing pain dropped a red veil behind his eyes. He'd been a fool to ride back alone, but at least he wasn't far from the house. And the rider wasn't coming from Dog Creek, at least not directly.

Of course, Holden Renshaw might use just such a trick to catch Sean off guard.

Reaching across his waist with his left hand, Sean eased the Remington from its holster. A trespassing stranger could hardly object to a man being careful. Sean wouldn't shoot until he was sure. Until he could plausibly claim that Renshaw had drawn on him first.

As if he recognized the danger, the rider slowed his mount. Though he didn't move his hands from the reins, Sean sensed that the stranger was ready to draw on an instant's notice. He was tall and lean, like Renshaw, but Sean didn't recognize the horse. He lifted the revolver halfway and hesitated.

The rider brought his mount to a stop and raised both hands level with his head. "Easy there," he said. "I come in peace."

Sean lowered the gun and let the man advance, certain now that he was indeed a stranger. It wasn't any wonder he hadn't been sure: there was a superficial re-semblance between the man and Renshaw.

Resemblance or not, Sean didn't like being caught at a disadvantage by anyone. "Who are you?" he demanded. "This is private property."

"Is it?"

"The Blackwells own this range."

The stranger squinted, deepening the sun-sculpted lines bracketing his eyes. "I didn't see any fences."

"No one contests our borders."

The man pushed his hat back, revealing strangely pale golden-brown eyes and close-cropped brown hair.

"My name is Jacob Constantine," he said. "I have business with the Blackwells."

Sean was hurting and in no mood for polite conversation. "What business?"

Constantine twisted to reach for his saddlebags. Sean went for his gun again, but the rider had his own weapon out and aimed before Sean could lift his own gun again.

"It isn't polite to threaten a peaceful stranger," Constantine said softly. "Stand down."

Sean's fingers twitched as if they had a mind of their own. He couldn't beat Constantine under these circumstances, as much as he enjoyed the idea of teaching the man some manners. Slowly he replaced his gun in its holster and waited, jaw clenched, as the rider pulled a rolled paper out of one saddlebag.

Constantine unrolled the paper and held it out so that Sean could see it. "I'm looking for this man."

The broadsheet was crudely printed; the drawing of the wanted man, dark with a heavy beard and thick black hair, showed light-colored eyes and a strong nose, but little else of the features. The crimes were rustling, robbery and murder. The reward was very generous.

Sean shrugged. "Who did he kill?"

"A man he was working for in New Mexico." Constantine snapped the paper to straighten it against the wind. "Ever seen him?"

"No."

"His name is Heath Renier."

"I haven't seen him, and I assure you the Blackwells haven't, either. I'm the foreman here."

Constantine cocked his head and looked Sean over in a way that was just short of insulting. "Mighty fine for a foreman."

Sean jerked on Ulysses's reins. "You're welcome to be on your way."

The bounty hunter rolled up the poster and tucked it back in his saddlebag. "He may be clean-shaven now," he said. "And one thing that doesn't show too well in the picture—Renier has a deep scar across his neck. He probably keeps it covered."

A fleeting thought darted through Sean's mind, there and gone in an instant, before he had a chance to grasp it. "There's no such man here."

"Have you seen a lone wolf in the area? Black fur, bigger than most?"

Startled as he was, Sean kept his countenance. "What does that have to do with this man?"

"Some say Renier keeps it as a kind of pet."

That ephemeral thought returned, tinted by the memory of the wolf's attack and the shame of his own fear. Sean drove it away.

"No wolves like that," he said coldly.

"What about the ranch south of the creek?"

"Dog Creek. It belongs to my uncle. I know every hand employed there. No stranger in Pecos County stays anonymous for long."

If Constantine was disappointed, he didn't show it. "Thanks for your help, Mr.—"

"McCarrick."

"Mr. McCarrick." Constantine touched the brim of his hat, turned his horse and rode south toward the creek.

Fuming with anger, Sean watched until the man become a speck on the horizon, then turned Ulysses back toward the house. Constantine was like so many men in Texas: crude, unmannered, believing himself the superior of men with twice his ability and intelligence. If he'd been the one to catch Constantine unaware…

Sean jerked the reins so sharply that Ulysses skidded and reared. The thoughts that had passed so quickly through Sean's head during the conversation returned, crystal clear and astonishing.

It couldn't be. The wolf. Renshaw. It had seemed complete coincidence at the time, as it would to any sane man.

But what if it weren't? What if Holden Renshaw…

Holden Renshaw. Constantine was looking for a man named Heath Renier. H.R. A man with a scar hidden by a neckerchief.

Sean laughed, giddy and disbelieving. It was too fantastic. Renshaw always wore his neckerchief, but so did nearly every other cowman in Texas. He had black hair and light-colored eyes.…

Hadn't he always believed that Renshaw must have some great darkness in his past? Hadn't he always been certain the foreman was a barbarian, a malevolent devil who had come out of nowhere to claim Jed's affections?

Ulysses shifted his weight, his neck stretched in the direction of his comfortable stall. Sean ignored him. He was busy remembering every last detail of what the bounty hunter had said. The part about the wanted man having killed his employer. A man who had done such a thing once could easily do it again.

All such a man needed was a motive.

Sean sat very still in the saddle, half-afraid this dream might vanish with the slightest motion. That skeleton of an idea had grown flesh, and all it required now was the breath of life. That breath might come when he questioned Joey again…or when he found the ideal time and place to obtain the most damning evidence of all.

As for the wolf…if he found the opportunity to kill it, he wouldn't hesitate, but it was far more important to avoid any premature encounter with Renshaw. Killing him in "self-defense" could not possibly be so sweet as exposing him as an outlaw who had just murdered his latest employer out of jealousy and greed.

It only remained to lay the trap. If he could use Rachel Lyndon as bait, he might be rid of the other obstacle that stood between him and his destiny.

He had kicked Ulysses into motion and was almost to the house when Amy approached on her chestnut Thoroughbred mare.

"There you are, darling!" she exclaimed. She peered into his face. "My, but you look as happy as a cow in clover. Did you catch the wolf?"

Even being compelled to admit that he had returned empty-handed didn't dampen Sean's mood. "It's a clever beast," he said, "but it has chosen the wrong enemy. I'll bring it down, I promise you."

"Oh, I know you will." She drew the mare alongside Ulysses. "You work so hard, darling, and you've suffered so. But once we're married…"

Sean reached across the space between them to clasp her hand. "Yes, sweetheart," he said. "I can't wait." He pretended to let his mind wander for a minute or two and then turned to Amy again. "I've been thinking… how would you feel about throwing a party for Mrs. McCarrick?"

Amy's pretty lips pursed. "A party?"

"It occurs to me that I have seriously neglected my uncle's wife since I left Dog Creek."

"I did offer to visit her, but you said that Renshaw—"

"I didn't want you to go alone, but a party seems a perfect opportunity for you to meet. There can be no risk of altercations."

"Why didn't you let me ask my father to gather a posse to drive Renshaw away? No one likes him, and after what he has done to you, no one would object."

"I believe that would only have made things more difficult for Mrs. McCarrick, even if I were to return to Dog Creek. I suspect that Renshaw has strongly discouraged her from venturing away from the house. There is no doubt that he hates her, but he must have seen the value in convincing her that she should listen to his advice. I can't in good conscience ignore the situation any longer. She must be very confused about whom she should trust."

"Then perhaps we ought to wait until Jed returns."

Sean knew he was playing a dangerous game, but the potential reward was well worth it. "I hesitate to say it, Amy," he said, giving her a troubled glance, "but since we're soon to be married…"

"What is it, Sean?" She leaned toward him, all feminine solicitude. "You know you can tell me anything."

Sighing deeply, Sean met her gaze. "I'm not sure that Jed is coming back."

"I beg your pardon?"

"He's been away too long. I believe he would have sent some word to me long before I left Dog Creek."

Amy's face blanched with sincere alarm. "Do you think your uncle is…do you think he's dead?"

"It's only a feeling, you understand. I have been

ignoring it for some time. But now…" He shook his head. "All my instincts tell me something has happened to him. Mrs. McCarrick may be a widow."

Amy looked away. "If what you believe is true…" She stroked her mare's neck. "The poor woman."

"She is probably heir to my uncle's ranch."

Her always-erect posture stiffened even more. "Aren't you his principal heir?"

"I was. I haven't seen his will since I learned he was to marry, but I can't believe that he would neglect his wife in any bequest."

"You should have told me."

"Would it make any difference, Amy? Would you cease to love me?"

For a while she was silent. When she spoke again, her voice was cool and remote. "What do you think could have happened to him?"

"Any drive has its risks, and my uncle has always insisted on running his operations with the fewest possible employees. He didn't personally know all the drovers. One of them might have turned on him for the money. Most of the West is still wild and infested with criminals and other hazards."

She nodded thoughtfully. "Do you plan to share your thoughts about your uncle's fate with Mrs. McCarrick?"

"I have no proof. But people will begin to ask questions if he does not return soon. In fact, it's difficult for me to believe that Renshaw hasn't come to the same conclusion."

Amy ran her riding crop through her clenched fingers in nervous, repetitive strokes. "Do you also think that he's withholding this information to keep control over the ranch and Mrs. McCarrick?"

At times Amy could be almost bright. "It seems a strong possibility. It is by no means certain that Mrs. McCarrick will receive the bulk of the estate, but if she *is* the sole heir, Renshaw would want to be in her good graces until Jed either returns or is found to be deceased."

"But surely a man like him could never win any woman's favor!"

You haven't met her, Sean thought. "Renshaw, like most of his kind, can occasionally be clever, and Mrs. McCarrick knows nothing of ranching. If he makes himself essential to her, he'll have all the control he wants. He won't let her sell Dog Creek to us even if she decides to go back to Ohio rather than remain in such a hard place alone."

She slapped her crop into the palm of her hand. "I still can't believe—"

"As long as she remains isolated at the ranch, she will be under his sole influence. That is why a party would be such an excellent means of making her aware of the social and business opportunities in the county—and perhaps of learning what Renshaw has been telling her."

The heat was beginning to rise, reflecting brilliantly on the high polish of Amy's English riding boots. "Perhaps you're right," she said slowly. "We ought to arrange a general introduction for Mrs. McCarrick. I shall invite all the ranchers in Pecos and Crockett. Mrs. McCarrick will find she has a better ally in the Blackwells than in a ruffian like Renshaw."

Sean smiled. "Clever girl."

"Someone will have to fetch her, of course. I could send—"

"Renshaw himself will bring her, my dear."

She gaped most unbecomingly. "Invite him? Have you gone mad?"

"I doubt very much that he would let her come alone."

"I hadn't thought of that." She bit the end of her crop. "How can we be sure she'll come?"

"If we invite him as well and he attempts to keep her from coming, there would be a great deal of gossip. He may not care what others in the county think of him, but he won't want to raise too many questions or ruin her reputation. And if he accompanies her…" He patted Amy's knee with his good hand. "Renshaw will be compelled to acknowledge that she does have other friends, and Mrs. McCarrick will see what he truly is."

After considering for a few moments, Amy nodded. Though it was very short notice for the majority of ranchers who lived many miles from Blackwater, she agreed to convince her mother to hold the party in two weeks.

Of course it was possible that Rachel had come to the conclusion that Sean had tried to bribe her…or that, in spite of Sean's belief to the contrary, she had learned the truth of the whipping. She might even be reluctant to attend because her attraction to Renshaw had turned her against Sean for no other reason than that Renshaw hated him.

But that might not matter in the end. She could hardly refuse an invitation to a gathering hosted by the most prominent family in Pecos County. She would have to continue to paint herself as a respectable member of the community.

The Fates were on his side, but he must continue to show himself worthy of their regard. By the time the party ended, he would know if his scheme would come to fruition.

Chapter Twelve

OVER THE NEXT four days, Heath taught Rachel how to ride. Every dawn he met her with a touch of his hat brim and a mumbled "mornin'," she asked if he had found Joey yet—always with the same worry he tried to ignore—and they began the lesson. They both pretended that nothing had changed between them; Rachel concentrated on her learning, and Heath tried to close off all his senses. Later in the morning, when they were finished, he and Charlie would ride out to take care of the season's remaining work—not too taxing now, which was fortunate, considering there were only the two of them left to do it.

By late afternoon Heath would be searching for Joey, covering a different area each day, looking for any track, any trace of scent, that might tell him where the boy had gone. He even sent Maurice to ask in Javelina, and Charlie to Blackwater, but no one had seen the boy.

By the time it got dark, Heath was generally in a filthy mood. That was when he went over the creek to Blackwater and started hunting for Sean. But Sean didn't take his bait; no matter how often the wolf taunted or how close he got, Sean never came after him. The fact that Sean always traveled with at least two hands said he was still expecting Heath to make good on his threat, but he wasn't even willing to risk facing a lone lobo. His pride wasn't big enough to defeat his cowardice.

If it hadn't been for that unfinished business, Heath could have been on his way. He'd heard nothing more about the bounty hunter, but that could change at any time. And everything else was just about ready. Gordie was as fit and strong as Lily's colt. He sat up and looked right at Heath whenever Heath came to see him, his eyes bright and his mouth full of funny little babbles that Heath almost thought he was beginning to understand.

Then there was the letter from Ohio. All Heath had to do was show it to Rachel. She could go back anytime she wanted.

But he didn't show it to her, and he didn't leave. He taught her skills she would probably never use: how to mount properly, how to hold the reins and guide Banner, their second-oldest and gentlest horse, in a slow walk. On the second day he let her ride a big circle around the outbuildings. On the third, he let her try a trot, watching her every second. She didn't grab the saddle horn once.

Every day was pretty much the same. Every day, even when they barely touched, even though he let her use the mounting block and wore his gloves so he wouldn't have to feel her skin, his cock reminded him exactly what he was missing.

On the fourth day, Heath watched her canter Banner around the corral, keeping a close eye on the gelding's gait and her balance in the saddle. He could be at her side in seconds if she started to fall, but she never did. That was the only thing that saved him.

He pulled his hat low over his eyes as if that could block out the overwhelming awareness of her that never went away. How in hell had he managed to lose all sense just because Rachel Lyndon had almost fallen a few feet off the back of an old gelding?

A few feet that could have killed her, if Jericho had decided to spook. That was his fault, for coming near the house as a wolf instead of Changing first. But even his worry didn't explain why he'd almost started something he couldn't finish.

She'd looked at him with heavy eyes full of need, opened her arms and her lips, ready to open her legs and her body. Not to Jed. To *him*…

Banner came trotting up to the fence, ears swiveled back as he listened to Rachel's praise. Her smile faded as soon as she met Heath's gaze.

"Had enough?" he asked in the flat, even voice he always used when he spoke to her now.

"Do you think I ought to continue?" Same kind of voice, prim and almost respectful, as if she was talking to a teacher at one of those fancy schools back East.

"You done good." He opened the corral gate and followed her to the mounting block. He stood ready in case she needed help, but she got down herself and shook out her skirts.

"If you have no objection," she said, "I would like to try a longer ride tomorrow."

For no good reason, the back of his neck started to prickle. "What do you have in mind?"

"Away from the house. Along the creek, perhaps. I could ride Jericho again."

It wasn't such a bad idea, considering that she would need to ride on ground a lot less even than what was around the house.

She don't need to learn anything of the kind, he told

himself. *She'll be going back to a place she won't ever need it.*

"I thought we might take Gordie," she said, as if she felt the need to fill up his silence. "I think it would do him good to get out in the sunshine, if we go when it's still cool."

That was what made Heath decide in favor of a longer ride. It would be a good test of Gordie's fitness to travel.

And having him along would make it damn near impossible for anything to start up between himself and Rachel.

"All right," he said, watching the swish of Banner's tail so he wouldn't have to look into her eyes. "Day after tomorrow. We'll leave at dawn."

She nodded, began to move toward the house, then stopped again. Heath could feel that heat building up between them, heat that had nothing to do with the way the sun was starting to bake the ground and bleach the sky.

"Thank you, Mr. Renshaw," she said. And kept on going until she was inside and he was outside, with a solid door between them.

Charlie was out on the range, but Heath was in no mood to join him. He searched for Joey again, riding south this time. He left Apache in the shade of an abandoned, half-collapsed dugout and Changed, running another twenty miles toward the Rio Grande and back around.

It was no use. Wherever Joey had gone, the desert had done a good job of wiping out his trail. At least he hadn't met with an accident; a rotting body was one thing Heath could have found without any trouble.

He tried to make sense of the situation as he rode north toward the creek. Why had the kid run away? Last time they'd talked was the night Joey had seen the money, and Heath had told him Jed had left it for the ranch. He remembered Joey had wanted to go with him to punish Sean, and Heath had said he should get that idea out of his head.

Was that why Joey had lit off? Was he mad because Heath wouldn't take him along? The boy could be flighty sometimes, but most of his kit was still in the bunkhouse, and he would still be hurting from the whipping.

"Fool kid," Heath muttered, earning a curious look from Apache. "Reckon you'll be back when you're good and ready." Better to think that way than think Joey was gone for good.

But worry gnawed at him, and he knew Rachel would be upset again, the way she was every time he told her Joey was still missing. Instead of going straight home, he turned east instead and went on to Javelina.

Sonntag was sweeping the street in front of the store as if it were paved instead of dirt. He watched Heath dismount, set the broom down and followed him inside. Heath pretended to look around and wandered up to the message wall. The wanted poster for the murderer Heath Renier was gone.

"Can I help you, Herr Renshaw?" Sonntag asked, coming up behind him. "Another cradle, perhaps?"

"You got one?" Heath muttered, staring at the blank space where the poster had been.

"*Nein*, but I can easily order—"

"Did they catch the outlaw?"

Sonntag moved to stand beside him and slid his spectacles farther up his nose. "So it would seem. The bounty hunter came in yesterday and took it down. He said the man had been caught elsewhere and he was returning to San Antonio."

Heath felt as if a whole passel of ants were scurrying around inside his skin. Someone else had been taken for him. Maybe someone innocent.

They'll let him go when they find out he's not the man they want. Meanwhile, Heath had just been given a little more time. Luck was on his side. Luck he didn't deserve.

"A relief, *nicht wahr?*" Sonntag said.

"Yeah." Heath turned for the door.

"Herr Renshaw, I have more of that jam you like."

Without thinking, Heath followed the storekeeper to the counter and bought two jars. It was Joey who liked the jam, not him. But Joey would be coming back. And Rachel would like it, too.

He walked out of the store wondering why he felt like a jail-cell door had just slammed in his face.

"THE BOY AIN'T come back," Charlie said.

Sean slapped the yearling calf's rump so hard that it jumped and kicked and raced away, tossing its short-horned head. The other beeves in the corral kept well away from Sean, sensing his sudden anger.

"I told you not to come openly," he snapped, opening the gate.

The cowhand glanced around, scanning the out-buildings, corrals and the distant house. "I don't see no one around."

In Charlie's small and unimaginative mind, that would be enough. He was lucky that he happened to be right. Sean removed his gloves and tucked them into the waistband of his trousers.

"Do you think he's left for good?" Sean asked the hand as he strode toward the barn, forcing Charlie to keep up as best he could.

"Don't know, Mr. McCarrick. Could be he got too scared to stay."

Sean scowled. The situation had seemed so promising until he'd learned that Joey had never returned to Dog Creek. Now he appeared to have lost one of his best sources of information…not to mention the location of the hidden saddlebags.

I should have had him followed, Sean thought. But he hadn't seen the need when he was so certain that Joey wouldn't dare cross him. It had simply never occurred to him that the boy would ride away from the only place he could call home, certainly not without the resources his secret cache could buy.

Of course, there was still the unpalatable possibility that there had never been any money at all, and Joey had believed that Sean would take full revenge when he learned the truth. In that he was certainly correct.

Perhaps the boy was a better liar than Sean had judged possible, but he wasn't clever enough to evade a determined, skillful pursuit. Sean would gladly have hired someone to hunt Joey down…someone like that bounty hunter Constantine, who had apparently left the area not long after he'd arrived. But with only a little over a week remaining until the party, it was unlikely that the boy would be found in time to tell Sean what he wanted to know.

"What d'you want me to do, Mr. McCarrick?" Charlie asked, aware enough of Sean's mood to keep his distance.

"Renshaw is still looking for him?"

"Yessir. He's startin' to seem a mite worried."

Worried because he was concerned for the boy, or because he and Joey shared secrets he didn't want uncovered?

"Continue to keep watch," Sean said. "If he does return, I want to know about it first thing. And if he looks as if he'll run off again, you get him alone, secure him and bring him to the old dugout at Dry Spring."

"Yessir."

"Go. And don't let yourself be seen."

Charlie disappeared, and Sean turned for the house. The setback was hardly to be dismissed, but he was by no means prepared to relinquish his plans. Tomorrow Amy and her mother would tender the party invitation to Mrs. McCarrick and her foreman. Sean had the will from Heywood in his possession, and the unquestioning loyalty of enough men to do whatever needed to be done.

The Fates had not abandoned him yet.

HEATH FINISHED saddling Jericho and Apache before the sun was up. Rachel's scent drifted to him across the still air as he tied the blanket roll onto the saddle, and he half turned to watch her walk across the yard.

She was dressed in the brown calico skirts she always chose for riding, and he figured she was also wearing the boy's britches he'd given her to protect her legs from chafing.

Hellfire. Last thing he needed now was to think about her legs and what they could wrap around. He looked away so he wouldn't have to notice the luster of her dark hair, the curve of her lips, the unconscious sway of her body. Lucia was right behind her, carrying Gordie all wrapped up in enough blankets to keep a horned toad comfortable at the North Pole in December.

"Buenos dias, señor," Lucia said.

"Mornin'." He glanced at Rachel. "You ready?"

Her hesitation was so slight that he almost didn't notice it. "Yes," she said. "Nothing about Joey?"

He shook his head. "He'll turn up."

Her tongue darted out the way it did sometimes when she was worried or scared, but she knew as well as he did that there was nothing more to be done. After a few seconds she moved closer to Jericho's head. "Hello, boy," she murmured.

"You ain't scared?" Heath asked.

"We've been through this before, Mr. Renshaw."

Her voice was crisp and businesslike, allowing for no argument. As long as she was prickly, he could keep pretending to forget the times when she'd been soft. Soft all through her body, ready to forget about Jed. Ready to let him in.

He must have cursed, because Rachel gave him a wary look and backed away. Heath busied himself with buckling on the saddlebags—filled with a hearty breakfast Maurice had insisted on preparing—to Apache's saddle, while Lucia helped Rachel fix up the sling she would use to carry Gordie against her chest. When they were finished, Lucia took the baby and Rachel approached Jericho again. Heath bent and made a stirrup out of his hands.

"Shouldn't I use the mounting block?" she asked, her voice quivering a little.

"Ain't no mountin' blocks on the range," he said. "Go on."

Her little foot fit easily in the cupped palms of his hands. He waited until she had a firm grip on the saddle horn and boosted her up. She settled easily, the skirts falling around her legs so that the hem brushed the tops of the boy's boots he'd found for her. She took up the reins and sat upright and easy, as if she'd been born in the saddle.

Another reason to admire her. Another strike of the brand, burning its way through flesh and bone and into his heart.

Except you couldn't burn what wasn't there. And never would be again.

Taking the sling from Lucia, he helped Rachel ease it over her head, then lifted Gordie and tucked him inside. Heath's fingers brushed her bodice, and she gasped. He clenched his teeth and went to mount Apache.

They started toward the creek, Heath in front. His human ears tried to stretch behind him to catch the creak of her saddle, the clop of Jericho's hooves, every little sound she made and breath she took. The smell of her, sharp in his nostrils, made his cock so hard that it was almost painful to sit in the saddle.

Rachel caught up, riding beside him but far enough away so they couldn't touch by accident. "Where are we going?" she asked.

"About seven miles west of here there's a bend in the creek with a stand of oaks for shade. Think you can ride that far?"

"Of course I can." She bent her head to smile at Gordie. "Isn't that so, little one?"

Setting his jaw, Heath pulled ahead again. They rode the first few miles along the creek in uncomfortable silence, broken only by Rachel's quiet chatter to Gordie, pointing out this bird or that scurrying lizard. Heath could see how interested she was in everything she saw. She gave a little cry of surprise when a jackrabbit bounded across the trail ahead of them, and listened intently to a meadowlark's call.

He'd been telling himself from the beginning that a woman like her couldn't find anything to like in a place so brown and hot and barren. But he was beginning to wonder if he'd been wrong.

No future, no past. That was what he had to keep on remembering.

An hour after they'd left the house, Heath called a stop for rest. He dismounted, took Gordie from Rachel and held the baby in the crook of one arm as he helped Rachel down, catching her around the waist as she climbed out of the saddle. He heard her suck in her breath and hold it until she was firmly on her feet and reaching for Gordie.

"You need to drink and stretch your legs," Heath said, letting Gordie go as soon as he was safely in Rachel's arms. "If you're hungry—"

"I'm not, thank you." She made a fuss over Gordie's blankets. "I believe that Gordie would like a drink from his bottle."

Angry again for no reason at all, Heath took the bottle out of the saddlebags and gave it to Rachel. She looked along the bank of the creek, picked out a rock big and flat enough to sit on and set about feeding Gordie. She acted as if Heath wasn't there, humming under her breath, and kicking at small rocks and pebbles with the toe of her boot.

Heath crouched a little distance away, not even trying to ignore her. He'd given up trying to figure out when she'd stopped being plain to him and started to be beautiful, or when he'd begun to think she could be the kind of woman who could love someone else more than herself. She and Gordie together were something whole and perfect, like a circle that could only be broken if someone else stepped into it.

He's my son. But that was just a bunch of words that Heath still didn't understand. Just like he still didn't know how to be a father. Or a—

Heath saw the scorpion scuttling from underneath the rock the second after Rachel kicked the stone aside. She didn't notice the creature climbing onto her boot until Heath was beside her, snatching her and Gordie off the ground and sweeping the scorpion away.

Rachel let out a *woof* of surprise and stiffened in his arms, turning her body as if to shield Gordie from his touch. "What do you think you're—"

"Don't move." Heath let her go and looked for the scorpion. It had disappeared, but he had a good idea where it had gone. He turned the nearest rock over with the toe of his boot. The ugly thing snapped up its tail, and he stomped down hard. Rachel gasped.

"Never kick things over out here," he said harshly. "You don't know what you might stir up."

"Is that a…?"

"Scorpion."

He turned around just in time to see her legs start to give out. He grabbed her again, circling her and Gordie in his arms. She shook her head frantically.

"Take Gordie. I'm not sure I can—"

"Hold on." He whistled sharply to Apache, who moved within his reach, and untied his bedroll with one hand. He shook it out, tossed it on a bare patch of ground and eased Rachel down, making sure she had the baby secure before he let go. She was trembling so hard that he thought she might shake right out of her clothes. Gordie's face was all bunched up in confusion.

Heath crouched beside them. "Ain't nothin' to be scared of now," he said gruffly.

The sound she made wasn't exactly crying, but it wasn't laughing, either. "It…it could have—"

"No one out here ever died of a scorpion sting," he said. "It would have hurt, maybe swelled up a little, but it couldn't have stung through your boot anyway."

She stared at him, all dark eyes in a white face, rocking Gordie back and forth, back and forth. "My boot?" she echoed, as if what he'd said hadn't made any sense. "It could have stung Gordie!"

Only if he'd been blind and deaf, but he could see that Rachel wasn't listening to reason. She wasn't scared for herself. She was thinking of what could have happened to the baby. Because of *her*.

"Listen, Rachel," he said in the kind of voice he would have used with a badly spooked horse. "It ain't your fault. You didn't know—"

"Take him!" She held Gordie out to him, the tears running down her cheeks. "I can't…I almost—"

"Hush." He knelt in front of her and took her in his arms again, the baby snug between them. "It ain't your fault, Rachel," he repeated.

The sobs came tearing out of her throat like a sickness he had no power to heal. Her fingers bit into his arm, and she pressed her face into his shoulder. Gordie started to cry, and all Heath could think about was keeping them both safe in his arms as long as they needed him, even if he had to hold them for the rest of his life.

Sometime later—he didn't know how long—Apache bumped his shoulder and nibbled on his ear. He came to his senses again. Rachel and Gordie had stopped crying. Gordie was settled in a cradle made by his chest and Rachel's arm. Rachel's fingers were still caught in his shirtsleeve, and her head was still tucked into the hollow of his shoulder. They were so quiet he wondered if somehow they'd cried themselves to sleep.

He eased away just enough so he could see Rachel's face. She stirred, her hand slipping away from his arm. Her eyes were red and puffy, and there were creases in her face where it had rested against his vest. She met his gaze, too exhausted to be wary or afraid or ashamed.

"I think Gordie's asleep," Heath said.

She looked down at the baby, and for a second Heath thought she was going to smile. Instead, she leaned away and wedged her arms under Gordie so she could hold him. Heath had no choice but to let them go. It was like dropping through a scaffold at the end of a noose.

"You all right?" he asked.

"Yes, thank you." All proper again, but humble and sad and weary. "You…you should take Gordie now."

He dropped back onto his heels, every muscle stiff and sore, a fist-size rock in his throat. "He's where he belongs."

Her hair, which had come loose sometime during her panic, fell across her face like a ripple of black velvet. "Don't you see? I'm not fit to care for him. I'm not—"

"You ain't perfect? Is that it, Rachel?"

He hadn't meant the words to be gentle, and she didn't take them that way. She stared at him through her hair while Gordie kept right on sleeping in her arms.

"You said you cared about him," Heath said. "Carin' don't mean givin' up when times get hard, or just because you made a mistake." He leaned toward her, holding her with his eyes. "You always run away when you think you ain't good enough?"

The paleness of her skin gave way to hot color. "You don't know," she whispered. "You have no i—" She closed her eyes and touched Gordie's cheek with hers. "No. I don't always run away."

Heath let out his breath and was about to stand up when he smelled human sweat and horseflesh downwind. He turned back to Rachel immediately and offered her his hand. She took it, cradling the baby close with her other arm.

Charlie Wood came around the willow thicket on the other bank, whistling softly. He reined in his horse at the edge of the water, looking surprised to see them.

"Mrs. McCarrick," he called, touching his hat brim. "Mr. Renshaw. Didn't know you was here."

Heath lowered his head. "What're you doing here, Charlie?"

"I was just on my way to check on a calf I saw limpin' yesterday out by Blue Spring," he said. He studied Rachel curiously. "Is somethin' wrong, Mr. Renshaw?"

"No. I been teachin' Mrs. McCarrick to ride."

"I saw that back at the house." Charlie showed dark, crooked teeth. "You're turnin' out to be a mighty fine rider, Mrs. McCarrick."

Rachel smiled without much enthusiasm. "Thank you, Mr. Wood."

"Well, I best be gettin' on my way, then." Charlie nodded to Rachel, turned his horse around and rode back the way he had come.

Heath stared after him. Charlie couldn't have seen anything that had happened or Heath would have smelled him long before. Once or twice Joey had been able to sneak up on him, but that was a rare event. Even so, he found himself bristling and inclined to ride after Charlie to…

What? Ask him if he was following them?

He shook his head sharply. "We'd best be movin' on," he said to Rachel.

She turned her head slowly, taking in the creek and the horses and the open range. "Perhaps we should go back."

"Is that what you want?"

Brushing her hair out of her face with a work-roughened hand, she steadied Gordie and moved to rise. "No," she said. "I would like to go on."

Heath didn't know why that felt like a victory. He should have wanted her to be scared, let her think that the Pecos was a deadly place no sane female would want to live in.

But he'd lost that chance. He'd lost a lot of chances, and he would go on losing them if he let himself keep on thinking that what Rachel felt should make a difference in anything he was going to do.

He's where he belongs. The words had come out of his mouth as if someone else had said them. He'd made it sound as if he wanted her to keep Gordie forever.

He was just as much a son of a bitch as Sean had ever been.

"I'm going to lift you into the saddle," he said. "You just hold on to Gordie."

Rachel fixed up the sling while Heath shook out the blanket and rolled it up again. Then he put his hands around her waist and lifted her and the baby into the saddle. If she was surprised at how easy it was, she didn't show it. She squared her shoulders and looked straight ahead. They finished the second half of the trip without another word between them.

Three-Oak Bend was one of the prettiest places along the creek, close to one of the springs that fed into it. Birds chittered among the leaves, and quail scattered as the horses approached. Small animals rustled the slender branches of the willows crowded on the bank. A blue heron spread its wide wings and lurched into ungainly flight. The ground along the bank was trampled, but there was no other sign of cattle. And no sign that any human being had been this way recently.

Heath led Rachel down the gentle slope to the shade under the trees. He dismounted, helped her down—careful to let her go as soon as he could—and untied the blanket roll and small crate he'd brought for Gordie to sleep in.

"He still asleep?" he asked her as she stood gazing at the clear water and the silvery fish darting near the surface.

She stroked her fingertip across Gordie's forehead. "Yes. I think perhaps the commotion exhausted him."

Heath set down the crate and rolled out the blanket. "You need to drink."

The way she looked over the ground told Heath she wasn't done worrying yet. "No scorpions here," he said. "It's safe."

With a soft sigh she knelt beside the crate and laid Gordie in it, tucking the blankets around him. He didn't even move. Heath filled his canteen with water from the creek, gave it to Rachel and unsaddled the horses.

After laying the saddlebags in the short grass beside the blanket, Heath went down to the creek and pretended to examine the hoofprints around it. When he went back, Rachel was sitting on the blanket, examining the cold fried chicken, biscuits and little cake Maurice had sent along.

"I believe Maurice should have been a chef for some wealthy French nobleman," she said in a high, light voice. "I wonder what brought him to Texas."

"Same thing that brings a lot of folks," Heath said, leaning against the tree farthest away from her. "He wanted a life where nothin' was holdin' him back or fencin' him in."

She looked out across the creek. "It does seem as if nothing could ever enclose this country."

"They already got bob-wire fences some places east of the Pecos," he said, "but the cowmen around here don't favor the Devil's Rope."

"I think I understand why." She smoothed her skirts over her legs.

"Do you?"

Hellfire. The last thing he wanted was to let loose more trouble between them, and asking her that kind of question was the worst kind of trouble. He turned his back on her, hoping she wouldn't answer.

"One builds one's own fences," she murmured so quietly he knew he wasn't meant to hear.

He should have left it at that. But he remembered her tears, the hurt in her eyes, the pain she had finally let him see. The feel of her sobbing into his shoulder, clinging to him, as if he could save her.

"You broke out of yours," he said. "All them jobs, that world that made you small. You traded 'em in for somethin' bigger."

Leaves rattled in a little puff of wind. Heath could hear Rachel's breathing, soft and fast.

"I never spoke about my previous employment," she said.

Not to *him*. He could say that Jed had told him, but all of a sudden he was sick of lying.

"I found your letters," he said.

He expected her to be mad, maybe storm at him in

that schoolteacher way of hers. But she kept sitting where she was, staring at her hands folded on her skirts.

"It seems you know more about me than you ever admitted," she said.

"I know that you was sent to live in an orphanage when you was a little girl and didn't have no way out except workin' jobs you hated."

Her head jerked up. "I never said—"

"You didn't have to." He pushed away from the tree and went down to the water's edge. "When you wrote about what you wanted in life…" He picked up a stone and tossed it into the center of the creek. "You told Jed a lot of things, but not everything."

The quiet was so deep that it felt like every living creature in the Pecos had gone to sleep. "You're right," she said in a voice weary and sad. "I didn't tell him everything."

His neck started prickling again. She was about to say something important. Something that would finally explain why she was so afraid—afraid of her own passion, of losing her dream, losing Gordie.

"You once asked me if there had been someone… before Jed," she murmured. "There was a man in Ohio. He—" She stopped, her eyes focused on a past he still couldn't see. "What does it matter now?"

But it mattered to Heath. She'd known another man. A man who'd wanted her, taken her in his arms, heard her soft gasps of pleasure…

His upper lip lifted in a snarl. "What did he do?" he demanded. "Why did you leave him?"

"You have no right to ask me such things," she whispered.

Heath spun around. "Who was he? What made you leave?"

A hawk cried above the willow thicket, and Rachel lifted her head. "I did not leave him," she said. "He left *me*."

Chapter Thirteen

THE BEAT OF HEATH'S heart was louder than the rumble
of stampeding cattle across hard-packed earth. "What
did he do to you?"

"It doesn't matter!" She closed her eyes. "Why do
you care, Mr. Renshaw? It has nothing to do with you.
You have no claim on me, and you never will."

No claim? He wanted to prove just how wrong she
was, grab her and throw her down on the blanket and
erase that other man's touch from her body.

"That's what you're runnin' from, ain't it?" he
demanded. "This man you thought you loved."

"You talk a great deal about love for a man who
knows nothing of it!"

She was right. He didn't know anything about love.
Not a damn thing. For most of his life he hadn't even
believed it existed except in stories.

He threw his last pebble into the creek with unneces-
sary violence, and paced back and forth along the bank,
tamping down his anger as hard as he could. He'd
apologized only a few times in his life, and he wasn't
ready just yet to add another one to the short list.

But the fact was that she'd trusted him with information she could have kept to herself, knowing what a son

of a bitch he could be. She'd trusted him just to listen, and he'd attacked her instead.

If she kept on trusting him, she would end up being hurt worse than he could stand. But maybe she would hate him less if she knew a little of what made him what he was. Not everything, never that, but just enough.

With a sigh, Heath walked back to the trees and eased himself down against one of the trunks, knees up and hands dangling between them. "You said I know more about you than I'd admit," he said. "Reckon it's fair you know more about me."

She looked at him narrow-eyed, as if she expected him to grow a pair of mule's ears on the spot. "Perhaps I don't wish to know more," she said.

But she did. Like so many times before, her eyes gave her away...her eyes and her lips and the scent of her skin.

"You asked me once what *I* was runnin' from," he said quietly. "When I was a baby, younger even than Gordie, my ma gave me up. She didn't want me because I didn't fit in the world she was born to."

Rachel covered her mouth with her hands. "Holden, I—"

He kept talking, knowing he would lose his courage if he stopped even for a moment. "She gave me up to a couple named Morton," he said. "They didn't have no kids of their own, so they was glad to have me to help on their farm. I wasn't much use for a few years, but I was always strong for my age. Soon as I could follow orders they put me out in the field to pick the weeds, fetch and carry, whatever they could find. They didn't have no time to raise me up as anythin' but a servant."

Heath had been careful to keep his voice level, but some of the feelings got through, the feelings he'd kept hoping were dead and gone. Rachel was leaning forward with her fists tight in her lap, her eyes big, shining pools.

"I'm…I'm so very sorry," she said. "Did you have any friends? Did you go to school?"

Easier to laugh than let her see even a little of the old hurt. "The Mortons liked keepin' to themselves. They couldn't spare me for no schoolin'. By the time I was ten, I was doin' more work than the few hands they hired on. If I ever complained, Pa Morton was ready with the belt."

"He beat you?" She swallowed. "What about your foster mother?"

"She tried to stop it sometimes, but she didn't care enough to make it stick." He shrugged. "For twelve years," he said, "I took it. Didn't reckon I had anywhere else to go. Then somethin' happened. I finally stood up to Morton, and he took out his shotgun. That's when I left."

Arms wrapped around her ribs, Rachel rocked just as if she was holding Gordie and needed to soothe him. "You were only a boy!"

"I should've left a lot sooner."

"Where did you go?"

He shrugged. "Wherever I could find a way to keep myself alive."

Tears squeezed out of her eyes. "Yes," she whispered, as if she really did know just what he'd had to do to stay alive. He barely kept himself from jumping up and taking her in his arms and telling her not to cry over him. Not *him*.

"It's over," he said roughly. "Over and done."

She wiped at her eyes and shook her head. "Is it?"

How many times did he have to remind himself that

she never let go of a notion once she had her teeth in it? "I stopped runnin' when I came to Dog Creek," he said, knowing how soon he would be proving himself a liar.

The big blue heron that had flown away when they arrived appeared among the willows across the creek and waded into the water, stately as a judge. Rachel watched its head dart down to catch a little fish in its long beak.

"What finally made you stand up to Morton?" she asked.

The question wasn't unexpected. "Pa Morton beat me one time too many," he said.

The way she looked at him gave him the feeling she didn't believe him. If it hadn't been for what had happened with Jed, he might have told her, taken the chance one more time. But he could still see Jed's face. No outright shock or horror or disgust, just a mask he would wear as long as he had to, until he could get rid of the creature he'd treated as a son.

Oh, Rachel had found the wolf beautiful. She'd believed it had helped Joey. She didn't want anyone to hurt it, and she said she wasn't afraid. But if she knew the truth, she *would* be afraid. And worse.

But maybe there was part of it she could understand.

"A week before it happened," he said slowly, "I saw a wolf runnin' in the woods near our farm. He was the prettiest thing I'd ever seen, and he was free. He could go where he wanted, and no one could tell him different." Heath removed his hat and rested his head back against the tree trunk, feeling the story unravel a knot beneath his ribs. "The wolf kept comin' to the same place, got really close to me sometimes, and I got to thinkin' of him as a kind of friend. One day I went to meet him and Pa Morton followed me. He shot the wolf right in front of me."

Rachel bounced right up from the blanket, fingers curled into fists like a boy in his first saloon brawl.

"Why?" she demanded. "Was the wolf threatening your livestock? Had it hurt someone?"

"He didn't do nothin'. Morton just wanted to punish me."

Rachel took a short few steps one way, turned and marched back again. "He was your friend!"

"As much as any wild thing can be a friend."

She lifted her chin and stood with legs apart and arms akimbo as if daring him to laugh. "If I had been there, I would...I would have shot the man instead of the wolf!"

His heart ricocheted around inside his ribs like a bullet in a tin can. Here was the she-cat in all her glory, the tigress Rachel didn't want to acknowledge. He didn't have any doubt that she could shoot someone if she had reason. Even if it was for him.

"Much obliged," he said, trying not to let her see how much she'd affected him. "Only I reckon it wouldn't be Morton you'd have shot if you'd had a gun before you came to Dog Creek."

She blinked, flushed and strode to the bank, wrapping her arms tight around her chest. "If I had had a gun..." Her head dropped as if she couldn't hold it up anymore. "The man I thought I loved...there was a baby. He refused to have anything more to do with me when I told him we were going to have a child."

Heath stared at her rigid back. "You wasn't married?"

"No. We were not married."

The knot that had started to come apart snapped back together again. *No one should be compelled to pay for a single mistake for the rest of their lives.*

Now he knew what that mistake had been. He'd started out looking for it so he could prove to himself that maybe she wasn't worth his concern, the same reason he'd challenged her about loving Jed. But all he could think now was what being unmarried and pregnant would have meant in her world—a world where folks measured other folk by rules that kept everyone, man or woman, in his or her place. She didn't have to tell him one more thing for him to know that she'd been cast out from her own kind, shamed and judged and condemned.

He didn't have a right to judge, not when he'd lain with a woman and gotten her with the child that...

The child.

A strange weakness washed through Heath's limbs, and a strident humming filled his ears. He stood, bracing himself on the tree trunk. "Where's the kid now?" he asked.

She tilted her face toward the sky, grief and longing and despair in every line of her slender body. "He died at birth. That is why I can no longer have children."

Shame came over Heath so hard that he almost couldn't catch his breath. She hadn't given the baby away or abandoned him. She'd wanted him, just the way she wanted Gordie.

But her man hadn't. He'd turned his back on Rachel when she'd needed him most.

"Why?" he asked hoarsely. "Why did the son of a bitch leave you?"

"I was to inherit most of my aunt's considerable fortune. That was all he wanted, and when she disinherited me because I..."

He wasn't even thinking when he went to her and

opened his arms. She walked into them, pressing her face into his collar. Heath rested his chin on her hair and shivered with wave after wave of rage and pity.

"I'd kill him," he said. "If I knew where he was, I'd—"

She gave a little hiccup of a laugh. "Shall I fetch your revolver?" Her fingers dug into his shirt. "No. I was very young then, and it was long ago. I survived."

Any way she could. Heath felt helpless, wanting to ease the pain she still felt and knowing he never could. All her secrets were clear to him now, from the reason she loved Gordie so much to why she was so scared of what her body wanted. It had betrayed her before. It was still betraying her.

"You never told Jed, did you?" he asked, hesitantly stroking her hair.

She started to pull away. "No," she said. "I'm not worthy of him. I never was."

He took her arms and made her look at him. "Maybe he was—isn't worthy of *you*."

Rachel searched his eyes, wondering how she could ever have thought that Holden Renshaw was a villain. In the past few hours he had become a different man. There was no disgust in his face as he held her now, no contempt, no judgment. He didn't regard her with lust in his heart. He was comforting her just as he had when she had endangered Gordie's life with her carelessness, as if she deserved such comfort. Such acceptance.

It could not be real. In a moment he would walk away. She could *make* him walk away.

"Most men would consider me a whore," she said, giving the word a bitter edge. "I thought I had changed, but I haven't. I haven't learned from my mistakes."

"Rachel—"

"If not for Jed and Gordie, you would have been glad to accept an invitation to my bed, wouldn't you? It would have been my sin, not yours."

His grip on her arms loosened, and she broke free, stepping back until her shoes splashed in the creek. "I lied to Jed. I didn't tell him about the baby, or that my own aunt threw me into the street for debauchery. Do you suppose he would still want me if he knew?"

Rachel could count on one hand the number of times she had observed any sort of vulnerability in Holden Renshaw, but she saw it now in the movement of his throat and the bewilderment in his eyes.

He doesn't know what to say. He can't deny any of it. He can't tell me it will be all right, that Jed will understand.

"He never knew me," she said. "He wanted a good woman, a companion who didn't expect anything more than a stable home and wholesome work. What he got was—" The words caught on her tongue, and she shook her head wildly.

He lunged toward her and caught her chin in his strong, callused fingers. "You think Jed's perfect, Rachel? He's not."

Now he was angry. At Jed? She had come to believe that his loyalty to his employer was real, not some bid for power as Sean had claimed, but that anger…

Water had begun to leak into Rachel's boots. She tried to move past Holden, but he put his hands around her waist and lifted her onto the bank. She walked quickly toward Gordie's crate as soon as her heels touched firm ground.

Miraculously, the baby had slept through the commotion, his face untroubled, innocence unsullied. Rachel lowered herself to the blanket. There were still things she had to explain before he woke. Holden had to know all of it, even though she could see no hope.

"I didn't lie only to Jed, you know," she said, silently counting Gordie's gentle breaths. "I lied to everyone when I came to Javelina. You see, I never married Jed, in Ohio or anywhere else."

Perhaps it was odd to expect outrage from him now, given what she had already revealed. But he didn't speak again until he was standing on the other side of the crate, looking down at Gordie with that strange, vulnerable expression still on his face.

"I knew you wasn't married," he said.

Gordie yawned, and Rachel held very still until she was sure he was sleeping again. "You knew?" she said numbly.

"It was clear from the letters you sent Jed."

The letters that revealed every dream she had come to cherish since she had lost Timothy, dreams she had never shared with anyone but the man she was to marry.

"You knew," she said thickly, "and yet you asked those questions, tried to make me—"

He dropped into a crouch, balancing on his toes with the careless grace that never ceased to fascinate her. "I was mad for a while," he said, "but I understand why you had to do it."

Rachel believed him. His very past spoke for his sincerity. But if he had felt that way, why hadn't he revealed his knowledge of her deception before?

Of course. Gordie. He'd treated her as a necessary evil when she'd first arrived at Dog Creek so that she could care for the baby, and he had continued to leave Gordie in her care even after he had briefly suggested she give the baby up to Lucia. He must have believed she would leave if her secret was exposed.

Was there any sense in thinking that his concern for Gordie was *not* his only reason for letting her think he'd believed her?

No. No sense at all. Yet if it was all for Gordie's sake, why did he sometimes behave as if he had only a passing interest in what happened to the boy? Why had he given her the cherished privilege of naming him? Why had he chided her for thinking of giving up when she had declared herself unfit to care for him?

She could think of only one reason in the world, the very reason she had almost dismissed only a few days ago. *I don't much care for folk who throw their kids away like rotten meat,* he'd once told her. It was so clear, and yet she was as much in the dark as ever. All the things she had learned from his story of his youth, and she still didn't understand why he would deny his own son.

Or why he would keep thrusting Gordie into her arms, as if he…

Hope for nothing. Believe nothing. Your heart can never be trusted again.

Rachel gazed past Holden's worried face. Why should she believe she had any pride left, let alone a future remotely like the one she had so foolishly envisioned?

"I told you I loved Jed," she said, her voice sounding remote and indifferent even to her own ears. "That was also a lie. I did not believe myself capable of that kind of love anymore."

She held her breath, but he said nothing, and he was no longer looking at her when she glanced at his face.

"I know now," she said dully, "that I can never marry

Jed. Not only because he is not likely to want me when he knows how I have misled him, but because I have learned that love is essential to me after all."

And if Holden Renshaw could not love, if the only affection he truly understood was the little he spared for Gordie, she would never marry at all.

Holden's boots scraped the ground, stirring last year's fallen leaves. "You deserve to be happy, Rachel," he said.

If she once looked into his eyes, she would begin to weep again, and she had had far too much of weeping. "I thank you for that. But no one can be responsible for another person's mistakes or expectations. I have chosen my own path."

"No," he said. "Someone else chose it for you."

"Is that really what you believe, Holden? That we do not control our own destinies?"

He scraped up a handful of soil and weighed it in his palm. "There ain't no such thing as destiny," he said, turning his hand over to let the dirt fall. "Just fightin' to survive."

Once, Rachel had believed the same. But something strange happened then, a peculiar, uncanny sensation of lightness that seeped up inside her like clear water rising through a poisonous murk. An inexplicable peace drove the despair from her mind and heart. She had but one responsibility now, and that was to Gordie. Even if Holden could not or would not acknowledge him, the child would never be abandoned. She would stay on at Dog Creek as long as necessary to make certain that he was adopted by loving parents, whether Jed returned today or in a year. If Holden loved Gordie even a little, he would help see that it was done.

She was free to make her own choices again, based not on society's dictates or the bonds of her own past, but upon the deepest desires of her body. Holden knew she had been reviled for getting with child out of wedlock. He didn't care. He, of all men, saw *her*, not a hussy who had failed to live as a good woman should. He had given her the only real compliment he knew how to give. Now that she had no dreams to defend, she carried no burdens. No pride to maintain, no use for a mask of prudence and respectability. No expectations, no need to do anything but live in this moment.

She held out her hand. Holden didn't see it at first. He was staring past the little grove of oaks, beyond the stretch of green that marked the spring, and out to the bleakness of the parched desert he called home.

"Holden," she said.

His gaze moved to hers as if she had jerked him by a chain bound tightly around his neck. His eyes were wide and strange, like those of an animal driven into a corner. He scarcely seemed to be breathing at all. But when she touched his hand, his fingers uncurled and a deep, shuddering sigh released all the tension in his unyielding frame. When she removed his hat and leaned forward on her knees to kiss him, she felt as if she were releasing them both from a cage built of empty fears and hollow rage.

Holden sprang free like a tiger escaping a lifetime of captivity, dragging her into his arms, hip to hip and thigh to thigh. She opened her mouth, welcoming the thrust of his tongue. His hands, spread across her back, moved down to cup her bottom, pulling her harder against him. His arousal seemed to burn through her skirts. Her breasts, trapped in their restraints of chemise and corset and bodice, begged for his caresses, and the ache between her thighs flared into something like pain.

She cried out in protest when he let her go, but he was far from finished. His fingers fumbled at the tiny hooks of her bodice, and she pushed his hands out of the way to finish the job herself. The edges fell open, and Heath pushed it away from her breasts and worked it over her shoulders until she was compelled to intervene again and remove it entirely.

But the corset still stood in the way. Breathing fast, she tried to focus her attention on unfastening the busk, refusing Holden's eager assistance. When she was done, she shrugged out of the stiff garment, which soon lay beside the bodice on the blanket behind her.

His hands were on her as soon as she was free, cupping her breasts through her chemise, working feverishly to uncover her naked flesh. She unbuttoned the placket of the chemise and pulled it over her head. Holden lifted her, one hand at her back and one supporting her bottom, until her breasts were at the perfect height to accommodate his mouth.

Then his lips were on her breasts, his tongue following a moment later with hungry little flicks that pulled her nipples into hard, aching peaks. She flung back her head and gave herself over to the wanton inside her, moaning and lacing her fingers through his hair as he suckled her, first one breast and then the other. He was not gentle, but she wanted nothing of gentleness after so long a wait. He kissed her again, almost savagely, and pushed her down on her back.

At last, the wanton cried. *At last!*

She tugged at the heavy folds of her skirts as Holden pushed them up over her ankles and knees and thighs.

The baggy boy's trousers underneath were a minor impediment, quickly disposed of and tossed aside.

Rachel's only thought then was to feel the hard length of Holden's shaft inside her, thrusting deep, filling the empty, aching space inside with his heat and power. Nothing else mattered, not even the fact that she might never feel such sensations again.

But he didn't lie over her and take her as she wanted so desperately. She felt the brush of warm air between her thighs, and then his mouth was there, moving almost gently now, and his tongue was gliding over those lips, licking and teasing until a gush of wetness spilled out, wetness he lapped up as if it were honey. He circled his tongue around and around until she was aching and thrust inside.

Rachel cried out, arching upward as he filled her, not as she had wanted, but so wonderfully that she forgot she had ever desired anything else. Her body began to quiver as he withdrew and teased her nub until she felt her body release with joyful ecstasy.

Closing her eyes, she lay still, savoring the deep, delicious throbbing and the peace that came after. Holden was pulling her skirts down, covering her again, hiding the vulnerability she had so willingly exposed.

And then he was standing, walking away, leaving her.

As she understood now that *she* had to leave. Because she had made her choice. Because she had betrayed Jed in every way possible. And because there would be no other time like this, no tender reprise, no declarations of devotion.

She had not expected any of those things. But hope, that merciless enemy, would not be silenced.

Until Holden walked away.

You deserve to be happy, he'd said. But not at Dog Creek. Not with him.

She sat up and began to pull on her clothes, chemise and corset and bodice. She rose and put on the trousers, buttoning them carefully. Then she knelt beside Gordie's crate. He was awake now, amusing himself with his own tiny fist, pushing it into his toothless mouth.

There was no doubt that he was healthy, changing so rapidly and learning so quickly that she couldn't remember ever having seen a baby so precocious. Jed would want him. He would find another woman, steady and reliable, to become his wife, to care for this remarkable child.

Or Holden would…

He would have to make his intentions clear once and for all. Even if he were to admit to being Gordie's father and commit to giving the baby a father's full care and affection, a bachelor cowhand could certainly not expect to raise a child alone. Or had *he* believed all along that Jedediah would adopt Gordie as he had once taken in an orphan boy named Joey?

One way or another, the issue must be settled before she could go.

"Holden," she said softly.

He stopped with a saddle in his hands, turning his head without looking at her.

"Swear to me that Gordie will always have a good home."

His body shuddered once, as if she had asked him for something beyond his power to give. But when he spoke, there was no hesitation in his voice.

"I swear," he said.

It was all she could ask for. Father or not, Holden had rescued Gordie. He would do what was necessary.

Gordie's life had just begun. Hers was over. Over and done.

Chapter Fourteen

THEY DIDN'T SPEAK again as Rachel gathered up the untouched food and Holden saddled the horses. Gordie gurgled and grinned while she fed him his milk, as if all the world had been made for his enjoyment.

Holden's touch was impersonal as he lifted her and Gordie onto Jericho's back. They rode back in the silence of strangers.

It was late afternoon when they reached the house. Lucia took Gordie off to feed him, and Rachel retired soon thereafter. She heard voices through the window as Holden talked with Charlie, and a little while later, he rode out again.

Rachel lay dry-eyed on the bed for several hours, unable to rest. Just after dark, Lucia came to inquire about her, passing on Maurice's concern, as well. She was able to answer quite steadily, and even ventured outside to thank Maurice for his interest and ask if Mr. Renshaw had gone to look for Joey. The Frenchman answered in the affirmative but eyed her intently, and she wondered if it was possible that her fresh sin was visible on her face.

Holden was still away the next morning when Mrs. Adelaide Blackwell and her daughter, Amy, arrived.

Lucia answered the door as Rachel changed Gordie's

diaper. She was astonished to hear strange women's voices after weeks of hearing no one else but Lucia, and she guessed immediately who it must be. She threw on her shawl, gave Gordie to Lucia in the hallway and continued with her heart in her throat.

"Fine ladies, the both of them," Holden had told her, and he hadn't meant it as a compliment. That, of course, meant little. They were the wife and daughter of the chief landowner in the county. Sean, whom she had hardly thought of for days, had gone to them when Holden had thrown him off the ranch. They might well think her unspeakably rude for not making herself known to them, though she knew it was usually the practice for the more established resident to call upon the newer.

What might Sean have said to them? Rachel had already concluded that he had very likely been behind the bribery attempt in Javelina and that he couldn't wish her well. He had certainly made no attempt whatsoever to renew any acquaintance with Mrs. Jedediah McCarrick. He might even have told them that he suspected she wasn't married, if he believed it would not incriminate him.

If they had even the slightest suspicion that she had been living at Dog Creek under false pretenses, let alone that she was a fallen woman…

Rachel laughed silently. *Remember that you have no pride left to lose.*

The ladies were looking around the parlor when she went to greet them, their expressions far too neutral to be approving. But they smiled pleasantly enough when she welcomed them and asked them to sit, painfully aware that she had nothing but hard, rustic chairs to offer them.

They were both attractive women, very "fine," just

as Holden had indicated…rosy and blonde, dressed in fashionable, snug-fitting gowns more appropriate to a very different setting. While Mrs. Blackwell was prim and formal, Amy's hazel eyes sparkled, and her smile held a surprising degree of warmth.

"My dear Mrs. McCarrick," she said. "I have been so longing to meet you. I see that everything Sean has said about you was true."

Rachel was sufficiently in control of herself that she didn't stiffen at Miss Blackwell's ambiguous remark. Miss Blackwell continued before she had a chance to reply.

"We sincerely hope that we haven't inconvenienced you by arriving so unexpectedly," the girl said. She glanced down at her gloved hands. "We have been unconscionably remiss in not calling upon you before. I hope you can forgive us."

Rachel would gladly have wished them to the devil, but there was no help for it now.

I could tell them the truth and be done with it. But she had no understanding of what such a revelation might set in motion. Holden clearly wanted her to maintain her masquerade, and she intended to do so until Gordie's future was secured.

"It is no inconvenience at all," she said, returning Amy's smile as if she truly meant it. "I have been remiss myself. May I get you tea?"

"That would be delightful, wouldn't it, Mother?"

Mrs. Blackwell nodded briefly, and Rachel rushed into the kitchen. She had nothing better than a few stained china cups to serve in, and only the common sort of tea offered in the store in Javelina.

She returned to the parlor while the tea was brewing and pulled a chair nearer the Blackwells. "You must think me quite a hermit, Mrs. Blackwell, Miss Blackwell. I am afraid that I was a little overwhelmed by the country when I first arrived, and with Mr. McCarrick absent..." She smiled again. "That is no excuse, of course, but I do very much appreciate your call. I am sure that Jedediah would be equally pleased if he were present."

"Thank you, Mrs. McCarrick," Amy said. "That is very gracious of you. We had been concerned that you have been finding it lonely here in your husband's absence. How difficult it must have been to arrive in a strange place only to find no one to meet you."

But someone did meet me, Rachel thought. "I am grateful for your concern, Miss Blackwell," she said carefully, "but I've found so much to do here that I've scarcely had time to be lonely."

Amy nodded sympathetically. "One becomes almost accustomed to the isolation, though we do our best to lighten it with gatherings among the various ranchers in this and the surrounding counties." She smoothed a crease in her gown. "Have you heard from Mr. McCarrick?"

There was no turning back now. "Not recently, but..." She bit her lip. There was no reason why she couldn't tell as much truth as possible. "I confess that I've been a little worried."

The young woman's eyes sharpened with interest. "In what way?"

"Jedediah and I corresponded for a year before he married me," she said. "It is not like him to fail to write, knowing that I would have arrived weeks ago."

Amy reached across the space between them and rested her hand on Rachel's knee with a gesture that seemed impulsive. "Please don't worry. I'm sure there's a simple explanation. Jedediah is not only a good man, but he has spent many years in Texas and knows what he is about. What is your foreman's opinion? I know that he and Jedediah have been close."

Amy's mention of Holden raised Rachel's guard. If Sean was living with the Blackwells, they might very well share his opinion of Holden. In fact, she was certain of it. Though she had seen Holden with very few people, all of them at Dog Creek, she would be willing to wager all four of her dresses and her threadbare shawl that he had far fewer friends than Sean McCarrick. And Sean had certainly been eager to tell *her* of Holden's manifold sins against him.

"The last time we spoke of it," she said, "Mr. Renshaw was not overly concerned."

"There you are." Amy met Rachel's gaze. "You must find Mr. Renshaw invaluable."

"He is accustomed to running the ranch."

"But he is hardly personable."

"I expect nothing from him but that he keep Dog Creek in working order until Jedediah—" She broke off. "I am sorry about the quarrel between Mr. Renshaw and Mr. McCarrick. I was ignorant of the situation when Mr. McCarrick left."

"Of course you were. It was best that they be separated. They were never well disposed toward one another, and Sean now has an excellent job as our foreman."

The girl spoke lightly, but Rachel sensed a thread of anger underneath the casual words. Though there was no reason for her to think so, Rachel was suddenly struck by the thought that Amy might regard Sean as something other than her father's employee. They were both young and attractive, and Sean, in addition to being handsome and well-spoken, had displayed a keen ability for the same scheming he had attributed to Holden. A man of ambition and modest means would regard the daughter of a wealthy family as a very profitable catch, as Rachel well knew.

But what were Sean's ambitions? She had only the vague notions that Holden, and Sean himself, had put in her head. That and the fact that Sean obviously hadn't wanted her at Dog Creek.

"Men can be trying at times, can't they?" Rachel said, rising. "If you'll excuse me for a moment, I'll check on the tea."

By the time she returned with the tea things, such as they were, Amy seemed uninterested in resuming the topic. Instead, she brought up one just as uncomfortable.

"And how is the child, Mrs. McCarrick?" she asked.

Of course Sean would have told them about Gordie.

"Very well, Miss Blackwell," Rachel said. "He has thrived since Mr. Renshaw brought him to Dog Creek."

"And you have not located his parents?"

"Unfortunately, there was no way of finding them, since they had abandoned him at a deserted farmhouse. In any case," she said more brusquely, "his parents clearly did not want him."

Amy nodded approvingly. "May we see him?"

Irrational as her feelings might be, Rachel didn't want to show Gordie to the Blackwells. Nevertheless, she rose, went to the bedroom and took Gordie from Lucia, holding him close as she brought him into the parlor.

She expected Amy to ask to hold him, but the young

woman only extended one delicate, silk-clad fingertip and brushed Gordie's cheek. "How delightful," she said. "It is clear he has your affection."

"Yes."

"It would be ideal if Mr. McCarrick were to adopt him. Surely he will be glad to see such a strong, handsome boy when he returns."

Rachel swallowed. "I hope he will."

As soon as Amy withdrew her hand and Mrs. Blackwell had looked her fill—without comment—Rachel took Gordie back to the bedroom. When she returned, Amy seemed content to pursue more mundane subjects, such as the weather, the lack of the most basic women's sundries at the general store in Javelina and the social opportunities in San Antonio.

"Of course, we are limited here, but, as I said, we make the best of what we have," Amy said. "In fact, we had hoped, Mother and I, that you might consent to join us at a gathering at Blackwater in ten days' time. All the ranchers in Pecos and Crockett Counties will be invited, and you shall be the guest of honor. I know that everyone will wish to hear about your life in Ohio and your correspondence with Mr. McCarrick."

Rachel set down her cup with such force that it rang against the tabletop. "I...I am very flattered, Miss Blackwell, but—"

"Come, Rachel! May I call you Rachel? You cannot disappoint so many people, and I assure you that you will find a warm welcome. All the women—and there are not many of us—are eager to bring you into the fold. I do so much want to get to know you!"

At a loss for words, Rachel raised her cup and drank the cooling tea. Amy Blackwell had made an invitation she could not politely refuse. Rachel would ordinarily assume that it had been tendered in all goodwill and friendliness, with no ulterior motive. And in fact, that was almost certainly the case, and her unease was no doubt only due to a lingering fear of exposure. Indeed, what harm could all the Amy Blackwells of the world and their judgment do her now?

But in her determination to maintain her fiction just a little while longer, she had never considered the necessity of entering the local social sphere. She had intended to live quietly until Jed returned or she could creep away like a little field mouse when the first snow covers the autumn stubble.

"Mother," Amy said, sensing Rachel's hesitation, "tell her she simply can't refuse."

Mrs. Blackwell gave an almost imperceptible sigh. "Let me add my pleas to my daughter's, Mrs. McCarrick."

"Come, do," Amy said warmly. "Mr. Renshaw may escort you." She waved a hand in airy dismissal. "I don't expect there will be any trouble between the two men, not with everyone else there. Sean is arranging a hunt for that horrible brute of a lobo who so badly injured him nearly two weeks ago. I suspect that Mr. Renshaw will wish to join in, whatever his quarrels with Sean. After all, any wolf is a threat to every cattleman in the county."

Rachel went suddenly cold. She couldn't imagine why Sean would suffer Holden as a guest if he had any influence at all over the proceedings. But this mention of a wolf…

"A wolf attacked one of the outlaws when he was whipping Joey." That was what Holden had said that night in the stable. She had asked if there were many wolves in the area, and he'd replied that there were not as many as there used to be.

He had also said they almost never went after people. *Nearly two weeks ago.* Could two wolves have attacked two different men in the same area at the same time?

Rachel came very close to bolting, but somehow she managed to keep her seat. If it was the same wolf, the black wolf she had seen at Dog Creek, there could be only two possible explanations. Either the lobo was indeed a dangerous animal that had to be eliminated before it hurt someone again.

Or Sean McCarrick and the "outlaws" were one and the same.

"May we count on you, then?" Amy asked eagerly.

Rachel blinked at her, too dazed to do more than mumble her assent.

Amy clapped her hands.

"Wonderful!" she exclaimed. "We shall expect you on the twenty-third." She rose, lending her mother her arm. Rachel rose with them, belatedly aware that she had just committed herself to something that had awakened a sense of alarm she could not dismiss. Alarm that had nothing to do with her tenuous position, and everything to do with Holden and Sean McCarrick.

You need not go. Leave today. Tomorrow.

Somehow she managed to accompany the Black-wells to the door, where she took Amy's offered hand.

"I have so much enjoyed our visit," Amy said. "I know we shall become fast friends."

Rachel stood on the porch while the ladies ascended into their carriage—an actual carriage, not a wagon—and set off. Holden rode into the yard a few moments later, staring after the carriage with a hard, set look on his face. He dismounted, left Apache by the hitching post and joined her in the doorway.

"What were they doing here?" he demanded.

Rachel went back into the house and sat at the table, poised between fury and fear. "They have invited us to a party," she said, gazing bleakly at the door.

"A what?"

"A party, in honor of my arrival in Pecos County."

"You didn't say yes?"

She looked up at him, hoping no trace of her emotions showed on her face. "Was it Sean who whipped Joey?"

He stopped in the middle of an angry stride and swung to face her. "Sean?"

"Miss Blackwell said he had been attacked by a wolf at the same time your 'outlaw' suffered the same punishment," she said.

Narrowed eyes fixed on hers. "It was Sean, all right," he said grimly.

"For God's sake, why didn't you tell me?"

After four long weeks he had finally learned when she was not to be foisted off like a child. He shook his head and rumbled that peculiar, growling noise she had heard him make only when he was dangerously angry.

"It wouldn't have done no good," he said. "You wouldn't have believed Sean could do somethin' like that, 'gentleman' that he is. Even I hardly believed it. You couldn't have done nothin' about it, and I—"

"Did you see it happen? Were you there?"

"I stopped it." A muscle twitched at the corner of his mouth. "I had to bring Joey back, or I would have—"

"Why in heaven's name would Sean want to hurt him?"

Holden paced a tight circle and came to stand before the table again, his fists knotted with corded tendons and blue veins. "Because he hates Joey, just the way he hates anything Jed loved. Joey reminds Sean that he was cast off by his own pa, who had better things to do than raise a kid. Jed was stuck with a whelp who'd rather see someone dead than let them get anythin' he couldn't have."

"But what could Joey possibly have done?"

"He didn't have to do nothin' but get in Sean's way. Sean wanted to be the only thing Jed cared about, the one Jed would raise up to be the 'gentleman' he thought he should be. Sean decided he didn't have to play by no rules, because Uncle Jed owed him the easy life his pa didn't give him. When he didn't have things just the way he wanted, he tricked Jed, stole from him, used him like he was some stupid old man instead of the one who'd taken Sean in and given him a fancy education and duds and money for wastin'. And Jed kept lettin' him do it until just before he left. He was goin' to run Sean off himself."

How was it only now, when so much was coming to a head, that Rachel was discovering the secrets that drove Sean McCarrick and Holden Renshaw to such extremes of hatred? Of course Sean had despised her. He was clearly a bad man, and she was yet another interloper to take his place in his uncle's affections.

But Joey…he was only a boy. A child who could never have intended to arouse such violent resentment in Jedediah's nephew.

How could Sean possibly have expected to get away with the whipping? Perhaps there had been no other witnesses, but he would have to be more than a little mad to commit such an act, even in such a seemingly lawless country as this. Joey might be only an orphaned boy, but he was not without friends. Friends who would not hesitate to punish Sean for his crime.

If she could, if she had influence and money and power like the Blackwells, Rachel would have gladly punished Sean herself in any way short of outright violence.

She closed her eyes. After he had brought Joey to the house, Heath had said the outlaws "wouldn't be back." He had implied that he would kill them if they ever tried. But he had just said he'd stopped the whipping, and aside from whatever injuries the wolf had caused, Sean was still apparently hale and employed. No consequences had been called down upon his head for the senseless maiming of a boy who could have done him no harm in return.

Yet she had seen the look in Holden's eyes when he had spoken of Joey's attackers. If he had kept the incident a secret and convinced Joey to do the same, he must have had his reasons, and they would not be to Sean's benefit. Holden would never let Sean get away unscathed. There had to be an explanation for why Holden had taken no action. Why he hadn't spoken of Sean's crime at all.

Holden must have sensed her question before she asked it. "He ain't gettin' away with it, Rachel," he said softly.

With vivid, violent clarity, a vision played out behind Rachel's eyes, an image of Holden and Sean facing each other with Joey lying injured at Holden's feet. Perhaps there had been no open threats, but none would be needed. A single look from Holden would have been enough, that and the hatred between them.

"He'll pay," Holden said, leaning heavily over the table. "He'll pay, Rachel."

Pay with his life. Holden would find the gun she had

hidden. He would belt it on and walk onto the range and challenge Sean to a fight to the death.

She had thought to tell him that she would soon be packing and would be leaving on the next stage. But how could she say that now, when something terrible was about to happen? Something...she might somehow prevent?

With exquisite control, Rachel began to fold the diapers she had washed that morning and stacked on the table. "When did you intend to kill him?" she asked.

His fists bumped the table as he jerked away. "I had to be careful, Rachel. I wanted to find Joey first if I could, and I—"

"Is that why Joey ran away? Was he afraid Sean would hurt him again?"

Despair crowded the simmering rage from Holden's eyes. "He knew I wouldn't let anyone hurt him again. But he was..." He trailed off and shook his head. "It's just as well he's gone now. I didn't want to bring no trouble down on his head, or yours. I was waitin' for the right time. But now..."

Now. What had changed in his mind? Was it the party? Rachel's mind worked furiously, pushing aside the more distressing aspects of Holden's revelation. The invitation itself made no sense in light of what he had told her.

"Could the Blackwells know what Sean has done?" she asked, sick with sudden horror.

Heath's lips twisted in bitter amusement. "You think Sean would've risked makin' himself look bad by admittin' somethin' like that to anyone? The Blackwells ain't as nice as they seem, but they have a reputation to keep up. They wouldn't approve of open violence against someone from Dog Creek. And Sean wants Amy."

As Rachel had guessed. "So this party is being given in complete ignorance of Sean's behavior?"

He hesitated, his eyes moving with his thoughts. "Ignorance of whuppin' Joey, yes."

Which made perfect sense. Amy had let slip the bit about the wolf attack in complete and blissful ignorance of how it had really happened. Yet Rachel could not shake the dreadful feeling that there was something very wrong in the timing of the party.

"Would Sean have any control over who is invited?" she asked. "He scarcely knows me. Perhaps he now has reason to believe that you have not told anyone at Blackwater of his crime, but what if you had informed me? He would scarcely be in favor of such a celebration if he thought I might expose him."

"Don't reckon he thinks you *do* know," Holden said.

"But *you* were invited! Can it be that he doesn't expect you to take any action against him?"

Holden barked a laugh. "He *knows* I will. That's why he won't let me get anywhere near him when he's alone."

"Then he must expect you to challenge him at the party."

"Challenge him?" Holden's slow smile was more terrifying than the deadliest rage. "He knows no one would take my word against a gentleman like him, a settled landowner's kin with friends in high places."

"Then what…?"

She could have wept at her own stupidity. The picture she had formed in her mind was all wrong. She had always recognized the leashed violence in Holden's nature. She'd known he couldn't have worn that gun just for show, and had been prepared to consider that he might have killed in self-defense. Even yesterday, she and Holden had half seriously spoken of shooting Holden's adoptive father and the man who had abandoned her.

But that had been only talk, unlike Holden's plans for Sean. He had never intended to challenge Sean to a fair fight, no matter how likely it might be to prove fatal for one of them. He wouldn't see any reason to bestow such a privilege on someone who had hurt his friend the same way Pa Morton, a man he despised beyond any common hatred, had hurt *him*.

Shaking, she clenched her hands together and met his gaze. "Do you intend to murder him before the party, or when the Blackwells and all their guests are present?"

"I may not have no education, but I sure as hell ain't stupid. I won't do anythin' to Sean where anyone can see. No one'll ever know I done it."

Of course he would have considered such things, unless he wished to be executed. She ought to be glad. Perhaps he would succeed, and a villain would be prevented from ever hurting innocent children again.

But Holden would still be a murderer. He would have surrendered to his most bestial nature. He would never be the same again.

"I can't let you do it," she said.

"You don't have no choice about it."

"If you attempt anything at the party, I'll try to stop you."

"You ain't goin' to the party. You're stayin' here with Gordie."

"I don't see how you can enforce such a command." Rachel felt a new calmness taking hold, a frigid sense of purpose even Holden at his most intimidating couldn't shake. "And you have not addressed my belief that Sean must expect you to confront him in some way. You are a danger to him in more ways than one as long as this situation remains unresolved. Do you assume he will simply allow you to get him alone? He may be an evil man, but he is no more stupid than you are."

"You think he's settin' some kind of trap?"

"If Sean had anything at all to do with inviting you, he must have some purpose for doing so."

"If he does, it won't be your problem, 'cause you won't be there to see what he has in mind."

"I most certainly will be th—"

With an explosive breath, Holden yanked one of the chairs away from the table and sent it crashing to the floor. "Fool woman," he growled. "There's a few more things you'd better understand. The Blackwells may not know what Sean's been up to, but they ain't askin' you to their party just to be friendly. Artemus Blackwell has wanted this place ever since Jed claimed the south side of the creek. Blackwater is one of the biggest outfits in West Texas, but Colonel Blackwell needs the whole creek for the spread to grow as big as he wants it to be. He would already have swallowed this ranch whole if Jed hadn't made clear he wasn't acceptin' Blackwell's offers and stuck by his guns."

"But that has nothing to do with—"

He slammed his flattened hand on the tabletop. "Listen to me. Sean has always figured he was goin' to get Dog Creek after Jed was gone. The ranch was goin' to be his ticket to everythin' he wanted. He'd sell it to the Blackwells, go in with them and move up while they did. But when you showed up, he knew it might not be near so easy as he thought."

Understanding struck Rachel like the iron-shod hoof of a frenzied horse. Sean didn't merely resent her coming to Dog Creek because she might supersede him in Jedediah's affections. She had meant a possible—probable—end to his dreams. A wife would jeopardize his claim to the ranch and any other property Jedediah might leave behind.

But if he had known she was coming and believed she was married, why had he tried to buy her off?

"A man came to me the evening of my arrival in Javelina," Rachel said slowly. "He said that Jed had changed his mind and didn't want me. He offered money if I would go back to Ohio."

Holden stared at her, his mouth opening with a startled demand. She told him the rest in flat, brief sentences, and when she was finished, his face had gone pale.

"Son of a bitch," he whispered. "Sean told you *I* did it?"

"I knew it couldn't be true soon after I met you, but Sean came back when you were away getting Lucia. He tried again to convince me that you would do anything to be rid of me, perhaps even resort to violence. Even when I realized *he* must have sent the man to bribe me, I couldn't make sense of it."

Never had she seen a man's expression change so terribly as Holden's did then. "I thought he was lyin'," he said. "About knowin' you was comin', when he said Jed had told him and didn't tell me. But he found out. Damn you, Jed, what the hell were you thinkin'?"

Somehow Rachel knew Holden's present fury had not been provoked by Sean's attempted bribery. There was something else behind it, something so horrible that Holden refused to speak it aloud.

"What is it?" she whispered, unreasoning terror striking like a scorpion's stinger.

Lucia appeared in the hallway just as he began to reply. Her dark gaze darted from Holden and Rachel to the chair that lay sideways on the floor.

"*Perdón*," she said. "I thought I heard a noise. You are well, *señora?*"

The smile Rachel gave her was the falsest she had ever bestowed on anyone. "I'm fine, Lucia. Is there anything you need? Is Gordie all right?"

"*Sí, señora.*" Lucia hesitated, glanced at Holden and disappeared into the hallway. By the time Rachel had turned back to question Holden again, he had shut himself away behind a rigid mask of steel as honed and deadly as a blade.

"Sean wants you at that party for reasons of his own," he said in a voice as flat as the expression in his eyes. "He probably put the women up to it in the first place. He can't think you figured out it was him who tried to make you leave, or he wouldn't be sure you'd come. And if he knows you ain't married, he's keepin' it to himself. He sure as hell doesn't think you know about the whippin'." He swore again. "He must still believe he has some chance to get on your good side and have a say in what happens to Dog Creek when Jed—" He stopped abruptly, the muscles in his jaw clenching and releasing.

What Holden said made sense. Sean had already made an attempt to talk her into vouching for him when Jed returned. But he truly must not suspect she was capable of discovering for herself that *he* might have the best motive for bribing her, or what such an act implied.

But he was making too many dangerous assumptions. He assumed Rachel would go on believing his lies about Holden, and that she would never listen to Holden's side of any story. He assumed, though he had spent so little time with her, that she was stupid and blind and incapable of assembling facts in a way contrary to his interests.

As I was stupid and blind and incapable with Louis.

She was blind no longer. Whatever Sean's schemes for her, they were nothing compared to what his malice must be where Holden was concerned.

"What you say may be true," she said, "but it does not change my intentions. I will accept the invitation. Gordie will be fine here with Lucia."

His gaze met hers, and she was flung back to that first day when she had sensed the full weight and power and danger of his presence. But he didn't growl or threaten her again. His voice dropped so low that she had to strain to hear it.

"Don't do it for my sake, Rachel," he said. "I ain't worth it."

His pain cut her to the quick. "I…I will decide what is worth—"

"You don't know what I am. What I've done. I've committed crimes. I was a bad man. Worse than you can imagine."

It was a measure of how much she had changed that she could imagine the kind of past he had spoken of and feel not appalled and disgusted, but deeply sad.

"It doesn't matter what you've been," she said. "Only what you choose to do from now on."

"I ain't changin' my mind, not even for you. And even if I wasn't goin' to do it, you'd feel—"

"You always assume you know what I feel."

But he wasn't listening. "I've got some money," he said, beginning to pace again. "I'll give it to you so you can get away from here."

She was stunned by his sudden reversal. Only a few minutes ago he'd demanded she stay with Gordie while he went to find Sean at the party.

He wants to keep you safe, a part of her said. But why would he think she would leave simply because he offered her money? Did he think lack of means and fear of an uncertain future were the only things keeping her here?

Of course he didn't. But if he wanted to send her away for her own safety, why wouldn't he send Gordie, as well? Because Gordie couldn't interfere in his plans for vengeance?

"If I go," she said coldly, "I will take Gordie with me. He will need someone if you fail to return."

Chapter Fifteen

HEATH TURNED AWAY, went to the door and opened it, leaning against the doorjamb with his arms crossed and shoulders hunched. "I don't plan on gettin' killed," he said.

"Then don't insult me again by suggesting I would run away now."

Her words had a funny way of hurting even when he didn't think he had anything left inside him to hurt. He would have given ten years of his life if he could *want* to be rid of her. Forget how he'd felt after he'd pleasured her by the creek, the longing and need he'd tried so hard to kill.

If he let himself stay a coward and didn't drive Rachel away, it would be a hundred times worse when it was all over and she found out everything. Everything he'd lied to her about. What she was going to lose, even though she would have wealth and kinfolk and a chance to start over.

Maybe she really would try to take Gordie with her if she knew about the letter from Ohio.

He's where he belongs. He'd told Rachel that only yesterday morning, as though he'd been planning to let her keep him. What if he finally told her that Gordie was his son?

Sure, then try to convince her anything would be better than letting *him* decide what was best for the boy. She would ask questions he couldn't answer, questions she'd already tried to ask before.

But if she stayed, she might get into serious trouble trying to interfere. She was right about a lot of things. Sean hadn't made Amy Blackwell invite him to the party without good reason. He would be on his guard. He couldn't just show up, drag Sean away and kill him. He didn't know yet what he was going to do or how he was going to do it, though right now it looked as if Sean was handing him the perfect chance with the wolf hunt he'd arranged to follow the party.

But what else was Sean planning? A few weeks ago, Heath wouldn't have believed Sean capable of doing anything that might seriously risk the reputation he was so eager to make, let alone whip a kid half to death. A few minutes ago he'd realized that Sean might be worse than just crazy. He might be a murderer.

Heath closed his eyes, listening to the rumble of Maurice's voice in the bunkhouse as he spoke with Charlie, Apache moving around in the stable, and the quarreling of chickens foraging in the yard. He'd figured early on that Sean considered Rachel a threat to his ambitions just because she existed. Now he realized Sean had known Rachel was coming, and the son of a bitch had probably known a lot more than that. Jed must have told Sean at least some of his intentions. There wasn't any other explanation that Heath could see.

He could believe that Jed might have made the mistake of letting Sean know that his bride was on her way. But if he'd taken it one step further, told Sean he was planning to disinherit him, told him about the wills…

Sean was malicious enough to kill Jed and then try to make sure there would never be anyone else who could claim Dog Creek. But would he go that far, knowing that if one thing went wrong he could be hanged as a murderer? Would he have the guts for it? Whipping a kid wasn't the same as attacking a grown man who could defend himself, a better rider and marksman than Sean could hope to be in a hundred lifetimes.

Maybe it had been an accident. They could have met up when Jed was on his way back and fallen to arguing. Maybe Jed's horse had spooked and thrown him, just as Heath had thought. If Jed's death was deliberate, why hadn't Sean taken the saddlebags?

Because Jed hid 'em when he saw Sean comin'. Or he knew Sean was comin' ahead of time.

Rachel's touch on his shoulder nearly made him jump out of his skin. She dropped her hand right away, but Heath felt as if she'd given him a hard shake.

"I don't believe our discussion is over," she said, stepping back out of his reach.

She's waitin' for me to yell or threaten her again, Heath thought, but that wasn't enough to stop her from poking at him like a bear cub with a beehive. Why couldn't she have been a different kind of woman…a woman he could have ignored, despised, betrayed without giving a damn? Why did she have to keep looking at him that way, angry and determined and sad and caring all at the same time? What made him think he could make her go or do anything she didn't want to do?

He'd thought about leaving with the baby right after he'd found out about the bounty hunter. He'd decided against it because back then he'd figured Rachel wouldn't leave Dog Creek after he was gone, and Sean would make her life miserable. But she wasn't planning to marry Jed now, and she had somewhere to go. If he left tonight and made sure she got the letter...

Sean would get away with everything. Joey would still be missing. And Rachel would go on suffering, because she would have lost what she cared most about. What he was taking away from her. Gordie.

There wasn't any answer that would make things right. No matter what Heath decided, Sean had to die for what he'd done. Rachel would be hurt. And he would have to raise Gordie up alone and keep on running from the law.

Unless, like Rachel had said, he didn't come back from the fight, and Gordie was left an orphan at the mercy of humans who would revile him—or worse.

Swear to me that Gordie will always have a good home. And he'd sworn.

He looked at Rachel, who was still waiting, her dark eyes scared but defiant. *You always assume you know what I feel,* she'd said. She was right. Maybe he couldn't really know what she would feel if she learned the truth about what he was. Was it a sign of desperation that he had started wondering again whether she was the one woman out of a hundred, out of a thousand, who could really understand and accept him? That he wanted her to be that woman more than he'd ever wanted anything in his life?

A shudder of dread and pure, shameful fear ran through him. He could test her about some things, like whether or not she could understand why he'd kept Jed's death a secret, and if she could really care about the kind of man he'd been. But the only way he could ever find out the rest was to *show* her. And once he did that, there would be no going back.

"You're a good woman, Rachel Lyndon," he said, hating himself but knowing he had to tell her what was in his heart one time before he left her. "If I weren't the man I am…if things were different, I would ask you—" He released a shuddering breath. "I would take you 'n Gordie away and ask you to marry me."

Her eyes went wide, and for just a moment she smiled—that open, radiant smile he'd seen only twice before. He saw again in her face that feeling he'd seen by the creek when she'd offered herself to him, warmth and hope and affection brimming so full that she could give it to Gordie and still have enough left for him. She was waiting again, waiting for him to tell her that he *would* ask her, no matter what kind of man he was.

But he didn't say it. Her smile faded like the rose Heath had seen once in a vase on a crooked table in Frankie's room at the bordello.

"Thank you, Mr. Renshaw, for the sentiment," she said at last. "It is an honor to be considered for such a position, even if you feel yourself incapable of engaging in such a binding relationship. I assure you that I have taken your words in the manner they were intended."

Heath wished he could slit his own throat. "Rachel, I—"

But she was already walking away.

Marry me.

How strange that for one blissful moment Rachel had believed Heath had meant it.

She closed the door to the bedroom carefully. Gordie was awake, moving restlessly in his cradle, but Lucia had fallen asleep on Rachel's bed, clearly too weary to remain awake even after what she had overheard in the parlor.

I'm sorry, Lucia, Rachel thought. *You should not have had to listen to any of that.*

Thank God she hadn't heard the "proposal."

Rachel knelt on the floor beside the cradle. *I'd take you and Gordie away.* How long had Heath been thinking such things? Since they had lain together beside the creek? Or had it been an impulse of the moment, an impulse he knew he would never have to fulfill?

If I weren't the man I am. Hurt by his childhood, bitter, angry, hardened against the world. A "bad man."

Rachel pulled the pins out of her hair and lowered her head over the cradle. Gordie caught at the long loose strands with delight. It didn't matter what she thought. Holden was going through with his plan, such as it was, and she could think of no way to stop him. He seemed so confident that he would succeed, even as he apologized—to *her*—for what he was.

I ain't plannin' on gettin' killed, he'd said. And yet he was still afraid. Afraid enough that he could see nothing but emptiness ahead. When she'd threatened to take Gordie, he hadn't said no.

Perhaps he couldn't bring himself to say it. Would he try to stop her if she left with Gordie before the party? Once, she had told Holden that she would find a way to care for the baby if Jed turned him off, but only yesterday she had set all such thoughts aside because she couldn't give him the life he deserved.

Could she leave Holden to destroy himself?

She lifted Gordie out of the cradle and held him close. She had insisted she would accompany Holden to the party, but she wasn't sure she could bear to remain here that long.

Ten days. That was how long she had to decide.

Slowly she set Gordie down again and walked into the kitchen. Holden's gun was still in the cupboard where she had hidden it. She picked it up gingerly, stretching her fingers to fit around the smooth wooden grip.

Tomorrow she would ask Maurice to show her how to use it. She would tell him she was still worried about the outlaws Holden had warned her about.

The next week would be the longest of her life.

"IT's TRUE," CHARLIE SAID. "Mrs. McCarrick and Mr. Renshaw are betrayin' Jed."

Joey squeezed his eyelids tight together, holding the shameful tears at bay. His belly was flapping against his ribs, he was dirty and sore and his back still hurt, but this was the worst of everything that had happened to him since he'd run away.

After nine days of surviving as best he could, he had decided to come home. It would be a sore humiliation, admitting to Holden that he'd tried to rustle Blackwater cattle and been caught by Sean all over again, worse still explaining how he'd turned yellow and told Sean about the money.

But in the end, he'd known he had to do it. Nine days was enough for Holden to have taken care of Sean. Joey would have to face something he didn't want to do, but at least he wouldn't have to worry about being hanged for rustling.

Charlie had found him a quarter-mile from the house. Now he sat easily on his mount, shaking his head and sighing over the things he'd seen while Joey was gone.

"You can ask Maurice, if you want," he said. "He's seen the same things. They've been sparkin' ever since you left. Renshaw pretends he's teachin' Mrs. McCarrick to ride, so's they can be together without raisin' questions. But they've been goin' away from the house alone. I saw 'em myself." He sighed again. "Wouldn't be surprised if they up and run off together with that baby before Jed ever gets home."

Joey slumped in his saddle. Maybe it wasn't true. Jed had once said that cowhands were worse gossips than women at a quilting bee. Joey had only been gone nine days, and when he left, Holden had still disliked Rachel plenty.

Or had he? From the first time he'd met Rachel, Joey had thought Holden was crazy for hating her. Maybe she wasn't pretty, maybe Holden wasn't in the habit of liking women, but Rachel was good through and through, a right proper lady. Joey had been sure Holden would change his mind sooner or later. He'd just never figured Holden would ever look at Mrs. McCarrick as anything but Jed's wife.

Joey racked his brains for some clue as to when things might have changed. Most of the time Rachel had been fixing him up after the whipping, he hadn't known what was going on. She had fixed Holden up, too.

Was that it? Had Holden been grateful and softened toward her then? She was probably lonely with Jed away, and Joey wasn't so stupid that he didn't know that loneliness made people do things they wouldn't usually do.

And Charlie had said to ask Maurice. The Frenchie wouldn't make up something like that. Joey could find out the truth without half trying.

"Wish I'd found some other place to work," Charlie

said, as if he hadn't noticed Joey's silence. "I didn't want to stay at Blackwater, Sean being what he is, but I always thought Renshaw was a good man. 'Pears I was wrong. He's really betrayin' all of us, not just Jed. You, especially, after what happened to you at Blackwater."

Joey stared at Charlie. "W-what do you mean?"

Charlie gave him a look of pure pity. "I met one of the Blackwater hands down by the creek, and he had a story to tell about Sean whippin' some kid. I know Holden said you ran into outlaws, but I got to thinkin' he must have been lyin'." He squinted at Joey. "Reckon from the look on your face it's true. That why you left Dog Creek?"

Joey's face was so hot he thought he might explode. Sean would never have told anyone what had happened, but someone hadn't kept the secret. You would think they'd be too scared after one of them had shot Holden. But maybe…

Fresh hope almost wiped out Joey's shame and hurt. "Did Sean get in trouble?" he blurted out.

"That's what I'm tryin' to tell you," Charlie said. "This hand said he heard Renshaw promise to punish Sean for what he did to you. That true?"

Joey nodded numbly, hope crumbling like a biscuit made with too much flour.

"Too bad Renshaw didn't keep his word. Guess he was too distracted by Mrs. McCarrick." Charlie sucked on his teeth. "Hear tell Sean is doin' mighty fine with the Blackwells. They think the world of him, and he sure ain't sufferin' for what he did to you."

Dizzy and sick, Joey wished he could get off his horse. The last thing he wanted right now was to let Charlie see how upset he was, how much he wanted to die right there and then.

"Funny that Renshaw and Mrs. McCarrick are goin' to the Blackwells' party in a week. You'd think Renshaw would want to stay away from Sean when he didn't have the grit to stick up for you."

A party? Sean had invited Holden to a party? It didn't make any sense, but Joey didn't much care if it did or not. Holden had broken his word. It had all been lies. He *was* betraying everybody, just like Charlie had said.

The biggest shame of all was that Joey had come to think that Holden really cared about him.

I wanted him to be my father. But that would never happen. Never could have happened.

"Reckon you could go to the Blackwells, tell them what happened," Charlie said. "Maybe whoever saw it will speak up."

Joey laughed, but only inside. It looked as though no one knew about the rustling yet, but he could hardly believe Sean hadn't sent someone for him since he'd been away. Sean could tell the Blackwells about what Joey had done anytime, see Joey strung up before he could say one word in his own defense.

And no one would even try to stop him.

"I ain't stayin'," he said.

Charlie nodded sympathetically. "I'm thinking of leavin' myself. I'd take you with me, 'cept I don't have much money."

That was the problem. Joey didn't have a penny to his name, no kin, and nowhere to pick up decent, lasting work this time of year.

But he knew where to get plenty of money. He didn't owe Holden anything now. And if Charlie was right and Holden was planning to run off with Rachel, he would probably just take the money himself, anyway.

You'll be stealin' from Jed, too. But Jed hadn't told anyone about Rachel, had he? He'd lied, too.

"I got to go," he told Charlie. "Thanks for tellin' me."

"Your stuff is still where you left it in the bunkhouse," Charlie said. "Want me to come with you?"

"No. I don't want Holden to know I'm back."

Charlie shrugged, reined his horse around and rode west. Joey kept going toward the house. As soon as he couldn't hear Charlie's horse anymore, the tears came. He blubbered for about ten minutes, his eyes all puffed up and snot dripping from his nose. After that, he was able to start thinking again.

He would have to be careful. Holden had a way of hearing and seeing things other people couldn't, and he would know if Joey went sniffing around in his cabin. The good thing was that he had a habit of riding out most every night alone and was usually gone for hours. If tonight was one of those nights, Joey could get the saddlebags, steal Jed's fastest horse and leave Dog Creek forever. Maybe Holden would figure out who stole the money, but he would have to kill Joey to stop him.

Once, Joey had hoped to make Holden see him for a man, not a boy. Now all he wanted was to show Holden that betrayal could go both ways.

He dragged his arm across his nose, turned Acorn south and chose a deep draw a few miles from the creek, where he could camp until nightfall. He ate the two hard biscuits in his pocket, and pretended he wasn't scared and hungry and wishing he were dead. Three hours after sunset, with a three-quarter moon to light his path, he rode within a quarter-mile of the house, left Acorn in another draw and walked the rest of the way. He stopped behind the bunkhouse, listening, hoping Holden was really gone.

The yard was quiet. So was the house, and he didn't see any lights in the bunkhouse. Charlie wasn't anywhere in sight. Joey snuck into the building and found a couple of empty bottles on the table. He tucked them under his arm and slipped into the cookhouse to grab whatever he could find.

Step by slow step Joey crept into the yard. Crickets, the lowing of the milk cow and the stamping of a horse in the corral were all he could hear. The cabin was dark. He went around it and into the stable.

Apache wasn't there. Holden must be gone. Still, Joey was careful to take a good look around before he went back to the cabin. As he dropped to the floor and crawled toward the bed, he could feel cold sweat trickling inside his shirt, stinging the little places where his wounds were still healing. Reminding him again why all this was worth the risk.

The saddlebags were just where Holden had left them, still stuffed with money. Joey threw the bags over his shoulder and crept out of the cabin, going straight back to the stable. It only took him a few minutes to saddle Twister. He led the horse outside and filled the two bottles from the pump, then rode out of the yard and onto the range. Ten minutes later, when he slowed Twister to a trot, he heard hoofbeats behind him.

Holden.

Joey pulled Twister to a stop and grabbed his rifle, too scared to think. His sweaty hand slipped, and by the time he got a fresh grip on the stock the rider was too close.

Charlie Wood grinned at him as he pointed his gun, showing his black and crooked teeth.

"Where you goin' in such a hurry?" he drawled. "Don't you know Mr. McCarrick's been lookin' for you?"

THE LAST TIME Heath had been to a party, the room was filled with whores and the men who used them, drinking themselves blind and dancing clumsily to music from an out-of-tune piano. The stench and noise had been so bad that he'd had to leave after a few minutes.

Still, that party had been honest. No one had pretended to be what they weren't. Everyone here was pretending, and some were going to suffer for it.

Heath took a measured sip of his whiskey, watching Rachel laugh and pretend just as much as the others. She was clean and bright in her plain dress, a sparrow among peacocks, beautiful in a way they could never be. If they knew she'd had a kid out of wedlock, or even that she wasn't married yet, they would scorn her forever. But right now Amy and her parents were being friendly to her for their own hidden reasons.

As for Sean, he was with most of the other ranchers near the table that had been set up for drinks, compelling their attention the way he always did and talking about the wolf hunt he'd arranged for tomorrow. He'd barely spoken to Rachel, and he'd ignored Heath so far, but that wouldn't last. The question was whether or not Heath could find out exactly what else he was planning.

Swallowing the last of his whiskey, Heath thought about the past week. He and Rachel had avoided each other; he'd tried once or twice to talk to her about the party, but she'd refused to listen. He'd not only failed to convince her to stay away, but he'd upset her more by telling her that he would have married her. He realized now that in trying to make it easier for her when he left, he'd only made things worse.

And he'd failed in another way. The night after he'd argued with her, Joey had come back to the ranch. Heath hadn't been there to talk to him, or stop him from what he was about to do. After running himself to exhaustion, Heath had fallen into his bunk with no more awareness than a head-shot human. When he woke the next morning, he'd smelled Joey in his room.

He'd met Charlie in the yard as soon as he ran out to look for the boy. The hand had been apologetic, almost ready to grovel when he'd told Heath he'd seen Joey riding away from the ranch with full saddlebags buckled behind his saddle. He hadn't tried to stop him; he'd figured Heath knew he was back and where he was going—south, toward the Rio Grande. When Heath went to get dressed and ride after him, he'd found the money-filled saddlebags gone from under his bed.

Following Charlie's directions, he'd ridden south, but there had been no sign of Joey; his trail had gone cold, and Heath couldn't smell him out even when he Changed.

Joey had stolen the money, as well as the letters and wills, but it wasn't his fault. It was Heath's. Everything he'd done since Rachel's coming had been wrong, from giving Gordie to her and being blind to Joey's unhappiness, to letting himself care for a woman and leading her to think he could be what he wasn't.

He had one last chance to do something right.

He set his empty glass on the table and ambled over to join Sean and the ranchers at the other end of the room. They were laughing at something Sean had said. Sean poured himself a drink and lifted it in salute to

George Saunderson, who owned a good-size spread on the other side of the Pecos River.

"Speaking of wayward beasts," Sean said, "I have every confidence that we'll bring down that brute tomorrow. How can we fail, with such good and true gentlemen working together?"

"Seems you got a personal grudge against that lobo," George said, gesturing at the arm Sean held stiffly at his side. "He got a damn good taste of you."

Sean kept his smile, though the muscles worked in his jaw. "Yes. And I intend to see that it doesn't attack anyone else. It's a big devil, cleverer than most. It's only a matter of time before it begins attacking your beeves, John, or yours, Finn."

The men nodded. "We're with you, Sean."

"So am I," Heath said.

None of them had noticed him coming. They all turned to look at him with various expressions of wariness, dislike and curiosity. They knew there was no love lost between Jedediah's nephew and his foreman, and they didn't feel any more comfortable with Heath than most humans. They would be more than inclined to take Sean's side of any argument. But Charlie had said Sean had told everyone a pretty story about deciding to leave Dog Creek on his own, so they weren't quite ready to condemn Heath yet.

"Ah. Mr. Renshaw," Sean said.

For a long, heated minute all they did was stare at each other. Heath was sure then that Sean believed he had Heath just where he wanted him. They both knew that what lay between them was going to be settled before the hunt was over, each of them figuring he was going to win.

All Heath wanted at that moment was to come right out and accuse Sean of killing Jed. All he needed was the look on Sean's face to tell him it was true.

But no one would believe him. *He* would look like a man gone crazy with hate.

The ranchers glanced at each other uneasily. "Renshaw," George said, lifting a gray eyebrow. "You heard anything from Jed?"

"Nothin' yet, Mr. Saunderson," Heath said. "Expect to anytime."

"I imagine Mrs. McCarrick is a little lonely there all by herself," John Powell said. "Coming from the East as she does."

Heath showed his teeth. "Reckon that might be true, since no one's come to see her."

"My wife kept meanin' to visit her," Finn O'Hara said. "Only, Adam's been sick, and Addy's ailin', too. They're gettin' better now, though." He scratched his chin nervously. "Heard about the baby. Right good of her to take it in."

"Jed done right in pickin' her," Heath said, fixing his gaze on each man in turn. "But it ain't polite to talk about ladies when they ain't around."

"You surprise me, Renshaw," Sean said. "I never would have thought you'd be interested in such niceties."

"I'm surprised at *you,* Sean, gettin' up the courage to go after the animal that brought you low."

Rage and hate transformed Sean's face just long enough for Heath to see. "Oh, I intend to make the vermin suffer once I have it," he said. "Take my vengeance and rid us all of a killer. Two birds with one stone, as it were. Wouldn't you feel the same?"

Heath knew his guess was right for the second time. The wolf hunt was where Sean planned to get both enemies if he could.

But Sean was human. He didn't know about *loups-garous*. Or…

Crazy thoughts spun through Heath's head. Did Sean somehow suspect there was a connection between the wolf and Heath? That it wasn't an accident that Heath had shown up right after the wolf had savaged him?

That was crazy. Crazier than Sean. "Yeah," Heath said. "I'd feel the same."

"I wonder if Joey would agree?"

Chapter Sixteen

HEATH ALMOST HIT him. Just as he began to raise his fist, he realized that was exactly what Sean wanted: to set him up as the villain in front of people who already disliked him.

"Joey has more grit in his little finger than you have in your whole body," Heath said, smiling through his teeth. "He can hold his own…in a fair fight."

Saunderson frowned, obviously knowing there was some particular battle going on that he couldn't quite understand. John Powell shifted from foot to foot, and Finn poured himself another drink.

"I wonder if *you've* ever been in a fair fight?" Sean asked with a savage smile of his own.

"I thought we were talking about a wolf hunt?" George said quickly.

"So we were," Sean said, turning to refill his glass. He sipped it almost delicately. "Are you certain you wish to join us, Renshaw?"

"I am, and I'll do you one better, McCarrick. I'll wager I can bring the wolf in first."

He couldn't mistake the way Sean weighed his proposal, searching it for traps. "What would you propose as stakes?" he asked.

"Whoever loses leaves the county for good."

It felt as if the whole room went quiet, though the women were across the room and only a few others could have heard them talking. "That's ridiculous," Sean snapped.

"Afraid you'll lose all this?" Heath said, waving his hand at the room.

Sean's face went red, and he took a step closer to Heath.

"I suggest you retract that remark," he said softly.

"Do you accept or not?"

A man like Sean could only be pushed so far. He swung. Heath dodged the blow easily. Saunderson and O'Hara dived at Sean and caught his arm before he could try again.

"Mr. Renshaw!"

Rachel caught Heath's arm and pulled him away with a determined jerk. Everyone was staring now: the Blackwells, the handful of women, the other ranchers and their foremen in their best duds.

"I believe Miss Blackwell was about to suggest a dance," Rachel said in a carrying voice.

Amy Blackwell joined them. "Yes, indeed." She looked pointedly at Sean, and he had no choice but to ask her. George Saunderson's daughter Annie, just growing into her womanhood and eager to show off her skill, sat down at the piano. She bent over the keyboard and struck up a waltz.

If they'd been alone, Heath would have told Rachel just what he thought of dancing. He'd maybe done it three times in his life, and he hadn't been good at it any of those times. But she wasn't likely to give up when her purpose was to separate him and Sean.

So he did what he had to, placing his hands the way he remembered, feeling Rachel's hand in its white glove rest on his back. Her waist was small and firm, her gaze steady as he began to move his feet. A few other couples joined them on the polished wooden floor of the Blackwells' big parlor, and instinct took over. After a minute or two he and Rachel were spinning around the room. Rachel's whole body transformed into something made of light and air. Her skin was flushed, and her eyes shone like sunlight on still water, and all Heath could think about was the way she'd looked after he'd loved her by the creek.

He was amazed to find himself thinking the dance had finished too soon. Rachel pulled free before he thought to let her go. She gave him a long look, a warning and a plea, and walked with Amy and Eunice O'Hara to the table stocked with vittles brought by the guests.

Sean came up behind him.

"Did you find that amusing, Renshaw?" he asked in a low voice.

Heath turned slowly to face him. "I ain't laughin'."

Sean looked across the room at Rachel, who was listening with a smile to Mrs. O'Hara babbling about her new stove. Rachel glanced briefly at Heath and Sean, her brows drawing down in worry.

"You certainly appeared to enjoy your dance with Mrs. McCarrick," Sean said. "Can it be that you two have become friends? *More* than friends, perhaps?"

Hellfire. Heath saw that he'd been a fool, so intent on his need to get Sean that he'd assumed McCarrick wanted to make friends with Rachel and manipulate her with the Blackwells' help. It wasn't that at all. He wanted to ruin her.

"You watch your mouth," Heath growled.

"Would you prefer to discuss the subject here? I'm

sure several of our guests might find the conversation quite fascinating."

Heath's muscles tensed with the need to Change and finish what he'd begun.

"Perhaps we should retire to the veranda?"

Another dance had started, and Rachel was accepting Rufus Mayhew's hand. Without answering, Heath strode out of the parlor and along the hall to the kitchen. One of the Blackwells' servants, a cook in cap and apron, glanced up from her pots in astonishment as he pushed through the door to the section of the porch that extended to the back of the house. Unlike the rest of the porch, which was lit by hanging paper lanterns, this area was dark except for the light of the moon.

Sean strolled out after him, whistling softly. He looked Heath up and down, leaned against the railing and smiled.

"Well, Renshaw. It seems you've been keeping more than your share of secrets."

Bide your time, Heath told himself. "You got somethin' to say, say it."

The railing creaked as Sean adjusted his position. "Tell me…how long have you and Rachel Lyndon been lovers?"

Sean never had a chance. Heath laid him low before he finished the last word. "You filthy son of a bitch," he snarled.

Blood dripped from Sean's nose onto the porch. He shook his head, got up on one elbow and kept on smiling. "I see I was right."

Heath dragged Sean to his feet by the lapels of his pretty frock coat. "Where did you hear these lies?"

"It couldn't be more obvious, Renshaw. The way

you look at each other, watch each other constantly… there are dozens of clues."

Heath shook Sean so hard that the man's teeth rattled. "If you've said this to anyone else—"

"I haven't. Not yet." Sean shook his head in mock regret. "Which do you think would cause a greater scandal, your diddling Jed's wife—or the fact that she's not Jed's wife at all?"

It wasn't any real shock to find out Sean knew, considering what Heath had already guessed. But why had Sean waited to bring it up now?

Because he wanted a fight. Heath had thought that Sean meant to do whatever he'd planned during the hunt, but maybe he had something else in mind, after all.

Heath let Sean go with a push. "You think you'll ever get the chance to tell anyone, McCarrick?"

"What do you propose to do, Renshaw? Kill me here?"

A howling storm raged inside Heath's head, a blackness that was nothing human. "You want a fair fight? I'll give it to you."

Sean pulled a clean white handkerchief from inside his coat and patted at his nose. "A pity Jed won't have a chance to witness such a novelty." He sighed. "Perhaps it's best that he'll never know how his fiancée betrayed him."

The storm shredded Heath's insides like paper. It wasn't just what Sean had said, but the way he'd said it, grinning at Heath because he *wanted* him to know. He wanted Heath to react so he could say Heath knew Jed was dead. Just like *he* did.

He'd murdered Jed. Heath was certain of it now, and he planned to make Sean suffer for that before he died.

Heath backed up, took off his hat and Jed's second-best coat, and unbuttoned his vest. Sean did the same, the sneer never leaving his face.

No fair fight was possible between a human and a *loup-garou*, but Heath managed to hold back just enough. Sean feinted a few times and connected once when Heath let him, but he mostly kept his distance, dancing around like a possum on a tin roof in summer. When Heath let Sean slip under his guard, Sean didn't even try to hit him. Instead, he reached for Heath's neck, caught hold of the tails of Heath's neckerchief and yanked down hard.

Warm air hit Heath's scar like scalding water. He fell back and jerked the neckerchief back into place. Sean took the chance to hit him in the mouth. Heath's fist smashed into Sean's face a second later. He jumped on top of Sean and drew his arm back again.

Someone screamed.

Heath let his hand fall and sprang to his feet. Amy was standing in the kitchen doorway, her hands pressed to her mouth. Crowded among the other women, Rachel hovered behind her, such a look of horror in her eyes that Heath almost felt ashamed.

George Saunderson moved past the women and helped Sean to his feet. "What the hell's goin' on here?" he demanded.

Sean held the handkerchief over his split and swelling lip. "A friendly disagreement," he said. "It was meant to be a private affair."

Amy hurried to him and began dabbing at a cut on his cheek with her own lacy handkerchief. "This is intolerable!" she cried. She turned to glare at Heath as she worked. "My father will have you thrown out!"

Rachel slipped past the crows clustered at the

doorway. "I do not believe that Mr. Renshaw provoked the fight," she said.

Lips tight, Amy stepped away from Sean and stared at Rachel. "You didn't see it any more than I did," she said.

"Mr. Renshaw," Rachel said, "did you start the fight?"

He met her gaze. "Depends on what you mean by 'start.'"

Saunderson looked from Heath to Sean and back to Heath again. "You should know better than to tussle around the womenfolk."

"I apologize," Sean said with a stiff bow. "I did not intend for the matter to get so out of hand."

Heath couldn't believe that Sean would take the blame so easily. "Reckon it was wrong," he said. "It won't happen again."

No one knew just what a lie that was. Heath nodded shortly and picked up his vest. Amy was still glaring at him as she chivied Sean into the house. The other women followed, whispering loudly and shaking their heads.

Rachel stayed behind. "If you intended to let everyone know that you hope to kill Sean," she said, "you could not have gone about it more skillfully."

"I had my reasons." He touched the already healing cut on his chin and sniffed the air. No one was near, not even the cook, who'd probably been the one to tell everyone about the fight. "You should have stayed away."

She drew a handkerchief from somewhere in her dress and held it out to him. "Nothing has changed, Holden," she said.

"Plenty has changed." He ignored the handkerchief and stared down at her as if she was still a stranger. He knew what he was about to say would hurt her, but if there was any chance of getting her to leave, he had to take it.

"Do you know what he said, Rachel?" he asked. "He knows you ain't married. And he's guessed that you and me…"

He didn't have to finish. Rachel's face lost its color. "How?" she whispered. "How is that possible?"

"I don't know. But you don't want to be out here with me right now."

Her jaw set. "I am here holding a simple conversation with my husband's foreman. No one—"

"Sean will tell everyone what he's guessed if it suits his purpose. Do you want to be anywhere around here when that happens?"

Her eyes were nearly black in the darkness, wide and scared. But her gaze never wavered. "Are you so certain he will be believed?"

"He can make anyone believe anything he wants."

"I am not so certain. I have spoken with Amy. She was far from pleased that Sean let himself be drawn into a fight. I'm no longer convinced that she intends to manipulate me on Sean's behalf."

Heath laughed. "You're makin' a mistake if you think that. She wants Sean as much as he wants her."

"It doesn't matter. I'm not afraid of either one of them."

Oh, she was afraid, all right, but she was ready to face the humiliation and disgrace of exposure if it meant she could stop Heath from going after Sean. He grabbed her shoulders, afraid that if he let himself soften even a little, he would take her in his arms and tell her everything would be all right.

"If Sean says anything before the hunt," he said, "I'm goin' to have to kill him here."

She didn't even try to get away. "The hunt," she said. "That's when it will happen, isn't it?"

He let her go. He wasn't going to tell her that had been his idea all along.

A warm evening wind picked a few dark strands free from Rachel's tightly bound hair and caught at her skirts, pressing them against her legs. "Sean planned the hunt, too," she said. She flung her arm toward the darkness beyond the house. "It *is* a trap. Anything can happen out there, can't it?"

Heath remembered Sean's mocking grin. He'd *wanted* Heath to believe he'd murdered his uncle. He knew Heath would never accuse him openly. It was still just between them. But Heath saw now that Rachel had to know everything about Sean, because the weak, soft part of him still wanted her to understand.

"Sit down," he said.

"You haven't answered my—"

He took her by the arm and marched her to the rocking chair by the kitchen door, pushing her down onto the seat. "Jed's dead, Rachel," he said.

It was hard telling her the rest, hard to look at her face…the shock and horror at first, then the despair that came over her when she was clearheaded enough to realize how badly Heath had betrayed her. Her breath was ragged, her face etched with grief and anguish.

"Why didn't you tell anyone?" she said in a voice hoarse with unshed tears. "Why didn't you tell *me?*"

It wasn't a long story. Heath had made it a point not to remember all the details of his life since he'd left the Mortons, and he'd already told her part of it. Just not enough.

So he told her about the weeks of near starvation

after he'd run from the Mortons, the desperation, the petty theft just to keep himself alive. The hard fights he so seldom lost. The petty crimes that got bigger as he learned from the most skilled and hardened outlaws west of the Mississippi. Years of rustling horses and cattle, and never being caught. The first bank robbery. The first train. The first time he'd killed a man who'd planned to kill him first. The killing he hadn't done but had been blamed for, setting him on the run again. The new life Jed had offered him. Everything but the betrayals, his real name and the wanted poster with the scar.

And what he could become.

"I thought it was an accident," Heath said, talking to the wall over her head. "I didn't see no sign that anyone else had been there, and I knew how it could look to them what already blamed me for the foreman's murder. So I kept Jed hid."

Rachel wrapped her arms around her chest, no expression on her face at all. "But it wasn't an accident," she said.

"When you told me about being bribed, I started to think Sean could have done it. Now I *know* he did. He knew you was comin'. He murdered Jed because he found out Jed was goin' to take away his inheritance."

"Then…it was because of me that Jedediah—"

Heath dropped to his knees. "It wasn't you. Jed would have cut him out even if he wasn't plannin' to marry you. Sean would have gone crazy when he found out, but maybe…"

Maybe I would have been there to stop him.

"He knows where the body is," Rachel whispered.

"I 'spect he's been back there since he done it, lookin' for anything of value Jed was carryin'." And

Heath wouldn't have been surprised if he'd gone out there again right before the party. In fact, he expected it.

"You see how it is," he said, touching Rachel's cheek with the tip of one finger. "No one'll believe Sean done it. There ain't no proof. I'm the only one who can make it right."

"But you won't." She reached to pull his hand against her face. "You said you tried to leave your old life behind. You can't go back to it now. It will destroy you."

He got up, even though he wanted to keep on touching her for the rest of his life. "That doesn't matter now," he said gently. "I got somethin' for you. It'll give you a chance to start over."

Suddenly she jumped up from the chair and closed the space between them in two steps, her chest rising and falling fast, and her eyes sparking with familiar fire.

"*You* can start over, too, Holden," she said. "We can do it together. You and I and Gordie. I'll tell them I never married Jed. We'll find some way to prove that Sean killed him, and then—"

A door opened for Heath then, gleaming heavenly gates that offered him a glimpse of paradise. He took Rachel's face between his hands and lowered his head.

Then the door closed, and the Pearly Gates snapped shut. Heath let his hands fall.

"It can't be done," he said. "Even if we could find the proof, they'd start wonderin' why you knew Jed was dead and didn't tell anyone. Even if you told 'em now, Sean would make somethin' ugly out of it. Maybe he'd even think of a way to blame you for it." She started to speak, and he covered her lips with his fingers. "I'm sorry, Rachel."

Her throat worked up and down, but she didn't do anything except step back again and walk to the porch railing, where the wind teased her hair like a lover.

"You said you had something to give me," she said.

"Meet me at the stable three hours past midnight. Make sure no one sees you."

She stood by the railing a little while longer and then went into the kitchen, passing him by without a word or a glance.

He didn't return to the party, which had gone so quiet that even he could barely hear the voices from the parlor. When Rachel joined the others, they sounded friendly enough. No shunning yet, no cruel gossip about a married woman and her foreman.

But that was cold comfort. Nothing Heath had said to her, from revealing Jed's death to telling her exactly what he was and what he'd done, had made her turn away from him. She would keep coming back, keep trying to interfere, keep hoping he would change.

Only one thing would make her realize the truth and answer the question that had festered in his heart since he'd started caring for Rachel Lyndon.

The alcohol in Heath's empty stomach seethed like a pit of vipers. He went out to the stable, saddled Apache and turned him toward the range.

Twenty minutes' ride out, when he was just about far enough away from the house to Change, he caught a scent that had him off Apache's back in a heartbeat.

The man who came out of the darkness on his rawboned dun looked like any other cowhand drifting between jobs, weary and wind-beaten and a little ragged. But Heath knew he wasn't any regular cow-hand. Apache jigged, flattening his ears, and Heath set his hand on the gelding's shoulder.

"Who are you?" he growled.

Swinging his leg over the saddle, the man slid to the ground. "My name is Gavin Renier," he said in a voice smooth and low and educated, like Rachel's. He peered into Heath's eyes, and his nostrils flared. "I've been looking for you for a long time."

Heath's hand went to his hip, but he didn't have his gun, hadn't touched it since Rachel had put it away. He knew he could get out of his clothes fast if he had to, but that wouldn't do him much good when this man who called himself Renier could do the same.

"I don't carry a gun," Gavin said. "And I wouldn't shoot you if I did." He pushed his black forelock out of his face and let his hands fall to his sides. "Unless I'm much mistaken, you're my brother."

After all the shocks he'd given Rachel, Heath couldn't say he wasn't due for at least one of his own. He wanted to deny it, wanted to Change and drive this *loup-garou* away from his territory like any self-respecting wolf would do.

But he couldn't deny what he saw: the black hair, the lean face, the eyes that looked so much like his own. He could smell it even better than he could see it, the unique signature that could only belong to another of the same blood.

"I ain't got a brother," Heath snarled.

"You do if your name is Heath Renier."

"Like hell!"

They moved with equal speed, shedding clothes with such ferocity that cotton shredded and wool tore at the seams. Heath finished first by a split second and leaped for Gavin's throat.

He couldn't get a grip. Gavin, as black as he and almost as big, ducked under his attack and bounded aside, swift and sinuous as a ferret. He snapped at Heath from behind, a feint that wasn't meant to wound but to warn.

Spinning around, Heath crouched for another leap, his wolfish mind torn between bitter rage and despair. Gavin held his ground, swiveled his ears and cocked his head in a gesture as eloquent as any human speech. *Do you really want to fight?*

The hair along Heath's back began to settle even before he decided to give up. He backed away, keeping well clear of the agitated horses, and waited until Gavin made the first move to Change back to human again.

"You've got nothing to fear from me," Gavin said as he gathered up his scattered clothes. "I'm not your enemy, Heath. I've come to bring you home."

A wolf's laugh was more like a moan, but it suited Heath's mood perfectly. He Changed and pulled on his torn britches and shirt, leaving his boots where they lay.

"I don't got no home," he said. He calmed Apache with a touch, letting the animal's sturdy warmth give him comfort in return. "You may be my kin, but I ain't got no family. My ma saw to that."

Gavin sighed and bowed his head. "That was a mistake. It was never our mother's intention to give you up."

"You think I didn't go lookin'?" Apache tossed his head, and Heath lowered his voice. "When the Mortons told me how I'd been thrown away and drove me out of their house, I found my real ma's people in a town called Salvation. Wasn't hard to find out she'd had a half-human bastard she couldn't wait to get rid of, just like she did his human pa."

"If you believed that, why did you take the Renier name?"

Heath didn't have an answer for that. He never had. "You'd best get on your horse and ride out. I got nothin' more to say."

"Even if I told you that what you heard was a lie? That our mother was forced to give you up?"

Once, a long time ago, Heath would have died to hear those words. Now they twisted like bob-wire in his belly. "A mite too late for regrets, ain't it?" he asked.

"It'll be too late for you if you don't come with me now," Gavin said, angry for the first time since they'd met. "There's a bounty hunter looking for you. I've been searching for years, following the rumors and the stories about Heath Renier. When I tracked you to Pecos County, I heard a bounty hunter was putting out posters here and in Crockett. Once I figured out where you might be, I kept watch on him, and I could see he'd figured out the same thing."

Heath reined in the urge to Change again. "Is he here now?"

"Not now. I led him to believe I was Heath Renier, and he took the bait. He followed me east as far as San Antonio. I lost him there, but I don't know how long he'll be deceived. He's *loup-garou* himself."

One werewolf hunting another. No surprise. But why would this man he didn't know risk his own life for a brother he'd never met?

"Obliged for that," Heath said gruffly, "but you don't have to help me no more. I can—"

"Our mother wants you to come home."

Heath laughed. "To Salvation?"

"She left a long time ago," Gavin said. "She defied the clan and married again. Elkhorn is a safe place, and none of the Salvation Reniers have ever bothered us."

"Is her new mate human?"

"*Loup-garou.* But she kept on looking for—"

"*You* ain't half-human. Why should you give a damn about me?"

Gavin snorted in frustration. "Do you think your being my half brother and not full-blood makes any difference to me or my sisters?"

Sisters. A whole damn family. Heath ignored his ripped stockings and pulled his boots on over bare feet.

"And it don't make no difference to you what I've done?"

Gavin pushed his hair back again, the lines in his face deeper than before. "The Reniers," he said, "regardless of branch, have plenty of black marks in their history. Do you intend to go on killing, Heath?"

Apache shifted sideways as Heath swung into the saddle. "Why should I trust anything you say?"

"You've got nowhere else to go, unless it's to jail. Constantine will find you sooner or later. Aren't you tired of running?"

Bone tired. And he saw now that he had an answer to the one problem he kept putting out of his mind. If he chose to believe that answer.

"Would you take in a boy who's only a quarter *loup-garou?*" he asked.

"Without question." Gavin eyed him narrowly. "What boy?"

"You know where Dog Creek is? Ride there and wait, if you mean what you say. If I don't come back by dawn the day after next, you get that boy and take him back with you."

"I don't understand. Where are you going?"

"I got business to take care of before I go anywhere else. Private business. That boy needs to grow up where no one'll turn on him because of what he might do someday." He swallowed. "Will you see to that?"

"Yes. But if you have business of the kind I think, I'm coming with you."

"No! The boy's all that matters."

"He's your son, isn't he?"

Heath closed his eyes. "You want me to beg?"

Gavin cursed. "I'll make sure he has a good home. But remember that you've got a home, too. Don't destroy your life because you can't stop hating."

Heath pulled Apache around and started back for the house at a gallop. Gavin didn't come after him. A half-mile from the house, Heath let the gelding slow to a walk.

A home. That was what he'd been offered. The kind of home he'd never known, with real kin, people like him who would never drive him or Gordie out because they were different. Who would accept a pair of 'breeds in spite of the life he'd led.

Like Rachel would do, if he gave her the chance?

Heath's heart jammed inside his throat. Wasn't he going to give Rachel that chance, even knowing how it would turn out?

He'd already made up his mind. Showing her what he was wasn't some kind of test. It was to scare her away, so she wouldn't suffer so much when he took Gordie and abandoned her.

Heath bent low over the saddle, hurting in places no one could see. *She might understand*, a small voice whispered. *She could be different.* There could be a safe place for all of them.

If there'd ever been a hell worse than prison, it was hope.

Chapter Seventeen

SEAN LOOKED IN the mirror and laughed.

It couldn't have gone any better if he'd been God himself, arranging every move like a puppet master bouncing his marionettes on a stage. Renshaw had fallen for his provocation, confirming Sean's certainty that he knew Jed was dead, proving that he had developed a relationship with Rachel and giving Sean the perfect opportunity to uncover Renshaw's scar.

Holden Renshaw was Heath Renier, wanted for multiple crimes and destined for hanging. His relationship to the wolf, if any, was more uncertain, but Sean had proof enough now to see Renshaw punished. Not merely killed, of course. That would be far too easy. Destroyed utterly. If the humiliation Sean had suffered was the price he must pay to see that happen…well, it would only make his victory that much sweeter.

Oh, it hadn't been easy to get Joey to tell him what he needed to know. Threats were no longer effective. The boy seemed determined not to speak at all. Persuasion of a different and far more painful sort had been required.

In the end, Joey had confessed to where he'd found the saddlebags. Jed's saddlebags, holding more treasures than mere money, though Joey had never searched them and found the letters and the wills.

Two wills. Perhaps Renshaw had been perceptive enough to destroy the one leaving everything to him, but Sean still had the copy from the lawyer's office in Heywood, which was now no more than a pile of ash.

Probing at his swollen lip and blackened eye, Sean reviewed the fight once more. The biggest risk he had taken had been allowing Renshaw to realize that he knew of Jed's death. It was possible that Renshaw had guessed Sean had killed the old man.

But Sean calculated that Holden would never dare share such speculation with anyone else, even if it hadn't been clear that the foreman was just as eager to ruin Sean as he had ever been. Perhaps Renshaw hadn't tried very hard to confront Sean after Joey's whipping—and admittedly Sean hadn't made it easy for him—but Renshaw had a much stronger motive now that his lover had been threatened with exposure.

That amused Sean most of all. Renshaw wasn't merely using Rachel Lyndon. He actually *cared* about the woman, just as he cared about the child. Perhaps he even felt some loyalty to Jed's memory. Yet if Renshaw was intelligent enough to realize that Sean had recognized his scar and his true identity, if he understood that Sean was laying a trap he might not escape…

No. He would never forgo the pleasure of killing his nemesis. Heath Renier had a primitive kind of courage, and with that courage came a fatal blindness. Blindness that would lead a man to fight instead of run, even when flight was the only thing that would save him.

Sean began to remove his collar, humming under his breath. All the pieces would soon be in place. He had spoken at length with Charlie after the cowhand had brought Joey to him, and now it was only a matter of taking the first steps. The hunt would proceed as planned, with a sunset rendezvous near the draw where Jed's body lay. Renshaw would understand that the choice of meeting place was deliberate and would no doubt be lying in wait, hoping to get Sean alone through some trickery. But Sean would already have his men in place even before the hunt began. They would keep Renshaw pinned down until Sean and the others arrived.

That was when the old man would be "found," and Sean would reveal his conviction that Holden Renshaw was the outlaw Heath Renier. The ranchers and other hands would listen to him, of course, no matter how much Renshaw denied it. With Renshaw in custody, they would ride back to Dog Creek, where proof would be obtained in the form of Jed's saddlebags, liberally painted with cow's blood, being "discovered" under Holden's bed.

The wills leaving everything to Renshaw and Rachel would be the crowning touch, and with only a little persuasion, Sean would convince everyone that Renshaw had had a perfect motive to kill Jed and recruit Rachel Lyndon to defraud Jed's rightful heir.

All Sean needed to do now was keep Renshaw and Rachel from leaving Blackwater before the hunt.

Pulling on a fresh shirt, collar and cravat, Sean cast a last glance in the mirror and finished with his vest and frock coat. For the rest of this evening, it would be as if Holden and his whore had ceased to exist for him. He would not spread rumors or provoke the foreman in any way.

Sean smoothed back his hair and walked out of his room.

Amy was hovering in the hall.

"Why were you gone so long?" she hissed. "Every-one is waiting for supper."

"They can wait a little longer."

Her unease was apparent in the way she pinched the folds of her skirts between her delicate gloved fingers. "Why did you fight with Renshaw?"

He smiled. "Would you have had me ignore him and show myself to be a coward?"

"I don't like it, Sean. First you simply disappeared, leaving everyone to wonder why you did not find our party worthy of your attention. And then we found you—" She grimaced, ruining her pretty face. "You looked every bit as bad as he did, an uncivilized ruffian with your shirt torn and blood on your face. You know Mama and Papa don't approve of—"

"Darling," Sean said, slipping his arm around her shoulder. "I always have a purpose in everything I do. It has been obvious to me for some time that Renshaw is planning some sort of mischief, and he made that very clear during our altercation. That is the reason I wanted you to invite him, so that I could discover his purpose."

"But you said—" She shook her blond head. "If you intended to make Rachel turn against him, I don't think you have succeeded. She obviously trusts him com-pletely." Her face grew pensive. "I expected to dislike her thoroughly, but I find I cannot. She has no airs about her and is far more engaging than any of the other women. And she positively dotes on that foundling." Amy hesi-tated. "If, as you implied to me, she is somehow involved with Renshaw, it is surely his fault, not hers."

He might have told her then that Rachel had never married Jed, that she was a liar as well as a silly fool taken in by a scoundrel. But he wished to preserve that revelation for a time when it would be far more humiliating for the little bitch.

"Are you condoning the possibility of an affair?" he asked sternly.

She slipped free of his hold. "Of course not. But she…she must wonder why Jed thought so little of her that he failed to be at the ranch when she arrived." She bit her lip. "Are you certain your uncle is dead?"

"Not entirely. But I have come to believe that Renshaw may know the truth."

"Surely Rachel doesn't."

"How can you possibly be so certain?"

Amy wrung her gloved hands. "I don't know. I just feel—" Conflicting emotions passed over her face like clouds. "She risked so much to come here without knowing anything about Texas or the kind of life she'd have with a man like Jed. It must have been so difficult to find him gone and herself alone."

"And so she turns to a man like Renshaw and breaks her wedding vows?"

"You cannot be sure she has done so. You know I despise Renshaw. I would never have believed such a man capable of caring for anyone. But he does care for Rachel. There must be something human in him after all."

Sean withdrew from her as if she'd spat in his face. "Can you be serious? He has threatened me numerous times. He has betrayed my uncle, a man he should have revered. And there is worse." He glanced down the hall toward the dining room, feeling the familiar rage burning in his chest. "I have learned that Jed made out two wills…one leaving everything to Holden Renshaw and one to Rachel in the event of their marriage. The first has been voided, and the signature on the second

was not written by my uncle. It has been forged. Unless
we expose—"

"Where did you find these wills?"

"Don't you understand?" His voice began to rise, out
of his control. "I know my uncle would never have disinherited his own nephew. I am certain that Renshaw
destroyed the will that deeded the ranch to me. I believe
that Rachel had some part in this scheme of fraud and
forgery. If matters proceed as I expect, neither Renshaw
nor Rachel will be able to claim a single section of Dog
Creek. They will be thoroughly discredited."

"What do you mean? What do you intend to do?"

"You have no need to know."

"In other words, you don't trust me!"

"All you need do is keep Rachel here at Blackwater
for two more days."

"Do you really believe you can order me about?"

"You are either loyal to me, without question, or—"

"Or what?" Her lips thinned, turning her nearly as plain
as Rachel. "I don't care what you say. I don't think Rachel
knew about these wills. If Renshaw did, he deceived her."

"But she still stands in the way of my lawful inheritance. I cannot tolerate that, Amy. I—*we*—will lose everything we have dreamed of, everything that should be
ours."

"But if Rachel—"

"You are as ambitious as I am," he growled. "You
want what I can give you when I've risen to heights even
your father can't imagine. All this—" He cut his hand
through the air, encompassing the elegant hallway.
"*This* is all that matters to you. Money and influence
and the groveling of lesser beings."

Her fair skin flushed red. "Is that what you think of me?"

"I know you, Amy. When I have Blackwater—"

She covered her mouth with her hand. "You don't love me, do you? You never did. I'm just a stepping stone you planned to purchase with Dog Creek."

"Love is nothing. Power is everything."

With a little cry she spun about and started toward the dining room. Sean caught up with her and grabbed her arm, tightening his fingers around the delicate bones of her wrist.

"You'll have no regrets when this is finished, sweetheart. I promise you. But you are to say nothing of this, do you hear? Nothing. You have been spoiled in this house. It is discipline you require, and I will see that you get it."

She leaned away from him, fear in her eyes. "I…I won't say anything," she whispered.

Sean smiled. "Good girl."

When he let her go, she was as meek as a lamb.

JOEY PULLED ON the ropes around his wrists and blinked as the door to the dugout swung open. Charlie stood silhouetted against the light, a grin on his face and a gun in his hand.

"Howdy, boy," he said in a friendly tone. "Slept well?"

"You damn—" Joey strained as hard as he could, but the ropes wouldn't budge, and the fresh stripes on his back burned all over again. His face was so swollen that he could barely open his mouth. "You're a stinkin' coward, Wood!"

"No more 'n you." Charlie leaned against the earthen wall, watching a bug skittle across the collapsing roof. "Couldn't take the punishment, could you?"

The tears kept on coming, no matter how hard Joey fought them. For a while he'd endured the pain, determined not to give in again, figuring Sean had some no-good reason for wanting so bad to know where the saddlebags had come from. But in the end, the coward in Joey had told him it was just a little thing, not worth getting killed over.

Now Joey knew it wasn't little. And there was nothing he could do to take back what he'd said.

If only they'd killed me first.

"Sean'll never get away with it," he mumbled. "Holden'll finish him first."

"Just like he did after Sean whupped you?"

"Go to hell."

"I might, but you'll get there before me."

"If you're goin' to kill me, do it now!"

Charlie shifted his weight, shooting out one hip like a drowsy horse. "I ain't got no orders to do it yet. Maybe Mr. McCarrick still has some use for you."

"I'll kill myself before I help McCarrick."

Chewing on a ragged nail, Charlie shrugged. "That ain't my lookout. I'm here to fetch the saddlebags. Pretty soon no one is goin' to doubt that Renshaw kilt Jed."

Joey closed his eyes. Sean hadn't even bothered to hide his plan from Joey after he'd let him down from the ropes. Oh, Joey didn't know all of it. Only that Sean was going to blame Holden for killing Jed, and use the saddlebags to prove it somehow. And it would be a great big joke, because Sean was the one who'd done the old man in.

Sean would never have told Joey those things if he thought Joey could escape. And he was right. The chances of getting out of here and back home in time were about as big as drowning in Dead Man's Draw.

But they were going to kill him anyway. He might as well die trying to get out rather than just sit here like a trussed rabbit waiting to be skinned.

"I got to piss," he whined. "You got to let me up."

Charlie spat. "Get on your knees and turn around," he said. Joey did as Charlie commanded and felt the ropes around his ankles loosen and fall away. "Take care of your business. Quick."

Struggling to his feet, Joey went to the corner of the dugout to empty his bladder while he searched for the rusty piece of metal he'd seen there when he'd first been brought in. It was still there, so broken and dull that he couldn't even guess what it had come from.

Without looking behind him, he leaned to one side and fell, striking the wall with his shoulder and coming down right on top of the metal piece.

Charlie cursed and came after him. "What're you playin' at?" he snapped, grabbing Joey's arm and hauling him back to his feet. "Go back to your place."

Joey went meekly, the metal tucked in his palm. He stayed still while Charlie bound up his ankles again. Charlie pushed him in the chest, forcing him back against the wall, and got up.

"You stay nice 'n quiet," he said, "or I might just decide to tell Mr. McCarrick that you was too much trouble to keep alive."

Whistling through his teeth, Charlie ambled to the opposite corner of the dugout, picked up the saddle-bags and slung them over his shoulder. The rickety door shut behind him with a thud. As soon as he was sure Charlie was gone, Joey worked the piece of metal in his fingers until he had it up against the rope binding his wrists. He might bleed to death before he was done, but a little more pain wouldn't make any difference now.

This was his last chance to do something right.

RACHEL PICKED HER way across the yard, glad for the moonless night but all the more careful because of it. She hadn't dared carry a lantern, though she wondered how it could matter now if someone learned she was going to meet Holden Renshaw alone in the stable.

But it *did* matter. She had lost her head when she'd spoken to him on the veranda, so desperate to divert him from his course that she hadn't considered all the consequences. She had said she wouldn't care if she was exposed as an impostor and Holden's lover, but that wasn't true. Whatever happened, once this horror was over, she would go back to Dog Creek and Gordie. Jed was dead, but Gordie still needed a good home. With Holden so bent on self-destruction, she could no longer trust him to keep the vow he had made by the creek.

I got somethin' for you, Heath had said. *It'll give you a chance to start over.*

Enough to start over with Gordie? Had that been what he meant? What else could it have been?

As long as I am Mrs. McCarrick, no one will try to take Gordie away until I am gone. And there was as yet no sign that any vicious rumors had started, or that Sean planned to speak against her. He had ignored her completely after the fight, but the other ladies had continued to be cordial and sympathetic in spite of the awkwardness that had lingered when the party resumed. Even Amy had been friendly, quickly overcoming her anger at Holden, and there had been no scheming in her manner or false warmth in her eyes. In spite of all that had happened, Rachel found that she could no longer believe what Holden had said about Mrs. Blackwell's daughter.

I might have been welcome here.

And she would have given it all up if only Holden—

Enough. She must go on, start over, think only of Gordie now. Holden was forever beyond her reach or her help.

A horse nickered as she approached the stable, and a deep awareness in her body told her that Holden was already waiting. As soon as she entered, he touched her arm.

"Come over here," he said quietly. "Sit down."

He offered her a wooden stool in an empty stall and stood just outside, his hands at his sides, his face expressionless. There would be no more displays of emotion. Only an ending.

Rachel rested her hands in her lap and stared beyond him at the dark shape of the horse in the opposite stall. Holden seemed to be waiting for her to speak, but she had nothing to say. He reached inside his waistcoat and withdrew a folded piece of paper the size of a letter.

"When I was in Javelina the day after Joey was hurt," he said, "Sonntag gave me this letter for you."

She looked up. "A letter?"

"From Ohio." He turned the paper around in his hands. "I should have given it to you before, but I—" He broke off, reached out and offered the letter. Rachel took it, the brief spark of curiosity flickering out even as she touched the pretty stationery.

She unfolded it. All she could make out was the fine and elegant hand of an educated woman.

"I can't read it here," she said dully. "It's too dark."

"I can." He took it back and cleared his throat.

It took some moments before Rachel understood what she was hearing. Three times before, her life had changed utterly: once when both her aunt and Louis had abandoned her, again when Jed had made his proposal, and at last when she had met Gordie and Holden. Now it had changed yet again. Or would if she wished it to.

"My grandmother was wrong, cousin," Phoebe Kaplan had written. "No one should be compelled to pay for a single mistake for the rest of their lives. You shall have your rightful share of the inheritance. Come home, and we shall be the best of friends."

Phoebe Kaplan, a girl so much younger than Rachel had been at the time of her disgrace, a child she had hardly known, now the sole heir to Aunt Beatrice's fortune. A young woman of astonishing generosity and goodness.

Come home. Rachel could return to Ohio a wealthy woman, to a place where she might be loved. A place where Gordie would have everything to make him happy.

She looked up at Heath. In the brief moment before his face turned cold again, she glimpsed the vulnerability she had seen only a handful of times, a profound pain that sent an echoing stab of agony through her own body.

"You have what you need," he said in a voice stripped of emotion. "You can go anytime."

Rachel tried to stand, caught her shoe in the straw and stumbled. She was in Heath's arms before she could draw another breath.

Heath could have stopped it. It would have been the right thing to do, to push her away and let her go, forget he'd ever known her.

But in just a little while she would be leaving him.

And he wanted to remember her the way she was now, looking up at him with skin flushed and lips parted, desire in her eyes. Still wanting him to up and take her and Gordie and run away. Still *caring* for him, in spite of everything.

So he kissed her. Not hard the way he'd done it by the creek, but gentle. Gentle like he'd almost forgotten how to be. Her lips opened up like a cactus flower, welcoming, wanting. Her tongue tangled with his, and her fingers gripped his hair as if she was afraid he'd stop if she didn't keep them there. He explored her mouth until there were no more secrets, nothing left for her to withhold.

He still could have ended it. Should have, for her sake. But she didn't want to let him go, and he didn't have the will to force her to. She was already working at the buttons of his vest before he put his hands on her bodice and fumbled for the hooks. She closed her eyes and let him do it, helped him take off the bodice and corset and skirts and petticoats, leaving her standing only in her chemise, unmentionables, shoes and stockings.

She shivered a little as he looked at her—not skinny, but slender and strong, with firm arms, a small waist and hips that curved just right. Her breasts were made to fill a man's hands, brown nipples already hard and waiting for his mouth.

But it wasn't enough to see her like this. He wanted her naked under him, her flesh against his.

He reached for her underthings, and her hand closed on his.

"Wait," she said. "I want to see *you*."

Now *he* was the nervous one, even though he had no reason to be. He wasn't ashamed of his human body any more than he was ashamed of the wolf's. But it meant more than just letting her see him naked. Somehow it meant she would see all the way to the heart of him, even beyond what she'd already known from all he'd told her.

Before he had a chance to start undressing himself, she was busy with his vest again, unbuttoning it, helping him shrug out of it. She laid it aside and paused for a moment to lean into him, smelling him the way a female *loup-garou* would smell her mate.

Then she reached for his neckerchief.

Her wrists felt fragile as birds when he stopped her. "Wait," he said.

She searched his eyes. "Why? What's wrong?"

He knew she had to remember the last time he hadn't let her take it off, when she'd been fixing his shoulder. Chances were she'd never heard anything about the wanted poster and the scar on the outlaw's neck. She wouldn't know what it meant.

Still, it was hard, because he'd kept it covered so long, hiding it from the men he'd worked with, and the whores and the few "respectable" women he'd known.

Rachel was more than any of them.

He reached up, tugged at the tight knot at the base of his neck and pulled the bandanna away.

Rachel gasped.

"My Lord," she whispered. "Holden—"

With an effort, he kept himself from touching the scar. "It ain't nothin'" he said.

"Nothing! Whoever did this must have…he must have almost killed you."

Damnation, her eyes were getting all wet again. "He didn't," he said gruffly.

He thought she was going to ask if he'd killed the man who'd done it, but she only got up on her toes and touched the scar, gently, as she would Gordie's cheek. He shuddered. No one had ever touched it before 'cept him.

"I'm sorry," she said. "So sorry."

He kissed her again, a little harder, just to make her shut up, but as soon as he let her go again she was stretching up and kissing the scar. He closed his eyes and shuddered.

"Don't be afraid," she said, as if *he* needed reassurance.

Maybe he did.

Heath didn't move as she unbuttoned the placket of his shirt. She uncovered the top of his chest and kissed the hollow of his throat. She worked her way down until she reached the last button and then tugged at the shirt impatiently. He got it off, and she fell to kissing the rest of his chest, running her tongue over his nipples, kissing the arch of his ribs and his stomach.

It was almost more than he could stand. He wanted more of it, but he was afraid. Afraid of how weak and happy it made him feel.

He didn't have much more time to think about his feelings, because she'd found the buttons of his britches. He stopped her again.

"My boots," he said.

Rachel stood back just long enough for him to pull his boots and stockings off. Then she was working at his buttons again, her tongue sticking out as if she was unwrapping a package she couldn't wait to see. She found out quick that he never wore anything underneath his britches. The second his cock came free

Rachel's hands were on him, and he had to concentrate on not coming then and there.

Hellfire. She was good. That other man she'd been with, the one who'd abandoned her…maybe he'd taught her. Or maybe she was just a natural. Either way, Heath wasn't thinking about how she'd learned. Her hands stroked him, teased him until he was harder than he'd ever been in his life. She fondled the head and caressed it with a fingertip.

And then she did something he would never have expected in a hundred years. She knelt in the straw and took him into her mouth.

The groan came up out of his chest unbidden as she licked and suckled him, taking as much pleasure in it as he did. No, that wasn't possible. But she seemed to enjoy it the way he'd enjoyed tasting her. She was a long time about it, and after a while he knew he wasn't going to last much longer.

He took her head gently between his hands and made her stop, though his whole body screamed to make it last just a little longer. She looked up at him, and he raised her by her shoulders. Before she could speak, he pulled her chemise over her head and started on the ties of her drawers. They fell down around her ankles, and she stepped out of them.

They were both naked now, on equal terms, like a pair of gunfighters ready to duel. Heath tugged the pins out of her hair, and it fell around her shoulders. She looked down. He tilted her chin up, bent to kiss her, then eased her to the straw.

He did again what he'd done by the creek, kissing and licking and suckling her breasts while she lay gasping with her hair spread out like a halo around her head. He kissed her all the way down, under her breasts and her belly and the place between her thighs. She was hot and pink and swollen, her body already weeping with joy. When he tasted her, she bucked like a half-broken filly, her breath coming in short, eager little puffs. He ran his tongue over her lips and around the nub between, sucking it into his mouth. He licked up her juices, taking time to let her know how much he liked the taste of her, liked seeing her quiver and pant.

She was as close to coming as he was, and he didn't want her released until he was inside her. She felt the same, clamping her fingers around his shoulders and pulling him down on top of her.

He touched her with the head of his cock. He was too far gone to take her gently. He thrust into her warmth and wetness, felt her clench and let go as she wrapped her legs around his waist.

Arching her back, she moaned as he began to move, pushing as deep as he could and pulling almost all the way out before he thrust again. He kept going until she was close to coming, and then he withdrew, silencing her protest with a long kiss. He lifted her, held her against him and turned her over onto her hands and knees. Raising her hips, he entered her again, her round bottom soft against his belly. She rocked with his motion, eager to take him in as far as he could go.

She came just before he did, lifting her head and crying out as her body clenched around him. He finished right after, holding her hips as he shuddered and let go.

He wrapped his arms around her waist, turned her around, held her tight and kissed her forehead, her chin, her lips, her hair. She held him with the same kind of desperation. They both knew this would never come again.

Easing her down beside him, Heath lay on his back in the straw. Rachel tucked herself into the hollow of his shoulder, her fingers brushing the hair on his chest and her leg wrapped around his. Heath closed his eyes and let all the tightness flow out of his muscles.

Was this what it felt like to be happy? To be able to pretend that he was like any other man…able, no matter what he'd done, to leave the past behind him?

Happiness had never been meant for him. But maybe Rachel could find it someday. He never prayed, but now he did. For her. He held her for a while longer, until he knew he couldn't put it off any longer.

Chapter Eighteen

HEATH ROSE SILENTLY and walked naked out the doors of the stable. Rachel watched him, reveling in the grace and power she loved almost as much as his fierce tenderness and stubborn refusal to let her share his pain.

She had come to the stable prepared to take whatever he'd promised to give her and walk away. There was nothing left to hope for now. And yet she'd offered herself willingly, wanting to hold him within herself one last time. She had no regrets.

Brushing off the straw as best she could, she got up and looked for Holden. She could see no sign of him when she reached the doors and looked outside. Without his clothing he could not have gone far and neither could she, but she crept out after him, glancing toward the silent house.

A dark shape, swift and low, glided toward her from across the yard. She knew it was the wolf well before it reached her, black and sleek and unpredictable. She could not have run even if she wished to.

The wolf slowed a few yards away, its tongue lolling from its long muzzle, and made a sound like a low moan.

Rachel did her best to keep still. "Please," she said. "I don't mean you any harm, and there are men hunting for you. I don't want you to die."

Yellow-green eyes blinked, and the wolf made another sound that in a man would have indicated the greatest pain. The air seemed to shimmer around the animal like waves of heat hovering over the horizon, and a blackness darker than the night settled over her vision. She scraped at her eyes in terror. When she opened them again, the wolf was gone.

Holden stood in its place, naked and so rigid that each of his muscles stood out in sharp relief.

"Rachel," he said in a broken voice, "I never wanted you to know."

But she *did* know.

The wolf was Holden Renshaw.

THE LOOK ON Rachel's face was enough.

She tried to control it. Maybe a part of her remembered that he had never harmed her or Gordie, that she had once wanted him enough to forget everything else he had been and done. But the horror reached her eyes and painted her face with the animal fear Heath had seen so many times before, a fear that went deeper than any respect or desire or the feeling fools called love.

He wanted to howl to the skies, tear at the ground, run straight into the hunters' guns and let them take his life. For a brief time, carried away by their loving, he'd seen those heavenly gates again.

But wasn't this what he'd always expected? Rachel was human. Tomorrow or the day after, once she got over the shock, she might make herself pretend that it didn't bother her. Maybe, unlike the others, she would try. But her acceptance would always be a mask, a skin worn over her terror and disgust.

"Gordie's my son," he said. "He's like me. Now you understand."

Her lips parted. She tried to speak, but her voice was gone, along with her trust and the faith she'd clung to in spite of all the lies. Heath Changed, spun on his hind paws and burst into a run.

He didn't see Rachel again, and she didn't come out of the house the next morning to watch the hunters saddle their mounts and check their rifles. Heath closed off his senses, praying he wouldn't smell her before he left with the others.

Sean didn't even look at him. He waved to Amy, who stood with her mother on the porch, and kicked his stallion into a gallop. Heath turned Apache away from the rest of the hunters, all the male guests and most of the Blackwater hands, and set off toward the south. He knew Sean expected him to try setting his own trap. It wouldn't matter if he made it look obvious by riding in another direction.

He couldn't feel his heart anymore, but his brain was still working. He wasn't sure what Rachel would do now that she had the letter, but he knew she wouldn't try to take Gordie. Gavin would be waiting at Dog Creek, and if Heath didn't return, he would see to the boy.

It wasn't his own possible death Heath mourned with what little feeling he had left, but the knowledge that he might never see Rachel or Gordie again. Even if he survived, the half-life that remained would have meaning only because of his son, and it would end when Gordie no longer needed him.

RACHEL REACHED AGAIN for the gun tucked in the waistband of her skirt. It felt cold and evil under her fingertips. She had thought long and hard about bringing it, but in the end she had decided such bitter precautions were necessary. She prayed she would never be compelled to point it at anyone. Not even Sean McCarrick.

In the distance, the dust left behind by the riders was still visible, but she was rapidly falling behind. She kicked her horse's sides and he broke into a trot, responding at last to her desperate need.

Her decision to follow Holden and the hunters had required only as much time as it took for her to dress, creep from the stable back to the Blackwell house and crawl into her bed. The world had become a maelstrom of emotion and disbelief—astonishment and horror and all the sensations that followed hard on their heels. The shocks had come one after another, building until it seemed as if her mind could contain no more.

Yet she had accepted all the rest because her feelings had not changed. It might be over for Holden, but not for her. There was a bond between them, between them and Gordie, that could never be broken.

And she came to understand, as she lay in bed shivering with the covers pulled up to her chin, that there was nothing in the world that could destroy them. Love was enough to overcome even the greatest fears and the gravest doubts. Even the impossible.

She hadn't slept during what remained of the night. She had thought back to every discussion or experience that had involved the wolf, and everything began to make sense. The dream in which the outlaw had been replaced by the wolf that had attacked Louis, the story of the wolf attacking Sean. The meeting with the wolf at Dog Creek, and the conversation with Holden that had followed.

He shouldn't have been there, he had said. *He shouldn't have been so close to the ranch after dawn.*

Rachel had asked him not to shoot the wolf if he came back. She had said the wolf was beautiful, and he had told her most people wouldn't agree with her.

Because his own foster father didn't shoot his friend the wolf. He tried to kill Holden.

She had wept, remembering the story of his life on the run. How much sense it made now. No one could accept him. He had nowhere to go, no home, no hope. Until he had come to Dog Creek.

Don't make the mistake of believin' a lobo thinks like a man, he had said. But Holden *was* a man. A man capable of compassion and loyalty and great devotion.

And Gordie was his son. That was why he had so often questioned her about her own devotion to the baby. He was afraid she would become like the Mortons. He was afraid to trust anyone with his secret. It was why he had seemed so driven to tell her about himself, to explain his past, and yet never spoke of a future. Why he had loved her with such fierce tenderness and then walked away as if it meant nothing.

Yet still he had told her not to give up on Gordie when she had thought herself unworthy to keep him. *Carin' don't mean givin' up when times get hard, or just because you made a mistake.*

In the end, he had tried to trust her, but she had betrayed that trust, recoiling from the great gift he had offered her, rejecting the miracle of his transformation. She had despised herself as she had lain in bed, her tears soaking the pillow, knowing there might never be a chance to set things right.

So she had risen before dawn, as the hunters were

just beginning to assemble. She had dressed in the skirt she wore for riding and secured Holden's gun. When Amy had come out of her own room a short time later, Rachel had told her that she wished to ride that morning. Amy had agreed, though with notable reluctance. She had offered to ride with Rachel, but Rachel had said she needed time to think over all that had happened at the party and promised she would not go far. She had asked in the kitchen for a bottle she could fill with water and a little food to take with her.

She had waited impatiently for one of the hands to saddle the Blackwells' gentlest horse, a gelding Amy had ridden when she was younger. By the time she rode away, the hunters had already left. Soon they had become little more than specks in the distance. Rachel knew they were bound for a place along the creek called Willow Bend, where the wolf had last been seen. She followed the dust trail until it had blown away on the wind, then continued in the same direction, following the prints of their horses' hooves on the hard ground.

Now, as the gelding carried her after the riders at a maddeningly slow pace, she wondered again what she thought she could possibly do if she caught up with them. The odds were very much against her. Yet she had too much to fight for, and fight she would, even if her greatest enemy proved to be Holden himself.

Three hours after she had left the house, she realized she had lost the hunters' trail. Nor had she found the creek. She had remembered Holden's warning about the desert, but remembering hadn't been enough when she had been so bent on finding him. She didn't dare dismount for fear that she might not be able to get into the saddle again.

The gelding blew out his breath and dropped his head. Rachel looked up at the sky. Holden had taught her a little about the angle of the sun and using the compass, and after a few minutes she realized she had gone in the wrong direction. Once again she set off, shaking her weariness away with a toss of her head.

She was certain her decision was correct when the sun reached its zenith and began its downward arc toward the west. But the gelding was beginning to droop, his pace slowing more and more, and Rachel had still not reached the creek.

By late afternoon her body had grown heavy and her eyes refused to focus. She dozed in the saddle, and when she woke again the gelding was standing still, his hip cocked as he, too, rested. The poor animal could go no farther, and in a few hours the sun would begin to set.

She knew then that she had made a terrible mistake— not in attempting to help Holden, but in failing to provide for Gordie in the event of her death. Lucia would certainly not abandon him, but even if she and Maurice found a good home for him, he would be alone, like Holden. Forever alone.

I must get back. She could rest the gelding for a while, share her water with him and wait until morning. She would not allow herself to die so easily. Someone was sure to find her sooner or later.

But Holden…

She did her best not to think at all and slid gingerly from the gelding's back. She offered the horse water in her cupped hands, drank, herself, and took a little of the food she'd brought. After a while she lay down, hoping to sleep a little to gather her strength for the next day.

But the sun was still in the sky when she woke to find a long shadow spilling over her and a rider watching her from the back of a big gray horse. She scrambled to her feet, shading her eyes against the light.

The rider dismounted and touched the brim of his hat. His face wore an expression of strain and worry. "I'm sorry if I frightened you, ma'am," he said. "I didn't expect to find anyone alone out here."

Rachel hardly heard him. She was lost in astonishment over the man's obvious resemblance to Holden, not only in face and coloring, but in build and natural grace. She backed closer to her gelding and laid her hand on his neck.

"Who are you?" she asked.

"My name is Gavin Renier."

She didn't know the name, but that didn't lessen her unease. She saw with relief that he wasn't wearing a gun and wasn't making any attempt to come closer.

"Are you lost, ma'am?" he asked.

Rachel wasn't prepared to admit any vulnerability to a stranger, especially not this one. "My name is Rachel McCarrick," she said. "I am a guest of the Blackwells."

"I've heard your name, Mrs. McCarrick. You live at Dog Creek."

"Yes," she said. "I have been looking for a band of hunters searching for a wolf."

"A wolf?" Renier's face became grim. "A black wolf?"

His sudden change of demeanor made her shiver. "Yes. Have you seen them?"

"Not yet. I'm also looking for a wolf of that description."

Rachel wished she dared reach for her gun. "Do you intend to hurt him, too?"

"I intend to save him." He searched her face with eyes more gold than green. "Why do you care, Mrs. McCarrick?"

Telling the truth was out of the question. "He...he is my friend."

"Your friend?" He took a step toward her. "How is that possible?"

"He saved the life of a boy I know."

He was silent for nearly a minute. "I understand that you have a foreman named Holden Renshaw. Do you know where he is?"

Rachel moved closer to the saddle, knowing that even if she could mount without help, she couldn't get away before this man caught up with her.

"If I knew," she said, "I wouldn't tell you."

The sun-etched lines around his eyes deepened. "I need to find him. He's my brother."

It couldn't be true. Holden had never mentioned kin other than the mother who had abandoned him. But she could not deny the amazing resemblance between Holden and this man.

A man who was looking for a black wolf.

"Mr. Renshaw doesn't have a brother," she said defiantly.

"He didn't know he had one until yesterday," Renier said. "I spoke to him and asked him to come back with me to our family. He said he had business to attend to, and I knew he was going to get himself into trouble."

Holden had known? He'd discovered he had family who might want him? Did that have something to do with why he had revealed his true nature?

He was in trouble. And he had no allies but her. Unless this man was telling the truth. Unless...

"Do you know what he is?" Rachel asked, throwing all caution aside.

Renier stared at her, and she could almost feel the threat radiating from his body. "What do you mean?" he asked softly.

"He and the wolf are closer than you can imagine," she said. "Closer than brothers. You might say they are almost one creature."

The threat was gone in an instant. "He told you?" Gavin asked.

"He showed me."

Gavin removed his hat. "You must be a remarkable woman, Mrs. McCarrick."

"I am not remarkable at all." She glanced toward the western horizon. Time was running out. "Are you like him?"

"Yes. And I may be the only one who can help him."

Her mind seized on an idea that seemed an answer to her deepest fears. "Is your family also…like that?"

"We are. That's why we want him back."

"Did you know that Holden has a son?"

"At Dog Creek. He said—"

"Will your family take him in if something happens to Holden?"

Once again he gazed at her as if she was something extraordinary. "Yes."

"Gordie must have a home if…if Holden doesn't return. If you care about Holden at all, please go to Dog Creek and be ready to take Gordie if the worst happens."

"I've been there. Holden already asked me to go. But I couldn't stay, knowing he was about to do something dangerous. Now that I know those men are after him—"

"He won't be alone. I intend to do whatever is necessary to stop them."

"You?" He made no effort to hide his astonishment. "How do you expect to do that?"

"I don't know."

Renier shook his head. "How will you find them?"

"Do you know where the creek is?"

He was quiet again, much longer than before. "I can track those hunters right now."

"Then take me to them. There isn't any time to waste."

"I can't let you—"

"You can. Would you condemn your brother's son to a life of rejection and pain? I cannot assure him freedom from such a fate. But I may be able to help his father."

He put his hat back on. "I don't know why," he said, "but I believe you."

"I don't think my horse can carry me much farther."

"Mine can carry two for a while. We'll lead yours."

Renier wasted no time in tying her gelding's reins to his horse's saddle and mounting, easily lifting her up behind him. She put her arms around his waist. With a soft click of his tongue, Gavin Renier turned his horse toward the setting sun.

THE HALF-DOZEN MEN Heath had led away from the rendezvous site had lost his trail. They'd already been riled up because the whole long, hot day they'd only seen the wolf at a distance, never close enough to kill. When he'd finally let them chase him, determined to rob Sean McCarrick of his allies, he'd realized that Sean couldn't have told them they were also after an outlaw. If he had, they never would have followed the wolf so far.

McCarrick was biding his time. As Heath had

guessed, he must have returned to the scene of his crime sometime before the hunt, found what was left of Jed's body under the overhang where Heath had buried it and laid out Jed's bones where anyone could find them with just a little searching. He'd stayed with the biggest band of hunters until the last couple of hours, keeping himself safe from an unexpected attack. But he couldn't give up on the chance to take Heath Renier himself and make the grand announcement of his victory right where Jed lay waiting.

The three men Sean had sent ahead of time to watch for Heath—El, Gus and Cash—might have laid a pretty good ambush if Heath hadn't smelled them a mile away. They'd been too scared to leave their places to chase the black wolf when it showed up to taunt them, but the ranchers hadn't been so cautious. Now they were too far behind to catch Heath before he went back to the place a quarter-mile from the rendezvous where he'd left his clothes.

But when he got there, he didn't Change. Sean's scent was heavy on the wind, mingled with that of his three men and two others who hadn't gone with the ranchers.

Heath hesitated. He'd set out from Blackwater without any real plan except to kill Sean, knowing Sean expected to be ready for him. The wolf told him to finish it now, while so few of Sean's allies where there to protect him. But the human...

There was no human here. The wolf had his way. Heath shook out his coat and set off at a trot, dragging the weight of his bitterness like a double-jawed trap. Right now Sean and the others were scattered behind the low hills overlooking the draw. All Heath had to do was lure Sean out from cover. When the men came running to help him, they would find his body along with the bones of the man he'd murdered.

Heath snarled, the taste of blood already on his tongue. He went straight for Sean's hiding place and trotted to the top of the hill, ears and tail erect, silhouetted plainly against the setting sun. He heard the rattling of pebbles and the scrape of Sean's boots as he saw the wolf. But Sean hesitated, weighing whether or not he should risk exposing himself when Heath Renier might show up at any minute. A cricket chirped in the brush. Nothing else stirred.

The quiet didn't last. Just as Heath expected, Sean couldn't let the opportunity pass. He'd suffered humiliation at the hands of the lobo, and he had too much to prove now, to himself and the men. He was angry. Too angry to think.

He came out of hiding, scrambling up the hill with his rifle in his hands, his faced distorted with hate. He took aim. Heath grinned at him and trotted back down the hill. Sean came after him, panting and cursing. Several times Heath allowed Sean to get just close enough to aim, gradually leading Sean in a wide circle back toward the draw.

Sean was too fixed on the lobo to notice where he was going until they were almost on top of the bones. He went stock-still, glanced around and then looked straight at Jed's remains.

Shifting his weight, Heath gathered himself for the burst of speed that would take Sean down.

And stopped. It was too easy. Once he got his teeth locked around Sean's throat, he wouldn't be able to stop himself until Sean was dead. The human in him knew that wasn't enough. He demanded more. Much more. Not only Sean's death in pain and terror, but his knowledge that he'd been beaten by the man he despised and shown for what he really was.

He spun around, loped over the next hill and raced for his clothes. Sean might go right back to his men, or he might follow again, but he wouldn't get far.

Sean was still standing in the draw, looking just about ready to go back into hiding, when Heath returned. When Heath walked over the hill, Sean looked up, his mouth open and his eyes stark with sudden fear.

"Renshaw," he said hoarsely. "About time you showed up."

It was a pretty good act, but not good enough. Sean was scared out of his wits. His trap hadn't worked out quite the way he'd planned.

"Looks like you lost your bet," Heath said softly.

Sean tried to grin. "It isn't over, Renshaw."

"It's about to be."

Panic froze Sean's face. He didn't want a fair fight. He never had. He raised his rifle, but his hands were shaking. His head turned in one direction and then another, looking for help. He backed away, and his feet crunched on Jed's bones. He flinched.

"What's wrong, Sean?" Heath asked. "You wanted it to happen here, didn't you?"

Sean retreated until he was well out of Heath's reach. "I see you don't have a gun," he said.

Heath crouched beside the bones and rested his hand lightly on Jed's skull again. *You'll get justice now, old man.* "I don't need a gun," he said.

"You won't get away with this, Renshaw. I have men—"

"They ain't here, are they? But you always was a

stinkin' yellow belly. Maybe you should start yellin'. Or shootin'."

The taunt shut Sean up just as he opened his mouth to shout. He aimed the rifle again.

"I won't shoot you yet, Renshaw. Or should I call you Renier? I expect my men will be here any moment, and then I'll tell them who you are and how you killed my uncle."

It wasn't any surprise to Heath that Sean had figured out who he was. He'd already guessed as much.

"Now, why would I kill Jed?" Heath drawled. "Wasn't me who had the motive to do him in."

"You had motive. And I can prove it." Sean laughed nervously. "I have the will my uncle wrote, the one leaving everything to you, the one he rescinded when he decided to marry Rachel."

So Sean had found another copy. That was why he'd been so confident yesterday.

"There was a will made out to you, too," Heath said, "only Jed figured out just what you were and crossed it out." He bared his teeth. "Did you find him here and argue with him over your future at Dog Creek? Did Jed tell you was through?"

"You're crazy, Renshaw. You'd never convince anyone of such a wild story, even if you lived to tell it."

"That's funny, McCarrick. I would have figured by now you'd know you're the one who won't be tellin'."

Chapter Nineteen

IT HAD ALL gone wrong.

Sean tried to hold the rifle steady as he grinned at Renshaw, knowing that any sign of weakness could be fatal. For a little while he'd actually believed that Renshaw wasn't coming, that he'd turned coward again and run rather than face his certain fate. It wasn't what Sean had wanted, but he could still blame Jed's death on the outlaw Heath Renier and make sure he was pursued until he was taken and hanged.

But Renshaw hadn't run. Sean had been careful to keep some of the other men around him during the hunt, but he'd lost his sense when he'd seen the wolf so close, too intent on showing the others that no mere animal could defeat him.

Now the joke was on him. There *was* a connection between Renshaw and the wolf. Renshaw had used the beast to lure Sean away, right to where the bastard wanted him. Renshaw had succeeded in ruffling him so badly that he had revealed that he knew Renshaw's real name and accused him of killing Jed with no witnesses present to hear.

All Sean could do now was distract Renshaw until the men wondered where he had gone and came looking. Shooting Renshaw would bring them running, of course, but if he missed…

Renshaw had no weapon, at least—although he might have one hidden, and he was fast. Too fast.

"You think you've won, Renshaw," Sean said, filling his voice with the confidence he had come dangerously close to losing. "But your guilt will be revealed whether or not you kill me…and then what will happen to Rachel and the baby?"

He thought he'd gone too far when Renshaw lunged at him, but the outlaw stopped just short of grabbing him by the throat. "What do you mean?" he snarled.

It was time to bluff as he'd never bluffed in his life. "I know how much you care for them," Sean said. "I also know that Rachel is a fraud. The two of you have been deceiving everyone. You knew my uncle was dead, and that he'd be found eventually. You wanted everyone to think that Rachel had a right to whatever he left behind. That's why you conspired with her to pretend she was already married and forged Jed's signature on the will to—"

"I never forged no signature."

"But you did, Renshaw. And when that is discovered, as I'll make sure it will be, your conspiracy will be evident to everyone. No respectable person in the county would allow such a woman to care for a foundling child."

The rage in Renshaw's eyes burned so hot that it took a supreme act of will for Sean to hold his ground. "No one's takin' the boy," Renshaw said. "Not if I have to—"

"Kill everyone in the Pecos?" Sean shook his head. "Even you, with your apparently well-earned reputation, can't manage such a feat. And if I should die at your hands, Rachel won't merely be disgraced and disinherited, she'll find herself accused of being the accomplice of a wanted killer."

He had the satisfaction of seeing complete comprehension transform Renshaw's face. *At last you begin to understand*, Sean thought. *You know I may be bluffing, lying to save my own skin. But you can't be sure. And even if I have no direct proof that Rachel knew who you were all along, you know I'm capable of seeing that she's blamed for harboring a dangerous fugitive.*

"You see how it is," Sean said casually. "You wouldn't be in such a quandary if you hadn't allowed yourself to care for your employer's intended and a foundling brat." He chuckled. "Ironic, is it not? You're the ferocious outlaw, I'm the educated gentleman, yet you have allowed yourself to bestow your affection on those weaker than yourself, and that has made you vulnerable. You have made the mistake that I never have and never will."

"You've made a mistake, all right," Renshaw said. "I can take you right now and keep you as a hostage until Rachel and the boy are a hundred miles away."

"And confirm to the world that she was your whore and your confederate? Set the law on her and force her to run for the rest of her life?" Sean tapped his chin as if in thought. "I have another proposition for you, Renshaw. Give yourself up now. Admit to being Heath Renier, and to killing my uncle. If you do, I will personally see that your lover and the infant are supplied with enough money to get them out of the county, where they will be free to start a new life."

He saw Renshaw waver, undoubtedly weighing his own life and freedom against the welfare of those he supposedly loved. Sean was betting that the emotional rot went deep, and he would give in.

But something happened he had no way of anticipating. Renshaw took a dozen steps back, his hands loose at his sides. He didn't reach for a hidden gun, or attempt to escape. Instead, he threw down his hat and began to remove his clothing, kicking off his boots, unbuttoning his vest and trousers, pulling his shirt over his head and throwing it aside. The bandanna came last, revealing the jagged scar.

He's gone mad, Sean thought, and lifted his rifle, waiting for some wild action that would force him to shoot.

Renshaw didn't move. He didn't even blink. He seemed to become almost transparent, the air shimmering around him, darkening, wreathing him about like smoke. His body began to change, hunching, settling low to the ground. When the mist cleared away, a black wolf stood where the man had been.

Sean got off one shot before the lobo reached him. The animal's weight dropped him and knocked the rifle from his hand. Powerful jaws snapped in his face, while vicious nails raked at his chest and tore his waistcoat. The wolf's eyes glared into his.

Renshaw's eyes.

Sean tried to scream. Teeth like razors closed on his collar, ground down, pierced his skin. Sean whimpered and emptied his bladder. All his plans had been for nothing, all lost to a creature that should not exist. He prayed for the first time in his life.

Then the man-beast hesitated for a breath, as if remembering the man it had been a few moments before. An explosion of hoofbeats echoed in the draw. The crack of a rifle deafened Sean, the bullet whizzing past his head. The wolf jerked and grunted in pain. Suddenly the weight was gone from Sean's chest. Rough voices shouted warnings, and someone knelt beside him.

"You all right, Sean?" George Saunderson asked, laying his hand on Sean's shoulder. Sean cursed in pain, and George withdrew his hand.

"I can see you're not," he said. "Boys, get on over here. Mr. McCarrick's hurt bad. We need to—"

"The wolf," Sean croaked. "Where is it?"

"O'Hara thinks he hit it, but it got away. We got to get you back to Blackwater."

"No. The wolf…" Nausea choked Sean's throat with bile. "You…you've got to—"

"Easy now." John Powell crouched beside George and draped a blanket over Sean. "Do you think you can ride?"

"Jed…Jed is here."

George's breath gusted into Sean's face. "Jed? You're shaken up, son. Just—"

"God in heaven!" Powell swore. "There's bones here."

Sean sighed and closed his eyes. They'd found Jed. One of the men would see his gold tooth and identify him. He had regained the upper hand. Everything he'd said to Renshaw would come to pass.

"George," he rasped. "Listen to me. Renshaw…is—"

Before he could form the word, he heard a voice he had never expected.

"Where is Mr. Renshaw?"

Rachel. Sean tried to sit up and felt a gout of fresh blood spew over his torn shirt.

"Lie still," George said. "We're goin' to bandage your neck. Don't worry, we'll take care of everything. All you have to do is…"

His words ceased to have meaning. Sean sank into darkness.

ALL WAS CHAOS. Rachel held the gelding still among the stamping horses and shouting men, knowing that Holden was gone.

But he had been here. Rachel saw the ugly wounds on Sean's face, neck and chest. Something had attacked him, savaged him, nearly killed him.

She closed her eyes tight and opened them again, as if she might change the world by sheer will. But it was all too solid. A few of the men hovered over Sean, binding his injuries. Another group bent over something on the ground, speaking in low, urgent tones. The rest huddled atop their mounts, and argued about the wolf and what it would take to bring it down once and for all.

Holden had escaped them once again. His brother was on his way back to Dog Creek and Gordie, prepared to do whatever was necessary to save the baby. She had no goal now but to find his father.

"Ma'am!" a voice said behind her. "What are you doin' out here?"

She recognized the rider as one of the Blackwater hands, a thin-shouldered cowboy with a hound dog's face. He looked genuinely alarmed, and she knew she had to set him at ease immediately.

"I went out riding," she said quickly, "and lost my way. I saw riders in the distance and followed them."

The man frowned with patent disbelief. "You've come a long way from the house, ma'am," he said. "I'll take you on back, and—"

"My horse is very tired," she said. "He needs rest before he can go on, and I require rest, as well. Perhaps in an hour or two…"

"It'll be dark then, ma'am. I think—"

Whatever he thought, Rachel never learned, for the hand's attention was caught by the raised voices of the men looking at the ground. Intent on escape, Rachel edged her horse toward the bank of the draw, riding in a wide circle around them. She caught a glimpse of something white; then one of the men shifted, and she saw the skull grinning up at the darkening sky.

Jed. Her stomach heaved, but she kept going. There was nothing she could do for him now. There had never been anything she could do, not even to punish the man who she was sure had killed him.

She had reached the foot of the nearest hill when the mounted men broke apart and set their horses into a run over another hill to the west. She didn't have to ask where they were going. Taking advantage of the momentary confusion, she rode after the hunters. None of them looked behind to object or send her back, but they moved too quickly for the weary gelding to keep up, and she quickly fell behind. Only when she heard a distant shout did she urge her mount into a gallop, bending low over his neck and holding on for dear life.

The wolf was trapped in a small canyon between steep walls of earth and stone. Blood seeped from a wound in his shoulder, matting the black fur; he snapped and snarled as the riders urged their horses closer and encircled him, their rifles bristling like spears.

Only one thought came to Rachel's mind. She slid off the gelding's back, her boots landing hard on the ground, and fumbled for the gun. She slipped and slid her way down into the canyon, her skirts dragging at her feet. She scrambled over shifting stones and low brush, and finally reached the bottom.

The wolf lifted its head and looked directly at her. His eyes seemed to plead, *Go back.*

She ignored the message and ran as fast as she could toward Holden, clutching the gun so hard that her fingers went numb. One of the hunters exclaimed in surprise and horror as she skidded to a stop between Holden and the riders. She lifted the gun and aimed at the nearest man.

"Stay where you are!" she warned him. Heath snarled behind her.

"Run," she whispered to him. "Go!"

He hesitated, a sound between whine and growl coming from his throat. Then he heaved himself up the steep incline, his claws scrabbling as they sought purchase. One of the riders—John Powell, she remembered—took a shot, and Rachel heard it strike the earth just above her head. Three of the hunters broke away, ready to set off in pursuit. Rachel pointed the gun toward the sky and fired.

Everything came to a stop. Astonished, angry eyes pierced her like cactus spines. Finn O'Hara and George Saunderson dismounted and jumped down into the canyon.

"Just what do you think you're doing, Mrs. McCarrick?" Saunderson demanded, snatching the gun out of her hand. "You could've been killed, or hurt someone!"

She didn't even attempt to answer. The two men half dragged her back up to level ground and got her onto the gelding. They pinned her mount between theirs, muttering about her apparent lapse into madness and wondering at the reason for her "fit." When they got back to the draw where the other men waited, Sean was sitting propped up against a pile of bedrolls, his wounds bound, pale but alert. Powell helped Rachel dismount and remained close, clearly determined not to let her commit any more rash and incomprehensible acts.

Rachel knew she must either come up with a reasonable justification for her actions and demonstrate that she was over her lapse into "insanity," or they would hold her prisoner until morning.

"I'm very sorry, Mr. Powell," she began. "I don't know what came over me. It must be the heat and the long—"

A shout cut off her desperate explanation. Holden was riding down the hill, fully clothed and as casual as if he'd just come back from a leisurely amble along Dog Creek. There was no sign of a wound anywhere on his body. He looked straight at Rachel, taking in the men around her. Then his gaze fell on Sean.

"What's goin' on?" he asked. "I heard shots. What're you doin' here, Mrs. McCarrick?"

Sean tried to sit up and gasped, his face as white as Jed's bones. "He killed Jed!" he cried.

The hush was profound. Everyone stared at Holden. George Saunderson murmured something to Sean.

"He did it, I tell you!" Sean cried. "He admitted it to me himself! His name is Heath Renier, and he's wanted for murder!"

Renier, Rachel thought. *Like Gavin.*

Belatedly, Saunderson and Powell started toward Holden. "I've heard of Heath Renier," Powell said, his eyes narrow in his deeply tanned face. "I've seen the poster. He's wanted for more than murder. There's a bounty on his head." He drew the gun at his hip. "H.R. Holden Renshaw."

Conflicting voices rose in argument. Heath moved

so swiftly that Rachel hardly had time to register the fact that he'd dismounted before he was at her side. A gun flashed in his hand, and the muzzle came to rest squarely against her temple.

"Nobody move a muscle," he said softly. "I'm Heath Renier, all right, and I've killed plenty of men. Won't bother me at all to kill a woman."

He backed away, one arm around Rachel's chest as he dragged her toward his horse. She struggled instinctively, confused and more than a little afraid of this sudden violent change. He threw her up into the saddle, ignoring the hunters, who were urging each other to go after him, and mounted behind her.

"Any of you come after me," he said, "and she dies." He gave the gelding a kick, and Apache sprang away like a jackrabbit. Rachel clung to the saddle horn, the wind bringing tears to her eyes.

As soon as they'd descended the other side of the hill, Holden holstered his gun and shifted his arm to her waist. Apache kept running, and her hair came free of its loose knot. She found it difficult to breathe.

"*Are* you planning to kill me?" she asked, the bitter words out of her mouth before she could stop them.

His breath gusted sharply against her hair. "I had to do it," he said. "He wasn't only goin' to tell everyone that you ain't married and been betrayin' Jed with me. He was goin' to make it look like you knew who I was all along and was hidin' me at Dog Creek."

Rachel's heart stuttered wildly. "So you *are* Heath Renier," she said.

"And I'm wanted, just like they said. That's why it needs to look like you never knew who I was." She could feel the heat of his hand penetrating her bodice like a blade of fire. "You shouldn't have come. You shouldn't have interfered."

Laughter rose, then died in her throat. "So I should have let you be killed?"

"If it weren't for—" He clenched his teeth with such force that she could hear his jaw crack. "If I'd finished Sean, he wouldn't be able to hurt you or Gordie."

She tried to twist in the saddle to see his face. "Hurt Gordie?"

"He threatened both of you. That's why you have to leave the county. I'm takin' you to Dog Creek. There's someone there who can help you get away."

She knew he must mean Gavin, but there was hardly any time to absorb what he had said. "You didn't kill Sean," she said. "Why?"

"'Cause I made the worst mistake of my life."

But she knew it hadn't been a mistake. In the end, he hadn't been able to go through with it. He had killed before, as the outlaw Heath Renier, but he had changed. He had become a decent man named Holden Renshaw.

But the law would never let him escape, even if he was able to defend himself against Sean's charges. He would remain a hunted criminal.

"You must run," she said. "Gordie will be safe with your brother. I—"

His chin bumped against her head. "You met Gavin?"

"While I was looking for you. He was on his way to help you, but I sent him back to Dog Creek. I know what he is, Holden."

The sun had been below the horizon for several minutes before Holden spoke again.

"You'll never be safe from Sean unless he's dead," he said. "I aim to get another chance at him."

"No! There must be another way."

"There ain't."

"I don't care what they say about you, or what you may say about yourself. You aren't a murderer."

He didn't answer. She could feel him pulling away from her, growing more and more distant, detaching himself from anything he might ever have felt for her. It wasn't only because he knew he was likely to be taken or killed. She knew he would never get over her shock and horror when he had revealed his other self. He assumed that she was suddenly willing to give Gordie up because of her fear that he would grow up to be like his father.

She could have tried to convince him that she had long since stopped feeling anything remotely like horror. If he had not been so set on his own death, she might have explained that she thought he was far more miracle than nightmare. If she had already told him that she loved him, he might even have believed her.

But she had waited too long. Her own fear of rejection, her own stubborn pride, had kept her silent, and now it was too late. Holden was more beast than man now, his mind awash with violence. Appealing to his reason, to his humanity, would be as futile as asking the desert to sprout apple trees and roses.

And yet, in spite of everything, she knew she had to try one more time.

"I'm not leaving you," she said. "Gordie doesn't need me now. I'm staying with you until you agree to go with your brother, wherever he wants to take you."

He refused to answer and set Apache into a ground-eating lope. He kept going for several hours, effortlessly finding their path through the darkness, then made a simple camp in a shallow draw. Rachel was too exhausted to protest his command that she sleep. It was still dark when he woke her.

The first patina of dawn had silvered the sky when the landscape began to seem familiar again. Holden finally broke the silence.

"When we get to the house," he said, "you just keep on pretendin' that you're my prisoner. We need to fool everyone, even Lucia and Maurice. You get a few things to take with you." His voice grew rough. "I'm sendin' you with Gavin as far as Heywood, and you ain't got no say in the matter. He won't hurt you."

"I know he won't. But I'm still not lea—"

In one motion he pulled the kerchief from around his neck and whipped it across her mouth, winding the reins around the saddle horn to free his hands so he could tie the cloth behind her head. The smell of him filled her nostrils. He ignored her muffled cry, took up the reins again and urged Apache into a run. They were near the place by the creek where Heath had first loved her, when he suddenly pulled Apache up and sniffed the air. His mouth hardened, and he kicked the horse into a gallop once more.

Even before they reached the house, Rachel smelled the unmistakable stench of scorched wood. Holden pulled out his gun and rested it on his thigh. As they neared the edge of the pasture, a fan of sunlight struck the blackened husk of the barn.

Holden slowed Apache to a walk, cursing under his breath. Rachel took advantage of his distraction to pull at the neckerchief, but he stopped her, pulled a knife and sliced off one of the reins. He tied it around her wrists, loosely enough that she was comfortable but not so loose that she could free her hands.

"Keep still," he said.

They rode into the yard. There was no sign of Gavin. Maurice was standing a few yards from the barn, gazing at it as if it presented a problem he didn't know how to solve. He started as he saw Heath and Rachel approach.

"Monsieur Renshaw!" he began. "Thank God—" He broke off in consternation, staring from Rachel's face to the gun in Holden's hand.

"What happened here, Maurice?" Holden asked softly.

"I…I do not understand."

"You don't have to. What happened?"

"There was a fire. We do not know…" He hesitated. "We do not know how it started."

"Was anyone hurt?"

"We saved the animals, but…" He trailed off again, searching Rachel's eyes. "*Monsieur,* surely you do not mean—"

The things Rachel would have said to Maurice were far too complex to convey with her eyes alone. At least Maurice seemed more confused than alarmed. He knew Holden too well to believe him capable of harming Jedediah's wife.

But he *was* afraid of *something*.

The door to the house opened, and Lucia, looking nearly as dazed as Maurice, came out. She stopped abruptly when she saw the tableau in the yard. With his knees and a shift of his weight, Holden turned Apache to face her.

"Where's Gordie, Lucia?" he asked.

Lucia's gaze darted to Maurice, then fixed on Rachel.

"A man came," she said, clasping her hands in distress. "He said he was your brother, *señor*. He gave only one name. Gavin. He said you had told him to take the child away for his safety. I could not stop him."

She had begun to weep. Rachel twisted furiously in the saddle. Holden locked his arm around her waist.

"It's all right, Lucia," he said. "You done the right thing." He looked back at Maurice. "Where'd they go?"

"I do not know," the Frenchman said, his nervous demeanor giving way to defiance. "Let *madame* go, *monsieur*."

Holden pointed the gun at Maurice's head. "Where'd they go?"

"South."

"Did anyone else come here?"

"*Non*." Maurice straightened. "I do not know what is happening, *monsieur*, but I cannot let you take Mrs. McCarrick."

Holden ignored him. "Where's Charlie?"

"I do not know."

"Are any of the horses hurt?"

"*Non*, but—"

"You want to help Mrs. McCarrick, you go saddle up Rip and Copperhead, and bring them out here right quick." Holden shifted the gun so that it pointed at Rachel's heart. "Get movin'."

Swearing in voluble French, Maurice trotted toward the stable. Lucia continued to weep silently.

"Lucia," Holden said in a gruff voice, "it's all right. No one's goin' to get hurt so long as you do what I say."

The Mexican woman was about to speak when Joey came pelting out of the house, his rifle in his hands. He skidded to a halt beside Lucia.

"Holden!" He grinned broadly and lowered the rifle. "I thought—" He noticed Rachel's gag and stopped.

Holden tensed, and Rachel could feel his heart begin to beat more quickly. "What're you doin' here, Joey?" he asked.

"I came back. To warn you. Sean killed Jed. He plans to—" The rifle came back up. "What's happenin', Holden? Why've you got Rachel tied up?"

Breathless and panting, Maurice ran over with two horses on leads trotting behind him. He glanced at Joey, and Rachel wondered if some silent message was passing between them.

Please, God, Rachel prayed. *Don't let Joey shoot Holden. Don't let anyone be hurt.*

"Maurice," Holden said, "put my saddlebags on Copperhead."

The Frenchman obeyed. Keeping his gun trained on Rachel, Holden twisted in the saddle, lowered her to the ground with his free arm and dismounted behind her. He gestured for Maurice to help her mount one of the horses he'd brought from the stable.

"Please, *monsieur*," Maurice said. "Let *madame* go."

"When I'm good and ready." Holden waited until Rachel was up and then mounted the other horse, sidling the animal close to Rachel's, so that his knee touched hers. He stared at Joey.

The boy's Adam's apple bobbed convulsively. "This ain't you, Holden. It ain't—"

"Do you still have the money?"

"No!" Joey bit hard on his lower lip. "Sean took it when he—you've...got to listen! He's plannin' to—"

"I know what he's plannin' to do, Joey. You're the

one who's got to listen. Put that rifle down and come over here."

Slowly Joey set the rifle on the ground and walked over to them, his thin shoulders sagging and his eyes glistening with unshed tears.

"I don't have nothin' to give you right now," Holden said, "but when I get some money, I'll send it to you. Maurice, you take care of Joey, and see that Lucia gets home to her family soon as you can. Maybe you'll have to find another job, but I'll do what I can to make sure you don't go broke."

"But, Holden," Joey burst out, "where are you going? Where are you taking Rachel?"

Holden reached out and laid his hand on Joey's head. "Better you not know, boy. You just take care of yourself, and if anyone else comes, you tell 'em Heath Renier still has Mrs. McCarrick."

"Heath Renier?"

"I need you to promise to take good care of Apache. He's yours."

"But—"

"Don't try to follow me, hear?"

"Holden—"

But Holden wasn't listening. He grabbed the lead rope of Rachel's horse. She clasped the saddle horn with her bound hands and tried to look back at the others as Holden kicked his horse into a canter and hers followed suit.

There was nothing they could do. She was grateful that Joey was safe, and that no one had been hurt in the fire. And she was certain Joey, at least, didn't believe Holden would hurt her. Would the boy make the mistake of following, though?

If Holden had any concerns about that, his face didn't

show it. It remained an expressionless mask, though for a short time, when he had spoken to Joey, she had seen that mask crack.

They rode south. Holden kept the horses at a steady canter, glancing often at the ground and pausing occasionally to sniff the air. Rachel wondered when Gavin had taken Gordie and how far ahead he had gotten. Were they safe? She prayed again, for Holden and his brother and Gordie.

Only two hours after they had left the house, Holden pulled up, lifted his head and took several deep breaths.

"Gavin and Gordie are up ahead, right over that hill," he said. "But someone else is with 'em. You got to stay quiet a little longer."

Rachel tried to protest, but he paid no attention. He urged the horses ahead at a cautious walk. They crested the hill, and Rachel could see two men by a jumble of rocks, one standing and the other sitting in the shade. The standing man was pointing a gun at the sitting one, who held a blanket-wrapped bundle in his arms.

Gordie.

Chapter Twenty

RACHEL KICKED HER horse, thinking only of getting to Gordie, but Holden kept a tight hold on the animal's lead. He drew his gun and kept going, guiding his mount with his knees.

The stranger was watching as they approached.

"Hold it right there," he said.

"Who are you?" Holden demanded.

"He's Jacob Constantine, a bounty hunter," Gavin said in a heavy voice, making no attempt to stand. "He was watching the house from downwind. I'm sorry, Holden."

"You might as well call him by his real name," Constantine said. "I've been looking for you a long time, Heath Renier."

Holden showed no reaction. "Is the baby all right?" he asked Gavin.

"Yes," Gavin said. "Hungry, but unhurt."

Rachel leaned forward as if she could reach Gordie merely by willing it, but Constantine moved to stand in the way. There was something familiar about him, something that linked him to Holden and Gavin. His hair was a medium brown, but his eyes had that same touch of wolfish gold.

My God, Rachel thought. *He's one of them.*

"Let the lady go, Renier," Constantine said calmly, "and we'll talk."

"You let my brother go first," Holden countered.

"I'm afraid that isn't possible."

"You'd hurt a baby?"

"Would you?"

Holden hesitated and slowly holstered his gun.

Constantine released his breath.

"Your brother did a brave thing, leading me away when I almost had you," he said. "I'll let him and the baby go—if you release the lady and give yourself up."

Rachel struggled to speak. Holden untied the kerchief, and she spat it out of her mouth.

"It's not what you think!" she cried. "His name is Holden Renshaw. He's trying to save me from a man named Sean McCarrick, who murdered my fiancé, Jedediah McCarrick."

Constantine met her gaze and shook his head. "I've met this Sean McCarrick. I can well believe he murdered somebody. But that's not why I'm here. This man is Heath Renier, wanted in three states and two territories, and he means you no good."

"I shall be the judge of that!" She tried to kick her horse forward, but Holden wouldn't let go of the lead. "That man you are holding is trying to keep Mr. Renshaw's son safe. You have no right to hold him."

"I have every right, ma'am," Constantine said. "Seeing as how he obstructed justice by interfering with a lawful arrest."

"How can it be lawful, when you don't even want to know the truth?"

"She's got nothin' to do with what you want, Constantine," Holden said. "But there's a murderer tryin' to make it look like she knew who I was all along, when she didn't. She has to get to safety with the baby."

"I can arrange that, Renier," Constantine said. "You've got a choice. Give yourself up, and I'll let your brother take the lady and the baby as far away as he wants to. Otherwise he comes with me, and the lady can take her chances."

Rachel didn't have to look at Holden to know how much he hated Constantine. But there was nothing she could say. He had to give himself up. Gordie had to come first, and she had no doubt that Sean would hurt him if he got the chance.

Her heart was crumbling, and she knew it could never be whole again.

Holden looked at her. He tried to conceal his feelings, but they shone in his eyes, everything she had once wanted from him and a hundred times more.

"You go on with Gavin, Rachel," he said hoarsely. "He'll take you and Gordie to my family. They'll help you, whatever you decide to do."

With a lack of grace she had never seen in him before, Holden dismounted. He held one hand high and carefully drew his gun with the other, tossing it on the ground several feet away.

"Holden," she whispered.

He didn't look back. "You can let Gavin and the baby go now," he said to Constantine.

With a jerk of his gun, Constantine waved Gavin to his feet. "Take that baby over to the lady and untie her hands. If you give me any trouble, I'll shoot your brother."

Gavin nodded, his expression as grim as the bounty hunter's, and walked slowly toward Rachel. He paused only an instant as he passed Holden, and they exchanged glances. Then Gavin continued until he was standing beside Rachel's horse. He carefully hung the baby's sling from the saddle horn, reached up to untie her hands and passed Gordie into her arms. He secured the sling around her neck with trembling hands.

Rachel uncovered Gordie's face. It was wrinkled with displeasure, and he looked on the verge of crying, but he was obviously unhurt. She held him close and rocked him, praying she would not begin to weep herself.

"Come on, Renier," Constantine said.

Holden took a step toward the hunter just as the report of a gunshot shattered the silence. Constantine ran toward Holden and pushed the muzzle of his gun into Holden's chest.

"This better not be trouble of your making, Renier, or I'll—"

He broke off as a horse and rider barreled over the hill.

"Sean," Holden said. He reached for his empty holster. Constantine spun him around and held him by the throat. Rachel grabbed her horse's reins and urged him to the opposite side of the rocky cairn.

Gavin turned to face Sean.

"Someone else is coming," he said.

"Joey," Holden said. He moved with his usual astonishing speed, wrenching himself out of Constantine's hold and jumping away.

"You can shoot me, Constantine," he said, "but if you don't stop McCarrick before he hurts someone else, I will."

Constantine, his face no longer calm, pointed his gun first at Heath and then at Sean, who had stopped his horse at the bottom of the hill. "Make a move and you're dead," he growled to Heath. "You get down off that horse, Mr. McCarrick."

Sean didn't move. He was smiling like a madman.

"Thank God!" he said. "You've caught him!" He looked over at Rachel. "And you're safe. I've been praying—"

Joey's horse appeared at the top of the hill. He reined in, his face flushed, and took aim at Sean.

"Don't believe anythin' he says!" he shouted. He stared at the bounty hunter. "I don't know who you are, but you got to listen! Holden didn't do nothin'! Sean's the one who killed Jed!"

"He's right!" Rachel cried. She stared at Sean. "You've lost. Once Gordie is safe, I'll do everything within my power to expose you for what you are."

"*You* will expose *me*?" Sean laughed with delight. "I hardly—"

"Shut up and get down," Constantine snapped.

"Get out of here, Joey!" Holden shouted.

"But he's goin' to kill—"

"There won't be any killing here," Constantine said. "Put down your gun, boy. And you," he said to Sean, "get off your horse."

Sean didn't move. "You're going to need my help to bring Renier in, Constantine," he said. "I have proof that this man murdered my uncle and conspired with this woman—"

"He's lyin'!" Joey shouted. "I found Jed's saddlebags! Charlie was a traitor, Holden! I caught him runnin' away from Dog Creek like a no-good polecat, 'n I made him talk. He started the fire so's he could put the saddlebags under your bunk without anyone seein'. He put blood all over 'em, too." He gestured wildly with the rifle. "Sean planned to make it look like you killed Jed to get the money, but he's the one who killed him!"

"Whatever happened here will be dealt with after I take Renier to jail," Constantine said. He looked at Sean. "I don't need your help. Get off that horse and throw down your gun."

Sneering in contempt, Sean dismounted. "You're making a mistake, Constantine."

"Gavin," Heath said, "take my horse and get Rachel out of here."

Gavin took the reins of Heath's horse and led it toward Rachel, careful to keep his free hand away from his body. No one else moved. When Gavin reached Rachel, she bent her head and removed the sling from around her neck.

"Take Gordie to your family," she whispered. "I can't leave Holden."

He met her gaze. "Heath wouldn't want—"

"I know. But Gordie will be loved. That is all that matters."

Gavin searched her eyes for a moment longer, then took the baby from her. He secured the sling around his neck and mounted.

No one seemed to notice him. Constantine was still aiming at Holden, but his gaze was fixed on Sean, whose smile hadn't faded. Joey remained at the top of the hill. Rachel walked out from behind the cairn.

"Mr. Constantine," she said. "Please listen to me."

He turned his head slightly. "I told you, ma'am…"

"Rachel, get out of here!" Holden snapped.

None of them were looking at Sean when he drew the tiny pistol from inside his coat and aimed it at

Rachel. Holden moved before Sean could shoot, throwing himself in front of her. Constantine aimed his gun with precision and shot Sean through the heart. Sean fell, an incredulous expression on his face. Rachel looked away.

"He shouldn't have done that," Constantine said. "You were a witness, boy," he said to Joey, who looked as if someone had knocked all the air from his lungs. "If I need your testimony, I'll send word." He jerked his gun at Holden. "It's time to go."

"No!" Rachel cried. "How can you turn on your own kind?"

"I can't let you take him," Joey said, raising his rifle.

"Don't be a fool, boy," Holden said. "You got your whole life ahead of you. All I care about is that you and Gordie and Rachel are safe."

Joey hesitated, his face wet with tears. Rachel pushed her way between Holden and Constantine.

"You want Heath Renier for the things he's done," she said, "but he isn't that man anymore. He could have killed Sean before, but he didn't. He saved Joey and me." She stared into Constantine's golden eyes. "He's spent his whole life running because of what he is, because people tried to kill him for it since childhood. How can *you* not understand?"

Genuine regret flickered in the bounty hunter's eyes. "I'm sorry, ma'am. I can't let him go."

"But you can! You can pretend you never found him. You can ride away and let Holden start over with the family he's been denied all his life." She clasped her hands like a supplicant. "Do you know what it's like to be robbed of your family, your own kind? To lose every shred of hope?"

His eyes answered for him. He *did* know. And that was *her* only hope.

"Rachel," Holden whispered.

She wasn't listening. "If you have ever wanted the chance to start over," she said, "you must let him go. If you've ever loved anyone…"

Constantine stared over her head, past Joey on the hill and up to the blue sky beyond. Rachel looked at Holden. His eyes were as eloquent as Constantine's, begging her to let go and find the new life he had wanted for her. Rachel had begun to despair, when Constantine slowly holstered his gun.

"Pity," he said. "Seems Heath Renier and Sean McCarrick shot each other in a standoff when no one was watching."

Rachel sagged. Holden caught her and held her close.

"Constantine—" he began.

Their gazes locked. "If I ever hear you've committed one more crime, even if it's stealing a piece of licorice from a candy jar, I'll kill you," Constantine said. "Now go, before I change my mind."

"I won't forget this, Constantine. If ever you need my help…"

Constantine didn't answer. He and Holden looked up at the same time and stepped apart, Holden pushing Rachel behind him. Joey turned his horse around, rifle raised.

The riders came at a trot around the hill, three dusty men on sweat-stained horses. They stopped, drawing up in a row and taking in the scene with expressions of bewilderment.

Constantine pulled his gun again and held it pointed at Holden's head.

"If you want to get out of here," he whispered, "play along."

The riders exchanged glances. George Saunderson dismounted, his hand on his gun, and walked toward Sean's body. He crouched beside it, turned Sean over and shook his head. John Powell stared at Constantine.

"Who the hell are you?" he demanded.

With his free hand Constantine reached inside his waistcoat and withdrew a badge. "My name's Jacob Constantine, Texas Rangers. I'm taking this man in for murder."

So he was not merely a bounty hunter after all. Rachel stood close to Heath, though his eyes warned her away.

"You all right, Mrs. McCarrick?" Finn O'Hara asked.

So Sean hadn't told them who she really was. She lifted her head. "I am perfectly well. And I am not Mrs. McCarrick. My name is Rachel Lyndon."

Saunderson stared at her. The other two men were clearly bewildered. "Rachel Lyndon?" Powell repeated.

"This woman is coming with me as a material witness," Constantine said. "You take the body, and I'll return when I can to account for this man's death."

A sharp conversation followed, but Rachel hardly heard it. Her heart had no room for such trivial concerns.

Holden was going to be free. Gordie would have a home. And she...

"Rachel," Holden said. "They're gone."

She blinked, clearing the tears from her eyes. The ranchers and Sean's body had vanished. Joey had dismounted at the bottom of the hill. Constantine stood back, watching silently. Gavin had come out from behind the cairn, cradling Gordie in one arm. He held the baby out to her.

The agony of loss almost brought her to her knees. She took Gordie and gave him to Holden.

"He's your son," she said.

He met her gaze. "He's yours, too."

She smiled. "You've found your true place, and so has he."

"I ain't leavin' you, Rachel."

"You must. You have your own people now, people who want you. You'll never be alone again."

"Are you sayin' you can't…" He swallowed. "Did you mean what you said when you talked about love?"

"I…"

"Do you love Gordie enough to accept what he is?"

Yes, she wanted to shout. *Just as I accept* you. *Just as I love* you.

But she would always be an outsider among his people. Perhaps they would accept her, but she would always be a burden to him, a reminder of his past. And Gordie would always know she was not his real mother.

She turned away. "I will return with Joey to the ranch and collect my things. Perhaps he'll be willing to escort me to Javelina."

Holden stepped very close, Gordie's little body nestled between them. "They know who you are now. They'll—"

Without another word, Rachel walked toward Joey. He looked from her to Holden in confusion. She had almost reached him when Holden came up behind her.

"If it's a choice between stayin' with you and goin' with Gavin," he said, "I ain't goin'."

"Please, Holden—"

"You want me to think you can't accept what we are. But I know you accept Gordie. You'd never let him suffer for not bein' human."

"He needs his own kind."

He put his hands on her shoulders and spun her around. He had given Gordie to Gavin, and his arms were free to hold her prisoner.

"Tell me you don't love him," he said.

She turned her face aside. "Of course I love him!"

"He still needs you." His voice caught. "*I* need you."

"You say that now, but—"

He dragged her against him and kissed her. She melted into him, opening her lips, opening all of herself for one glorious moment.

"You're my family, Rachel," he murmured into her hair. "You and Gordie. Oh, hellfire…I love you."

Her heart burst in an explosion of joy and fear. It couldn't be true. No one had ever loved her before.

But he does. He does.

"It won't be easy," he said, holding her away. "I'll still be a wanted man. But I'll do everything I can to keep you and Gordie safe, no matter what."

"I'll come with you," she said. "To your family. If they'll have me."

Holden bared his teeth. "They'd better." His eyes, so full of love, searched hers. "You sure, Rachel?"

She cupped his rough face in her hands. "I love you. I think I always have."

He shuffled his boots in the dirt. "You reckon…you think you'd still be willin' to marry me?"

"I can't go on being a fallen woman, now, can I?"

They held each other for a long time after that, Holden's face against her hair.

"What should I call you now?" she murmured. "Holden or Heath?"

"You said it yourself, Rachel," he said, kissing her forehead. "I'm Holden Renshaw now. Reckon I always will be."

She sighed in deepest contentment. "Holden, my love."

Someone cleared his throat. Rachel opened her eyes to find Constantine standing behind Holden.

"I think you'd better go," he said.

With a short nod, Holden released Rachel. He walked over to Joey and spoke with him in a low voice. When he was finished, he pulled Joey into a hug. Joey clung to him fiercely. They parted, and Joey mounted his horse.

"Goodbye, Mrs. McCarrick!" Joey called with a wave of his hand. "I'll be seein' you!"

With a yell, he kicked his horse up the hill and flew up it at a gallop. Holden returned to Rachel and pulled her into the crook of his arm.

"What will happen to him?" she asked anxiously.

"He'll be all right. He's goin' back to tell everyone about what Sean confessed to him when Sean kidnapped him." He shook his head. "I reckon they won't let Joey keep the saddlebags. But he'll have Maurice, and I'll see they get some money once I'm in a position to send it."

"We'll help in any way we can," Gavin said, coming to join them.

"I'll earn my own keep," Holden said, and grinned. "Honestly."

Rachel didn't smile. "What will happen to Dog Creek now?"

"I don't know. If they can't find some distant kinfolk,

reckon it'll be put up for sale." He frowned. "You still don't think you'd want to go back to Ohio? I can try—"

"Don't be ridiculous. You'd fit in there about as well as a wolf in a schoolhouse, and Gordie needs this wild land to thrive. As for my inheritance, it will be there if we need it."

Heath pulled Rachel close again and kissed the top of her head. "You'll still be leavin' here with nothin', Rachel," he murmured. "Just like you came."

"Nothing?" She reached out for Gordie, took him from Gavin, and smiled up at Holden as the pieces of her heart came together again. "I have everything. Everything in the world."

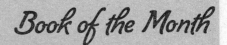

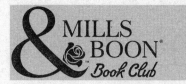

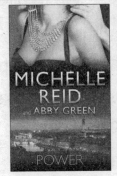

The World of Mills & Boon®

There's a Mills & Boon® series that's perfect for you. We publish ten series and with new titles every month, you never have to wait long for your favourite to come along.

Blaze®

Scorching hot, sexy reads

By Request

Relive the romance with the best of the best

Cherish™

Romance to melt the heart every time

Desire™

Passionate and dramatic love stories

Browse our books before you buy online at
www.millsandboon.co.uk

M&B/WORLD

& 🌹 Have Your Say

You've just finished your book. So what did you think?

We'd love to hear your thoughts on our 'Have your say' online panel
www.millsandboon.co.uk/haveyoursay

- 🌹 Easy to use
- 🌹 Short questionnaire
- 🌹 Chance to win Mills & Boon® goodies